THE ONYX DOOR

A Gaslamp Trinkets Novel

THE LUELLA WINTHROP TRILOGY
BOOK III

KENNETH A. BALDWIN

EBURNEAN
BOOKS

Published by Eburnean Books, an imprint owned by Emberworks Creative, LLC.

www.eburneanbooks.com

EBURNEAN
BOOKS

To Cedric. With you, we are complete.

COLD AND DARK

"Luella, what's wrong?"

Edward leaned against a tall coil of thick rope. He was wrapped in a patchy sheet of old canvas in a feeble attempt to ward off the incoming cold. His breath cast nearly invisible clouds of hot steam into the dark, a byproduct of dragging the large, unconscious body into the dock house.

Gerald's body.

My fingers were practically frozen over a similar stretch of canvas, but I didn't feel cold. I didn't feel anything. Cyrus crawled out from under my makeshift blanket to shake the water from his fur for what must have been the fifth time since we got off the boat.

I stared at my fiancé, pathetically trying to forget the passionate and accusatory voices of the fae choir. They had struck me dumb, and I'd said nothing since Edward held me in the ferry's engine room.

I could only sit and stare.

I had come back from the Netherdowns into the freezing Severn river. Cyrus had rescued me while Edward brawled with Gerald on the boat. I sang Hirythe's song to test Edward. He failed miserably.

Even in Byron's room with Jeremy nearby, I'd never heard such a strong confirmation: Edward had interfered with high magic.

Surely, there was an explanation.

After all, the song was wrong about my sister, and the song didn't function as expected with Byron.

But I failed to conjure up any rationale to prolong this sentence. The song must be wrong about Edward because...

Because what?

I was so foolish. It had been directly in front of me the entire time. Everyone I trusted told me to test him. I had refused to test him. Why?

Deep down, did I know the man I had promised to marry, the man to whom I trusted my lasting devotion, had been lying to me?

Trust is as fragile as an eggshell.

What excuse could he have for keeping his involvement in high magic from me, knowing what I faced?

My only consolation was that at least I had kept secrets of my own, and I held small parts of myself he couldn't claim. Had I opened up to him more fully... I shuddered to think of it, the consequences of giving a liar, a traitor, access into my heart.

I stared at him as if he were a violent kidnapper. I wanted to hate him. I wanted to lash out at him. Scream. But when I reached down for my anger, I came up empty. Even the magical illness that had infected me for so long had abandoned me.

I was on my own.

Gerald groaned on the floor between us.

"He's stirring," Edward noted.

"I know him," I whispered. It wasn't easy to admit even that much. My innate survival instincts wanted to keep my knowledge from him. Why reveal my hand to Edward? He had enchanted me. I wasn't sure why, but if I divulged my discovery, there was no telling how he might react. He was a stranger to me, my fiancé.

He looked at me, brows knit.

"You do?"

"Yes. This is Gerald," I said.

"The Gerald we were to meet in Reading?"

"The same. If you hadn't been arrested, you'd have met him."

"What the devil is he doing here? And why did he try to destroy the diary?" Edward coughed, releasing a puff of steam from his mouth. We needed to warm up in earnest soon, or the cold would be more than an inconvenience.

But where could we go? I was a fugitive. The Dawnhurst Police would soon discover that I was no longer in my cell, if they hadn't already. They hunted me after Luke Thomas' murder. Now, the night of my escape, they would discover Charlotte Thomas had disappeared as well.

I closed my eyes. That was another secret my instincts told me to keep from my enchanter. If Edward knew about his mother...

Cyrus let out a low menacing growl as Gerald started moving. Edward had tied his hands and legs with sturdy rope, but in a flash, Gerald lunged at Edward.

The Lord of Fernmount skittered backward as quickly as he was able and watched the big man trip over his tied feet, landing on the wooden dock house floor with a crash. Cyrus lowered onto his haunches beside me, hair bristling on his back but, he remained deathly silent.

"Release me!" Gerald cried, writhing on the ground as he tried to escape the ropes.

"You are in no position to make demands," Edward replied, the canvas draping off his shoulders like a cape as he stood.

"You think some cords of rope can keep me from pulling your limbs off?" Gerald snarled and spit.

"I beat you on deck, and I'd be happy to beat you again." Edward folded his arms. Once, Edward's pugilist proficiency had been a comfort to me. I'd once seen him brawling with a constable several stone larger, but he wasn't a clear victor in that case. Now, the idea that he bested Gerald made me tremble in fear. Still, now the adrenaline was spent from his veins, and, noting the fresh bruises on his side, I wondered if Edward could best Gerald again.

"Why not untie me and give it a go?"

"You set out on the boat for the sole purpose of throwing a book into the water. Why?" Edward asked.

Gerald grunted.

"What do you care?"

Edward breathed in and let out a slow, measured breath.

"Did you find it yourself or did someone give it to you?"

"Find what?" Gerald's voice was low and dismissive. But I detected traces of sick amusement, as if he enjoyed toying with Edward, as if none of this had any real implication.

Edward let out a roar like a lion and grabbed a yard-long metal hook hanging on the wall. He stared at Gerald and hefted its weight in his hand.

"Let's skip the bit where you feign ignorance. Why did you destroy it?"

Gerald leaned against a vertical wooden beam, a slight smirk creasing his face. I didn't move, cloaking myself in darkness and stillness.

"Destroy what?" Gerald asked again. Edward reacted like a stick of dynamite. He lunged forward with the hook raised, ready to strike. I did not believe my eyes. This was not the Edward I thought I knew. Rage glinted wildly in his eyes. This was not right. My Edward would have never...

But even the sting of his discovered betrayal didn't dull my protective instincts.

"Edward, no!" I shouted too late. Gerald swung up an arm, loose rope dangling from his wrist, and caught the hook in midair. He took advantage of Edward's surprise and overpowered him, forcing his hands at his sides. He swiveled him around to face me. I stared in horror. Edward struggled against a firm and terrible hold, made more deadly by the metal hook now resting near his neck. Behind him, Gerald glared, wild with fury. I thought I knew these faces, but devils stared at me.

"Who's there?" Gerald yelled. Cyrus started growling again, inching forward. I paused, wondering why Cyrus would posture so aggressively. Gerald was no stranger.

"Gerald," I whimpered.

"Luella Winthrop?" Shock broke through his voice.

"Luella, run. Get out of here," Edward said, before the point of the hook bit into his neck, shutting him up.

"Quiet, you," Gerald said. "What are you doing here, Luella?"

"I should ask you the same," I replied, shifting my way out of my little hiding place. Noticing my movements, Cyrus barked a warning.

"Don't come near!" Gerald warned. "I'll kill him!"

"You'll do no such thing," I countered. Cyrus matched me step for step as I closed the gap between Gerald and myself.

"Call off the dog!"

"What, Cyrus?" I asked. "He's your friend. I've watched you give bones and scraps of meat to him. He's not going to hurt you. No one is going to hurt anyone. Stop acting like a child."

Gerald shook his head erratically, as if he was trying to shake water from his ear or a fly from his nose.

"Why did you take the diary?" I asked.

"Are you in league with the police, then?" Gerald tightened his grip on Edward.

"I'm running from them," I said. "It's no different from when we talked at Reading."

"Reading?" he asked, a small glint in one eye. "Then what are you doing back here?"

"I was trying to work out a plan to clear my name. It went poorly. Why don't you let Edward go?"

Gerald laughed nervously.

"If you're running from the coppers, why are you running with one?" he asked, indicating Edward with a cruel twist of his arm.

"He's no longer a police officer."

"How do you know what he is?" Gerald yelled. I paused, trying to shed the feeling that he was right. Who was Edward? Why should Gerald let him go? I could run now and never turn back, leaving him behind.

But Bram still awaited trial for a crime he didn't commit, a crime he might hang for. And whatever monster Edward might be, his mother didn't deserve to be trapped in the Netherdowns as she was.

"He's my fiancé," I said steadily. Gerald peered at me like he was putting together a puzzle. The sound of the river lapped against the dock outside and beneath us. He shook his head again.

"Lies."

"It's not a lie," I said. I held up my hand, a gold band shining in a shaft of moonlight. Seeing the band hurt anew. It was a lie, just another piece in Edward's greater deception. It made my stomach churn that Edward would use a family heirloom so callously to deceive me. I swallowed back emotion. *Don't start now.* "Why did you destroy the diary, Gerald?"

He struggled to form words, shaking his head again.

"I can't tell you," he said, finally.

"Why not?"

His eyes stretched wide.

"I don't know!"

"What do you mean you don't know?" Edward cut in, bristling with annoyance. Gerald shook him.

"I meant what I said," Gerald replied.

"You're not yourself," I continued, stretching a hand toward him. "You aren't going to kill this man, and he's certainly not going to kill you. You're not in danger."

"I am. I am in grave danger!"

"From who?"

"I can't tell you!" Gerald looked like he was in physical pain. His face strained like someone was strangling him.

"That's fine, then. Don't strain yourself. Do you want to tell me?" I asked. He set his jaw firmly and nodded. Edward gaped at me from over Gerald's large forearm.

"Why not let Edward go? You don't have to tell us anything, and I promise he won't try to hurt you." I bit my lip. Edward had been about to hit him with a hook for naught but more information, but the fury had faded from his eyes. Then again, I no longer trusted I could his emotions.

Gerald paused and considered.

"Come now, Gerald. You may not be able to tell me something, but surely nothing compels you to hold my fiancé hostage."

Gerald didn't let go per se, but Edward must have sensed some loosening of his grip, for he climbed out carefully from the large man's burly grasp and quickly sidled over beside me. Gerald did not lower the iron hook, however.

"Thank you," I said. "We're both grateful. Aren't we Edward?" I shot my fiancé a stern look to quiet any incoming objection. He awkwardly turned back to his adversary.

"Yes, thank you, for letting me go from the life-threatening grip you had me in."

"Would you like me to try it again?" Gerald retorted, salt in his voice. "Might I remind you, I committed no crime. I received a book with instructions to throw it in the river at its deepest point. You were the one who boarded my boat and attacked me."

"I did not. You started—" Edward took a step forward, eliciting further defensive posturing with the gleaming hook. He backed up hurriedly, raising his hands in surrender.

"I was surprised to find an intruder on my boat."

"Enough, both of you!" I cried. Cyrus hadn't moved more than an inch. He still stood, teeth bared. "Who gave you the book? I assume you didn't take it from Edward's private chambers."

Gerald's eyes squinted as though in pain.

"What have I done?" he lamented. He stepped backward and bumped into a wood beam. It knocked a chain from a shelf with a loud, metallic racket.

Cyrus growled again. I bent beside the dog.

"Cyrus, down! Relax! It's just Gerald."

In a flash, words Hirythe once told me came swimming back to me. *I'd trust the diary with Cyrus before I would Bram.*

Why should I calm or quiet this pointer? He had led Edward to the river and rescued me. Was it possible Cyrus was more than a garden variety canine?

I looked at my hand patting his neck and wondered.

"What are you doing?" Edward asked out of the side of his mouth.

I stood and walked toward Gerald until the tip of the iron hook touched my neck.

"Gerald never wanted to destroy the diary. Did you, Gerald?"

Gerald's panicked eyes shot around the room. He was afraid of something. This large, powerful man acted like a spooked child. I recognized those eyes. I had seen them in the looking glass.

They were touched by magic.

It unfolded in my mind like the answer to a riddle. The only reason

Gerald would destroy the diary is if he either feared it, which was unlikely, or if he'd been put up to it. If he'd been put up to it, he'd need either a good incentive or a harsh stick ready to strike. Given his current state, I had to think it was the latter.

Jeremy. Who else?

But I was afraid to talk about Jeremy in front of Edward. I was afraid to reveal any magical information in front of Edward. If he had enchanted me, was he in league with Jeremy? Why rescue me from the water or fight Gerald on the boat. Was it all for show?

Nothing made sense.

If this was a plan, I wanted to disrupt it.

"You can go, Gerald," I said. "We won't follow you."

Gerald leveled his brows.

"Luella, we can't let him go," Edward hissed behind me.

"You're lying," Gerald said.

"What purpose would I have in trying to prevent your leaving? We're friends." I put a hand on the iron hook and lowered it.

"He's seen you." Edward stepped closer behind me, trying without purpose to whisper. "He'll go to Cooper."

"And tell him what? That I'm not in my prison cell? That I'm somewhere outside?" I folded my arms. "Telling Cooper that he saw me in a dock house somewhere in Dawnhurst won't exactly have the hounds at our heels. We'll be long gone by the time he can get an audience."

"I'm not going to the police." Gerald shook his head erratically.

"He would say that." Edward scoffed.

"You're on the run again?" Gerald asked me. Inch by inch, his temperament was returning to the sarcastic friendship I'd enjoyed in the past. "Is it the same thing you told me about in Reading, at the Forbury Gardens?"

I nodded.

"It's worse. They have Bram in custody now. He's confessed to the crime, though I know he didn't do it." I clenched a fist as I left out the part where I asked Bram to confess on my behalf.

Gerald slumped back against a worktable. It protested under his weight.

"They have Bram for murder?"

"Not necessarily," Edward replied. We both turned to him. "We've arrested him in connection to a supposed murder, yes, but a magistrate will have to determine whether there's enough evidence to charge him."

"So, his willing confession about killing your father won't be enough evidence for a magistrate?" I asked flatly. Now, anything Edward had to say about Bram triggered a heightened sensitivity.

"I just wanted to be accurate," Edward muttered. I turned back to Gerald.

"Where will you go?" Gerald asked me.

I shrugged. My mind still reeled from Edward's betrayal. How was I supposed to focus on anything, let alone this conversation? "Back on the run."

I could feel Edward holding back his response. Doubtless, he would want us to go back to Fernmount. There he could barricade us in the propriety of status and cross-jurisdictional difficulties.

But I wouldn't abandon Bram to his prison just to be trapped in Edward's mansion.

"What will you do?" I asked.

"Back to Reading, I suppose," Gerald replied. "Try to find the rest of the fair workers."

"You'd abandon Bram? He's your friend." Perhaps it was too much to hope that Gerald might become a fruitful ally. Really, I just wanted a chance to meet with him again out from under Edward's watching eye. Perhaps if we were alone, I could prompt him to divulge what happened, how Jeremy had reached him, and what leverage he had.

"There's not much I can do for him if he's gone and confessed to murder," he said. "The damned fool. Did he do that for you?"

I didn't respond. Uncomfortable creaking and Cyrus' growls filled the room.

Gerald stared at me derision tugging at the crow's feet around his eyes. "You never appreciated him," Gerald said. "Bram was a good man. It's a shame he gave his heart away to a terrible woman."

"I deserve that," I said.

"Well, enjoy your wedding. Try not to let Bram's fate bother you too much when you're nice and situated." Gerald lumbered over to the door.

"People can change, Gerald," I called after him. "Especially with help."

Gerald dropped the iron hook unceremoniously.

"What could you do to make up for all this?" Gerald laughed cheerlessly, shook his head, and disappeared into the night.

SAFEHOUSE

The dock house felt all the more empty and cold without Gerald there. Edward, usually eager to speak his mind, brooded quietly in the dark.

Gerald's parting words stung. He never had been afraid to tell me how he saw things without censure. I valued that honesty.

He was right, in any case. Everything was my fault, and this time, I couldn't hide behind the comfort of ignorance. I schemed, connived, denied the truth in front of me in order to manipulate my life into what I wanted it to be.

As a result, the man who had sacrificed more on my behalf than all but my father stood behind bars, awaiting an unfair trial and an unjust verdict.

As tears fought their way to my eyes, my teeth chattered. The cold pressed on my body heavily like an icy blanket.

"Can't we start a fire or something?" I asked, rubbing my hands together. "We'll die from exposure here. My hands are numb."

Edward looked at me, mouth twisted into a wounded grimace.

"How do you know Gerald so well?" he asked. I gaped. Really? Edward wanted to ask me about the extent of my relationship with the strange carnival and its workers now?

"What does that matter, Edward? I'm freezing to death."

Cyrus trotted around and sat on my feet. Edward shook off his emotions, but not without evident effort.

"Right. We can't start a fire. It'll draw attention to us."

"Don't you have friends in the city or something?"

"My father had friends in the city. They'd ask questions. Too many questions. What about you? Don't you know anyone that—"

He cut himself short.

"That what? Wouldn't mind housing a criminal?"

He shrugged sheepishly.

"Well, yes."

"Just because I'm not wealthy doesn't mean I associate with thieves and robbers," I said bitterly. This comment would not have incensed me a few days ago.

"I thought that—"

"You should know better. You served the city. You know its inhabitants. Has it taken so brief a time to look down from Fernmount, Lord Thomas?"

I spat the words, expecting my anger to feed itself, the magical illness within me to exacerbate, but nothing happened. The magic inside me was gone. I never thought that finally being rid of the ailment would leave some type of void, yet when I reached for that ever present anger to give me power, I came up empty. It was gone.

Edward sighed.

"You're angry with me because I let Gerald destroy the diary," he said. "I understand. After all we went through to get it, I should have been more vigilant."

It wasn't Edward's fault Jeremy stole the diary. It was mine. But Edward's attempt at remorse did not inspire any sympathy. This was an act. The grey eyes that reflected the moonlight coming through the window were cold and calculating. They filled me now with fear. He was a shell of the dream I allowed myself to believe.

That I still relied on him, that he had leverage over my situation, filled me with dread. My only tool now was the secrecy of my discovery, and I wanted to prolong that advantage as long as possible, even if that meant play acting.

I swallowed.

"I'm sorry, Edward. That was uncalled for. After all you've done for me, I should be grateful. I don't blame you for the diary. It's just so cold. I'm not myself."

"There's no need to apologize." He crossed the gap between us and pulled me into his arms. I let him, trying not to jump or wince. I was playing a game of chess. Both of us were setting up our gambits, lining our defenses. Heaven help me when it would all inevitably unravel "If there's no place you can think of, we may have to risk returning to my family's for the night. In any event, we'll need to track down Rebecca and Doug to warn them about what happened. They may need to go into hiding as well."

Returning to his family's tenement was out of the question. It would be the first place Cooper would look. Doug's pub would be second. Rebecca's flat third. If only I had more friends.

Then it hit me.

"Come to think of it, I may know someone."

If Mrs. Crow was startled by a wet, shivering trio on her doorstep in the middle of the night, she didn't show it. She opened the door with a tallow candle in one hand and an old table leg turned club in the other. It was a side of her I'd never seen before, but one that naturally fit the story of her life. Widows are, more often than not, frail or ferocious.

When she recognized my face and the haggard fear on it, she ushered the three of us in without a word.

It wasn't until she had locked the door firmly behind her and set her candle on the table that she wrapped her arms around me and wept.

"I never thought I'd see you again, my dear. Oh, but you're freezing. Come sit near the stove. I've spent it for the night, but it'll have some heat still until I can get it started again." She hurried me over to a chair. I took it gratefully and put my hands near the stove's metal to catch any residual warmth. Edward bowed his head.

"I owe you my most sincere gratitude, miss," he said. Mrs. Crow sized him up before looking at me askance.

"Now, what's a proper man like this doing with you in the middle of the night?"

"It's a long story," I said, shivering. "Cyrus, come here." The pointer bounded over and sat between me and the stove. Mrs. Crow fumbled with kindling and pulled a log from a sad reserve of firewood in the corner.

"A beautiful dog," she said as she worked.

"I owe him my life," I replied. That much was true. If I could trust anything, I knew Cyrus to be a loyal and benevolent Burgos Pointer.

Edward pulled a kitchen chair beside me and sat down.

"We'll need to do something about those clothes, or lack of them," Mrs. Crow said after she had ignited a small flame. Edward had ripped off the skirts that weighed me down in the river, down to my corset cover and petticoat. I still clutched the canvas I'd stolen from the dock house, but I was not what you'd call presentable.

"Please, don't trouble yourself too much," I said. "Edward can go and retrieve something for me."

"Don't worry," my old neighbour replied. "I think I may have something your size. A remnant of my youth."

I nodded. "Thank you." Flamelike pins started pricking the tips of my fingers, a merry sign that I may yet save them from frostbite.

"As for you, Mr.—?"

She paused to allow Edward a chance to fill in his name on her behalf. He stuttered and looked to me.

"Oh, it's all right," I said. "I trust her with my life. You can trust her with yours."

"Thomas," he replied. "Mr. Thomas."

"Well, Mr. Thomas, I may have something for you as well. It'll be a bit old-fashioned, if you don't mind," Mrs. Crow went on without missing a beat. She must have been referring to some remnants of her late husband's wardrobe. I winced. The cherished keepsakes of Mrs. Crow's late husband on the shoulders of this man...

"Old-fashioned is quite fine. Thank you," he said, rubbing his hands together.

"As for you..." She looked at Cyrus before opening a cupboard and pulling out a stale biscuit. "We should get you dry as well. I've a towel somewhere in here. Come, then."

Cyrus looked at me as if to ask permission. I nodded towards her, and he eagerly followed Mrs. Crow from the room. I turned to Edward.

"I don't mean to rush you finding warmth, but one of us must go find Rebecca and Doug."

"You can't be seen. In a few days, I'll have a carriage take you to Fernmount by night."

"We can discuss that later, but first, our friends need safety." I put a hand on his shoulder and looked into his eyes. "Please. Once Cooper learns I'm on the run again, he'll apprehend them for questioning, if not for more. I won't have anyone else in a cell because of me."

He took my hand and kissed it. His whiskers scratched my cold skin, and a sick nausea rose in my throat. His touch frightened me, and I took my hand back quickly. A brief flash of his eyes hinted that he noticed.

"I'll change my clothes and go. Stay here until I'm back."

As if I had anywhere else to go...

He left the room to inquire about his new outfit, leaving me alone to stare into the flames. As they licked at the small log in the stove, memory of Hirythe's study plagued me. If I closed my eyes, I could all but see Charlotte's portrait hanging above me.

What had I done?

It was strange sitting in Mrs. Crow's kitchen. It looked so similar to the one across the hall, the flat my sister and I had rented for so long. Mr. Stringham would have undoubtedly found new tenants already. I was sure they'd have adjusted everything to fit their own tastes. Now it was just a door across the hall from Mrs. Crow's flat. The past is always a locked door.

Except in the Netherdowns.

I wrung my stiff hands. The diary was gone, resting at the bottom of the Severn, as waterlogged as the copy of Dr. Rupert's Uncantation, the spell I'd considered using on Bram to disconnect us, to kill him, perhaps, at Edward's suggestion...

Now, Jeremy was inside his old comrades' memory, hell bent on destroying it, and I could not assist them. There was a single page left of the diary, and it was sitting in a prison cell on the outskirts of the city.

I could not retrieve it without getting arrested again.

There was an idea. Turn myself in. Cooper's officers would arrest me, and if I was lucky, they'd put me back in the same cell, with the page still there. I could use it to go back into the Netherdowns and stop Jeremy somehow. Then, I'd manage to find a cure for Charlotte. Of course, we'd all exit the Netherdowns back into my prison cell, assuming the police didn't burn the page in a rubbish bin.

I shook my head. The word "if" multiplied like country rabbits.

Even if I managed to stop Jeremy, Bram was still arrested. Every pathway led me there in the end. I had ruined Bram. He would either hang, Jeremy would destroy his memory, or both.

Mrs. Crow sat down beside me and rubbed my back.

"Now, now, dear. Let's just get you warm." She tucked a threadbare blanket around my shoulders, fussing a bit to get it laying just right.

Edward emerged from her room wearing a long coat and a loose collar. He kissed me on the head, sending a shiver of revulsion down my spine. Then, he instructed Mrs. Crow not to answer the door under any circumstance and stole into the night. She locked the door behind him.

As soon as he left, a heavy weight lifted from me. My whole body started quivering as the anxiety rushed out and my pretenses gave way.

Mrs. Crow stoked the stove gently.

"You probably have no small number of questions," I started. She waved a hand.

"As far as I'm concerned, you're innocent. And if you're not innocent, the gentleman likely deserved it." I blew out a large sigh of relief, but her shoulders sagged. "I told you wrong those months ago. I never should have suggested seeking out Byron for help."

I coughed. That was becoming a ready theme for my life. Never ask Byron for help. Recognizing the irony helped to calm my nerves.

"You've more than made up for it. Despite everything, listening to you pretend to be a desperate lover in front of the police will remain one of my fondest memories."

"You're too young to talk about memories like that," she replied. "You have your entire life ahead of you."

My entire life seemed so far away, a shore miles from a shipwrecked sailor.

"I've ruined everything," I said.

"It can't be all bad," she replied. She scratched Cyrus' head. He looked very comfortable beside her, a change from his posturing toward Gerald. "What's this here?"

She leaned forward to inspect the dog more closely and pulled the fur back behind an ear. A nasty looking cut lay beneath.

"Poor Cyrus," I said. "I haven't inspected him since we were reunited."

"This doesn't appear self-inflicted," Mrs. Crow said. "Someone must have beat him."

It might have been Gerald. It would explain why the dog had been so aggressive toward him.

"I can't even protect a dog," I said, rubbing my forehead.

"Come now. It's not all your fault."

"It is. I was meant to keep him safe. I was meant to keep Anna safe. I was meant to be a good friend, a good daughter. Mrs. Crow, I've made the most terrible mistakes."

The small fire had thawed my frozen eyes, and tears leaked from them.

"We all make mistakes, Luella."

"Not like mine. I've played with people's lives and with powers that were so far beyond me. I was arrogant and foolish and intentionally blind. I've hurt so many people I care about."

"Perhaps you can turn it around," she said.

"It's hopeless. I have nothing to work with." I caught myself before babbling on about magic. I did not want to risk Mrs. Crow thinking I'd gone crazy. "There's something wrong with me."

We sat without speaking for a minute. The fire crackled like a third party to the conversation.

"Do you see that portrait on the wall?" she said, motioning with her head toward the likeness of her late husband. I struggled to lift my head up. "About a month before we married, I was despondent. The entire world caved in on me. We'd been courting for about two months at the time, and I my emotions got the better of me. He was so charming, his energy was so infectious, that I reluctantly opened up my heart to him."

I looked at her curiously. She stared at the portrait on the wall and mechanically continued petting Bram's dog.

"Why were you despondent?" I asked. She took a deep breath.

"Because about a year before, in a moment of terrible weakness and foolishness, I had lain with another man."

My mouth fell open. A feeling of awkwardness chased out all of my dread.

"I—Mrs. Crow—"

"He proposed, and I was scared, so confused that I said yes. Immediately after, I feared he'd find me out. I tried to put off the wedding, but I failed to come up with any valid excuses. The date came hurtling toward us, and my shame would be discovered by the person who mattered most in the world."

"What did you do?" I asked.

"I worked the courage up to tell him. It was the most frightening day of my life. Now that I knew what love was, how could I risk letting it go? I sat him down and as stoically as I could manage, explained what had happened."

She leaned back in her chair and closed her eyes.

"I'll never forget the pain on his face. It was terrible and so human. He cried in front of me, and I couldn't do anything but sit there. Sit there and suffer. What's worse, feeling pain or causing pain? When he composed himself, he looked at me and took my hand."

Cyrus rested his head on her knee.

"He said, 'We are not the choices of our past, not even the sum of them. We are tomorrow and today.'"

The words brought a fortifying smile to her face as though she tasted sweet syrup.

"We had hard times. Neither of us forgot about the road behind, but we lived that credo together to the best of our ability."

I abandoned my stolen canvas wrap, feeling warm enough now to attempt drying my clothes. Once, I imagined Edward could be as honorable as Mr. Crow. Now, I doubted that belief.

"I mean no disrespect," I said. "I'm happy that your husband was such a forgiving and saintly man, but I don't have that luxury. My relationship with Edward was built on a lie."

"I'm not talking about Edward." Mrs. Crow turned impatiently. "Luella, enough is enough. I don't know the details of your situation, but you are defined by more than your relationship with Edward, or another man, or your sister. You are tomorrow and today. You're a writer. You're a powerful woman with more strength in her than you're willing to let out. You've made choices, as we all have. You can't erase those consequences, but don't imagine for a second that the eldest daughter of Jerry and Emma Winthrop can't conquer whatever it is you're facing."

A kettle started singing. I gaped at her as she crossed the small kitchen to pour some tea.

"Bram is in prison," I said. She didn't know who Bram was, but it hardly seemed to matter at this point.

"Does he deserve to be there?" she asked, handing me the teacup. I shook my head. "Then get him out."

"Edward betrayed me," I muttered. She scooped a spoonful of sugar into my cup.

"Then leave him."

My mouth dangled open.

"They're hunting me for the death of his father." She poured a small portion of milk in after.

"Prove them wrong. But first, get changed before you catch pneumonia."

3

PLANS AND PROBLEMS

A dry set of clothes improved my mood considerably. Thankfully, the outfit she had in my size was more akin to a walking dress than a social gown. I was tired of caring so much about lace and frills. In an effort to placate Charlotte Thomas, I'd worn them since Reading.

But I doubted I'd be looking for any social attention now.

Edward had found our friends waiting at the Thomas tenement, the lights spent and the door all but barricaded. Now, a dismal group of five made a crowd in Mrs. Crow's small kitchen. She sat beside the stove, knitting nervously and draining another cup of tea. A gloomy Cyrus lay beside her. Rebecca and I had two chairs by the table, and the men stood—that is to say, Doug stood—Edward paced.

"I'm sorry, Doug," I said at length. "You would have never been mixed up in this if you weren't so kind. Now, you can't even go back to the pub you love so much."

Doug waved me off.

"It's not the first time I've withheld information about a criminal from the police. No offense, Edward. It won't be the last either. I'll head back there, eventually." His words were soft and nonchalant, but hesitance changed their inflection.

"You apologize to Doug before you do me?" Rebecca asked, hitting my arm.

"I don't even know where to begin, Rebecca. You gave up your work, your security—"

"It was a jest, Luella. Nothing more. You need not apologize."

Rebecca would try to anchor my sanity even in hell's waiting room. I exhaled to relieve tension, but my shoulders did not relax. Since Edward had returned to the flat, my whole body had clenched again, as if I were expecting a blow to the face.

He stopped pacing and leaned against the kitchen counter.

"It's simple," he said. "We must return to Fernmount. Once there, we can take full advantage of my family's resources to protect the three of you."

"You know as well as I do that leaving the city won't be as simple as last time. Your carriage and driver will be known and recognized. They'll suspect Luella is inside from a mile off." Rebecca circled the rim of her teacup with her finger.

"There are ways around that. We won't use my usual carriage. We can disguise the three of you. These objections are easily overcome."

"Once they find out we've escaped to Fernmount, coming back won't be easy. Edward, you'll be implicating yourself by assisting a fugitive," Doug argued.

"That's only true if they can prove Luella is living at Fernmount."

"Do you expect to lock me in a room, then? Swear all the service to secrecy? Word will get out," I replied tersely.

"Even if they do find out, what interest do we have in coming back, anyway?" Edward asked, frustration mounting on his grim face.

"How long do you believe you can keep the Queen's justice out of your family's mansion?" Rebecca asked. "A week? A month?"

"With the right lawyer, longer than that. Perhaps indefinitely. It's a better chance than she has here. We should leave tonight." He slapped a hand on the counter. I had rarely seen him so worked up.

"You'd leave Dawnhurst as fast as that? What about your mother? How would she know?" Rebecca countered, folding her arms.

A creeping discomfort crawled up my spine. I wondered how long it would take for Edward to discover Charlotte's disappearance.

"We can leave her a note. She's perfectly capable of traveling on her own," Edward said.

"I'm not leaving the city," I stated at last. My utterance silenced the room. Edward gaped, but I could almost feel a proud smile forming on Mrs. Crow's lips.

"Luella, I must have misheard you—"

"Edward, I can't leave Bram to fend for himself. He's in a cell because of me."

At mention of Bram's name, the color drained from Edward's face. He locked his eyes on me with an uncomfortable intensity.

"Bram Lowhouse is in a cell because he killed my father," he said evenly. That was an escalation, or so I would have thought until now. Edward had never accused Bram openly like this before. I thought his misgivings about the magician were based on jealousy. When did Edward stop believing his father had killed himself? Had he ever, or was he always searching for a credible cover story?

These were dark thoughts, but Edward had gained much since his father's passing, and the two had not been close.

I stood my ground and shook my head. While I was here with Doug and Rebecca, Edward could not hurt me.

"Bram is in a cell because I asked him to take the blame for an accusation against me. What evidence do you have that Bram killed your father?" I proposed my question carefully, a gentle probe to see if I might not start unraveling Edward's true motivations.

"Luella, you told me yourself that Bram got you mixed up in the magic at the start, then persuaded you to write more elaborate stories, to mine deeper and see what happened. He should have known better."

I frowned, wondering if Mrs. Crow was listening to mention of the word magic with interest.

"You would condemn a man because he encouraged me to write more elaborate stories?"

He balled his fists, slack jawed and struggling to compose himself. No, I had never seen him this way before. Cyrus lifted his head and let out a quiet growl.

"In any event, when did you take it as certain that your father didn't take his own life?" I continued.

An angry confusion possessed his features. Doug interjected.

"I don't like to pick sides here, Luella, but I've a mind to agree with Edward," Doug said. "I'm unsure what help you might provide given your current situation. If a police officer recognizes you, they'll arrest you. It's as simple as that."

"Perhaps I can help organize efforts to break him out," I said. Rebecca sighed.

"It may be possible, but it'll take a lot more than the theatrics we used when we helped you escape the city. We'll need to steal keys. We'll need to keep the guards occupied. Then we'll need a way to disappear." Rebecca's tone bordered condescending as she counted each action on her fingers.

"Not to mention, we'd need more manpower," Doug said. "We're all marked. I'm not sure how broadly you want to extend this circle of trust."

Rebecca put a hand on my shoulder.

"Edward is right, Luella," she said. "He has valid points. I don't like them, but I can't disagree with them. Perhaps you should go back to Fernmount."

I turned a dark gaze at Rebecca before standing up. When did these three become such a team? Doug and Rebecca wanted what was best for me, but none of them knew all I did. They lacked necessary information, yet prescribed solutions to me as if they were doctors. I hated doctors.

"Let me make one thing clear," I said to the room. "I am not leaving Dawnhurst-on-Severn without Bram Lowhouse." I spoke clearly, and the conviction coursing through me made my hands tremble. I held on to my chair to keep them still.

"I understand your concern for me," I went on, vehemently, "but this is not your decision. Bram is innocent, and I won't allow him to hang for something he didn't do. You can help me, or you can leave me."

The room had been stunned to silence. I had never issued such an ultimatum in my life, but I was tired of being a pawn in someone else's game. For once, I finally knew where to point my boat. I needed to free Bram, and sooner rather than later. I needed to work with him to destroy or subdue Jeremy and release Charlotte Thomas.

Then we would deal with Edward.

Rebecca grabbed my wrist and tugged me gently back into my chair.

"I'm sorry," she said quietly. "I didn't mean to impose my will. I merely urge caution that breaking Bram out of prison may be dangerous. Do you have any other ideas?"

My holy determination simmered. I could always count on Rebecca for loyalty.

"There is still a page of the diary left," I said. "Gerald threw the book into the river, but I used a single page to get to the Netherdowns from my cell. If we can retrieve that page somehow, and deliver it to Bram, he could at least get out of prison."

"But without the book, won't he be forced to return to the real world wherever that page ends up?" Rebecca asked. Edward had sat down on the floor, his elbows on his knees.

"Yes, but perhaps we can steal it back again, or Bram knows something I don't. There may be a way to make more pages. I don't know."

The room was quiet. If I'd hoped to keep talk of magic from Mrs. Crow, I had another failure to add to my record.

"How did you escape?" Edward asked, raising his head. "I left the jail after you instructed me to find Bram. Did you have a page from the diary the entire time? Why didn't you tell me?"

I swallowed.

"After you left, I figured Bram might be kept in the same building. We hid the page on his person before he confessed. It turned out he was in the cell beside me. He managed to slip it between the bars."

"Wouldn't that trap him there?" Rebecca asked. "Did he have another one?"

I shook my head.

"You're telling me that you convinced this bloke to take the fall for you, and then once he was in his cell, you took his means of escape?" Doug asked gruffly. It hurt to hear it. But I had my reasons at the time. I needed to warn Hirythe about Jeremy. I wanted to explain myself, to dull Doug's pointed look of disbelief, but I couldn't risk it with Edward in the room. That would take details, and I feared to give Edward anything more.

"You can understand now why I'm so adamant that we help him," I said coolly.

Edward turned his head to study the floor. Evidently, me owing another man didn't sit well with him. Was this streak of jealousy an act, or did Edward really hope to possess me as a wife?

"How do you propose we retrieve the page?" he asked without looking up. I bit my lip. Edward was our best chance at getting into the prison. He could pretend he was there to visit me and feign outrage when he discovered I was missing, demand to examine the cell, or any other number of requests the Dawnhurst police were likely to concede as deference to a former beloved colleague.

But then Edward would have possession of the diary page. What if he traveled into the Netherdowns? What if he destroyed it?

What could I trust him to do?

"Well, I'd think Edward is most equipped for that," Doug said, crossing his arms. "Mrs. Crow, do you mind?" He held up an old biscuit from a basket on the counter. How long had it been since we all ate fish and chips together?

"Help yourself, dear," Mrs. Crow said, looking up from her knitting. "It's a shame I don't have something fresher for you."

"How can you eat at a time like this, Doug?" Rebecca gawked at him.

"I think better on a full stomach," he replied, mouth full. He swallowed quickly. "Edward is least likely to rouse suspicion. The rest of us are on a list somewhere in that office of suspicious characters. Known associates."

"You're not too bad off, either," I said. "You and Mrs. Crow helped distract the police to facilitate my escape, but I'm sure that's cooled off by now."

"He's right," Rebecca said, leaning back in her chair. "Edward is the only one who can arguably claim any innocence, and that only because of his outstanding record of service."

"Cooper knows I'm aware of her arrest and her possible charges, but my only interaction with him since I left Dawnhurst the first time was to provide Bram as an alternate." Edward's tone was rueful. "In some ways, he might think I was still doing police work, police work with tainted judgment, but still police work."

"Would you still have access to the prison?" Doug asked.

"Yes and no," Edward said. "It's not as though I have keys or anything, and unless I have a case that pertains to one of the prisoners, I won't have any special privileges in terms of visits apart from what I could persuade the guards to allow."

"Do you think that'd allow you enough room to investigate Luella's cell and pocket a piece of paper?" Doug asked.

"It wouldn't hurt to try," Edward replied. The logistics of our plan did something to calm his temper. I wasn't sure that made me more or less comfortable about things.

"Unless you discovered the page and then failed to retrieve it," I said. "If one of the guards finds it and confiscates it."

Edward knit his eyebrows.

"In all honesty, it'd be easier to take the page back should it end up stored as evidence," he said with a stroke of his chin.

"Except at the point you wouldn't be picking up a bit of litter, but stealing evidence," said Rebecca.

"Perhaps it's time I took my share of legal discrepancy," he replied, practically eager to sacrifice his good standing.

"Isn't it wise to maintain at least one of us who won't get arrested on sight?" I said, shooting him a dubious glance.

"Do you have any better ideas, Luella?" Edward crossed to warm his hands by the stove, an excuse to study me. He continued in a low voice. "If we want the page, what other choices do we have?"

I massaged my temples. He was right. I struggled to invent an objection short of directly telling him I didn't trust him alone with the page.

Was I overreacting? He'd had opportunities alone with the diary in the past. I'd trusted him with it many times. He'd never entered the Netherdowns before.

Of course, now the rest of the diary was destroyed.

"It's only one plan," I said, trying a new tactic. "Assuming the page isn't in the cell, what is our backup plan? If we can't smuggle it in to Bram, we'll need another way to get him out."

"What about letting the trial go through?" Mrs. Crow said, breaking her silence. We all turned to face her. "Sorry, dears. I am the least informed about this extraordinary situation, but if what you're all saying is true, and this man has been using some type of magic, how do you expect any judge to convict him of anything? I was always told that evidence was needed to convict criminals—that is, in the absence of an accusation from someone well-to-do."

Doug scratched his beard.

"Juries are just unpredictable is all, Mrs. Crow," he said. "But I've seen mates get out of real tough scrapes with a good enough lawyer."

I swallowed. Lawyers were expensive. I willed myself to reach for Edward's hand.

"Well, we should be able to afford one," I said. It made me uncomfortable to touch him, but Edward had planned on using his family's lawyers on my behalf. I hoped to persuade him to extend the same benefit to Bram.

Edward set his jaw.

"Let's hope it doesn't come to that," he said. "It's expensive and a gamble. Why not try a route that doesn't require a public trial first?"

"That seems fair," Rebecca said. I shot her a glare that made her stumble over her next words. "We have a primary option and a secondary. What about lodging? We can't very well inconvenience Mrs. Crow and put her welfare in danger."

"Sadly, I don't have the beds for it," she replied.

"I may have some friends that could help," Doug said. "May be best if we split up. Luella, could you stay here?"

"Of course, she can," Mrs. Crow said. "She's family."

I smiled at her tenderly and nodded. I could count on Mrs. Crow, at least. Doug and Rebecca, as well. I also knew my sister, content in the Rigby home, to be trustworthy. Hirythe. Bram. That was my family now.

"What about me?" Edward asked.

"There's nothing in it," I replied. "You have to live as normal a life as possible. You'll stay in your family's tenement building."

"You mean away from you?" he asked, shaking his head. "I don't like it."

"Naturally. I don't either," I swallowed again, "but if you're to be moving about on behalf of the rest of us, you can't retire for the evening here on Harbor Street."

"Then can't we find somewhere else?" he asked. Doug and Rebecca looked on curiously.

"Edward, it's unwise for us to find common lodging together right now. We aren't married as of yet, after all."

He started, and I thought I saw a look of genuine concern shadow his brow. But that was all part of the show, wasn't it? I had been taken in too many times by it already.

"Nothing will happen to me," I said, trying to soothe him. "And, I won't be going anywhere, either."

We locked eyes as he searched my gaze desperately. I wanted to look away. He nodded at last.

"It's settled," Rebecca said. "Doug and I will stay with whatever seedy friend he has up his sleeve—"

"He's not seedy. He's misunderstood!"

"—Luella will stay here. Edward will be the public face of our little operation. He'll search out the first chance to retrieve the page, and should that fail, we will look into hiring a lawyer."

She let out a tired breath.

"Thank you," I said. "All of you. I hope you don't think me selfish."

"We do," Rebecca said. The room held its collected breath before she let out a burst of mischievous laughter. "What? If I'm not going to be honest with you..."

The tension snapped, and something more comfortable than taut anxiety found space in the atmosphere.

Then we separated with plans to meet back the next night. As Edward collected a coat, I took him by the wrist and drew him to a shadowy corner for some semblance of privacy.

"Edward," I whispered, "promise me you won't destroy the page."

"What?" he asked.

"I know how you feel about my friendship with Bram. But I swear, if you destroy my last route into the Netherdowns, I won't marry you."

He balked, as though he saw something nasty in my features, but nodded his assent before kissing my forehead and leaving the flat.

Soon after, I fell asleep on a bed of cushions prepared by Mrs. Crow. It was the first time in months I'd knowingly drifted off without fearing dark magic waited for me in my dreams.

The thought made me so very lonely.

4

THE TIGHTROPE

I woke late in the morning to the sight of Mrs. Crow tying a bonnet under her chin. Dawnhurst's river-born chill bit at me, countered only by a meager fire warming the stove. I brought my blanket with me to a chair by the stove.

"Where are you going?" I asked.

"Out. As you said last night, it's important that those of us not already sought by the police maintain some air of normalcy. I have my usual rounds to make, but I'll be back soon with something to eat."

I rubbed my hands together.

"I apologize for the state of the place," she quickly added. "I'm afraid it will be hard to keep the humility of my lifestyle a secret should we be living together."

"How can you say such a thing? You're risking much by helping me."

"I only wish I could tell Mrs. Barker. Her run-in with you while you were disguised in men's clothing a couple months back has had her in fits. It would do good for her to know you're well. She never believed you were capable of what the papers said."

I failed to suppress a smile, remembering when I had locked Mr. Barker in an alleyway and rushed through Mrs. Barker's shop, trousers on and Rebecca in tow. That her opinion of me had not degraded warmed me more than the fire.

"Do you like her iced buns?" Mrs. Crow asked. I nodded dumbly. I loved them. "I'll see if I can't talk her into letting me take a few home."

"Please, just don't mention me," I asked. Those two women were in it like thieves.

"I wouldn't dream of it," she responded. "Don't leave the flat. There's no telling if the neighbors might not recognize you."

When she left, the emptiness of the room enveloped me. I heard the old familiar creaks and muffled conversations. The sound of horse hooves on the cobblestones outside felt close and dangerous.

I didn't bother changing from my nightgown. I wouldn't see any of my friends until that evening. In the wake of a night's sleep, I tried to collect my thoughts, but it was no use. Fear and hurt from Edward's betrayal cut me short of any progress.

Could Edward have truly enchanted me? Did I imagine his betrayal?

The song had marked Anna, hadn't it? Hirythe had explained that she transgressed against our sisterly bond by telling Byron I lacked mental competency. That was a betrayal worthy of offending high magic.

The song had also incorrectly marked Byron, but that was because I couldn't manage to maintain eye contact with him. The fae chorus must have sung because Jeremy was nearby or his presence lingered in Langley's Miscellany.

Could the song be wrong about Edward?

Edward had a history of interest in magic; his mother had confirmed that. And since meeting me, he'd gained a magnificent inheritance from a father he despised and concocted a plan to strip Sergeant Cooper from his position with the Dawnhurst Police. Given the admiration I'd seen his fellows offer him, he might very well be a candidate to take Cooper's place.

What else would Edward want? A bride enamored with him to the brink of blind loyalty?

I swallowed a painful lump in my throat. My first magical dream with the fog creature had occurred the night after Edward shared his story with me. What greater condemnation did I need?

Still, the shock of its discovery had so far left me confused and dazed as to exactly of what I accused Edward. We met. He shared his story. That night, I had my first magical dream. Why enchant a reporter he'd never met before? And how?

I called for Cyrus to come, but he lay out of sorts and unresponsive to my invitation. Even trying to pull him to my lap did nothing, as he padded back to lie down by the stove with a huff.

Instead, I found a spare pair of knitting needles and tried my hand to outrun my thoughts. Before long, I had succeeded only in forming a tight, tangled mess of yarn. I set to work unraveling it, embarrassed to have Mrs. Crow return and see the waste.

She returned in the early afternoon laden with food, and I nearly devoured the bread and cheese she'd brought with her, hoping to save the buns for last. Mrs. Barker's buns weren't meant to be devoured. They were the foie gras of pastry, as far as I was concerned.

"Thank you, Mrs. Crow. I will pay you back one day for all your kindness," I said.

"Don't you fret about that. The Lord of Fernmount has been most generous," she replied, smiling. I knit my brows, causing her to track back on her words. I should have predicted this before. Edward stepped in as our benefactor? "Oh, Luella. I know you have suspicions about him or his intentions, but I can't refuse a tuppence or two to help fill the table for your midnight meetings. Besides, if I've learned anything in life, it's to make those who wrong you pay double for their actions."

I winced. It wasn't long ago that Mrs. Crow, Anna, and I all tried to share one another's burdens. I remembered the fear of an empty table. I swallowed a large lump of brown bread as I realized how much I'd come to rely on Edward. Knowing that we all lived on his purse now rendered my conviction about his betrayal or innocence all the more dire.

The sun went down early, and Rebecca met us at around seven, right as Mrs. Crow was finishing a fish soup. She hurried in the door, jackets and scarves covering everything save her eyes. Her arrival cheered my mood. Mrs. Crow was excellent company, but conversing with those a generation or two superior is never the same as spending time with peers. Besides, Rebecca knew the details of my magical history, and I wanted to talk with her about Edward's betrayal.

"Doug will be on his way shortly. We figured it'd be best if we weren't wandering the city together." She handed me her coat.

"Your hands are freezing," I said. "Come over here next to the fire."

"Gladly. Doug's friend lives about as east as you can before hitting the factories. It's no pleasant winter stroll either with these old gloves."

"Have you eaten, dear?" Mrs. Crow asked.

"Yes, Mrs. Crow. Thank you. Now, Luella, I've been simply tortured all day. After last night's meeting together, it was clear something was wrong."

"You know me too well, by now," I replied, sitting beside her. "It's Edward."

"What about him? What happened? The last I saw, you were headed to Dawnhurst prison in chains."

In low voice, I recounted all the terrible proceedings since then: my debate with Bram over who should use the diary page, my trip into the Netherdowns where I discovered Jeremy and Charlotte, my near drowning, the diary's destruction, and the magical confirmation of my fiancé's betrayal.

When I'd finished, she leaned back in her seat, dumbfounded.

"Edward? Your 'Steely-eyed Detective?'" she asked.

"Yes."

"But Luella, what does it mean that the fae chorus sang along? What exactly?"

"It means that Edward has interfered with high magic," I replied.

"Might he not have interfered with some other high magic that had nothing to do with you?"

I shook my head.

"Possibly. But if he had interfered with any high magic, any magic at all, why keep it from me?"

Rebecca knit her brows.

"Your sister had transgressed the magic of a sisterly bond. When she told Byron you'd gone crazy, she wasn't purposefully employing magic, it was an unintended consequence. Might not Edward have done the same? Your his fiancée. What if he offended your bond?"

"How?" I asked. "I've gone through the same questions, Rebecca. I'm not a master magician, but I've failed to conjure up any high magic for him to offend. He's been nothing but loyal to his mother. He has no siblings. And, if he had never betrayed me, his support for me has been almost godly."

Rebecca tried, pathetically, to smile.

"There. Perhaps his unwavering loyalty to you is what offended high magic?"

"I wish it were so. Perhaps it is. But if not..." I shook my head. "We have been very blind, I'm afraid."

Rebecca sniffled and dabbed her eyes. I put a hand on her arm to comfort her.

"I'm sorry. You have it much worse, but I've known the man for a long time now. I just can't believe he'd be capable."

"You can understand the delicacy of our situation," I said. "If he did enchant me, Edward cannot know that I'm aware. In any case, I believe his jealousy toward Bram is sincere enough. Bram's the only one who can help me sort all this out, and I've had to ask Edward to intercede with the law on his behalf. I'm balancing between panic and collapse."

Rebecca put a hand to her mouth.

"You can't mean that you intend to feign affection for him just to play the part of his bride to be," she said.

"What other choice do I have? I want nothing more than to discern the truth, but I have no control over Bram's timetable, which means I must do everything I can to help him. Don't you see? I'm walking a tightrope."

At that moment, the door swung open and Rebecca jumped in surprise.

Our male companions swept into the flat, Doug looking perturbed and Edward furious. The latter locked the door aggressively behind him.

"What's the matter with you two? I about thought the book of

Revelations was manifesting as truth at my front door!" Mrs. Crow stood with her hands on her hips.

"Sorry, Mrs. Crow. Edward is having an episode," Doug said as he shuffled over to Rebecca.

"Damn right I am, Doug. What were you doing greeting me on the street?"

"We were practically here," Doug retorted. "Don't be such a meater."

"Edward what's wrong?" I asked.

"This whole escapade is rotting and finished," he said. I recognize a glint in his eyes that I'd only see once before when he grabbed an iron hook to coerce Gerald's interrogation. It scared me now as much as it did then. In wake of his fury, my hopeful reservations about accusing him waned.

"Did you go to the prison?" Rebecca asked, gripping the chair with white knuckles.

"I went all right." Edward tossed his hat on the counter.

"What happened?" I asked again.

He took several deep breaths in a conscious effort to calm his emotions. It took longer than socially comfortable. Mrs. Crow offered him a glass of water. He drained it in a steady motion.

"Mrs. Crow, I apologize for my outbreak in your home. You've been only kind to us," he said after a minute or two.

"You'd better sit, dear. I can recognize a man's empty stomach when I see one," Mrs. Crow said. She grabbed Edward by the arm and dragged him to the table. Rebecca stood up and offered her chair.

"I fear you may be right," Edward said. "I haven't eaten since Doug's pub yesterday."

Mrs. Crow ladled a generous serving of soup.

"Don't you worry," she said, plopping the bowl down on the old wooden table. "You just answer as you eat now."

We all watched him finish a bowl before I restated my question.

"Thank you, Mrs. Crow. That soup has a distinctly Dawnhurst flavor." She swooped the bowl away to refill it. Edward sighed. "It didn't go as we planned. I went to the prison early this morning, hoping to gain access to the cells before someone disturbed them. By the time I arrived, there was no shortage of horses outside, and uniformed officers were milling about everywhere."

Mrs. Crow put a fresh bowl in front of him.

"They'd already discovered I was missing," I said. Edward nodded grimly.

"What did you do?" Rebecca asked.

"What else could I do? I played the part of a frantic lover, bounding into the prison and demanding to see you, working myself to froth with threats in case you'd been harmed. I didn't calm down until Johnson explained the situation. What he was doing at a crime scene is beyond me."

"The red-haired desk lad? The one always going on about missing persons?" I asked. Rebecca nodded as Edward took a few more spoonfuls.

"The guard had discovered your empty cell early in the morning and raised the alarm. You can imagine Cooper wasn't thrilled that you'd escaped Dawnhurst's finest yet again."

"And what about the poem?" I asked.

"The situation was complicated. I couldn't very well start asking about a piece of paper in your cell without looking completely mad. Instead, I demanded to see the cell myself, in case the boys had missed something. That's when I was escorted the Sergeant." He finished his second bowl of soup and waved off Mrs. Crow's attempt to fill the bowl again. "He told me I was to be nowhere near your cell, that I was too personally connected to the case to see clearly. Any requests to review the evidence would be denied."

"So the police have the page?" I asked, dread dawning on me.

"It would appear so," he replied. I searched his eyes, looking for a flash of deceit. It was possible that he was lying and he had the page but wanted to keep it from me.

"This is bad. I hope none of the officers enjoy the poetry enough to read it in earnest. The Netherdowns may be welcoming some new visitors in that case."

Edward folded his arms.

"That's just it. This had all transpired by ten this morning. Cooper invited me to the station for what he called a friendly chat, but that quickly turned into an interrogation. He had me there for hours. It was only interrupted by news that Johnson had gone missing."

"Missing?" I asked.

"Cooper was furious, and while he was distracted, I asked Big Bill what the fuss was about. Johnson, apparently, was tasked with transporting evidence from the prison back to the station. But he never showed up."

I stood up and paced, my hands on my head. My heart raced at the implication.

"Now, now, Luella. It's not necessarily all that bad. He could just be taking his time. Johnson always had his head in the clouds. He may yet turn up," Rebecca said.

"So the last page of the Mystic Diary is either with some new-to-the-field police officer who has gone missing or has entered the Netherdowns, leaving the page lying out wherever he happened to read it."

"I'm only saying—" Rebecca started. Doug cut her off.

"Becca..." He shook his head.

"I tried, Luella," Edward said. I looked at him, wondering if he did. "I did. Truly. I tried."

We stared at one another. I was sure he remembered my warning from the night before.

"To make matters worse," he continued, "I haven't seen my mother since yesterday morning. I'm sure she'll turn up, but given all the strange happenstance, it has me anxious."

I tried not to look at Rebecca, who knew the truth about his mother. Charlotte wouldn't turn up, but I was afraid to share that with Edward. Lately, he was more volatile than ever before, and, given his relationship with his mother, I doubted he intended to involve her in his magical mischief.

I stood and walked to the window, my hands on my head.

"So that's it then? Our first plan failed. What about our second? Have you contacted your lawyer?" I asked Edward. He turned his face downward in a dark and awkward expression.

"No. I haven't yet had the opportunity with all the trouble at the prison and the station," he replied.

"Well, you'll need to do it first thing," I said. "How long does Bram have before his trial?"

"He may have some time, yet," Doug said. "I've had a few friends go through the gauntlet, never for murder mind you, but he'll first be examined by a magistrate to find out what charge the crown will bring against him."

"Look at you, Doug," Rebecca said, smiling. "Perhaps you should be our lawyer."

"This is no time for jests, Rebecca," I said, crossing my arms. "No offense, Doug."

Edward had not stopped looking at me, his gaze steady and scrutinizing. I stared back at him, all my stubborn indignation bolstering me into an unflinching wall.

"May I speak with Luella alone?" he asked the room.

"Anything you can say to me can be heard by our friends," I replied. He blushed.

"Luella, please."

"Well, it's not much, but please take my room. You can close the door behind you, and though the walls are thin enough, you can talk in low voices," Mrs. Crow said, eager to interrupt any awkwardness.

Edward stood and extended his arm to the other room in invitation. I accepted stiffly and opened the door to Mrs. Crow's personal bedroom, decorated with out of fashion knickknacks and worn linens, emanating an overall feeling of tidy ruin. Edward closed the door behind him, leaving me in a state of trapped vulnerability. I had to remind myself that my three closest friends in the world were just on the other side of the wall.

"Well, what do you have to say that must be so secretive?" I asked. He stuffed his hands in his pockets.

"Are you upset with me over something?" he asked.

"Why would you say that?" I felt foolish pretending I wasn't, all the while knowing that the tension in my back had me straight as a board. Edward raised his eyebrows.

"You are acting strangely," he said. I took a breath. If I didn't want Edward knowing I'd discovered him, this wouldn't do at all. I needed to coax him, soothe him. Yet surely I couldn't just wipe away my personality. Would that not be just as suspicious?

"I'm sorry," I said, clenching my hands together nervously. "I'm just so worried about Bram."

"That much is clear, which doesn't make this very easy at all," he said. I narrowed my eyes as he took a steadying breath. "I'm not going to pay for his lawyer."

"Why not?" I asked. I had feared this, expected it, but it made me no less upset.

"I think you know why."

"It's because you're—what? Jealous? Is this still about jealousy?"

"It's more than that," he said. "What do you expect of me? I am only human. I told you before I wasn't proud of my jealousy. I'm trying to be honest with you!" He threw his hands in the air.

Jealousy. Deception. Schemes. Plans. Our chess game continued.

Did Edward fall in love with his victim, or was his affection an act? I had seen him go to great lengths to try and heal me. Was that remorse or a plot?

"Is that any reason to abandon an innocent man?" I asked.

"Is he innocent? He cheated you. He withheld information. Is that innocence?"

"He didn't force me to write anything. Do you hold me guiltless?"

"No!" he cried, stumbling backward. I gawked at the dramatics. "No, I do not. But I love you, and I cannot come to grips with all of this. My father is dead. I'm in love with the woman who brought it about, and I'm afraid she's in love with the man who pushed her to folly. People are vanishing in and out of a book, for heaven's sake, Luella. I don't know whether the ground or the sky is beneath my feet, and now you're asking me to pay for his lawyer."

His words stole my breath. Could anyone be so manipulative to construct a deception so many layers deep?

"You can't ask me to," he continued. "I can forgive your involvement in my father's death. Don't ask me to pay for his out of my own pocket."

I closed my open mouth. Something in my heart wanted to trust him. If he could give me the smallest opening, the smallest explanation, I'd be willing to take it.

"If he pushed me to kill your father, why did he do it?" I asked. "Did you know him before? Did he wrong you somehow?"

Edward hung his head.

"Will our whole life be about Bram?" he asked.

"I'll carry him with me always if he hangs," I said. It wasn't the answer he wanted, but stalemates made no one happy. Edward slowly nodded to himself before exiting the room and straight out of Mrs. Crow's flat. A part of me wanted to chase him, another wished he'd never return.

No heads popped into the vacant bedroom doorway in his wake to peer at me with inquisitive eyes. When I came out of Mrs. Crow's room, all of my friends were busy, attention rapt in some menial task. Mrs. Crow knit furiously, Rebecca read a newspaper. Doug was all too interested in the backs of his own hands. Even Cyrus feigned gnawing on a bone—the most exertion he'd showed all day.

"You don't have to pretend you didn't hear," I said. They all looked up at me, but pretended, anyway. I put my hands on my hips and sighed. "It looks like we need a third plan."

5

THE EAST SIDE PLAYHOUSE

I sat alone in the backstage wings of a small playhouse on the East Side of Dawnhurst, heart still racing from the walk over. I could recall a time when my father had brought me to this playhouse when I was a girl. We saw what I considered then to be an absolutely magical show. A man had juggled. A woman sang a beautiful song. And if I recalled correctly, some fellow with a stately beard had made a bird vanish.

It was a bright memory, but now the theatre was illuminated solely by a handful of candles. Long flickering shadows danced through the curtains and empty seats, giving off a haunting glow. If I looked out past the stage, the audience seemed to be filled with ghosts, both from my past and present.

I pulled my heavy coat closer. It was a man's coat, but not Edward's. It didn't carry his scent or presence. Doug had asked to borrow it from his friend—the same friend who worked the front of this playhouse. It kept my body warm, at least.

"Someone's coming," Rebecca called in a stage whisper from behind the absent audience. I took a breath to steady myself. Tonight was a gamble but a necessary one.

Usually, accused criminals represented themselves. Bram might do a fine job at that at his best, but there was no telling what Jeremy was doing to his mental capacity.

If attempting Bram's escape was too risky, we'd have to win with the magistrate. And if Edward was not going to pay for legal help, I would.

I had only one skill, but I had a relatively successful run under a pseudonym before. Why not try again?

I heard a bustle at the front door.

"You unhand me at once! What is this? I'm not going in there!"

"You will if you know what's good for you." Doug's heavy voice called out. This was risky. Mrs. Crow had about had a fit when we formed our idea.

Byron Livingston bumbled through the theatre door and surveyed the room.

"What do you plan to do with me?" he asked Doug, whose large form loomed behind him like a shaded gargoyle.

"Forward." Doug held out his hand and pointed to a chair in the audience.

"I won't go another step," Byron insisted, "until you make your intentions known. I have friends in very high places I assure you."

"How high?" Rebecca said as she stepped forward. Byron jumped and squinted to make out her features.

"Wait a minute, now. I know you. You used to bring me stories from one of my writers. And you, you were the proprietor at that pub the other day when I came to warn Luella of the police. What is the meaning of all this?"

"We want to talk. That's all," Rebecca said. "We'd have come to your office, but for some reason, we can't travel by daylight anymore. The police are searching for us, what with some failed attempts at keeping our mutual friend from arrest."

Byron's face fell.

"I didn't want to harm her," Byron said. "God knows how much I cared about Luella."

"Look at you, speaking like she's already gone," Doug said, cocking his head as though to mock his fear, "already convicted of the crime."

"You fought for her reputation after she escaped the first time. But tell me, did you believe she was innocent?" Rebecca asked.

Byron crumpled the brim of his hat in his fist.

"I don't see how that question is relevant to anything," he replied, his courage betrayed by a crack in his voice. Doug put his hand on Byron's shoulder menacingly.

"Then there's no harm answering," he said in a deep, raspy voice. Byron paled.

"Well, I'm confused," Byron replied. "You weren't there that day. Luella told me that she was somehow magically affected, that she wrote up the story of Luke Thomas' death before it happened. I thought she was crazy. How could she have written the article when she said?"

Silence filled in the answer to his question.

"The only feasible explanation is that she somehow knew," he said. "That she was involved."

"And yet you defended her?" Rebecca asked again.

"As I told you before, I care about Luella Winthrop. She is a particular weakness of mine. That's why my fiancée gets so jealous."

Rebecca nodded.

"Very well," she said. She raised her voice to me. "I believe him, Luella."

On these words, I strolled out from behind the curtain. Byron turned toward the stage and dropped his hat. I must have looked like the finale of a magic trick.

"Hello again, Byron," I said icily. He slumped into the nearest chair.

"It can't be," he whimpered.

I picked up a small, lit candelabra and descended from the stage.

"Answer truthfully, Byron. Was it a relief when they took me? At least, in part? Wouldn't it feel so right to have this whole messy business finally put to bed?"

He buried his face in his hands.

"Forgive me," he said. "I never should have allowed Carolina to read that story."

"You never should have kept it in the first place," Rebecca said.

"Byron, look at me. Look at what I've become. We are shadows now, forced to hide in the dark! You believe I had something to do with Luke Thomas' death—and you're correct."

He looked up at me, the wretched image of a man whose wrinkles were etched into his face in dark, shadowed relief.

"You did?" he asked hoarsely.

I nodded.

"But I am not guilty of murder," I went on. "Nor is Bram Lowhouse, who now sits in a cell, awaiting his charge. I will not allow the crown's justice to claim him wrongfully."

"What do you want of me, Luella? Please, just tell me."

I sat on a chair across from him and set down the candelabra. It was odd having Byron here, trembling, in the palm of my hand.

"I want a job," I said.

He gaped.

"A what?" he said.

"We would like to pay for a lawyer to represent Mr. Lowhouse," I said.

Byron looked between the three of us.

"That's why you had this man drag me from my home in the middle of the night? Because you want a paycheck? Why not just ask me to cover the cost of the lawyer myself?"

"That's what *I* said. You wouldn't believe how stubborn these two are," Doug added. I shook my head. "Sorry."

"Cooper is suspicious. If my ex-fiancé begins sponsoring Bram's defense, what do you think he'll do? I don't mean to offend you Byron, but you don't respond well to pressure."

"That's entirely untrue," Byron replied, sitting up taller.

"This isn't a debate," Doug barked. Byron shriveled instantly.

"I'm not asking you to be my publisher. I'm asking you to be my agent. My perspective on this case gives me unique insight that would be very interesting to the readers of Dawnhurst. There's value in that. I need you to find a peer who'd be willing to publish the stories for a good price, pay you on my behalf, and not divulge your involvement to anyone."

Byron bit the bottom of his graying mustache.

"You're using me as an extra layer of protection," he surmised. "But how can you trust me?"

I folded my hands in my lap. We all quieted as the sound of a few drunkards wandering by on the street outside faded.

"As you've said, you actually care for me. I'm sorry to take advantage of those feelings, but you've let me down twice already, once from mistake, once from negligence. I doubt you will do so again. Will you do this for me, Byron?"

"Are you asking me as your friend or your editor?" he asked, a nostalgic smile tempting his face.

I laughed, and Rebecca shot me a questioning glance. Convincing her that Byron could be trusted was no small feat. After all, she'd sat by and watched the two failures I'd just mentioned. She was right that this plan had its share of risk, but I would not sit on my laurels while Bram faced the law alone.

Somehow, Byron's previous shortcomings convinced me he would not fail a third time. He couldn't.

"I suppose I'm asking you as a fugitive without many other options," I said. Byron considered and reached for his pocket, where he usually kept his pipe. His hand came up empty. Instead, he paced down the aisle. I noticed Doug lean forward, ready to pounce after him if he tried to run off.

"We would need to choose the right daily," Byron muttered. "Something with enough reach to merit a hefty wage but not so large as to attract too much attention." The old editor was at work.

"We will also need to find a typewriter I can use," I replied. "It would be best if we didn't leave it up to someone else to transcribe my handwriting."

"Naturally. I can bring one here the next time we visit," he said. I exchanged looks with Doug and Rebecca.

"About that, Mr. Byron," Doug said. "You won't be visiting with Luella again."

"You mean you won't allow me to return here?" Byron asked.

"You can come back here all you like. I'm sure the owners would be happy to have you as a patron. But don't expect to find Luella," Rebecca added.

"Then, where will she be?"

"Come now, Byron," I said. "You surely don't expect us to tell you that. I trust you will do your best to represent our financial interests, but in case Cooper gets to you, it's for the best you don't know enough to compromise our safety."

Byron stared at us, his fingers frozen at his lips in thought.

"How am I to get her stories then?"

"They will find you," Doug said.

"And the typewriter? Or her payment in turn?"

"Leave the typewriter behind your building when you leave the office tomorrow. As for the payments, you can drop them with Mrs. Barker at Barker's Bake Shop. Tell her it's for flour and be on your way," I said. Mrs. Crow had already arranged this, asking if Mrs. Barker wouldn't mind receiving and storing payment for the discreet sale of some flowers. She told Mrs. Barker not to ask many questions, as the customer was procuring flowers for a woman other than his wife, and he'd be making judicious use of the double spelling: Mrs. Barker sold flour. Mrs. Crow sold flowers.

"Will you agree, Byron? Further, will you promise to breathe not a word of this arrangement to anyone, including, but especially, your fiancée?"

I held out a hand. Byron regarded it as he might a ghost, eyes wide on a pale face.

"I don't know, Luella," he said. "This is quite a risk. Helping you is one thing, but all this secrecy? If Carolina finds out, it could jeopardize our relationship. I may deserve some form of punishment for my previous failings, but you're asking me to endanger my domestic and professional life as a whole."

Doug shifted uneasily. I could almost hear Rebecca's doubt acting up. I needed to prove the merits of my plan to all of them.

I lowered my hand and walked slowly up to him, narrowing my eyes and screwing up my courage. He backed up in retreat until he bumped against a row of chairs. I leaned in.

"Byron, I won't ask you again. I'm giving you an opportunity to redeem whatever puddle is left of your manhood. You will help us. You will not tell Carolina. That is final."

His eyes stretched wide, and I softened my tone.

"And," I went on, "when Bram's trial is over, whether he is set free or put to death, we will go our separate ways. I promise you that. You will never need to worry about my effect on your fiancée again. Now, won't you shake my hand so we can get to work? One last go of it? Editor and writer?"

I smiled, not with menace or rancor, but with warm friendship. It melted the apprehension from his posture as though we were about to sit down to tea.

He took my hand.

"One last go," he said.

"The past is behind us. Let's save a man from the gallows."

Without another word, I turned and swept toward the front of the building, grabbing the candelabra on my way and blowing out the light by the time I reached the door. Rebecca and Doug fell in behind me. Darkness closed in on us immediately, and we pulled the hoods of our capes down low before greeting the moonlight.

6

THE MAGISTRATE'S DECISION

A few days later, I sat at Mrs. Crow's table, cleaning a filthy and hardly functioning typewriter. A thick coating of grime collected at the corners of the keys, and the middle letters on some keys had all but worn away. Some levers stuck, and the ribbon reel didn't spool properly.

But at least I had something.

As I sat trying to polish and oil its inner workings, my mind drifted to the beautiful Remington that Edward had given me for Christmas, its shiny, beautiful keys an eager invitation to create. Had only a couple of weeks passed away? Every day felt like a month.

I shook my head. That typewriter was nothing but a gift to keep me occupied. It was an insult.

Edward had been scarce lately. After his refusal to pay for Bram's lawyer, he had only stopped by once briefly after nightfall to check in and compensate Mrs. Crow for her trouble. It might have been my imagination, but each time I saw him, he looked less handsome.

Doug, Rebecca, Mrs. Crow, and I had kept our plans to pay for a lawyer from him. I'm sure that if he put his mind to it, he'd figure it out with little trouble, especially now this old typewriter was sitting on Mrs. Crow's kitchen table. But, in a way, Edward forced us into this scheme. He couldn't very well complain about not being included.

Even so, as much as I hated to admit it, I still relied on him. He brought important news from outside and compensated Mrs. Crow for my support, like I was a child or a pet. I was in a tricky position. Being under her roof put Mrs. Crow, but I had no means to pay her for her trouble. At the same time, I had no where to turn elsewhere in the city, and I couldn't very well ask her to refuse Edward's money.

Instead, I tussled with the never-ending back and forth on whether I was being unfair to assume the worst of him or whether I was in the right to guard myself against future harm.

In any event, tonight, I expected him eagerly. Today, Bram appeared before a magistrate, who would hear the evidence presented by police and determine which crime the crown would charge against him.

I wished I knew more about the law. I hoped the magistrate would see the lack of evidence and let Bram go, but somewhere in my bones, that felt very naïve. He had confessed, and nothing is harder to put back in a box than a confession.

I wanted to be out doing more than cleaning a typewriter. A page of the diary was out there somewhere, but I couldn't risk going out by day to search—even if I knew where to search.

Meanwhile, Cyrus was despondent. It was surreal to see a dog descend into deeper throes of melancholy, but no other word would aptly describe it. I wondered if some animal instinct told him that his master was in dire straits. Perhaps it was just being so cooped up all the time.

Mrs. Crow was the only person who could even get him to eat anything.

Cyrus walked over and rested his chin on my leg with more attention than I'd received from him in days.

"What a sorry lot we are," I said to him, with a gentle scratch behind the ears.

"Come now, dear," Mrs. Crow said, turning around in the kitchen. "Why not have a meat pie?" She offered me a tray and beamed. Edward paid her more than was necessary to keep me, and

Mrs. Crow was in considerably high spirits. I wondered if this was the first increase in income she'd enjoyed in many years. Modest upgrades to her lifestyle materialized. Meat pies were one such example. I caught her muttering to herself one day about what a marvel it was to afford sufficient butter and lard to execute the recipe.

"Thank you," I said, taking a lumpy pastry and putting it beside my machine.

"And don't go begging. There's one for you as well," she said merrily as she tossed the most disfigured pie to Cyrus. He picked it up and crossed to the corner of the room.

A fervent knock at the door startled me. I looked to the window. Night had fallen already. Apparently, even cleaning the typewriter was enough to speed up the clock.

Mrs. Crow loosed the bolt and invited Edward in. He hung his hat and coat and took a seat near the stove.

As he silently blew hot air into his hands and rubbed them together by the fire, I noticed dark wells under his eyes and a fatigued slump in his back. This was not my imagination now. His hair sat at funny angles, and I wasn't sure he had changed clothes since the day before.

"Edward, are you well?" I asked, despite myself.

He didn't look at me, instead steeling himself for strength. I thought he might start crying.

"You're undoubtedly eager to know about Bram's hearing," he said, his forehead drooping toward the floor.

I was. Yet, it seemed improper to ask, given his condition. I pushed down his betrayal, my heart instinctively trying to nurture him.

"We can wait for the others," I said.

"Edward, you're a right mess. What's happened to you?" Mrs. Crow said. She offered him a pie to eat but without the enthusiasm from a moment before.

"It's my mother," he replied, staring at the pies as if they were foreign artifacts. "I haven't seen her in days, and I've had no word."

Mrs. Crow set down her tray and motherly rubbed him on the back.

"Poor dear. That must be harrowing," she said. I swallowed.

"Your mother is a tremendous woman," I said. "She's probably just gone back to Fernmount."

It sounded limp even to me. He turned and looked at me for the first time that evening.

"I just got word from Fernmount," he said. His penetrating gaze struck a vein of nervous perspiration in me.

"And?" I mumbled.

"She's not there, either," he said. He searched my eyes, and I tried to meet him squarely. Did I stare back too long? I broke the contact and glanced away, but I still sensed his gaze on me like he had questions.

"She'll turn up," Mrs. Crow said. "Mark my words. Men are always worrying about the women in their life, but we're more capable than you think."

"I trust your gender to be very capable," he said with a forced smile. "It's just that given the circumstances, I'm quite at unease. I last saw her at our flat, and that night, an intruder stole Luella's diary from our rooms. I haven't seen her since, and I'm afraid that the two incidents may not be disconnected."

"What would someone want with your mother?" I asked. I had been chasing this question in my own head. Why did Jeremy take Charlotte? Was it just to ensure I'd be hunted if I made it back to the city? He knew Bram was locked up when she disappeared.

"I don't know. My mother hates magic. If whoever broke into our rooms only stole the diary, I can't imagine my mother possessing something of much worth to him."

He turned his gaze back to the fire in the stove. His mother hated magic. So why?

"I may need to go search for her," he said. "But I don't want to leave you in any dire straits."

"We can manage just fine," Mrs. Crow said. "I've a mind to take good care of Luella. Your family is the most important thing in the world."

He coughed. It sounded sickly.

"That's why I'm asking for Luella's permission to leave."

I put down my rag. The way he emphasized the phrase to leave sounded cold and monumental. Was he asking to leave the city or leave something more?

He looked at me pitifully, and I became all too conscious of the engagement band I still wore.

"You hardly need my permission, Edward," I said.

"Do you think it's wise for me to go in search of my mother right now?" he asked.

This question was calculate to trigger a confession, I was sure of it. I couldn't very well tell him it was wise, knowing that he would not find her, but how could I say that?

If Edward left, I'd breathe without worrying about his intentions and his history.

"It's always wise to listen to your heart," I told him. Strangely, he looked lighter, as though relieved I'd given my blessing in his search for Charlotte. He reached out and took my hand. His was still mottled with areas of cold from the winter air outside. After a moment, he nodded at the typewriter. His finger brushed across the plain gold band he'd given me for our engagement. I still wore it.

A sick feeling wrenched in my stomach. If I was right about Edward enchanting me, withholding information about Charlotte from him might be strategically important. But if I was wrong, it was naught but cruel.

"If I go, I could bring back your Remington," he said. "I'm not sure what you're writing, but I can't imagine working on this machine will be very enjoyable."

Despite my misgivings, warmth and sincerity appeared to emanate from his eyes, startling me. Even now, those eyes kindled heady feelings in my bosom. Yet, his gaze was so void of this warmth not moments before.

"Thank you, but I'd prefer to keep the Remington at Fernmount," I said.

"If I leave—that is to say—you won't—"

I held up my hand.

"It changes nothing."

His eyes lingered on the ring, a memory of his mother and our promise to each other bound in one object. This could not be an act. I satisfied myself to know that whatever plans he had when enchanting me had not gone as he hoped. I doubted he expected to develop feelings for me. Those were feelings I could manipulate, and in the middle of that manipulation, pretend to take refuge and comfort in. But it was pretend. I could not forget that it was just pretend.

A knock sounded at the door. Mrs. Crow scampered over to let Doug and Rebecca in. Their arrival broke me free of the trance that was Edward's eye contact. She sat beside me and stretched her hands toward the stove.

"It gets colder every evening," she said, shivering a bit.

"If we walked faster, you'd be warmer," Doug replied, hanging a scarf by the door.

"If we walk too fast, we look suspicious."

"If we walk too slow, we look suspicious," he mumbled.

"What was that?" She turned to him with a stern expression on her face.

"Nothing."

Rebecca brimmed with nervous energy. I watched her leg bounce up and down, as though she jittered from several cups of coffee.

"Well?" she asked, turning to Edward. "What happened?"

"Always to business, Miss Turner," Mrs. Crow said. "You haven't even had a bite to eat." She set two meat pies out on plates and put them on the table. Doug beamed.

"Mrs. Crow, I meant all of those words I said when we distracted the police. I think I may be in love with you," Doug said as he sat down at the table. Rebecca joined him and dug into the widow's offering.

"Thank you, Mrs. Crow," Rebecca said between mouthfuls. "But if I don't hear, I may burst. Edward's probably told Luella already, but some of us are still in the dark."

"Luella wanted to wait until we were all here," Edward said.

"Here we are!" Rebecca replied with a wave of her arm.

"Right. Well, as you know, Bram attended his hearing with the magistrate today. The point of the meeting was for the magistrate to review the arrest by the police, and make a formal decision as to what charges the Crown will levy against him. Often the victim is present at these hearings. Being that my father is dead, and my mother is missing, they asked me to stand in this role. You can imagine it started with a somber attitude."

He leaned against the wall.

"That can't have been easy," Doug said.

"If it were a robbery or assault, I could have called the whole thing off. But they don't treat accusations of murder lightly. Nor did I want to appear too willing to forgive him without cause. If I act suspicious, it won't do Bram any good."

I nodded blankly, considering Edward's effort to wash his hands of responsibility in Bram's fate.

"They produced Bram, who wore standard prisoner's garb and a thin face. The magistrate asked what Bram was allegedly accused over, and Sergeant Cooper stood forward to present the arrest, the preliminary evidence, and his recommendation. Cooper recommended that Bram be tried for murder or conspiracy to commit murder."

"Good heavens," said Mrs. Crow behind me. All the joy had drained from her face, and she held her tray of pastries limply. Edward's mechanical explanation drove home the severity of our circumstance.

"It's common for the police to recommend the most severe charge they can," Edward said, fingering the hem of his sleeve. "After all, the magistrate can disregard or adjust the recommendation with his verdict, and the trial court, ultimately, will decide the accused's guilt. Police are trained to expect the worst, and it's not our role to determine the particulars of punishment. So, Cooper's recommendation did not surprise me.

"The magistrate's temperament and predilections are significant in these hearings. Bram was heard before honorable Sir Mortimer Silverson, who has a bit of a reputation of being volatile in his decisions, albeit thorough in his investigations. He did not mince words."

I searched my memory for the name. I remember, vaguely, seeing Mortimer Silverson appear in an article here or there, but I had never paid the name of a magistrate much mind before.

That he had a reputation like this may not fare well for Bram, but at least it meant my stories might enflame an existing public persona. They'd sell more readily and hopefully afford us the funds we needed.

"He quickly made it clear that Sergeant Cooper had done a lousy job at police work. As we know, the only real evidence Cooper had to bring forward was Luella's statement from last week detailing Bram's alleged plan, the article written by Luella filled with sordid details on my father's demise, Carolina Drake's statement that the article was written under suspicious circumstances, and, most importantly, Bram's confession to the crime.

"Silverson told Cooper he wanted nothing to do with the case, that the evidence was paltry, thinner than cheesecloth. But given the high profile of the victim, and that the evidence was given weight by the accused's own confession, he had no choice but to move forward."

My heart sunk.

"They will charge Bram with murder," Edward said. "Silverson went on to say that, should the case go in front of a jury, the jury may find him guilty of a lesser offense included in the crime of murder."

"Lesser offense?" Doug asked.

"In other words, if it comes out at trial that Bram is likely a conspirator, and another culpable party did the dirty deed, they may still find him guilty of conspiring to murder Edward's dad. Did I get that right, Lord Thomas?" Rebecca asked.

Edward nodded. No one looked at me.

"That doesn't make sense. How can the man be guilty of conspiracy if they haven't proved someone killed your dad?" Doug asked.

"A fair point," Edward replied. "One, in fact, that Bram raised in his own defense today. He was told—and I wrote this down so as not to get it incorrect." Edward produced a slip of paper from his pocket, "Silverson explained Bram could be guilty of conspiring to murder even if the murder never occurred. Apparently, in the eye of justice, 'societal harm takes place when two or more people plan to commit a crime in the future, whether or not they actually commit a crime.'"

We sat silently as it sunk in. That was exactly what we had come to expect of the law. It never seemed to be on our side, cutting both ways, wielded by those who would never feel its sting.

Now Bram would have to face scrutiny not only for his involvement in Luke Thomas' actual death, but for any perceived involvement in a plan to end the banker's life.

When the jaws of justice take hold, only the beast itself can choose to let go. I feared Bram was too tempting a morsel to expect such a release.

"What a load of rubbish," Doug mumbled.

"What happens now, then?" I asked.

"Silverson believes that since the case is so public, it must be dealt with publically. He will submit Bram's case to a grand jury. They will decide whether there is enough evidence to continue to a full criminal trial."

"I thought the magistrate already did that," Mrs. Crow said. Edward shook his head.

"Today's hearing was simply to classify the arrest and decide under which charges to view the evidence."

Doug slammed a fist on the table.

"This is ridiculous. Every time, it's the same. By the time you get through the courts you'll have lost your mind from the tedium."

Rebecca put a gentle hand on his arm.

"Easy now, Doug," she said, drawing a sigh from him.

"I'm not frustrated for me, or even for Bram. I just feel for Luella."

A bitter smile stretched my lips. From what Edward recounted, Silverson likely would have let Bram go if he hadn't made a false confession to protect me. Why did I have to invent a plan that required such self-incrimination? Surely, there might have been other ways to position him as the suspect more indirectly.

I'd damned him three times over. He stepped forward on my behalf. He confessed. He gave up his means of escape.

I squeezed my eyes shut, heat trying to escape from behind my eyelids. I had taken and accepted too much. I would not be a beneficiary of other's madness any longer.

It was time to be a little mad myself.

I rushed over to grab a sheet of paper from the open parcel near the door, the packaging for Byron's gift, and dialed it into place on the typewriter. My friends shifted uneasily on their feet, understanding that I might be occupied for some time.

"There is one other thing," Edward said as he rubbed his neck. "I hesitate to bring it up, but it was singularly odd. When Bram was asked to stand forward, he seemed aloof. Silverson asked him to confirm that he was Bram Lowhouse, and for a moment I thought he might refuse. He just looked back at the magistrate with a puzzled expression. The magistrate had to repeat the question several times before a light finally went on and Bram responded."

I froze. It was a small incident, reasoned away by any number of explanations. Silverson might have pronounced his name awkwardly or he might have slept poorly the night before. But Jeremy's threats in the Netherdowns drifted into focus. What if Hirythe was losing? What if Jeremy was corrupting the magic? Hadn't he told me that I wouldn't recognize Bram by the end of things?

Time was running out, and I couldn't stand how slowly Bram's case was going. I needed to free him, and quickly.

I clacked and clacked and clacked the night away and didn't even notice when my friends left.

7

THE SOLICITOR

SILVERSON STUNS BY SHIRKING THE LOAD

The ever so most honorable holiness Sir Mortimer Silverson plans to add to his collection of audacious performances by presiding over the circus that is surely to be Bram Lowhouse's criminal proceedings in the aftermath of Luke Thomas' demise.

In Mr. Lowhouse's hearing just yesterday, Silverson went on a lengthy tirade, censuring Sergeant Cooper of the Dawnhurst Police Force for bringing terrible evidence forward to recommend a charge of murder against the humble carnival worker.

In such a proceeding, one might expect to see a connection presented between the accused and the victim, or perhaps a weapon and method by which the accused deprived the victim of his most honorable life. Instead, Cooper presented only a news article that was never printed and a confession surrendered by the accused.

Despite Silverson's admitted doubt over the credibility of Cooper's proposal, his worship agreed to submit the case to a grand jury determination. Why, one might ask? Perhaps from Silverson's chair, a pedestal on which he looks down at the working class, he desires to appease the raging mob that would surely storm

Dawnhurst's streets should a culprit not be found and tried for the murder of such an eminent banker and noble.

Why not use an extension of the Crown's benevolent justice to provide a culprit for such mobs and maintain civil rest? And if a culprit must be fabricated, who better than a wandering vagrant who lives in a hut with a traveling fair, like Bram Lowhouse?

A vagrant like that is a much more attractive and easily manageable suspect than the previous suspect, Luella Winthrop, who was last seen being escorted into Dawnhurst's prison on the east side, even if Charlotte Thomas, the late banker's wife, appears to have gone missing around the same time.

Fortunately for Sir Mortimer Silverson, it is beyond thinking to consider the submission of this case to a grand jury as an act of cowardice. After all, if one were to consider such a thought, the label would also taint his entire history of flamboyant rulings.

At least Silverson's peers can be proud and grateful. He has stumbled upon a method to pass his gavel to the masses for a case which might be difficult, alas even too difficult for him.

I leaned back in my chair and set down the paper.

"Well, you didn't let him off easy, did you dear?" Mrs. Crow asked with wide eyes, an uneaten biscuit on her tea saucer. "It's about time someone stood up against all those wig wearing buffoons."

"I'm just happy they paid us," I said.

I took a sip from my teacup, warmed by a sense of pride. My article had made its way to the first page of *The Dawnhurst Herald.* Byron was better than his word. He had told me the article would be best placed in a paper that wouldn't draw too much attention. I supposed he changed his mind, and it was fortunate, as the pay of an anonymously authored article like this one was considerably lower. It's difficult to negotiate fees when you argue on behalf of a shadow.

Still, it should be enough to get us started. Rebecca had found a lawyer that advertised himself as having experience defending against prosecution and, more importantly, he came relatively cheap.

We had entertained the thought of asking my sister's father-in-law for his assistance, but in the end, we concluded it would only complicate things. Besides, we weren't sure how they would react to my recent notoriety. I hoped my arrest didn't reflect poorly on Anna in her new home.

I longed to reach out to her, but though she sent letters to Mrs. Crow detailing life at the Rigby house in the country and asking if she'd heard of me, I forbade any correspondence in turn. I would not risk getting her involved.

A stray lock of my hair fell across my vision, now raven black. The residue of the dye spotted my fingers in faded tones. I couldn't scrub it off.

Mrs. Crow shifted in her seat at the table.

"Is it wise that you mentioned yourself by name?" she asked.

"I'd trade places with him if I could," I replied and meant it. I wished I'd never brought Bram back to Dawnhurst, that I was the only one Cooper implicated in this crime.

Perhaps we were wrong to fear the court system so much. If the evidence in my case had been put in front of Silverson, I imagine he'd have tossed the whole thing right out.

"That's not a very comforting thing to hear knowing what you're about to do," she replied. "A bit of dye won't change who you are. I'd still recognize you."

"That's because you've known me for my entire adult life, and you know I've dyed my hair."

I stood and put on a heavy cloak. It was midmorning, and I could not wait to feel the sun warming me through the thick fabric. The decision to listen in on the meeting with our lawyer was fueled, in part, by cabin fever. I couldn't continue languishing in poor Mrs. Crow's flat for the rest of my life. Besides, I wouldn't interact with him directly. I'd be hiding in another room, tucked out of sight.

I caught a glimpse of myself in the looking glass mirror. My new reflection would take some getting used to. Framed by such a dark color, my face took on a dramatic, perhaps overly artistic, view. But I was surprised to find the change didn't bother me. In fact, the darker hair set off my eyes in a lovely way. They would be most pleasing to—

Well, I supposed they would be most pleasing to me, and that was plenty.

Mrs. Crow answered a knock at the door, and Rebecca walked inside, a bonnet shielding her face from all but direct lines of sight. She looked at me and smiled.

"You look exotic," she said. "I envy the allure this color lends you!"

"I'm only glad it didn't turn green," I replied. I had heard many tales of ill-fated hair dying misadventures, and I had worried that instead of granting me a disguise, the dye would leave me a spectacle. "Are you ready?"

She nodded.

"The walk is much more bearable in the sunshine. Though we'll have to hurry. We are behind schedule."

Mrs. Crow rushed over to tie a bonnet around my own head.

"You two be careful," she said as she fumbled with the ribbons. "I've grown accustomed to company now. It won't do to have yourself arrested."

"Thank you, Mrs. Crow. We'll be back this evening."

"I'll have soup for you." She squeezed my hand, and I followed Rebecca out the door.

We walked arm in arm through what seemed like a dream. It's amazing how a few days indoors can alter one's sense of reality. The sun shone brightly, making me squint as it reflected off of old, ice-crusted piles of snow here and there. Closer to the pavement, it had turned to a gray, filthy slush that threatened my stockings. The cold, angry wind off the nearby river bit at my nose and snuck through my clothes.

We walked briskly but tried our best to seem unhurried. My thoughts were summoned to a memory of the last time Rebecca and I had walked like this in Dawnhurst, trying to evade police hot on our heels.

This was much more pleasant. I quickly realized that I was fortunate to never have sat for a portrait. My visage was not commonly known, even among the officers of Dawnhurst. As we whisked by side alleys and storefronts, I understood that the pressing danger that felt so heavy in Mrs. Crow's flat was not nearly as imminent as I'd feared. We didn't even see any police until we crossed Thompson's South Bridge to the east side, and even then he was a way off.

Strolling through my home in this way immediately lightened my mood. With any luck, Rebecca's lawyer would intercede on Bram's behalf. Silverson already considered the case against him thin.

There was hope yet.

I pushed from my imagination thoughts of what Bram must be experiencing. Was he despondent? Did he believe I'd abandoned him or suffered some fate at the hands of Jeremy?

If only I could speak with him.

We walked deep into the east side. I saw trails of smoke floating through the air, expanding from chimney pots from the factories on the city's outskirts. This was an area of town I visited often, and memories came readily as forgotten details from my childhood sprung up: the uneven cobbles, the windows too dirty to see through clearly, the stench of neglect...

Rebecca dragged me from my stupor into a small alleyway and through a door that once was red set in a brick facade. Inside, Doug paced nervously on a threadbare rug.

"Took your time, didn't you?" he asked.

"Were you worried about me?" Rebecca asked as she untied her bonnet and kissed his cheek.

"More for Luella," he said. She whipped him lightly with a ribbon.

"Liar."

"In any event, Bart will be here any minute," he said, adjusting a few rough wooden chairs. The dwelling was more modest even than Mrs. Crow's. Some areas of the floor had been trodden so many times the wood had lost all its distinguishing features, morphed into what looked like a shiny, melted brown iron.

"Where should I hide?" I asked, looking around the room. A couple of cupboards clung to the walls, but they were much too small. A doorway to another room in the corner didn't have a solid door, just a hanging bit of fabric.

Rebecca ushered me through this door where a mattress stuffed with a mix of feathers and straw laid on one side and a rough roll of blankets lay on the other.

"Have you two been sleeping here?" I asked, embarrassment creeping across my face.

"The mattress is for me. The roll is Doug's," Rebecca replied softly. I nodded and bit my lip. "Don't start. These are desperate times. And, I'll have you know, Doug has been a perfect gentleman."

"I thought you were staying with some of his friends."

"We did for one night, but they suggested we just take this place, as it was a bit more secluded. Truthfully, I doubt they wanted us there for too long. Who can blame them?" She looked back to the main room and turned again in a whisper. "You know how Doug eats..."

She sat down on the mattress, leaned against the wall, and motioned for me to join her. Scraping in the other room indicated that Doug still deliberated on chair placement. He was nervous.

I sat down beside my friend.

"Are you well, Rebecca?" I asked, nudging her with my elbow.

"What do you mean?"

"It's just that since you met me, I've upended your life in every possible way. I'm worried about you."

"You mean because I now live in a damp, grubby hole by the factories? Or because I'm sleeping in the same room as a man I'm romantically involved with? Or because I haven't had an opportunity to bathe properly in about week?"

She leveled her eyes at me mockingly.

"What could I have to complain about?" she asked.

"What would your family say?" I asked, ruefully. "I feel responsible."

"Luella, you remember I told you that my mother and I have made ourselves strangers. You feel more like family than anyone ever has."

"Why?"

She sighed and cast her glance around the room.

"Well, because here we are sitting together in a damp, grubby hole. It's only natural that our parents and siblings judge us, but ultimately, true family gets right into the grime beside you to pull you out of it."

I shook my head, freeing a lock of my newly black hair.

"But I didn't you pull you from the grime. I pushed you into it."

"No, dear friend, you did not. Think of who we were when this all started. I worked as a typist for a police station, convinced that my life had reached its peak. I had a job, I believed my family situation was firmly cast, and my days blurred together one after the other."

She struggled to get out the next words.

"I was lonely. The everyday people around me never wanted to know me more deeply than they did already, and nothing could change that, until Luella Winthrop came through the door."

I smiled, conjuring the scene in my head. She pushed me with a shoulder. She went on.

"The grime is not always material poverty. Complacency is the currency of the truly poor."

The conversation lapsed as I allowed her speech to sink me into reflection. When we'd met, I planned to marry Byron Livingston, a living, breathing shade of beige. More than anything in the world, I wanted to make my father proud by winning the Golden Inkwell. It took nearly all my courage to head to the police station.

I had been a child.

In the other room, Doug answered a knock at the door. Rebecca put a finger to her lips and left me alone on the mattress. I breathed quietly and strained my ears.

"Hello there, Bart. Come in," Doug said.

"Please, Mr. Tanner, Mr. Milton if you don't mind altogether too much." The voice high and stringy. I imagined him as being tall-legged, though short in stature.

"Mr. Milton, then."

"And this must be your charming wife," Bart Milton said.

"My wife? Ha! I—"

"I'm Rebecca. It is a pleasure, Mr. Milton," Rebecca said. "Thank you for agreeing to meet with my husband on this terrible affair."

"To business, then. I'm afraid I am a terribly busy man. Terribly busy! My appointments have appointments, and those have all been scheduled for weeks. It's a miracle I got you in." The chairs scooted with a sound like gravel on wood. "I understand you wish me to represent the interests of Mr. Bram Highhouse."

I knit my eyebrows. *Highhouse?*

"Bram Lowhouse," Rebecca corrected.

"Yes, of course, Lowhouse. It is a charitable cause. As you likely know, my services are not cheap."

He drew out the last part of his sentence as though the state of the room nearly blocked them in his throat.

"We're aware," said Doug. "But we think we have enough."

I heard a paper uncrumpling and tsking sound.

"This will do to start," Milton said, "but I will require more. Do you agree to pay me this up front? Mr. Highhouse's defense—"

"Lowhouse," Rebecca corrected.

"—Lowhouse's defense will invoke certain expenditures that I would otherwise be taking from my own pocket. Surely you understand. Time is money, and a timepiece an accountant's ledger."

There was a silence. I heard coughing from a passerby outside.

"I trust that won't be an issue?" Milton asked again.

"What type of expenses?" Doug asked.

"If nothing else, it will cover the nutrients I will require during the lengthy first interview I'll have to conduct with the client," Milton said through an embarrassed, guttural chortle.

"You mean a midday meal?" Rebecca asked, surprise lacing her voice.

"You must never discount nutrients, Mrs. Tanner. Never! And—of course, we will need to ensure that the client looks presentable. There are costs there as well. Trimming of hairs and what not! Then I have to pay my clerks as we prepare our arguments. Please, Mrs. Tanner, surely you won't require me to explain my entire ledger book to you at present. As I've said, I am an exceedingly busy individual."

"She doesn't mean anything by it," Doug said. "You'll understand that this is a lot of money to us, and we're just a bit nervous parting with it."

Chairs creaked in their places.

"Ah! Well, that is a decision you will have to be comfortable with. If I am to defend the client, it will cost a considerable sum. And there is no possible way in heaven or on God's green earth I could tell you how much that is upfront. The thought is preposterous, I'm afraid. Sheer lunacy! Normally, I require more at the outset, but given the position you are in, I'm willing to make an exception. But if you are having second thoughts, please let me know now. Time is money, as I've mentioned... Have I mentioned that?"

I gritted my teeth. Were all solicitors like this? Mr. Milton seemed obsessed with his schedule and his pocketbook and cared too little about the details of his prospective client.

"We are sure," Doug said. "We'll bring the money by your office first thing tomorrow."

"Wonderful," Mr. Milton said. "Then I'm happy to take your friend's case. The law is severe, and I cannot promise you that its iron jaws can be loosed in this case, but I will try my very best. In any event, in my line of work, new though it may be, we say that any lessening of a charged offense is a victory worth celebrating. In this man's case, I understand the noose looms over. If we can avoid that, well... That's a victory."

A chair scraped against the floor again.

"What should we do to help?" Rebecca asked.

"Do to help?" Milton asked, laughing. "You've already done more than any man has a right to hope for from a friend. Sit back and wait for my word and my bill! You're welcome to attend the grand jury proceedings."

Two more chairs scraped.

"Oh, before I leave," Mr. Milton added, "I saw that cheeky article in *The Dawnhurst Herald*. Is there anything strange I should know about the client before I meet with him?"

A pause.

"He might be losing his memory," Doug admitted.

"What do you mean? Is he of old age?"

"No. It's just as it sounds," Rebecca said. "He's losing his memory."

"You mean to say he may be losing his mind?"

"It's likely just the stress of the situation, but you'll be able to assess that when you speak with him," Doug said.

Milton scuffled to the front door.

"Very well. I hope this isn't too unpleasant. I'll send word and my next bill soon. Perhaps not in that order, I'm afraid."

The door closed, and I sprang to my feet.

"That's our lawyer?" I asked as I came from the other room, bewildered.

"Now, Luella, I know he seems rough, but he's the best we can afford," Doug said, hands raised in self-defense. "If we can afford him. Nutrients... I'll give him nutrients."

"He's a mess. He doesn't care at all!" I said.

"He cares about the money. Perhaps that's all we can hope for. We can't expect him to get emotionally invested. He's never even met Bram," Rebecca said.

I leaned against the wall.

"I suppose I just expected a little more sensitivity. He spoke more about billing than anything else. And what was that? He hopes 'this won't be unpleasant?' For who? Bram, us, or him?"

I crossed my arms and fumed. Doug approached me carefully.

"We haven't paid him yet. We can still call the whole thing off. Try to find someone else."

I felt my shoulders sag. There wasn't time, and perhaps they were right. Milton had come recommended by one of Doug's friends—a friend who had achieved one of the victories Milton described—and Rebecca made a point about the cold professionalism.

"No," I said as I traced a circle on the floor with my foot. "No one else will take the case for how much we can pay. It looks like Bram's fate is in the hands of Bart Milton." I felt as feeble and helpless as when I was infected by my magical malady.

Suddenly, a thought struck Doug.

"Luella, you've colored your hair," he said. "It suits you."

I looked at Rebecca and shook my head. At least I had one thing moving in my favor.

8

THE GRAND JURY

The week passed slowly. Although I'd gone to and from the meeting with our solicitor without incident, we all still felt it would be for the best that I remain inside as much as possible.

I wrote a couple of articles for Byron to submit for publication, but we received little interest. I couldn't blame the publishers. The case was interesting, but nothing had developed since the hearing. I was reduced to announcing that Bart Milton, Esquire, was taking on the case. That update, at least, found its way to the papers.

Meanwhile, Edward visited only once before leaving for Fernmount. My mention of his mother's disappearance shocked his nerves. And he'd been an absolute wreck, hardly able to string together a series of coherent thoughts.

"Why did you write this?" he asked me one evening at Mrs. Crow's holding up *The Dawnhurst Herald* with my first article.

"I needed money. You weren't interested in sponsoring my endeavor," I replied, rubbing my eyes. I had been squinting and peering at a typewriter for hours.

"You told the city my mother was missing. That's private family business!" He said, going red in the face.

"It's hardly private if there's a missing person. I thought that some publicity on the matter might help us find her." This was a lie. I knew where she was, but at least, it was a defensible position. It worked. Edward's temper cooled instantly.

"I should have thought of that myself." He looked back at the paper. I noticed a slight tremor in his hand. As he read, something enflamed him again. "But why in heaven's name would you accuse yourself in this article? Didn't you consider what that would do to your friends and family? That was selfish, Luella, and you know it!"

I peered at him.

"What's the matter with you?"

His eyes darted around the room as he tried to avoid my gaze.

"I should go. I must find my mother." He slapped the paper down on the table and retrieved his coat. I winced, knowing full well his search would come up empty. Seeing Edward's anxiety build ate at my scruples. Yes, his search kept him occupied, and I'd made the decision not to reveal her whereabouts, partly because I worried the truth would unhinge him entirely. I feared what Edward might do on the brink of desperation. But it didn't make withholding the information any easier.

"Will you be here for the grand jury proceedings?" I asked before he reached the door.

"Grand juries are a farce. The search for my mother is more important. I'm sorry, you'll have to find another sentry to go watch. Or do you disagree?"

I couldn't respond otherwise, and he left without ceremony. In his wake, a frown settled heavily on my face. I relied on Edward to bring news from the court proceedings. How else would I write my articles to pay for our solicitor? How else would I know what was happening to Bram?

I mulled over these concerns in the days leading up to the grand jury trial, and in the end, my curiosity overwhelmed me. I needed to see Bram myself, and I could only write articles based on the details I knew.

I simply had too many questions. How would Mr. Milton perform?

What was the state of Bram's mental decay? What juicy details could be plucked from the proceedings themselves?

I admitted that attending was a foolhardy proposition. Heading to the courthouse would be like walking into the jaws of a wolf, and I squirmed when considering sending Rebecca or Doug as they also might face questioning.

But I couldn't keep it from them either.

"It's a bad idea," Rebecca said, pushing an empty plate from her at Mrs. Crow's kitchen table. "We already have too many things going right."

"What do you mean?" I asked.

"It's just nature, perhaps even a dark magic. Call it what you will. We've had a lot of risky plans turn out lately. The scheme with Byron is working perfectly. Edward is giving you considerable breathing room. We found a solicitor. No one has recognized you yet. I think our luck might be up."

"Bah. That's just superstition," Doug said. "No one will look for Luella at the court."

"Everyone will look for Luella at the court," Rebecca countered.

"But how many police have really got a good look at her? With her dark hair, and whatever costume I'm sure we can arrange—"

"I can't believe you're encouraging this," Rebecca said, cheeks flushed.

"I'm only saying it may not seem as grave as it sounds. I wager she can get in and out without a problem. Go in. Sit in the back. Don't draw attention. Slip out before it's over. Who's going to feel confident enough to make an arrest?"

Between Doug and I both urging Rebecca to let me go, her protestations only lasted so long before giving way to a shaky allowance, "If this turns sour don't blame me."

Once we tasked ourselves with finding an adequate disguise, the week rushed by. Before I knew it, I was walking toward the courthouse on the northwest side of the city.

I refused to disguise myself as a man. It had worked once before and, with all my time traipsing around the Netherdowns in trousers, it felt natural enough. But Rebecca insisted that if someone took a second glance at me, they'd notice. Instead, I added some weight by padding my dress and sponges in my cheeks to give the impression of a more stocky, sturdy woman. Doug also found me a pair of tinted lenses to wear in order to hide my eyes.

Rebecca even went so far as to do war against my eyebrows, saying they were far too feminine. She took a bristle brush and roughed them up all coarse.

I was grateful for it now, though, as the courthouse came into view, and my heart began racing. A handful of scattered police officers milled around outside. I didn't recognize any of them, but I tried not to look their way all the same. The building stood on an island of stone surrounded by roads. It was circular in construction. I'd heard once that its design was copied from the Crown Court building in Gloucester. I'd seldom had occasion to come to this part of Dawnhurst, but I'd always thought the building looked incomplete.

I thought the same now. It looked like Hirythe's tower in the Netherdowns, if someone had chopped it off at the second story.

I turned my head downward, using the cold as cover under my bonnet. I was happy to see that I wasn't the only one planning to attend. A scattered crowd milled about, grouped off in pairs and threes. I melted into one group of four, just a half step behind them.

I passed through the tall front door and held my breath as I crossed under the watchful eyes of two guards elevated by the entrance. The crowd shifted slowly upstairs to a viewing balcony. As we ascended the steps, I spotted my article tucked under one gentleman's arm.

To stay anonymous, I took a position in the middle of the back of the spectators. A wooden pillar blocked my view of a portion of the room, but I doubted the prudence of elbowing my way to get a better view.

Below, in a round clearing toward the center, I saw a thin man in a dark suit and a bright, powdered wig. Was this our Mr. Milton? I should have asked Rebecca for a physical description. He fumbled with papers on his long, polished table.

To the side, I saw a row of benches filled with gentlemen looking quite pleased with themselves. They evaluated the onlookers down upturned, self-important noses. Slick smiles hid behind their mask of severity.

A door at the back of the room swung open, and Bram was escorted to a second table in front of the judge's podium.

When I saw him, my heart leapt into my throat. I had to swallow down tears of relief just to know he was still real. He looked terrible, dark bags hanging from his eyes. He was thinner than I remembered, and his hair, usually unkempt, looked positively wild. Chains hung from his limbs, restricting his movement and straining at the cuffs of a rough prisoner's uniform.

The spectacle and gravity of the whole scene had an immediate impact on me. The jarring musicality of the clinking chains rattled in my ears. And when a court officer called for all in attendance to rise for the magistrate, who marched to his elevated podium with downplayed but pedantic pomp, I wondered if I were dreaming.

On the second-floor balcony, no one had chairs, but the first floor attendees, primarily city officials or representatives from wealthy families, took a cue from the magistrate and took their seats.

It was then I realized Bram sat at his table, flanked by police, but alone. The chair beside sat empty and hopeless.

"Are all assembled?" Magistrate Silverson asked. He appeared younger than I had assumed, given his judicial reputation. His wig fell in curls down his shoulders, and he peered at Bram and the prosecutor over a beaked and crooked nose. Despite this aquiline feature, the rest of his face might have been jovial had he chosen a different profession.

"The Crown is here, represented," the prosecutor said.

"Very well. Mr. Lowhouse, I assume you are to represent yourself?" Silverson asked.

Bram cast a longing glance at the empty chair beside him and opened his mouth to respond when the sound of shuffling feet and a murmuring crowd interrupted him. A stout man wearing a fine coat carried a briefcase to Bram's side in a hurry.

"I apologize, your worship," the man said. "Mr. Bart Milton for the defense."

So this was my money.

Whispers circulated around me. I had named this man in my article, and apparently, my readers had come to witness the joust.

"Mr. Milton, you exhibit a flagrant tardiness," Silverson said, indignantly upturning his nose.

"My most humble apologies. It shan't happen again."

"I pray you are more prepared for this man's case than you were with travel plans this morning. Must I remind you, that your profession is already peculiar enough without your marks against its professionalism."

Milton blushed bright red and stood with his feet touching together.

"My apologies once more, your worship."

"Let us proceed." Silverson stood and addressed the room in a loud voice. "Today, we are gathered in an ancient body of noble purpose. The grand jury proceeding is a time-honored tradition forming a vital part of that great system of justice which so distinguishes our kingdom and enhances the reputation of our courts of law. You, the gentlemen of the jury, have a straightforward, albeit solemn, responsibility, to assess evidence without bias or prejudice and determine whether this man, Bram Lowhouse, should face a full criminal trial for murder or conspiracy to commit murder."

A hot flush rushed to my cheeks. Edward had told me this was the charge, but to hear it in so formal a setting was something altogether more set in stone. The theatricality of the court room accomplished its aim of communicating the severity of its charge.

"I remind you, gentlemen of the grand jury, that you need not aspire to the standard your peers must adopt should this case go forward. It is enough that you believe the evidence, if credible, to be sufficient to merit a criminal trial. You do not bear the burden of deciding this man's guilt. On the other hand, I caution you to treat this grave responsibility with the due care and attentions that it merits. While Mr. Lowhouse's condemnation is not in your hands, your hands, his liberty very well may be."

Silverson motioned with his arm to the prosecutor. I felt a pang of guilt for the way I had treated the magistrate in my writing. I had purposefully made my report sensational with the intent to sell as many copies as possible. Bram taught me how to sell stories months before. Fond memories played before my mind of dogs stealing paintings, bread transforming to mutton, mysterious lights in nearby woods —the memory was bittersweet.

But Silverson did not appear to harbor any ill feelings toward Bram. Although he had allowed the criminal process to continue, he showed no signs of the prejudice he cautioned against.

The prosecution stepped forward and gestured with arms wide.

"Gentlemen," he began. "I have no desire to deceive any of you. My position in representing the crown is one of justice and fair dealing. I've been informed by the Dawnhurst Police Force that this man has critical connections to the death of Luke Thomas. I will admit that, at first, I was dubious of the evidence that accompanied the claim. But as I probed deeper, coincidence and correlation shocked me deeply. Perhaps the same thoughts will occur to you, as well."

He sat down again, and the room was silent for several moments.

After an awkward pause, Silverson cleared his throat and stared at Mr. Milton. Milton looked up from his papers, startled.

"Oh, right. Mr. Highhouse has nothing to add at this time. We ask that the presentation of evidence begin."

"Mr. Lowhouse, you mean," Silverson corrected with a stern voice.

"Yes. What did I say?"

Silverson nodded and turned back to the prosecutor. I knit my brows. Shouldn't Milton have said something? The speech I just heard to the grand jury must have had some impact. Would our lawyer do nothing to diffuse the effect?

I craned my neck and saw a puzzled expression on Bram's face as well. I hoped Milton knew what he was about. We were as helpless in his hands as a wounded animal.

As I expected, the prosecutor first brought out a sheet of paper and held it up. Gentlemen in the jury craned their necks to get a better look at it.

"This is a damning piece of evidence," the prosecutor said in a loud stage voice. "It bears the accused's signature and details a confession that he was, indeed, the author of a scheme to end Lord Thomas' life and deflect blame to another."

A gentle murmur went through the courtroom. Silverson gently tapped his gavel on the stand to quiet the sparse crowd.

"It is not for us today to determine whether this confession is true or not," the prosecutor continued. "But I would think, it is evidence enough, even alone, to allow the good people of Dawnhurst-on-Severn and its neighboring communities to inspect and examine in the final stages of this man's trial."

He brought the paper to the jury.

"You can see that the document was created in accordance with the police force's ordinary protocols. The signature of a Sergeant George Cooper accompanies that of the accused here at the bottom. There is no fraudulence or forgery here. We are also willing to produce testimonies from the officers who took this confession. They can state this man did so without coercion."

I shut my eyes. He confessed for me. He was never meant to be here. The plan was to free him. What had I done? What could Milton possibly say to ease the gloom and foreboding of a signed confession?

The prosecutor sauntered back to his table, nose in the air.

"Mr. Milton," Silverson said, leaning forward in his chair, "do you have anything to add on the issue of this document?"

Milton took his time standing, studying a document on the table as he did so. I held my breath.

"Your worship, the defense has nothing to add at this time."

Another murmur swept through the room. Silverson pounded his gavel again, but it wasn't as loud as my heart pounding in my ears.

Nothing to add? If he wasn't going to refute the confession, what were we doing here at all?

"I will have order," Silverson cautioned the court. "The prosecution may proceed to the next item." As he said it, I thought I detected a pitying glance in Bram's direction.

The rest of the evidence was paraded out in a blur. I could hardly focus. I considered the evidence brought forward complete rubbish: tangentially circumstantial at best and altogether irrelevant at worst.

In every case, I hoped Milton would finally stand and present his own arguments to discredit the prosecutor's theory, but after every item he parroted the same thing.

Bram had apparently kept an account at a bank other than Luke Thomas', thereby allegedly creating a tie with some of his great commercial rivals.

The defense had nothing to add.

Bram had apparently been a known acquaintance of several pickpockets and cons.

The defense had nothing to add.

Bram had reportedly been sought for arrest in other cities across the kingdom for alleged crimes of fraud.

The defense had nothing to add.

Several hours passed without my knowledge. I was too wrapped up in anger and disbelief. Bram's chance at freedom was slipping away before my eyes.

Finally, the prosecution brought out a copy of Byron's weekly magazine. On its front page was my never published article.

"The crown's final evidence for this proceeding is this article, recalled from printers by a Byron Livingston, editor and owner of Langley's Miscellany. It is hard to believe, I know gentlemen—but truth is so very strange at times. This story was submitted to a printing press fin time for a late morning batch of print on the very morning police discovered the remains of the late Luke Thomas."

As my involvement was paraded in front of the grand jury, a fresh wave of fear sprung from my chest. I realized in a moment just how foolhardy coming today had been.

"The article was penned by a certain Travis Blakely, a name the Dawnhurst Police have identified as a pseudonym. The true author behind this writing is none other than Luella Winthrop, a woman who would rather flee the city than be questioned on this matter by police. The inference is clear. The details of Lord Thomas' demise were known before they occurred."

I set my jaw as the people around me, appreciating the drama, whispered and chattered. Some looked afraid, as if I might pop up from behind a pillar somewhere at any moment and commit another murder.

"Again, gentlemen of the grand jury," the prosecutor put his fists on his hips, "I do not come before you to connect the inferences that can be made from these differing pieces of evidence. Rather, I submit to you, that when taken as a whole, there is no logical alternative to trying Bram Lowhouse in front of a full criminal court, and I insist that it be done so in haste. If he is guilty, the people of England deserve to know, and know yesterday!"

He pumped his fist in the air, and several members of the grand jury pounded their canes on the ground in agreement. I frowned. This prosecutor had a gift of speech and presentation. Sizing up Milton now, I doubt there was much he could have done to prevent what I considered the inevitable next step.

Silverson quieted the courtroom and shifted to observe Milton with grave expression.

"Mr. Milton, you have elected not to dispute any of the evidence brought by the prosecution. Do you have any comments you desire to share with the jury today as is your right and duty?"

Silverson lowered his brows at Bram's barrister, laying a heavy inflection on the word duty. Mr. Milton stood once more, straightened his waistcoat, and took a deep breath.

"I have spent my time neglecting an opportunity to expound on the weakness of the evidence. I have done this for two reasons."

Bram straightened in his chair, and everyone in the room leaned forward, eager not to miss a word. Perhaps I had misjudged Milton. Did he have a hidden dagger ready for the kill?

"The first is simply that the weakness of the evidence speaks for itself. What value is there in a confession if you have to grasp at straws to prove its veracity? Which brings me to my second, and more important point. The issue is moot in any event, as I believe Bram Lowhouse to be of unsound mind. He belongs in an asylum, not a prison."

The gavel pounded. A storm of speculation from the onlookers.

"Order! I will have order!"

This was Milton's great strategy? Rather than condemn Bram to the gallows, divert him to an asylum? I ground my teeth in frustration. I had paid for this overwhelming genius?

Bram suddenly stood, his chains rattling with a violent energy.

"Perhaps Mr. Milton is correct," Bram called. "I would have to be crazy to allow this man to represent me here today!"

This outburst set the courtroom ablaze in shouts and conversation. Police seized Bram, yanked him from the table, and dragged him back to the door from which he came. Milton adopted a bright shade of fuchsia while Silverson bellowed for order.

Some men on the balcony threw balled up paper at Milton. Court officers closed in to maintain the peace.

I grabbed the elbow of the closest woman to my right.

"All the excitement has made me a bit dizzy. Would you mind escorting me down the stairs?" I asked, turning my face to her only halfway. All the commotion appeared to make her uncomfortable as well. She inclined her head, took me by the arm, and we descended together.

Outside, I thanked her and turned toward Mrs. Crow's flat. My head swam. The sky was beginning to darken. I must have spent several hours in the courthouse.

I walked quickly, fueled by the pent up frustration Mr. Milton had set off in me. We hadn't paid him a fortune, but certainly enough to inspire a competent performance. How much preparation was required to stay silent for hours before finally accusing his client of lunacy?

By Bram's reaction, he was as surprised as I was. I fought an urge to curse Rebecca for finding such an idiot.

Was I being too harsh on Mr. Milton? Presumably, Bram was not his first case. If he believed this to be Bram's best defense, shouldn't I trust him?

After all, if Bram was in an asylum, it would be much easier to visit with him, and perhaps from these visits he could advise me on a way to get him back to the Netherdowns.

I sighed, eliciting a visible puff of air in front of me. There was too much uncertainty with an asylum. Perhaps they wouldn't let me visit him at all.

"Woah!" I heard a cab driver cry. He pulled back on the reins of his horses, and I stumbled back out of the street. "Pay attention to the road, miss!" he called to me. I held up a hand in acknowledgement, afraid and embarrassed. The horses had come so close to stamping me with their hooves that I felt the warmth from their bodies.

I took a moment to collect myself. What was I, a little girl with her head in the clouds? I looked around to see if anyone had witnessed my mistake, and then I saw it.

The sun had settled low now, and the lamps were lit in uneven distances down the street. Behind me, I saw a hulking figure heading in my direction. My racing heart froze. I don't know how I was convinced it followed me, but I would have sworn to it in front of that grand jury.

My mind raced through possible explanations. I had no shortage of enemies. Trying to appear casual, I continued on, but found the first opportunity to cut through an alley to a neighboring street.

After clearing the corner of that alley, I labored on as quickly as I dared without drawing too much attention. How dangerous life must be for those afraid of the police! My breath huffed out in great puffs of steam. When I got to the street corner, I glanced back over my shoulder.

The shadowy figure gained on me. He, too, was moving at a very brisk pace. What could I do? At this rate, I wouldn't make it back to Mrs. Crow's in time. But there was no where else to go in this part of town?

Only Edward's tenement was nearby. I winced. It would have to do.

I took a left onto one of the main roads that cut through the northwest quarter. Wealth bred safety, and in these streets, the lights were more plentiful. Evergreen boughs still hung from occasional lamplights, remnants of the Christmas season, and though it was dark, it couldn't have been later than five thirty. Couples on strolls or on their way to dinner littered the avenue.

But still my pursuer continued, closer now than before. I wanted to turn and get a good look but didn't dare.

I passed a roasting chestnut stand and took another left. At the end of this small street, the elaborate gothic facade of the Thomas' tenement building stood tall. I had only to get there. Then the doorman might recognize me, or at least protect a woman from an assailant.

I didn't get close.

A heavy arm wrapped around my shoulders and pulled me behind a brick building into a narrow alley. I tried to scream, but a massive hand covered my mouth, muffling it.

"Blimey, Luella. If I were you, I wouldn't be out on the streets so openly. Raven hair and extra padding or not."

Gerald stared tenderly down at me like a disappointed elder brother.

❧ 9 ❧

GERALD'S STORY

"At first, I thought I'd take the boat down the Severn and leave it at Bristol," Gerald said, savoring a cup of a particularly strong batch of Mrs. Crow's tea. He closed his eyes and breathed in the aroma. "The carnival folk split. Some found a small cottage outside the city there. I figured I'd sit through the winter with them until show season was back on in Spring, then meet back up with the group still in Reading."

Mrs. Crow put a plate of rough cheesed buns in front of him. He nodded gratefully.

"Why'd you come back?" I asked.

"I never really left. When I got back to the boat, I realized it wasn't mine. Truth be told, our conversation scared the daylights out of me. I'd never felt like I couldn't say something I'd wanted to before. Inside, I tried to answer all your questions, but my mouth simply wouldn't form the words."

He took a crumbly bite from one of the buns.

"Hell," he said through a full mouth, "it was harder than apologizing to someone when you feel you're in the right."

"So where did you go instead?"

"Without the bed, I turned back toward Reading. I nearly knocked down a stable door until they'd rent me a horse, complaining the whole time about the hour. I rode until I my I'd practically fallen asleep and had to stop to rest in Swindon. I fell fast asleep into a fit of the blinking odd dreams."

Mrs. Crow, who had been tidying the kitchen counter, scurried off to her bedroom. Cyrus, who had kept a wary eye on Gerald since he'd come in, followed her. I looked after, fearing that I might be starting to overstay my welcome after bringing another stranger in to be fed.

In any event, the dog's trust in me had diminished considerably.

"When I woke late in the morning, it all came back. I remember everything," he said.

"You mean you remember how you came to be on a boat throwing a book into the Severn River?"

"Just about. He was a devil, Luella. I've spent my adult life around people who do feats and tricks to amaze crowds. It's their profession to flip the world upside down, or at least make it look that way. Our hypnotists hypnotize, sure, but this man was a devil."

"Where did you first see him?" I asked, the hairs on my arm prickling up.

"In Reading, the night after you found me in the Forbury Gardens. I was at a pub when he approached me. Thin like a chimney and wearing a coat that was too fine for the establishment. At first, I wasn't afraid of him at all. He didn't look like dangerous, even when picturing him with a weapon in his hand. But he asked if I knew Bram Lowhouse, and my face must have given me away.

"He ordered me another pint and sat down, asking all about the fair. I'm usually quite tight-lipped about that, as you might imagine. But he claimed to be a connoisseur of that type of entertainment, that he'd traveled as far as Germany and Egypt to observe different acts and effects. He said he'd met Bram on one of those journeys. Then my head got foggy."

"He drugged you," I suggested. Gerald swallowed another bite of bun and leaned back in his chair.

"Perhaps," he said. "But my thoughts grew thicker, like simmering treacle. It was as though someone else had control of my body until I woke up in Swindon, as I told you."

"He hypnotized you." I stood and crossed to the window. It was dark outside, and talking about Jeremy like this pushed me to check that the curtains were drawn tight.

"How's that possible?" Gerald asked. I shook my head. "Our hypnotists use plants in the audience. Sometimes we get lucky and a spectator is impressionable. But this? We're talking weeks, Luella, weeks I did someone else's bidding."

"His name is Jeremy Evans, and I'm sorry that I led him to you. He must have been following Edward and me. When I found you in the park, he would have made a connection."

"Luella, what are you mixed up in?" Gerald asked. I wrung my hands.

"Did Bram ever do something you couldn't explain?"

"Sure. He was our resident illusionist. Would have been right terrible at his job if he hadn't."

I turned back from the window.

"That's not what I mean. When he wasn't performing, behind the curtain, so to speak, did he ever do something that defied explanation?"

Gerald stood up.

"Nothing that couldn't be explained," he said.

"That's the thing about magic though, isn't it, Gerald? It camouflages itself. It can always be explained."

A chill breeze swept in from under the front door and drifted through the air. Gerald worked his jaw and stared at me, unwilling to accept what I suggested outright but unable to refute it, either. Hadn't he just spent weeks under a type of hypnosis?

"I was drugged," he said at length.

"For weeks?"

A gentle knock on the door broke the silence. I pursed my lips and opened it carefully. Doug and Rebecca crammed inside and closed it behind them.

"We're in a mess," Doug said, "an absolute mess of it."

"What happened? Is the grand jury done so soon?" I asked. Doug and Rebecca both straightened like poles upon seeing Gerald. The two men eyed each other up. Seeing both of them in the kitchen of such a small flat was almost comical.

"This is Gerald," I explained. "He's a friend. He knows Bram well."

"Not well enough, it seems," Gerald said.

"Doug Tanner," Doug said, extending a dubious hand. Gerald eyed it warily before taking it.

"Gerald Fields."

They postured awkwardly for a moment before releasing. *Men.* I had stopped trying to understand their social protocols.

Mrs. Crow appeared in the doorway from her bedroom, took one look at her kitchen, and turned around to disappear again.

"Well, what happened? Why are you both in such a state?" I asked.

"It's Milton," Rebecca explained. "He came to us as soon as the jury was dismissed to deliberate. He's dropping Bram."

"He's what?" My mouth fell open.

"Said he's never experienced such an embarrassment in his life," Doug said. "Apparently, Bram humiliated him in front of Silverson and the prosecution."

I folded my arms. "He deserved it. He tried to tell the court Bram belonged in an asylum. I think your mention of concerns about Bram's mental being may have inspired him."

"Bram's not insane. Anyone can see it," Gerald said.

"He might not be quite as lucid as you remember, Mr. Fields," Rebecca replied. "Jeremy is loose in the Netherdowns doing who knows what to his memory."

Gerald stared at the three of us. "The nether what?"

Rebecca paled. "I'm sorry, Luella. You said he knew Bram... I assumed—"

"He's learning more all the time. As are we, especially about lawyers."

Mixed emotions mingled in my breast. Seeing Milton's presence at the trial was uninspiring, but at least, it turned out to be some sort of legal strategy. Wouldn't it be better to have a barrister at the full criminal trial? I planned to have Doug express our displeasure with the insanity defense and expected a new one to form in its place.

Could Bram defend himself to any adequacy after he had confessed to the crime?

"You hired that lawyer?" Gerald asked. I nodded, and he looked around the room. "How'd you afford it?"

"It's a long story," Doug said quickly, but Gerald's question chilled my blood.

The money.

"Doug, did Mr. Milton give back the money we'd given him?" I asked. It sounded naïve and pathetic, even to me.

"He's not going to give it back. He's said it's already been spent and invested. Most likely on ruddy nutrients," Rebecca said with a grimace.

"He abandoned the client. He has no right—"

"He has every right! As far as he is concerned, he did the work. Why should he return the funds? Didn't he tell us he practically took us on for charity?"

I sank into one of the kitchen chairs.

"How will we afford a new lawyer?" I asked.

"You can write another story, can't you?" Doug asked. "Isn't that why you attended the grand jury trial today."

"Yes, but we'd already paid Milton everything from my last story, plus the small advance Byron worked out for my up and coming. And Bram publicly humiliated him. Where will we find another lawyer eager to take on a case that pays poorly and involves a troublesome client?"

We fell into a heavy silence.

"Perhaps it won't get that far," Rebecca suggested. "The grand jury may yet acquit him."

"Milton offered no defense on any piece of evidence," I replied. "His plan all along was to whisk Bram out of the mouth of a prison cell and into the arms of an asylum."

"What about Edward?" Doug asked. I closed my eyes and shook my head.

"He won't do it. I fear he believes, truly, that Bram is involved with his father's death."

Gerald let out a grunt in disgust.

"Bram Lowhouse would do no such thing." He stood and picked up his hat.

"Where are you going?" I asked.

"I need some air. I'll come round tomorrow some time. Doug. Miss." He tipped his hat at my friends. "Thank Mrs. Crow for the buns on my behalf, won't you?"

He ducked out the door and into the night air. When he was gone, Rebecca joined me at the kitchen table.

"There must be something we can do," she said.

"I can sell the pub," Doug suggested. We both gaped.

"What?" Rebecca asked.

"Absolutely not," I said. "For one thing, it would take too long. For another, it would require too public a transaction."

His brow gave away his relief that I turned down the help. Rebecca's expression had warmed in a strange way. She looked at him with a new countenance.

"And besides," I continued, "I can't ask any more from either of you. Doug, you came to my aid without any thought of return. I will never forget that. How could I ask you to give up your life's work?"

He shuffled his feet and busied his gaze on the ground.

"Truth be told, I'm glad to have met you. The positives outweigh the bad," he mumbled, scuffling his shoes softly on the ground. His eyes shifted quickly to Rebecca. She had suddenly found great interest in the grain of the table.

In spite of everything, a smile escaped me. As far as I was concerned, if anyone deserved happiness at the end of all this, it was these two.

It hurt me to bring their attention back to the issue at hand.

"Rebecca, I know it was a miracle you found Mr. Milton in the first place, but you must try again."

She snapped out of her reverie and replied, "Of course."

"In the meantime, it looks like I have more stories to write. Perhaps we can squeeze additional pay from the publisher somehow, but to do it, these had better be good."

"Skewer that Milton," Doug said. "If he's going to abandon Bram over a ruined reputation, let's make sure his reputation is good and ruined for certain."

I laughed.

"Doug, that's positively malicious."

He shrugged and pulled my typewriter out of the cupboard for me.

"He's a big lad. I'm sure he'll recover. Nutrients."

MONEY AND MOTIVE

The typewriter keys stuck. I struggled, straining my eyes by the light of a single candle. To make matters worse, I could hardly string a sentence together.

I was too worried about Bram to concentrate. In the morning, the grand jury would announce their verdict. It was all but a formality. I was at the trial. No one sitting in those benches would believe Bram was beyond his accusation. Not after Milton's gamble.

When the tallow had all melted down and dripped onto the table in thick lumps, I realized there was little hope of producing anything worthy of publication that night. I tried to sleep, sliding into bed beside Mrs. Crow, feeling guilty as a child. She had put up with so much already on my behalf. I had practically converted her home into an inn.

When at last I fell asleep, dreams of Jeremy and Mr. Milton dancing triumphantly under a gallows tortured me. I woke several times and imagined in my half-asleep stupor that Lady Thomas' portrait hung on the wall.

My nerves were frazzled, and panic seeped in through all the cracks of my composure.

I considered what failure might mean. In the worst case, Bram would swing. Edward's mother would never be recovered. Hirythe, the last of the fae, would be trapped forever in a half-world of memory. There was no telling what would happen to the Netherdowns if Bram died.

I wished I could do more. If only there was a way to track down the missing page from the diary. At first, I dreamed of retracing Johnson's steps between the jail and the station, but that hope shriveled the more time passed. My only hope to enter the Netherdowns was if Bram had some other hidden method of entry, but I wouldn't have the opportunity to discuss it with him anytime soon.

I balled my fists. It was infuriating to be so helpless. A twisted and sick part of me missed my magical ailment. I wished the fog creature would haunt my dreams and propose some other devilish gambit to me. Hadn't that creature told me to instruct it, give it directions? I resisted because I didn't want to be its slave.

Well, here I was. Free.

At the earliest light the next morning, I left the bed and dressed myself with more care than I had since my arrest. If Edward enchanted me, I wanted my money's worth. Doug had seen Edward's carriage roll back into town. It irked me that he hadn't called on me yet. If he insisted on playing his role as devoted courtier, what right did he have to neglect it?

The streets were mostly empty, populated only by those industrious men and women who braved a January morning chill in the name of business. I passed only three police officers, two standing on a corner chatting in their thick coats, one exiting a shop with pastry in hand.

They paid me no mind as they tried their best to soak in the sun on a cloudless morning. It occurred to me that paranoia and alert guards were a thing for evenings and late nights. Whoever heard of burglars roaming at the wholesome hour of nine o'clock?

Even the facade of the ornately carved building that housed the Thomas' Dawnhurst tenement building looked plain and unassuming in the waking light.

I walked confidently past the man at the door with a wave as though we were long friends. He hardly looked up from his morning paper.

On arriving at the door to Edward's tenement, I hesitated, trying to steel my nerves. He had already refused once to pay for Bram's lawyer, to say nothing of the pit in my stomach whenever I stood beside him.

But Bram could hang if I didn't at least try. I raised a gloved hand and knocked. My gaze lingered on the gloves. They were a dark leather, and the fur inside was the softest I'd ever felt. Edward had bought them for me while we traveled through England together.

My heart wanted to warm at the memory. I choked down the impulse. Beneath the gloves, the engagement ring he'd given me made my hand heavy. I still had not removed it, even while Edward was away...

There was no answer.

I knocked again but heard no stirring from within. Had Doug been mistaken about the carriage? I tried the handle. It turned, unlocked, and I poked my head inside. The sight took my breath away.

I had been in these lodgings not long ago, and the luxury of it made me feel uncomfortable. It was too neat, too clean, and too expensive for my tastes.

Now it looked as though it had been torn apart. Paintings on the wall hung at crooked angles. The floor was littered with coats, shirts, and boots. Books were strewn across chairs, open face down, pages crumpling between their covers and the floor.

I ventured inside and closed the door behind me. For some reason, fear accompanied me through the entryway and grew with every step.

Half-eaten plates of food balanced on the edges of tables and credenzas, some spilling their contents over finely finished wood.

Entering the dining room, a complete tangle of maps, documents, mostly empty tumblers, and solidified chunks of tallow wax hanging from a pair of expensive candelabras littered the cabinets and floor. More jarring though, especially given my current state, were the banknotes haphazardly littering the dining table beside Edward Thomas.

He sat hunched over, head resting on the solid wood, by all appearances, dead asleep.

I eyed the money shamefully, wondering what my chances were of successfully taking some and disappearing before he woke. There had to be more than enough to hire a lawyer—or at least to get one started.

I reflected on just how different Edward's life must have been from my own. We'd been crazy to think we could have joined our lives. It had been so easy to get swept up playing a noble lady, but deep down I was inherently different from him.

When had Edward wanted for anything? How could he so callously refuse to help a man in need? When money is abundant, does it really become so easy to believe its value is symbolic? What right had he to withhold the resources through a sense of snubbed pride while others were in such desperate need?

I crept up to the table and reached out a hand.

Edward moaned. I retracted it at once, appalled by what I'd nearly done.

Edward raised his head slowly and squinted around the room. He hadn't shaved since I saw him last. His cheeks were hollow, and dark circles hung below his eyes. Sweat matted his usually well-mannered hair to his head in haggard splotches, and his lips were dry and chapping.

When our eyes met, he froze and stared, as if trying to determine if I was truly there or I was some illusion.

Despite how he'd hurt me, sympathy bubbled from my heart.

"Edward," I said, searching for words.

"Luella?" he asked hoarsely. He cleared his throat, drawing some energy and vitality from within himself. He straightened in his chair and rubbed his eyes. "What are you doing here?"

"I came to talk with you—"

"You should be hiding in Mrs. Crow's flat."

"Edward," I looked around, "what happened here?"

He stood up slowly, a steadying hand firmly on the table.

"There's still no trace of my mother. I have made inquiries everywhere I can think of."

"Have you not slept?"

"I was sleeping just now, was I not?" He touched his neck tenderly and winced.

"You need rest."

"That's a luxury I can't afford. What time is it now? I've wasted hours." He patted his waistcoat, searching for a pocket watch.

"You'll be no good to your mother if you don't have strength," I argued.

"She's missing, Luella!" His voice bellowed through the dining room. "It's been over a week. There's no sign! Could you sleep in my position?"

I bit my lip as he sifted through papers on the table.

"I've sent messages to her usual stops in Dawnhurst, the seamstress, the hatter, even my father's old club. I've sent dispatches to her close acquaintances all over this side of England. She's not at home. The last I saw her was here, before you were arrested. I fear—" He swallowed back his emotions. "What if my father didn't take his own life after all?"

I stared and considered divulging the truth. Was the harm of him knowing as dire as I previously imagined? He was clearly in great pain. Whatever he had done to me, losing Charlotte could not have been part of that plan.

If he was in league with Jeremy, couldn't I use the information to turn them against one another?

"I've tried urging the Dawnhurst Police to conduct a more thorough search, but they're completely disorganized at present."

I paused, confused at that unexpected bit of information.

"Disorganized? Why?"

Edward stumbled to a nearby credenza, where he picked up a pitcher and poured a glass of water into the nearest tumbler, which still held a half finger's remains of brandy.

"Sergeant Cooper announced his resignation."

I steady myself on the back of a chair.

"He what?"

"It was after Silverson's public rebuke of him. I think my father's case was the boiling point."

I thought the sergeant would hold his position until he died at his desk or in the field. He certainly voiced that conviction to me when we spoke in his office. To think, we had planned to launch a defamation campaign against him. It might have worked.

Now, I was left with the worst of both worlds: Cooper disgraced, Bram on trial. Only one man benefitted. A hesitant, ironic smile tugged at my mouth. Edward had been sly. If Charlotte hadn't gone missing, he'd have everything...

"What will happen to the force?" I asked.

Edward downed the water mechanically.

"My name has been suggested as a replacement."

"You? Sergeant Edward Thomas? I wasn't sure you still wanted to work with the police," I said carefully.

"I didn't, at least not under Cooper. I lost respect for him after the way he chased you. But being a sergeant is a different question. I would have resources to do much good."

"I'm not sure it's resources you lack," I said, tipping my head to the bank notes littering the table.

"Money can only buy so much. It didn't buy my father's safety, did it?" He clenched his jaw as though nauseous.

"Are you planning on taking the position?"

He turned to me. "I wanted to talk with you first."

I pursed my lips. Edward was either devilishly strategic, a trait he might have inherited from his mother, or incredibly arrogant. On what ground would I tell him to refuse the position?

"Isn't it odd that you'd be considered? After all, you're engaged to a fugitive."

He shook his head.

"Few know of our engagement. Imagine, Luella. If I were sergeant, I could decide to drop your charges. Especially when Bram's case is resolved."

"You mean when he hangs?" I dug my fingernails into my palm.

"Whether he hangs or not, this trial will put the issue of my father's demise to rest, at least for the courts."

"So if you took this position of power, we could be married in public without the shadow of the law hanging above me."

He folded his arms. "It may take some time, but yes."

I closed my eyes and massaged my temples. The fortune. The estate. The power. And now the woman. At first, I had no motive and no means to assign Edward. Now...

There were still holes. I didn't know what high magic he used to enchant me or how he knew it would cause me to kill his father. The chain of events didn't make sense in my head. Of course, I didn't even know if I had a firm grasp on cause and effect. Sraith no longer infected me, it was true, but had it left lasting scars on my understanding?

"Are you sure you still want to marry me?" I asked.

"You can't be serious," he replied, roughly. "After all this, you doubt my conviction?"

I opened my eyes to see Edward growing angry. I didn't expect my question to provoke such a strong reaction.

"I'm sorry—"

"How much more can I do to prove my feelings?" His face was turning red. "I lost my father, and I sided with you against the police. I sheltered you, I hid you, and I rode by your side for months while we looked for another man to treat your condition."

"I didn't ask you to come with me," I cried defensively.

"It was hard to see you pine after him. Do you think I ignored your attempts to prevent my use of the diary? Do you think I'm terribly stupid and didn't recognize what feelings must have motivated your behavior? Now, when I've lost my mother, you question my devotion." He planted both hands squarely on the table.

He pretended he was so innocent. I didn't consider him stupid, but he clearly thought I was. My nostrils flared.

"Isn't that why you've come here?" he asked, standing back up. "You aren't concerned for my mother. You're only concerned about him. I heard what happened yesterday at the trial. No doubt you've lost faith in the solicitor you've somehow inspired to take his case. Did you hope to persuade me to reconsider covering his legal expenses?"

I stood up.

"You're so smart, aren't you, Edward?" I spat. "If I'm so terrible, why did my question upset you so? Why do you want to marry such a terrible human being?"

"I want to marry you because I love you."

I jutted out my jaw. How could he dare?

"I'm not sure you know what that means," I said. He rounded the table.

"I'm not sure either of us know. But who does at the outset? Luella, please, I'm heading back to Fernmount tomorrow. From there, I will conduct a proper search for my mother. I'm begging you. Come with me."

His eyes glistened. He looked terrible, a ghost of the man I knew. Despite all the time we'd spent together and all the knowledge I'd gained since, I could not tell what lay behind those eyes.

Did he truly love me? If he had a plan at the outset, it had not gone smoothly. His mother went missing, and perhaps he fell in love with the pawn he planned on using.

He took my hand and kissed it.

Or did he play with my emotions still?

"I can't leave him helpless," I whispered.

He looked down and swallowed.

"Even if I need your help, too? And my mother?"

It was too much.

I set my jaw and kept my silence. In a moment, Edward cleared his throat, looking away from me. A sense of finality filled the air.

"Leave me," he said. "I have to prepare for my journey."

He let go of my hand, and it hurt me more than I wanted. I fled the room.

666 JUDE ROW

AGAINST ALL ODDS, LOWHOUSE HEADED TO ASSIZES

Early yesterday afternoon, a grand jury ruling came from a panel of distinguished gentlemen with no legal experience that Bram Lowhouse may, indeed, be guilty in the case of Lucas Thomas' death.

In a baffling turn of events, Lowhouse's solicitor tried a risky legal strategy: do nothing whatsoever. After the prosecution paraded unconvincing evidence and tenuous connections for the jury, Mr. Bart Milton, solicitor with legal offices on 646 S. Winding Lane, opted not to refute any of the prosecution's evidence, instead relying wholly on a relatively new actionable legal defense: that of claiming a defendant insane.

Mr. Milton then demonstrated a technique that other barristers may want to mark as a learning example. If you plan to present a defense of insanity, it is best to explain such to a client beforehand, especially if the client is, as is evidently the case with Mr. Lowhouse, a man of sound mind.

Mr. Milton demonstrated a lazy effort, seeing as resting on one's laurels and declaring a defendant insane takes all the skill of a young woman of twelve years.

As a result, what started as a case deemed suspect at best by Magistrate Silverson, is now headed to the Dawnhurst Criminal Assizes later this month, *where the Crown's more experienced justice will administer proceedings. This is assuredly a loss for the public. Mr. Lowhouse's case has become more of a spectacle than the carnival that used to employ him. The poor defendant has been spat on first by a magistrate, then by his own solicitor, then again by the dated and ineffectual relic called a grand jury. Now, he must take a chance with a full criminal trial and must do so knowing the justice system has already failed him twice.*

I peered over my newspaper and stared at the reduced winter traffic of boats on the river. I stood in the middle of South Bridge, and there was a palpable difference in the temperature while standing above the water. It chilled me through.

Gerald had asked me to meet him here at this hour. He insisted that police rarely traversed this bridge, preferring the others that lay closer to their barracks. I'd lived in the city almost my entire life, but I was apparently blind to some of its facets.

It had been days since I'd last seen Edward. After our fight, he left for Fernmount without another word, off to look for his mother. He wouldn't find her. Everyday, I tried not to imagine his pain, not to let my sympathy for him distract from the fact that Hirythe's song had unmistakably marked him.

In the meantime, my next story published, I had nothing to do but worry. I'd try to start a draft of another article putting Cooper's resignation in the spotlight but felt stuck.

The assizes were in just a couple of weeks, but those weeks might have been years. Who knew what would happen in the Netherdowns in two weeks? What would be left of Bram's memory by the time the trial was over? And what would become of Hirythe?

These questions haunted me.

Yet, I could do nothing. Any attempt to visit Bram would surely end in my arrest, and without speaking with him, I had no hope of entering the Netherdowns.

Even if I could, what use would I be in the fight against Jeremy?

If only I had that last page. One night, I gathered enough courage to venture out and trace a path between the prison and the police office, hoping that it lay crumpled against an alley wall or stuck under a merchant's crate.

It was a desperate grab at a withering hope. We were helpless. Rebecca had no luck finding another willing lawyer in his place.

I had failed Bram. I'd sent him to prison in my stead. Now, I couldn't even help with his legal defense.

Despair glued my feet to the bridge, my elbows to its stone railing.

I wished that I still had my magical malady. The fog creature had asked me to command it, to make it do something. I'd refused its offers, but out of principle alone. Were it with me now, I'd be willing to barter. Was that wrong? Hadn't Bram traded portions of his life for his wife? There was something noble in it. Had not God himself laid a pattern of benevolent sacrifice?

I glanced over my shoulder, anxiously re-examining what I thought was a police officer's uniform. On second glance, it was nothing, just a man in a cape.

After my fingers had all but grown numb, Gerald's lumbering figure approached. He stopped a quarter of the way into the bridge, dropped a note on the ground, and turned immediately back toward the direction he'd come from.

I tucked my weekly beneath my arm and followed. When I bent to retrieve it, Gerald's scrawling hand had scratched out, *666 Jude Row, For Bram*.

My brows crinkled. Why bother sending me an address if I could just follow him? He was still easily visible above the crowd.

With a furtive glance behind me, I continued in his tracks across the bridge. But when I reached the east side, Gerald turned north. I paused.

Jude Row was most certainly south. If Gerald intended me to go to the address he left on his note, he meant for me to go alone.

My heart skipped. Why would he ask me to go alone?

Paranoia had become a constant companion, urging me to reassess how well I knew the man. Was this a trick? Gerald had destroyed the diary. Perhaps Jeremy found a way to rekindle his hypnotic hold.

I unfolded the note in my hand and stared at it.

For Bram. Perhaps it was bait, or else an entreaty to trust him.

Gerald had always been frustrated with the way I treated his friend. Would he invoke Bram's name just to ensnare me?

Then again, I had no reason to suspect Gerald would lay a trap for me, let alone one he couldn't attend himself. If the police waited for me on Jude Row, he'd be rewarded for bringing in a fugitive.

Once, I'd walked these streets fearlessly. Now, I had no shortage of enemies.

As I considered these competing theories, Gerald shrank further from view until I was left alone in the open afternoon holding nothing but a newspaper and the address.

I was tired of these games, tired of waiting.

Trap be damned.

I turned south, following the river until I arrived at an intersection. I remembered Jude Row from years before. Anna and I had frequented a laundry on that street. It wasn't far from the river, perhaps a few blocks in.

I headed east, and my heart began pounding. I breathed in the painful winter air as if I were running. When I saw the laundry, unchanged from how I remembered it, I had to steady myself on a lamppost. I scanned the street until I found a black, roughly painted door set in a grimy brick facade, flanked by filthy gray windows. The numbers 666 hung in muck-crusted iron above.

For a brief moment, it reminded me of the black onyx door from my dreams of the fog creature.

I looked around, searching for shadows in my pursuit. I pulled out Gerald's note again.

For Bram.

I walked quickly through the street, trying to generate enough momentum to render any abortive efforts futile. When I reached the door I didn't pause, instead grabbing the handle and willing myself inside.

Once in the building, however, fear gripped me in a paralytic vice. I stared at the closed door behind me, one hand on the handle, one on the wood, and tried to pretend I was invisible. I'd worked up the courage to enter. If this was a trap, I braced for the spring.

If it was not, benevolence would wait.

"Are you going to come in?" A weathered voice called from behind me. "I don't bite. Often."

The voice was colored with an accent from the highlands. It filtered through my ears and rang something from my past. Though I could not place the sound, the resonance of the man's voice was familiar. Vaguely, anciently familiar.

When I turned, I saw a pleasant-looking gentleman, hair graying under a well-maintained top hat, sitting in a chair. He took the hat off and smiled, deep crow's feet creasing the skin around his eyes.

"I don't have milk, I'm afraid. I hope sugar will do. And I took the liberty of procuring a small luxury. Iced buns. The best in the city."

In front of the man was a humble table, with tea set out and a pewter plate with a solitary iced bun sitting in front of a vacant chair.

I'd recognize Mrs. Barker's hand anywhere. My mouth watered. I hadn't eaten since the previous morning, too consumed by anxiety. But something still held me back. This man was a stranger.

"Luella, how are we to be acquainted if you won't at least sit. The food is not poisoned. I promise. Nor is the tea."

I inched forward and slowly descended into the chair, studying the man's face, trying desperately to discern his intention. But despite how I dug, I only found pleasant soil.

"Who are you?"

"My name is Alastair McHenry. Would you like one lump or two?"

I shook my head.

"Straight then? I suppose I should expect no less from Jerry's girl."

I narrowed my brows.

"I beg your pardon."

"You are Jerry's girl, aren't you? Jerry Winthrop?"

This felt too much like one of my feverish dreams.

"He was my father."

"He took it straight as well. Usually." Alastair smiled again. He had a trimmed beard of gray and red.

"How did you know my father?" My arms were cradled against my chest.

"A lot of people knew him. He was a good man. A leader among his friends, myself included. You don't remember, but we've met before. You were just a wee lass."

I searched my mind for an Alastair, but couldn't conjure this man's face or any mention of his name in my home. He must have noticed my effort.

"Don't go breaking your mind trying to remember. You were very young. Try the bun. It's very good. I bought two, but as you can see, I gave in to the temptation."

He took a sip of tea as he motioned to an empty plate beside him.

"I'm sorry, but what are we doing here?"

He put down the teacup.

"Well, your friend told me that you might be in a bit of trouble. If you would allow me, I'd like to assist you."

"Assist me? How?"

"I understand you may be in need of an barrister."

I tried to suppress a laugh. It came out as a snort.

"Bless you," he said, unfazed.

"You're a barrister?"

"Aye."

"Forgive me for doubting, but this doesn't exactly look like an barrister's office."

I looked about. The room was not dirty like the exterior, but it was very humble. A small coal-burning stove sat in the corner. There was a desk against the wall, but otherwise there were no large pieces of furniture besides the table before me.

"Fortunately for me, the building is cursed," he said.

"Cursed?"

"666. The rent is half what it'd be anywhere else. I keep this office as a place to meet clients, like yourself."

"What type of client would prefer a place like this to a more sophisticated office?"

"Clients who've had a wee bit of trouble with the police. Do you understand, little Luella?"

A defense lawyer. I commended the peculiar logic. If I were a criminal, and I supposed I was, I'd be much more comfortable meeting here than strolling up to legal offices in the west side.

I blinked. Gerald had found us a barrister.

"You mean to say that you intend to take Bram Lowhouse's case?" My mouth fell open, hesitant to believe Bram might actually have a chance at justice.

"Very likely, yes. I wanted to meet with you first. I wanted to see if you were like your father."

I blushed.

"In what way?"

"In that courageous, noble-hearted kind of way. Your dad would often put himself in harm's way to help his friends."

I touched my teacup, eager for the warmth. A thought hit me.

"You told Gerald to write that note the way he did, didn't you? He turned the other direction on your orders. Walking through your door was a test?"

Alastair laughed gruffly.

"Smarter than your dad ever was, too. Yes, Luella. That was me."

I sipped the tea and grew more comfortable by the moment.

"How can I convince you to help him?" I asked.

"Well, you can explain why it's important in the first place. Is this Bram your darling?"

I shook my head.

"Not really," I said. Romantic inclinations were a distant concern. I cared for Bram, yes, but how could I parse the particulars of that emotion? "It's complicated."

"Then what?"

I bit my tongue and considered what to reveal.

"I was accused of killing Luke Thomas."

"I know that. I read all the papers. I also know that this man confessed to that crime."

"Yes, but what you don't know is that he confessed because I asked him to."

This quieted Alastair for a moment.

"And he agreed?" he asked at length. "Why?"

"Because he loves me. And because I had a plan to get him out before he ever faced trial."

He leaned back in his chair and stroked his beard.

"Ah, thought you could outsmart the law, did you?"

"When the law is stupid, it shouldn't be too hard."

He stood up and smiled.

"Let me ask you something, Luella," he said as he sat down on the table quite close to me. "And I only want a straight yes or no answer. Did you intentionally kill Lucas Thomas?"

I stammered at first, wondering if he asked the wrong question.

"Yes or no?" he repeated.

"No," I said. When the word came out, it brought with it a millstone. An enormous weight came off of my shoulders. It was embarrassing to realize, but admitting to him and myself out loud that I did nothing intentionally to harm Luke Thomas made me feel lighter.

"Did Bram Lowhouse intentionally kill Lucas Thomas? Yes or no?" he asked.

"No," I said, then quickly added, "not to my knowledge."

"Is your knowledge on the subject any good?"

"It ought to be," I said. "He never even knew Luke Thomas from what he told me."

He stared into my eyes. His gaze was gentle, but probing.

"Very well," he said, standing. "I will take Mr. Lowhouse's case."

"You will? Just like that?"

"From what I hear, Mr. Milton was a fool in front of the grand jury. Most likely, he was too wrapped up in the finances."

My blood drained again. Alastair surely wanted something, or else he was not to be trusted. Who was this man to meet with me in secret at such a devilish address, bringing me my favorite baked good, no less.

I bit my lip, considering the word "finances" which he let linger in the air. Please, let it only be finances that he be after. There would be no trust needed if economic incentives were adequate to bind him to the task.

"We can pay you," I said. "Just not right away. Please, don't let that deter you. I promise I will be good on the debt if you give me time."

He stared at me, one hand on his waist, a grim expression on his face.

"You'll be good on the debt?"

I nodded, trying to keep tears of desperation from my eyes. He shook his head and turned toward the stove.

"Luella, when I was a young man, I was dirt poor. I'd moved to Dawnhurst because a friend of my cousin told me there was a position here in a factory. When I arrived, I started working, and life looked quite pleasant. I met your dad at that job.

"Then things took a turn. I was fired, and young fool like I was, it didn't take me long to get caught for stealing a purse of pennies from a pub. I was arrested, alone, and they were talking about using me to teach a lesson to all those other out-of-towners."

He looked at the floor and laughed bitterly to himself. When he turned his face upward, his eyes were misty.

"Your dad came to the station, and talked with the officer in charge of the case, a George Cooper, for seven and one-quarter hours. Cooper reluctantly let me go, saying he should have just paid the ruddy pub owner from his personal wages for the same trouble."

He sat down again and took my hands across the table.

"Since then, I've never stolen another penny. I moved from Dawn-hurst to London, where I convinced an old barrister to apprentice me. Your dad inspired my entire life. Now, I can't promise I can save your friend. But I will sure as hell try my best, and you are never allowed to talk to me about payment again."

Relief, so much sweeter than the bun on my plate, flooded from my heart. Hot silent tears ran down my cheeks.

"There, there, now. Look at us, two fountains in the middle of winter. We can't keep here crying. There's work to be done. We only have a couple of weeks before the assizes."

I tried my best to stop crying, but Alastair's kindness had set something off in me. After so much darkness, so much bleak horizon, I finally recognized a glint of light ahead. I hadn't seen the moondust trail since I ate my silver currant in the Netherdowns, but suddenly it occurred to me that trails like that existed invisibly in many corners, in the riverbeds of those who loved us.

He helped put my bun in a small bag, and after a few more questions about Bram, promised he would meet with him the next day.

"Oh, one last thing," he said as I reached the door. "Do you have any messages you'd like me to pass on to the accused?"

12

ALASTAIR'S PLAN

Alastair's offer caught me completely off guard, and for all the time I'd spent wishing for an opportunity to communicate with Bram, I'd spent little effort deciding what exactly I would put in it.

There were so many things I needed to tell him about Jeremy, Hirythe, the Mystic Diary, Charlotte, Edward... The list stretched on long.

But I didn't want Alastair thinking we were both mad. Frankly, it was a miracle that he was taking the case in the first place. What would become of me if I scared him off by sending his new client a message full of alleged magical information?

I supposed he might not read a sealed envelope if I gave it to him, but why risk it? I wanted to maintain, in his eyes, that Jerry Winthrop's little girl was without blemish.

For that reason, I wrote a simple letter, and hid within its prose a message I hoped Bram would recognize.

Dearest Bram,

You must forgive me for my earlier attempts at assisting you. Mr.

Milton is a rat, and I should have sniffed that out on him from our first meeting.

I hope you've been treated well. Imagining you alone in that cell makes me feel so helpless. As it is, I don't do much, and I don't go anywhere. I feel like I'm trapped in my own prison. And to think of how I wronged you the day you were arrested. It burns.

I can't even make contact with our mutual friend. The last I heard, he had requested your assistance with a difficult relation named Jeremy, who seems to be giving him a spot of trouble. I told him I would relay that message. I hope he's getting along all right.

The road we took to see him last has been closed because of some damage. Do you, by chance, know of an alternate route of travel? It's just that I do worry about him.

As for me, you might be happy to learn that Edward failed the test you designed for him. That knowledge has rendered our relationship awkward, to say the least.

You can trust Mister McHenry. He knew my father, and I hold him in very high esteem. We're lucky that Gerald was able to reunite us and just in time for your trial.

Keep your spirits up. There's hope yet. If there's any magic I can work on my end, please let me know. I would do anything for you.

Love,

I paused, my hand frozen before writing the word "Luella." If the police saw the letter, they would confiscate it at once and scrutinize it for clues. If they knew for certain I was in the city, I doubted I'd ever be able to leave Mrs. Crow's flat again.

Love,
  Anna

Alastair and I agreed to meet at the same time and place the following day. It was one of the longest days I can remember. I was practically giddy with excitement, like a child trying to fall asleep before her birthday.

I don't know what I'd done to deserve such a reversal in fortune, but Alastair was a godsend. There was no telling if he would succeed in freeing Bram of his charges, but for the first time, I felt such hope.

I paced around Mrs. Crow's flat with an open book in my hand, wishing to dive into a novel so time might move faster.

I smiled. High magic.

But it was useless. My thoughts flew around the room like a summer skylark. Perhaps we need not even go to trial. If Bram had some magic he could use to procure his escape, and I could help him with it...

Rebecca and Doug came over that evening, and I shared the news with them.

"That's incredible!" Rebecca said, almost spilling her drink. Mrs. Crow's nighttime tea had become a tradition by now amongst our group of vagabonds. "He won't charge a penny?"

"He explicitly forbade me to even bring up payment. I don't know what to do with myself."

"Well, he may not like it, but if we get through this thing, Alastair McHenry will never pay for a fish nor a chip in my pub the rest of his life," Doug said.

"I'm sure once he tasted the quality, he wouldn't refuse." I laughed. To hear me, you'd have thought we'd already won the case.

The next day, I arrived just a little early to 666 Jude Row. The door was still locked, and I had to busy myself inspecting a print stand to avoid looking out of place.

Alastair nodded at me when he arrived, though he did not greet me in the street. He was smart, that Alastair. Once he had safely closed the door behind him, I waited another few minutes before following.

"Did you see him?" I asked almost before I'd closed the door behind me.

"I certainly did," he said, folding his hands on the table. His face was grim, and it deflated my mood in a heartbeat.

"What's wrong?"

"Nothing is necessarily wrong, but I fear that this man has been dealt with unjustly. The effects on his mind are noticeable."

I slumped into the chair across from him without taking off my heavy cape.

"Effects?"

"It's difficult for me to judge because we're newly acquainted, but he seems vacant at times. When I asked him certain questions, his eyes just went out for a moment before responding with a muddled answer."

"Is he being evasive?" I asked, biting my lip.

"No. Nothing like that. I've seen this before, often in soldiers. It's almost as though he is tormented by something I can't see. It affects his memory, his cognition, everything."

I swallowed back tears. If only Alastair knew.

"Did he at least provide what you need for his defense?"

"Aye. Well enough, I suppose."

"And what is that defense? You'll forgive me for asking, but our last lawyer just labeled him a lunatic and hoped for the best."

This, at least, generated a small smile on the northerner's face.

"I won't be doing that." He sobered. "Though, I'm afraid the strongest approach might not sit comfortably with you."

"What is it?"

"Well, they are accusing Bram of murder or conspiring to murder Luke Thomas. In a way, that's good, because murder will require the prosecution to prove not just coincidence but motive, means, a plan. From what you both tell me, that won't be easy. The easier claim will be the conspiracy. After all, your news story and his confession paint a hard picture."

"I can explain--"

He held up a hand.

"You don't have to. In all honesty, it may be better if you don't. But I'll have to provide the jury an alternative reason he might have come forward to confess as he did."

I held back a nervous grimace. I knew where this was headed.

"It's all right. I want you to do it," I said.

"You didn't let me explain—"

"You want to say he was hopelessly in love with me and came forward to protect me. Isn't that right?"

He nodded once.

"That will require a strong suggestion that I'm actually the one who killed Luke Thomas, and I did so independently."

"At the very least, it would require convincing the jury that Bram thought as much. I have no desire to paint you as a murderer. As far as I'm concerned, Luke Thomas died by suicide. I still scratch my head that anyone believes differently."

"People love a show." I shrugged.

"That they do." He leaned back in his chair. "You took that better than I expected. I suppose you won't need this to soften the blow." He pulled another iced bun from his bag.

I laughed.

"How did you know I love those so much?"

He shrugged.

"You have to be a right fool not to love them. It's not magic, Luella. It's common sense."

"Did you give him my letter?" I asked. It had been mature not to jump to that question as soon as I arrived, but it took no shortage of willpower.

"Ah. See, I was saving that in case the iced bun didn't soften the blow as much as I hoped."

He reached into his bag and produced a folded sheet of paper. I did my best not to snatch it from his fingers.

At once, I recognized Bram's handwriting. It had been all over *Poems from the Wanderer*. But it looked more deliberate now.

Alastair stoked a small fire in the range, giving me a shred of privacy.

Anna,

Thank you for your letter. You could not have known about Mr. Milton. I'm grateful for everything you're doing on my behalf.

I was very sorry to learn about our mutual friend, though I suspected

Jeremy had shown up to cause trouble. Call it an intuition, something resonating in my bones. I wish there were others who were adept as I at calming down our friend's impending episode, but there is no one. Even I struggle with some of his moods, and I fear he will go positively wild before this is over.

In fact, if Jeremy has put him in one of these moods, it may be best for you not to see him alone. Though, it sounds like I may not need to worry about that. You said the road was damaged? I'm not sure what you mean.

I'm happy to have Mister McHenry. He seems infinitely better than that Milton.

Unfortunately, I have to keep this short. I'm not meant to look as though I'm writing a letter, but writing a statement for McHenry. I will just say this, if you are in contact with Gerald, he's been looking after a chest of mine. Inside may be some items that could be of use for you or Mr. McHenry.

I was so happy to hear from you. It's felt like ages, and I can't say how concerned I was for your welfare. I hope to see you soon.

Always yours,

Bram

P.S. You may want to avoid Edward until we can speak in more detail about him.

I instinctively pulled the letter to my chest.

"You told me yesterday that you and Bram weren't romantically involved," Alastair said with a teasing smile. He indicated the letter with his finger. "But the way you hug his words leads me to reconsider."

I blushed. How could I explain my feelings for the Meddler, even to myself? How could I tell Alastair that I trusted Bram with my whole soul, that from the moment I met him, I could not keep myself from getting closer to him?

"These might be some of his last words to me," I said. "You'd hug them, too."

"I hope you'll forgive me for reading the letters. I need all the information I can get to defend him." He straightened and came back to the table. A small fire worked in the stove.

"I suspected you would. I imagine you have some questions."

"I'm not interested in this friend of yours you two keep going on about. I asked you yesterday if either of you intentionally killed the Lord Thomas, and I believe your answer. The rest is your business. I am curious, though, about what item Mr. Lowhouse thinks might help me. Can you shed any light on that?"

I scoured my memory. When I had spoken with Gerald in Reading, he mentioned that Bram still owed him money for—what was it, keeping an eye on something?

Did Bram leave his chest of trinkets in Gerald's protection before entering the Netherdowns? When I brought a letter from my sister into the Mystic Diary, it produced a terrible monster. Who knew what items Bram had in the chest. He would have to leave them somewhere.

But I couldn't exactly tell Alastair that Gerald was custodian of a chest of magical trinkets. Given how Gerald responded to his own encounter with magic, I doubted I could even tell Gerald such a thing.

"Gerald may be in possession of a chest full of Bram's personal effects. I don't know what item he refers to in the letter, but it's likely worth investigating."

Alastair stroked his beard thoughtfully.

"I assumed as much, which is why I invited Gerald to meet with us here, today. He should be around shortly. I hope you don't mind a short wait."

I smiled.

"It turns out I have little to do today."

We sat and shared the bun he brought me, making small talk about my father. It was a joy to discover a story or two I had not previously known about him. The accounts were trivial, just silly outings in a pub or occurrences in the factory, but discovering something new about my dad made him alive again somehow.

His words to me in the Netherdowns came to mind: "Parents never leave us. Not really." I supposed that was true if we kept finding little pieces of them hidden throughout the world.

It had only been ten or fifteen minutes before Gerald opened the door. The sudden sound startled me out of the quiet intimacy of our conversation.

"Alastair. Luella." Gerald breathed into his hands and rubbed them together warmly. He bustled to the modest stove and tried to warm himself.

"Gerald, I'm glad you came," Alastair said.

"You made it sound important enough," Gerald said. "Luella, I'm sorry for the way I just dropped that note yesterday. It was his idea."

"I've explained everything, and she doesn't hold a grudge. Do you, Miss Winthrop?"

"Just a small one," I said. Gerald smiled toothily. We'd come a long way since he first tried to humiliate me at the gates of the carnival.

"I've met with your friend. He mentions that you have a chest of his personal effects, and that one of these items might help me in his defense. Do you know what he may be talking about?"

Gerald squinted at the fire before the color drained from his face.

"I don't," he said.

"But do you have such a chest?" Alastair asked.

"I do."

"Can we see it?"

"It's in Reading," Gerald said. "But I'm not sure you'll find what you want."

Gerald's hands twitched suspiciously.

"Why not?" Alastair probed.

"Because a man stole some things from it."

I narrowed my eyes at him. He shot a look back at me that confirmed my suspicions.

"You let a man steal from your friend's chest?" Alastair asked.

"I was—I was under the influence at the time."

"Shame on you, Gerald. I thought you were more trustworthy than that. Did this man have a gambling debt over you or something of that sort?" Alastair sounded almost fatherly in his disappointment.

"I can't remember," Gerald said glumly.

I knew why, and it was hardly the man's fault. Jeremy taunted Hirythe in the Netherdowns, saying he had brought some of Bram's trinkets. Now I knew where he got them.

"Did he take everything?" I asked. Gerald screwed up his face, as if trying to concentrate.

"I don't think so. Just the items he considered valuable."

Valuable. We all likely had very different ideas of what might be considered valuable.

"Then it's possible the item is still available to us in Reading," I said.

Alastair paced the room.

"It's possible, but who can say?" He sighed. "I'm afraid of gambling on something like this. If I divide my efforts and go to Reading, it will take away from the time I have to prepare for the assizes."

"Then I'll go," I said. Gerald and Alastair looked at me. "Gerald will accompany me."

Alastair rubbed his neck.

"Luella, are you certain?" Gerald asked. "You've been holed up since Bram was arrested."

I clutched the letter.

"Bram's life is in the balance. I've been so cautious thus far, in part because I didn't know what to do. If there's even a chance I can help him, it's worth the risk."

"Gerald, do you agree to accompany her?" Alastair asked.

The carnival worker swallowed, his face still pale, but he nodded. I wondered what Jeremy had done to pull Gerald under his spell. Whatever it was, it still haunted him.

"Then it's settled. I'll continue here, as if no item existed, preparing my best for trial. But please, move quickly, both of you."

Gerald set his jaw.

"We'll leave tonight."

13

THE FAIR WORKERS

Gerald wanted to leave as soon as the sun set. He insisted nightfall would lower any chance of me being recognized. I thought it would be suspicious to be traveling in the dark as we would, but he assured me that in winter, when night fell so early, it wasn't that peculiar.

He was disappointed to discover that I didn't know how to ride a horse and muttered something about calling in a favor.

"I'll cover the cost," Alastair said. "It's a trial expense."

I had little to pack. After living in borrowed clothes for weeks, I found a plain traveling skirt and grabbed a heavy coat. It was Edward's, but I didn't have time to find another.

Still, I thought it best not to leave without notice. As Gerald rounded up our means of transportation, I hurried back to my old building. Rebecca and Doug would be upset I hadn't consulted them, but perhaps it was for the best.

I didn't want to risk being talked out of my idea. For the first time in weeks, I could do something more than write a ruddy article. If there were items in Bram's chest that could help the trial or help an escape, I'd risk about anything to have them.

"What do you mean you're going?" Mrs. Crow asked as I stuffed a small bag full of essential bits of clothing. It was humbling to see that I couldn't even fill the bag with my own possessions.

"We found a new lawyer, and Bram said there may be some exonerating evidence in Reading. Gerald and I are leaving tonight."

"Gerald? That big brute of a man?"

"He's kind under the crust."

"Can't you at least wait until morning?"

"The assizes are in two days. If we don't get our hands on the evidence immediately, it won't be worth anything."

Mrs. Crow's face reddened as she plopped on a chair.

"I don't like this, Luella. I don't like it all. Aren't the police still looking for you? Sneaking around the city for an hour or two at a time is one thing..."

"I'll be safer out of the city than I am here. Who will recognize me in Reading?"

I bit my lip. I knew one person who might. I fooled Reading's Inspector once. I feared if he saw me now, he might understand who I really was. It all depended on how widely the stories in Dawnhurst had traveled.

Mrs. Crow sucked in her cheeks.

"I just wish things weren't so complicated," she said. I turned to her.

"Mrs. Crow, I can never thank you enough for your service to me and my sister. You've been family to us when we had none. And now, more than ever, my heart has grown very fond of you. I'm not sure things are any less complicated now than they were before. Perhaps life is complex, and we only recognize just how much when our hearts grow the courage to want something out of reach."

Mrs. Crow smiled sadly and put a hand to my cheek.

"Luella Winthrop, your mother and father would be very proud of you," she said. I furrowed my brows and looked at the ground.

"Not yet," I replied. "But they would love me all the same, and I've realized that's enough. I used to think my life's goal was to realize my father's dreams for me."

"And now?"

"Now, I think it's time to refine them."

Someone knocked at the door. I looked out the window. The sun had just set, and darkness sped on.

"You'll tell Rebecca and Doug? They won't be happy with me."

"I'll tell them."

I kissed Mrs. Crow on the forehead and, drawing back, saw her perhaps for the first time not as a woman to be dealt with, but one to care for.

"I'll make all of this up to you when the dust clears," I said.

"You have no debt to me. Oh, but Luella, I'd nearly forgotten! A letter from Anna came for you."

I halted. I wanted to stay and read it. Words from Anna would be like fresh water.

"Let's get moving!" Gerald's muffled voice called from outside the door.

"It will be too dark to read by night," I said. "Will you hold it for me until I get back?"

She nodded, and I embraced her one more time before leaving.

The journey to Reading was not nearly as comfortable as my first journey out of Dawnhurst in Edward's carriage. Gerald had satisfied his intention of finding a discreet devil to drive our horses.

We jolted along in a carriage, tumbling through the outskirts of Dawnhurst without incident, but even before the city diminished behind us, I was fueled by such an energy. I seized the exhilaration of being liberated from my den and rejoiced that I had a task, an important task.

"We'll stop in Swindon," Gerald said.

"No." I shook my head.

"We'll need to rest," he insisted. "The horses can't go straight through."

"Then we can stop long enough to exchange horses, and if necessary, a driver, but no longer."

Gerald stared at me.

"Luella, I understand that you're eager to get on with this business, but you'll be no good, *I'll* be no good, to Bram in Reading if we're dizzy with fatigue."

"You can sleep in the carriage," I suggested as one of our wheels struggled across a divot in the road. We jolted violently.

Gerald folded his arms and muttered something about the difficulty of finding a fresh pair of horses and driver past midnight, but he didn't protest further.

I didn't think I'd be able to fall asleep. The night became almost a fever dream, a medley of differently shaped shadows dancing past the light of our carriage lantern.

My mind race. It wasn't yet that late in the evening, and I speculated wildly what items might lie in Bram's chest. I had to admit to myself that in my heart, beyond my desire to help Bram, the possibility of interacting with magic again thrilled me.

It was wrong, but in some ways, I missed the fog creature, or at least the feeling of singleness that it gave me. For a brief period, when I knew how to use the ink to manage my attacks, it felt more like a weapon than anything else, as if I could unleash a terrible inhuman fury should I so desire.

I shivered. I had never desired it. This was madness.

I dozed off and woke only briefly to overhear Gerald talking outside of the carriage with someone.

"These horses are positively lathered. I'll have to charge you extra if you intend to ride mine as hard," said a gruff voice.

"The missus is right mad. Insufferable, really, but what's a man to do?" His voice filtered into the box from outside.

"If it were me, I'd hit her upside the head once or twice," replied a gruff voice, "but I won't turn down your business."

"I might hit her three times if it's the same to you." I smiled sleepily, empowered to know that big, tough Gerald couldn't seem to keep up with me.

I fell asleep soon after we started up again.

. . .

W e arrived in Reading at around ten in the morning. Poor Gerald was famished, having skipped dinner the night before. By the bags under his eyes, it didn't look as though he slept as well as I did in the turbulent carriage.

We pulled through Castle Street, and I recognized buildings as though from a dream. My time here with Edward seemed so long ago. To the south was the Hare and Hounds, to the north the Forbury Gardens where I'd found Cyrus, and drove directly by St. Mary's cathedral with its tall tower reaching to the heavens.

"Where is Bram's chest?" I asked, pulling myself away from the window.

"Hopefully," Gerald stifled a yawn, "it's in a small hovel near Queen's Street. I haven't had a chance to let the folks with the carnival know we were coming, and they haven't seen me since..."

"Since you were hypnotized," I finished. He grumbled.

"Perhaps we shouldn't show up empty-handed. I'm not sure if you remember, but carnival folk know how to eat."

My own stomach growled, betraying the strong face I tried to put on.

"I'm afraid I don't have any money."

"Well, if you're willing to spare me just a quarter hour, you don't need money. Alastair was thorough in his compensation."

He patted his jacket. I nodded through a pain in my neck from sleeping sitting up. Alastair had equipped us well enough. I was surprised there wasn't an iced bun hidden somewhere for me in the carriage.

"You're right. By all means, let's stop and grab a bite."

"Or several," Gerald muttered as he opened the door to lean out of the carriage and inform the driver.

We dropped off the horses first. The poor beasts looked exhausted, steaming like a locomotive engine in the cold. I patted them gently before Gerald led me to a nearby tavern. I kept my head down on the walk over, just to be cautious.

The tavern staff recognized Gerald immediately. We ate quickly, dispatching baked beans and sausages, before leaving with a bag of scones, bread, and a block of butter wrapped in wax paper.

"Now, before we go in there, I should warn you, some people living here aren't overly fond of you," Gerald said as we walked toward an old, dirty building made of brick and stone.

"What do you mean? I remember nothing awkward when I frequented you in Dawnhurst."

"Well, that's just it. Bram left the carnival after Dawnhurst, didn't he? Some think it's your fault."

"It was my fault," I admitted. "But it was also his decision."

Gerald held up his hands, embodying a better mood after breakfast.

"I'm not saying I agree with them. I'm only trying to prepare you."

I jut out my lip, the block of butter cold through my gloves. My warm memories of the carnival tarnished as I digested this new information.

"Well, fortunately, we're not here to make friends. We just need to get to Bram's chest."

"Right. We can try to get in quickly."

He knocked on the door, and the curtain in the second-floor window cracked open before loud steps sounded inside, and the door swung open.

"Gerald, I was beginning to think you'd never come back." A woman in a daring robe stood in the doorframe. She looked like a doll. Her lips were painted a deep shade of red, stark against shadowed cheekbones. She wore a beaded necklace, and her thick hair was pulled up behind a sash where it curled in wild strands.

Once, I'd spoken with the Reading Inspector about fortune tellers. I'm certain that when I had suggested I was Edward's mystic, this was the image the Inspector conjured.

She swept her gaze across me and curled a lip in a rehearsed, come-hither pout.

I recognized her at once. This was the hypnotist I'd watched the first night I met Bram.

"I see you brought a person with you."

"Sadie, you look stunning," Gerald said with a boyish grin that looked strange on his rugged face. She did not move an inch.

"That's a bold color choice, darling," she said, curling her fingers at my hair.

"It wasn't made per dictates of fashion," I replied.

"Sure." She turned from me. "You just left us, Gerald. It hurt many feelings. No goodbye—just gone one morning."

"I'm sorry about that. We come bearing gifts," Gerald said, holding up the bag of bread. Sadie leaned forward to peer inside.

"Bread and scones?" she asked, a little disappointed.

"And butter," I added as I held up the block of waxed paper. She eyed it suspiciously, but grudgingly stood back and swung the door wide.

We entered timidly into a beautiful mess. I had never paused to consider how performers filled their days during the off season. The polished acts that sparked such wonder and imagination at the fair were, doubtless, the result of endless practice. One can't just wake up juggling knives or cooking perfect versions of the recipes that mark fair food.

The room inside was littered with bright shimmering clothing, caged and uncaged animals of varying sizes, sashes, throwing axes, iron weights, and heavens only knew what else.

Sitting amidst the chaos were the carnival's workers, playing cards or reading books, all looking terribly bored and a little hungry.

I recognized a few of them, but none were my friends. I had always been Bram's guest, and no one but Gerald ever really bothered to know me.

"Gerald's back, everyone," Sadie said. I expected some congenial cacophony, but the return of one of their comrades only roused some half-warm mumbles. "And he brought bread and butter."

There was the commotion. We were unburdened of our offering in moments. Sadie looked almost embarrassed at how ravenously her comrades tore into the food.

"How has everyone been, Sadie?" Gerald asked.

"Since Samuel left for Bristol and took the wagons?" She rolled her eyes. "I think we've overstayed our welcome in Reading. Some local residents have scuffled up against a few of our more colorful lot."

She nodded to a man balancing a knife point first on his finger.

"It'll be time to move on, then," Gerald said.

"As much as I hate Bristol, we'll have to meet up with the others."

"Why do you hate Bristol?" I asked, trying to make polite conversation. Sadie stared at me with sharp eyes that made me wonder if her hypnotism routine had more true magic in it than she let on.

"Truth is, Gerald, I didn't want to leave without hearing from you."

"I'd have figured you went to Bristol." He shrugged.

"Sure, but you kept going on about important things you were watching over. You know me. I like to travel light. It didn't seem right sorting through and discarding your personal items."

"Are my things still here, then?"

"Under the bed." She gestured with her thumb toward the stairs.

"Which one?" I asked.

"Are you some sort of princess?" Sadie asked. "We have but one bed."

"You mean you all share a bed? There must be seven of you here."

She glared at me.

"We get creative."

A sharp knock cracked on the door behind us. Every face in the room turned.

"Are you expecting visitors?" Gerald asked. Sadie held up a finger.

"Who is it? I'm in no state to come to the door," she called.

"Reading Police, ma'am. We insist you open at once."

My heart raced.

"Gerald, they can't find me here!" I whispered.

"This isn't that type of house, constable!" she called back.

"How much trouble are you in, Sadie?" Gerald asked quickly.

"I haven't opened the door yet, have I?" she replied. "Ask Jean."

"Ma'am, please don't resist. We need you to open this door!" called the voice outside.

"Jean? What did you do?" Gerald asked. I could see pain on his face beyond the anxiety of being apprehended. This group was his family.

"*Rien,*" murmured a man in braces and a mustache. "I am a man. She was a woman. It was a natural thing."

"Jean!" Gerald stomped over.

"Open this door or we'll break it down!"

Sadie struggled to push a damaged cabinet against the door. I helped before grabbing her by the elbow. "Where is the bed?"

"And why should I tell the murderess of Dawnhurst where Gerald keeps his personal things?"

"Because they're not Gerald's. They belong to Bram, and he needs them."

The doorknob rattled roughly. The knocking continued. Outside, disgruntled voices jabbered about breaking something down.

Sadie narrowed her eyes at me.

"You took him from us," she accused.

"I'll give him back if I can save him from the noose. I promise."

"I already told you." Sadie swung her eyes toward the staircase. "We only have one bed."

"Thank you." I dashed across the room and up the stairs, praying there was some type of back door. Once, I had escaped police through a second-story window. I could do it again if necessary, even though I wasn't wearing trousers this time.

The door at the top of the stairs dangled on its hinges. When I pushed through, it gave no resistance at all. I surveyed the bedroom. There were sheets everywhere, hung from hooks in the ceiling to form makeshift hammocks. A small window let in dramatic shafts of morning light.

Under a rickety iron bed frame, I recognized the curious chest from Bram's yurt. The chest from which he'd first produced the pen and inkwell that started our tumultuous relationship.

Downstairs, a crash like splintering wood urged me quickly on. I rushed to the chest and pulled it from the bed, but the lid was locked.

Shouts echoed downstairs. It didn't appear that the carnival workers would be going quietly. I doubted whatever romantic rendezvous Jean had admitted to was the only grievance against the tenants.

I searched for something hard to pry open the lid. There was a juggling knife in one of the hammocks. I thrust the point into the lock as heavy footstep came upstairs.

Gerald appeared in the doorframe.

"What are you doing?" he asked, his face red.

"It's locked!"

"Luella, you need to get out of here."

"I'm not leaving without whatever is in this chest."

"There might not be much left in there at all," he said with a scowl as he pushed the bedframe against the door.

"Of course. Jeremy came here with you. You showed him the chest, didn't you?"

He didn't reply for a bit, instead fishing a small key from his waist-coat pocket.

"If I ever find the man that did that to me I'll beat him bloody."

He opened the lid and, true to his word, there wasn't much inside. I'd never seen the interior of the chest before, but it wasn't at all how I imagined.

There was a small locket, a sphere made of rubber, a closed vase-shaped object painted like a doll, a pair of simple rings, and a cutting of cheesecloth.

"This is all that's left?" I asked, collecting the items and stuffing them into the pockets of my jacket.

Gerald clenched his jaw.

"I'm sorry. He took them."

The police pushed through the door, scooting the bed frame across the floor, and squeezed into the room.

"Oi! You two! Downstairs!"

"Have we broken any laws?" I asked, pretending to be meek by burying my face in the floor and curtseying.

"We'll find out, won't we? Innocent folk don't often go barricading themselves in rooms like this." He motioned at the bed with a baton.

"It was like that when we came in," Gerald said.

"Wha—You—Like *that* when you came in? Think you're a funny-man, do you? Save your breath. Downstairs. I'm sure the Inspector looks forward to interviewing a comedian."

❧ 14 ❧

OLD FRIENDS

We sat with the carnival workers against the walls in the small room downstairs.

Gerald and I had come quietly when confronted by the Reading officer. By the looks of it, downstairs had been a different story.

The room was in a shambles. An overturned table, a mess of colorful scarves, and no shortage of sponge balls, knives, and even a pair of grumpy rabbits all strewn around the floor.

Sadie, Jean, and the rest looked a little worse for wear, some of them with bruises darkening on their cheeks or hands.

My heart raced.

"Keep calm, and we'll be fine," Gerald muttered beside me.

I took deep, silent breaths, but I didn't share his optimism.

A few Reading officers snapped to attention when a familiar, imposing figure strode into the room.

The Inspector of the Reading Police force.

He hardly glanced our motley crew over, instead exchanging some words with his inferior officers and taking two of them upstairs. The sounds of scraping furniture sounded above us before one constable stepped forward.

"Right, then. In a moment, the Inspector would like to interview you one by one upstairs. He has a keen knack for ferreting out the truth, so I suggest all of you abstain from any falsehood. It will be better for you in the long run."

Gerald released a low grumble.

"What did Jean do, rob a bank?" he whispered to Sadie.

"No talking!" one officer barked.

The door at the top of the steps creaked open, and a constable with curly blonde hair came down to retrieve the first victim.

I fingered the objects in my pockets nervously, trying to form a plan. If they were interviewing us one on one, perhaps I'd have enough time to—

"We'll start with you, miss." The man grabbed me brusquely by the arm and helped me to my feet.

I glanced back to Gerald, who gave me an encouraging nod. He didn't know my history with this Inspector, though. Everything might go to ruin, right here, right now. No items back to Bram and Alastair, just a one-way ticket to join Bram at the upcoming Assizes.

The constable ushered me into the room and shut the door behind. The Inspector faced away from me, his hands clasped behind his back as he gazed out the window. The Reading Police had righted the furniture to form a makeshift office.

"I've conducted many of these interviews," the Inspector began coolly without turning around. "More than I can remember. You might have some misguided notions of heroism that urge you to present a distorted version of the truth. Perhaps to save yourself. Perhaps to save your friends. But I swear to you, I will detect the moment you deviate. I can smell dishonesty, sense the fear that lives in lies. You cannot outsmart the law. You cannot fool me."

He turned around menacingly, and his gaze settled on my face before melting.

"Oh, hell. Not you."

"Inspector!" I performed a slight curtsey. "I didn't expect to see you again."

"This is why I skip church services. If there is a God, He could not wish this misery on me."

I fought back a smile.

"I don't want to be here any more than you do. Why not cancel our meeting? Surely, you have the power to dismiss me."

"The power to dismiss you? Bah." He slumped to a chair and motioned that I should sit.

"I take it you've deduced my true identity, by now?" I asked, sitting.

"I'm not a blooming idiot, though how would you know that? Yes. I read the papers, and I put two and two together."

I nodded. The story of Edward Thomas running through the streets of Dawnhurst raving like a lunatic while chasing a police wagon with his fiancée inside apparently had been too juicy a story even for reporters as far as Reading.

"And I wasn't the only one," he went on. "When my colleagues heard I released a woman who claimed to be Luella Winthrop, they had a great laugh."

I smirked.

"I know you work very hard to maintain your reputation. That must have been taxing."

"Quite." He glared at me. "To think, I had the suspected culprit of Luke Thomas' murder in my custody."

"Do you believe the case against me, then?"

"That's not my job, is it? I deliver justice, not administer it."

His words conjured up memories of Edward. He said something similar to me only days before asking to use a potentially lethal spell on Bram. Did the police believe the lies they told themselves?

A small vibration buzzed in my jacket pocket and resisted the urge to reach toward it.

"Ah, you see, I had always understood judges to ascertain justice. How does one deliver it before it's been defined?"

The Inspector rolled his eyes so far I thought he might knock himself over.

"Why come back to Reading, Miss Winthrop?" he asked. "You know this carnival scum?"

"Scum? That's hardly a decent thing to say."

"You don't know why we arrested them, now do you?"

"No. But I know a few of them personally. I'm sure they're innocent of—"

"Assault? Mugging? Beating a man senseless? Demoralizing a young woman?"

I searched for a response.

"Do you have proof?" I asked.

"Proof. Witnesses. Everything but a confession. Of course, where you're from, a confession isn't worth very much is it?"

I ignored his jab at Bram.

"Well, there must be some mistake."

He held up a hand.

"Miss Winthrop, don't bother. You can still befriend a villain. You don't need to pretend they're saints. If our friends don't love us despite our faults, what worth are they?"

"That's very wise, if not hypocritical, coming from a Police Inspector. Do you jail your friends when they make mistakes?"

He smiled without warmth.

"Many from your station rail against the police until our mission serves their interests," he said.

"And what is my station, exactly?" I asked.

He paced across the room.

"I am tired of hearing about you. In the papers, in my conscience, from my inferior officers, from Edward Thomas..."

My pulse quickened.

"You've spoken with Edward?"

"He was here two days ago, looking for his mother."

I knit my eyebrows.

"What would his mother be doing here?" I asked.

"I wondered the same thing. I didn't have the heart to tell him you were the one he should be asking."

The room grew colder as the Inspector stared at me.

"You suspect I had something to do with Charlotte's disappearance?" I asked, taken aback.

"Charlotte? You two are friendly now?"

"An engagement has a funny way of bonding people," I muttered.

"I think it highly suspicious that the date of your arrest and escape corresponds with the date Lady Thomas was last seen."

I squirmed under his gaze, any hope of escaping from him quickly diminishing.

"How can you think that of me?" I asked.

"Think what, Miss Winthrop? That you are involved in the murder or abduction of both Edward Thomas' parents?"

I balled my fists.

"Why?" I cried. "Why would I do that? Why won't anyone pause to consider what I would have to gain from any of this?"

The Inspector curled his lip.

"In my humble career, I've rarely, if ever, began an investigation with an answer to that question. It comes out slowly, in hideous piecemeal."

My pocket buzzed again. I stood. The chair scraped violently on the floor under me.

"What pieces have you seen from me? This is our second, if not third, interview. If you're so good at this, you must have a theory by now."

He glanced at the door behind me.

"I will share it, if you promise to confirm whether I'm correct or incorrect."

I folded my arms.

"How can you trust me to give you an honest answer?" I asked.

He smiled genuinely this time.

"I'm not looking for something that can hold up in court."

"Then why ask?"

He leaned back and put both hands on his knees.

"Edward Thomas abandoned his riches because he believes in justice and doing right by the community. That's not true of every officer. Some of us simply love the game."

"The game?" I sat down and stuffed my hands into my coat pockets. There was no denying the vibration now. Could the Inspector not hear it? In the midst of Bram's trinkets, the doll-faced wooden vase hummed like a bee.

"I see it like this. You and Bram Lowhouse have been working together for a long time. You fell in love and dreamed of a better life. But that was a tall order. A poor girl from Dawnhurst's east side and a roaming carnival magician? What kind of future is that?

"So the two of you concocted a scheme. Seduce a marriage proposal out of the prince of police. Then, kill his father so he inherits the estate, marry him, and do away with his mother. Then, once his family is gone, you withdraw your affection, and Edward Thomas returns to police work, the only thing that can fulfill his bleeding heart. At that point, you either live alone in his estate with ample time to travel or rendezvous with your lover. Or, if you are the heartless woman I believe you to be, an accident easily befalls him on the job. With no other family to inherit his wealth, suddenly a rich eccentric widow has the world wide open to her."

He folded his arms and leaned back smugly in his chair. It took all I had not to slap him. Fury wrenched through my neck.

"Am I right?" he asked.

"How dare you."

My fists shook. His version of my crimes struck a powerful nerve, and I understood why in a flash. As he voiced them, I realized I heard the a plan very similar to the one I accused of Edward. It had taken me weeks to understand exactly how or why Edward might have enchanted me, and here it was, voiced in part by his great Reading rival.

Edward was ambitious. He wanted greater influence in his police precinct and to right the wrongs his father committed against him and his mother. It would be a simple plan, brutal, vicious, but simple. Kill his father and remove his superior. All he needed to do was enchant some poor journalist, have them write a story that framed his father's murder as a suicide, then discredit his superior officer in the ensuing investigation. It would have been simple, but somewhere along the line, he fell in love with me.

The crude, naked version of my accusation stunned me. Was that really what I thought happened? Patricide? Framing an innocent person to cover up his crimes? It seemed ludicrous.

"Am I right?" The Inspector's smirk widened. I snapped back to conversation at hand with renewed contempt.

"Not only is your idea vile and indicative of the pathetic view of the world you must entertain to live with yourself, it's completely unimaginative."

He frowned. I doubted the Inspector could wrap his simple mind around the truth of my story.

"Perhaps it's more complex, then," he said. "Perhaps you didn't anticipate the genuine affection you developed for your mark."

I glared at a bedpost and checked my cheek. It would not do to lose my temper with the Inspector. I was wasting time, and I wanted to waste no more of my time on men's imaginations. I needed to get back to Alastair.

The wooden vase hummed wildly in my pocket.

"Is it so easy for you to assume the poor will do anything for money?" I said.

"I've seen desperation. I assume nothing. Criminals rely on assumptions."

"You claim to be an expert on criminals, but you've failed to identify the innocent woman right in front of you."

A guttural laugh escaped him.

"Innocent woman?" he asked incredulously. I blushed. Perhaps suggesting I was innocent was a bit of a stretch. My hand grasped the wooden vase. A slim crease around its center warmed my fingertips. I had magic dormant in my hand. If only I knew how to activate it. I wanted to.

Had I not learned my lesson about meddling with forces I didn't understand?

But what choice did I have? My road could not end here. Too many people depended on my freedom.

"You're not letting me go free, are you?" I asked.

"I imagine the credibility of my career hinges on the opposite," he replied.

"No one else knows I'm here. If our association tarnished your reputation before, why expose yourself to greater risk? What if I'm proven innocent in the end? You'd be the man that let a suspected woman slip through your fingers and the cruel Inspector that locked up the innocent fiancée of Edward Thomas, all at once."

As I said this, a spark jolted against my fingertip from the crease in the wooden figure. I glanced down at my pocket.

"A paradox," he said with an appreciative smile. "I must admit, Miss Winthrop, you are more inventive than the garden variety con. Usually, they swear innocence on the life or grave of a loved one, or try to bribe me. I give you credit for creativity."

I squinted at him. Did I detect the faintest change in his demeanor? Or was this all part of his usual twisted appreciation for his line of work?

"You don't dismiss my conjecture, then?" I asked.

"It's certainly true that the masses can be irrational. But I can't imagine that, even if you manage to clear your name, my work delivering you to the Dawnhurst police will provide any lasting damage to my reputation?"

"No? Not even if I do become Lady Thomas of Fernmount?" I continued. "A moment ago, you said the masses befriend the despicable while police were free to abuse them. Shouldn't we hold our constabulary responsible for keeping wolves out of the flock?"

He furrowed his brows.

"I didn't say the police were free to abuse the despicable," he said.

"No, just to lock them in prison without knowledge of their guilt."

"I said one should not withdraw friendship to those who have made mistakes, even terrible ones."

I smiled.

"Then you are a paradox to be hated by the masses, Inspector. Despite my suspicions to the contrary, you look human yourself and must be included in the target of your advice. However, you cannot befriend those who stray from the law. You must imprison them, as your duty dictates."

By now, an energy surged from the fingertips in my pocket up through my arm. It was familiar energy, strong and heady. Whatever direction this conversation moved, one of Bram's trinkets appreciated it. It frightened me and urged me onward. This was dangerous and intoxicating all over again.

The Inspector laughed nervously.

"Are you saying I have no friends?" he asked. "What of my fellow police officers?"

"Yet another paradox, Inspector. You, the ever vigilant eye of Reading justice, cannot be naïve enough to pretend that your men downstairs are free from the stains of any criminal behavior. Yet, you choose to ignore their indiscretions. Why? Because they're your friends."

"Enough," he said. In my mind, it sounded like the pocket was screaming. I panicked. The Inspector was closing himself off from me. If I needed to secure my freedom, I had to do something now.

"But if you allow your friends to escape justice while they mete out justice on the fallen, and you profess that we should all befriend the wicked, what does that make you, dear Inspector? Corrupt? Foolish?"

"I said enough!" The Inspector stood, knocking his chair over in the motion.

Open me!

The voice was similar to the fog creature of my magical dreams. It resonated in the same section of my gut.

I yanked the wooden container from my pocket. A smiling figure painted on it looked up at me vacantly. I settled it in my hand and found that it twisted on the horizontal seam, splitting down the middle near its belly.

"What is that?" the Inspector asked, still angry at my accusations. I looked up at him and shakily set it down on the floor, allowing the magic to guide me.

"Would you like to open it, Inspector?"

He stared at the doll on the worn wood floor. In an instant, his eyes glazed as though in a trance. I could nearly hear his heart hammer from across the room.

"I fear to," he said.

"Would you feel better if I opened it first?" I asked. My own pulse pounded in my neck. I didn't know what magic waited inside the wooden container, but I needed it.

The Inspector was uncharacteristically silent. His jaw clenched. Perspiration beaded his brow.

"I've feared this," he muttered, transfixed by the doll. The sense of foreboding lay thick in the air.

I reached a hand forward. The painted eyes scrutinized my conscience with a hot iron. What paradox did I live? My reluctance to test Edward haunted me. Why had I waited so long?

Did I harbor any similar hypocrisy or lies now? Somewhere in the recesses of my heart, did I not still entertain a hope that somehow I was mistaken, and Edward was still the man too scrupulous even to lose himself in romantic passion?

My hand hovered above the doll as flashes of that night in my bedroom returned to me. His grief. His hunger and desire. The look of shame.

Was it an act? How many proofs did I require of Edward's betrayal?

But what was proof? Perhaps I pushed Edward away. Perhaps his distance was not condemnation but proof I had failed him. I could not get close to Edward because he might wish me malice. But I could not distance myself from him if there was even a small chance he did not.

I shook my head. Despite the difficulty, perhaps because of it, my life had become more straightforward. My aim was now singular and uncomplicated. I needed to right my mistakes and free Bram.

But as I reached my hand forward to open the container, my mind writhed again, as though some type of worm tried desperately to burrow its way inside. What else? Where else could it feed?

My thoughts flew to Rebecca. Her face stretched through my consciousness, beautiful and wise. She was my closest friend. I doubted she would ever betray me. Friendship is a gift. A blessing. A relationship built of selflessness and sacrifice.

If I cared for her, why did I continually threaten her safety? Even now, I asked her to hide away, meet in secret like a common thief, live a shadow of the life she deserved. How could I allow a friend to make those sacrifices for me?

But how could I deny her the blessings that came with such selflessness? If I denied the opportunity to prove her sisterly love, how could she ever feel comfortable relying on me in similar ways should similar needs arise. Give. Take. Selfish. Selfless.

Friendship was a paradox I felt comfortable holding inside of me.

I reached out again, more quickly this time, and before my mind could recoil from its magical pryings again, I opened the container. Inside, I plucked an identical container, painted the exact same way. After I set it down on the floor, I closed the original.

Sitting beside each other on the floor, my eyes played tricks on me. Neither doll was smaller or larger than the other. They were exactly, impossibly, the same size. But if they were the same size, how did the sturdy wood of one fit within the other?

"Your turn," I said.

The Inspector's hand shook as he opened the next doll. When he replaced it again, three dolls of identical proportions looked at us.

"No," he muttered. "This is a trick. Again."

Opening the next doll was easier for me than the first. My thoughts spiraled over Bram. I cared for him, and I had endangered him. But the gnawing magic found no satisfaction there. Though my actions had not stood in line with my convictions in the past, now they did not deviate. I recognized my wrongs and made no excuse for them. Grasping this thought freed me from the pain of dolls. The understanding tasted like cool water.

Though my life lay in ruins, I no longer had any desire to scheme or cheat fate. I was Luella Winthrop, nothing more, and I would live without deceit. The dolls had no purchase on my conscience.

The same could not be said for the Inspector.

We went through the routine several times. Each turn, the Inspector found it more difficult to open the next doll.

After four rounds, I opened the tenth doll and pushed it toward him. A small, impossible army stared up, eager to continue. Silently, he began to sob.

I listened for a moment as a sign of respect before collecting the dolls. They slid back together smoothly, ten becoming one again. I stuffed them in my pocket and walked out the door.

15

ON THE RUN

A few of the constables heard the sound of the Inspector's increasing cries and rushed past me with bewildered looks. The fair workers seized the opportunity, and in the confusion, they reintroduced pandemonium, scattering in every direction.

I made a mad dash for the door, but struggling bodies blocked my path.

"What the devil just happened?" Gerald growled at my side.

"I need to leave immediately. This may be my only opportunity. Gerald, please."

He set a grim jaw and nodded.

"Here. Give Alastair my best." He shoved a fistful of coins into my pocket, grabbed me by the collar of the coat, and rushed me toward the door, doing his best to shield me from flailing limbs and airborne props. Sadie, Jean, and the others all pushed to get out of the flat, overwhelming the scattered police.

Somehow, I tumbled out first. My exit unstopped the dam, and people sprawled from behind me, scattering in different directions, rendering it impossible for the police to chase everyone down.

I ran and ducked through an alley behind a row of table vendors.

They paid me little interest, instead curling into themselves to fight the cold.

I turned up the collar on my coat and snatched a cap from one of the vendor's tables, depositing a penny in the woman's outstretched hand.

Before I could piece together all that happened, I was on the run again.

It didn't take me long to find the train station. I tried not to marvel as I purchased a ticket to Gloucester. I'd never ridden on a train. There was a station at Dawnhurst, but it was used mostly for transportation of coal and metal. Alastair had warned me to stay clear of trains, that they'd be watched, but I required speed now more than cover. Besides, I doubted they'd be looking for me in Gloucester. I could travel there, then pick a more stealthy route back home.

In any event, I needed to put the city to my back before the Inspector collected himself.

Heavens, what had those dolls been on about? I wrung my hands uncomfortably, remembering how the magic had wormed its way through my conscience, searching hungrily for deficiencies. Opening each doll felt like jumping off a high cliff, inviting more scrutiny into my soul.

How had the dolls replicated as they had? And what did using such a magical trinket cost me?

As I pondered on this, the train left Reading, and I breathed a sigh of relief. What a rush it was to watch the world streak by outside of the window, to remove myself from the suspicion and reach of the Reading police at such a speed. As the train picked up speed and claimed distance, my paranoia gave way to weariness.

The gentle sounds and rocking of the train soon put me to sleep.

I woke with a start, as a train attendant loudly announced we were arriving in Gloucester. I wiped a small trail of drool from my chin and kept my face down as I exited the train.

On closer consideration, it was likely unnecessary. After traveling all night, the mess of the Reading flat, and sleeping on the train, I likely looked a mess in an oversized coat and under a cap. The better dressed people around me turned the other direction, avoiding my eyesight, as they did with most street urchins.

It was late afternoon, and my hopes of getting back to Dawnhurst that night quickly vanished. I tried to speak with some carriage drivers, as Gerald had, but I lacked his persuasive abilities. Whether it was my appearance, my gender, or the meager sum of money I offered, who could say? The train ticket was expensive and hiring a carriage to start a journey out to Dawnhurst at this hour would not come cheap.

As the sun quickly dipped and temperatures fell with it, I was forced to find some frugal lodging.

My stomach twisted as scents from nearby taverns wafted into the avenue. I should have had some of the bread and butter we brought Sadie and the workers when I had a chance.

Intuition led my feet to a clean but inexpensive public house. The landlady must have taken pity on me, seeing my state of dress and how fatigue slowed my feet. She promised me a good night's sleep and fed me a bowl of watery potato soup with a very stale bite of bread before leading me to my room for the night.

I dreamt of Edward and Bram and wooden dolls. In the dream, I opencd a doll and found another painted like Edward. When I opened that doll, it looked like Bram. When I opened that doll, it looked like Edward. It went on and on.

I returned to the streets the next morning only to discover that my funds were inadequate to secure a private ride back to Dawnhurst, and panic crept in.

The assizes started today. If I didn't get back in time, I'd miss them altogether, and whatever benefit my excursion might afford Bram would be wasted. If I was fortunate, the trial might run into the following day, but how could I risk it?

To calm my nerves, I took a seat near the Severn river and pulled Bram's trinkets from my pocket. Perhaps one of them could assist me in finding a way home.

I avoided touching the wooden doll any more than I had to. The discomfort persisted, inspired by my dream the night before. I didn't want to encourage whatever high magic fueled them.

I laid the others on the ground before me: the dolls, two rings, both plain and unadorned, a sphere of rugged and notched rubber, a hemmed cheesecloth, and the silver locket clasped shut. Frankly, it terrified me to consider what lay inside.

My breath puffed in the air in front of me as I considered them all. Here they looked harmless, innocent, unextraordinary even.

If there was magic in them, I had no idea how to wake it up. The dolls had buzzed to life through no intention of mine, ignited by the subject of my conversation with the Inspector. The rest? Would they operate in a similar fashion? I lacked the courage to test them. Instead, I clumsily wrapped them all carefully in the cheesecloth and put them back in my pocket.

When I looked up at the river, I noticed a small fleet of ferries carrying wares, ore, and other goods downriver, headed to delivery points waiting for them in other cities.

An idea struck me. I hurried down the riverside until I found a set of docks. A filthy man, glistening like an onyx gem stone from soot and sweat, shoveled coal from a cart into his boat.

"Excuse me," I said, breathless from my jog over.

"Bugger off," the man replied. "Can't you see I'm working?"

"Are you headed toward Newport?" I asked.

"I told you to leave me alone. I won't ask again." His tone wasn't hostile, only hurried and tired.

"Are you running behind?" I asked.

He stood up, annoyed, and wiped his brow.

"What does it look like? Do you see any other coal ferries still in dock? I was to leave an hour ago, but you can't buy good help these days now, can you?"

He thrust his shovel back into the pile of coal with a scrape.

"Do you have another shovel?" I asked. "I could help you."

"What is it, miss? You need a lump of coal for your stove?"

"I need to get to Dawnhurst." He stopped shoveling again and looked at me curiously. "As soon as possible."

"Why not just take the train or a carriage?"

"I'm short on funds. And I need to get there in a more, well, subtle method, if you catch my meaning."

"Subtle method?" He shook his head ruefully.

"I can pay you what I have," I added quickly. "In addition to my labor. Come on, now. You're already behind. Why not accept the help and make a profit? How many people pay you to work for you?"

"Something smells foul here, doesn't it?" He leaned on his shovel.

"That's probably me. I haven't bathed in a couple of days. That's part of why I'd like to get home."

This made him smile.

"What's your name, miss?"

"Anna Rigby."

His smile broadened.

"Well, you're a good enough liar. I'll take the help and the money, but when we get to Dawnhurst, I'm going to make you hide under this stuff until I think it's safe for you to come out. I'd have this confiscated if they thought I was smuggling or somewhat."

I grabbed a shovel.

16

GEORGE COOPER

I never learned the ferry driver's name. He never asked for mine again.

I had never taken a ferry in either direction on the Severn, and the beauty of the winter landscape was a site to behold. Patches of snow dotted the riverside, and the ferry driver had to pull some deft maneuvers to avoid floating chunks of ice.

It didn't take us long at all to get back to my home city. It couldn't have been much past noon. As planned, the man helped bury me in coal before we pulled up to the docks. I thought this was excessive, but he insisted random checks were performed on incoming boats like his. Between my shoveling coal and my little hiding place, I must have looked like my father after a long day at the factory.

In the end, it was just precaution. I emerged from the pile of coal like a nightmarish Netherdowns monster.

"Let's not forget payment," he said with a laugh.

"The laughs aren't free," I replied, digging the rest of Alastair's money from my pocket.

"Nothing in life is," he said. "Will you be helping me unload?"

"That wasn't part of the deal."

"Worth asking." He laughed again as he set to unloading.

I considered stopping by Mrs. Crow's or even going as far as Doug and Rebecca's small wretched flat to clean myself up, but I was too anxious. Besides, what better disguise could I have than a dirty street urchin?

I walked quickly, and soon the fortress-like architecture of the courthouse rose before me. The foot traffic indicated that the building was well attended, a by-product of the case's notoriety and my own recent stories stoking the fire.

As I entered and tried to elbow my way up the stairs, I enjoyed the uncanny, almost magical ability of the lowly and unwashed to clear a path for themselves. Others were all too eager to get out of my way and avoid receiving their share of the filth that dusted from my coat and hat.

The chairs on the first floor had been removed to allow more spectators. Raised voices called from the central judge's area below. The proceedings had already started.

My breath caught in my throat. Bram looked even more pitiful than before, a mere shell of his former self. His eyes drifted around the room vacantly, as if he was trying to understand why he was there at all. Alastair sat beside him with a studious and solemn air, so different from the aloof character of Mr. Milton.

"The Crown recognizes the Prosecution's evidence as peculiar, but as Mr. McHenry indicated, it does little to tie the accused to the untimely demise of Mr. Thomas." The judge's voice boomed in a rich baritone.

"It would do little, your Worship, save for the accused's own confession." The prosecutor stood at his table, a hand deftly placed on a large stack of papers. He looked as though he posed for a Renaissance portrait.

"There are any number of reasons a man might confess to a crime," the judge returned. Magistrate Silverson was nowhere to be seen, and in his place was a much sturdier looking man. Alastair had told me that judges would come from London to preside over these proceedings. I was grateful this one had a clear head on his shoulders.

"I admit it does paint the accused in a very poor light," the judge continued, "but my interest is one of justice, and the question we have before us today is a simple one. Did Bram Lowhouse murder or conspire to murder Sir Lucas Thomas? To that end, the only interest I have in Mr. Lowhouse's confession is whether it is accurate."

"Your worship," the prosecutor said in a mighty voice, "the confession has value beyond the substance of his statement. I propose that the very act of making a confession about the crime implicates Mr. Lowhouse in its commission. The man is accused, as you said, not only of murder but of conspiracy to commit such. What purpose had he in confessing to the crime if not to advance a greater plot? And if he has knowledge of a greater plot, is he not a conspirator?"

A wave of murmuring and discontent swept through the room. I realized, feebly, that I had not seen the strength of the prosecutor's skill against Mr. Milton. He had no need to exhibit it against such a weak opponent.

The judge hit his gavel on the podium to quiet the crowd. I surveyed the room again and was surprised to find Byron Livingston across the balcony, looking on beside a proudly dressed woman in an overly large hat—a woman I assumed was Carolina Drake. Evidently, her theft of my article was not enough to prevent their engagement.

Alastair stood.

"You are no fool, your honor, even if the prosecution believes you to be one." Another round of murmurs circulated, more amused than the one before. The judge held up a hand and stifled a smile.

"Let's not turn this into a sideshow, Mr. McHenry," he cautioned. "If you have a point, please lead us there directly."

"I'm embarrassed to make it for its simplicity. The prosecution states that the only plausible reason Mr. Lowhouse would confess to a very public crime, a crime that has been in this city's papers more than news of her Majesty's war with the Zulus, is because he is involved somehow in the crime itself. Well, your worship, if that is true, I have but to give one alternative reason for Mr. Lowhouse's confession before the prosecution's entire theory topples to the ground."

"Can you offer such a reason?" the judge asked, leaning forward.

"I could offer hundreds, your worship, but it is gentlemanly to allow our opponent to retreat from such a tactical blunder. Surely, if the case against Mr. Lowhouse is so clear, this fallacy was a simple misstep, and I wouldn't want this court to waste its time playing it out to its pathetic end. I would prefer that we get to the meat of the prosecution's case, and I would like to hear their central argument explaining how Bram Lowhouse is involved in the death of a man he never met, a man from a vastly different social station, a man who had never wronged him."

I almost cried. It was as though Alastair wielded a sword on a battlefield, courageously fending off the paltry enemies that would do Bram in. I said a quiet prayer and thanked my father for his kind deeds. Their echo lived to bless me still.

"Have you a response?" Coldworth asked the prosecutor.

The prosecutor conferred with an assistant at his table before replying.

"We do. But if it pleases your Worship, we would request a brief recess before we transition."

"Very well. We shall resume in one quarter of an hour."

He pounded the gavel, inviting a sound like a crowded aviary to erupt in chatter. Alastair sat down beside Bram and put a congenial hand on his shoulder. The magician did his best to smile back. Across the aisle, the prosecution's table buzzed like hornets. I wondered what new attack they planned.

Hope sprouted inside me like a spring bulb. The way Alastair spoke and commanded the respect of the court, I believed perhaps, somehow, Bram might emerge from this after all.

That hope spurred me into action. It would be risky, but I had to deliver what I found in Reading. Besides, caked in soot as I was, hair dyed under a cap, and Sergeant Cooper nowhere in the room I could see, I calculated my chances were quite high of avoiding detection.

I pushed my way through the chatting onlookers, descended the stairs, and, with some difficulty, arrived near the bar separating the public from the parties. I hid in the smattered view of the second row.

"Alastair!" I called vainly from my secluded position. "Alastair McHenry!"

Somehow he heard me and casually came to my position. I could feel the people around us trying to glimpse our interaction from the corner of their eye. "I didn't recognize you. Where have you been?"

"It's a long story, but please, this is all I found among Bram's old things." I handed him the bundle of cheesecloth. "Perhaps he can tell you if anything can exonerate him."

Alastair eyed the items carefully.

"I was really hoping for something more akin to a letter that would prove his innocence. I'm not sure what some jewelry and a rubber ball can accomplish."

"You'll have to ask him," I replied. "Oh, and be very careful with those wooden dolls."

His shoulders sunk.

"I'm not sure how asking him will help," he replied. "I'm afraid his condition has not improved. He's on and off now."

I swallowed a painful knot and turned my face toward Bram. As though he sensed friendly eyes, the chains at his wrists rattled and he turned my way.

His eyes broke my heart. The havoc Jeremy had wreaked in the Netherdowns was plain to see on Bram's tormented features. Yet, somehow, when he saw me, a layer of worry melted from his expression, as though he witnessed a mirage in the desert.

He inclined his head.

"I'm here for you," I mouthed to him. A tear fell down his cheek, silently.

"I'll ask him, love," Alastair said reverently. The judge approached his podium again, and I nodded at Bram's barrister before melting back into the crowd.

I didn't go too far, interested to see Bram's reaction to the trinkets. When Alastair unfolded the cheesecloth, confusion scrunched up Bram's face. Alastair wrapped them back up and stuffed them in his bag.

If we hoped that the trinkets would be an immediate savior, we were either very mistaken, or Jeremy's assault on Bram's memory had taken a terrible victory.

"Order," shouted a bailiff to the unruly mass. The room quieted slowly before the judge continued.

"Has the prosecution had an adequate rest before their continuance?"

"We have your Worship. With your permission?"

The judge nodded.

"We would like now to turn to one of our important witnesses, Sergeant George Cooper, recently resigned from the Dawnhurst Police Force."

"Very well." The judge motioned to one of his bailiffs, who disappeared through a door near his desk. My heart began racing. Instinctively, I shrank further into the crowd.

In a moment, the bailiff had produced the old sergeant and led him to a stand between the judge's podium and the jury bench.

"Sergeant George Cooper. Do you believe in Almighty God?" the judge asked.

"I do, sir," Cooper replied solemnly.

"And do you swear by Almighty God that the evidence you shall give shall be the truth, the whole truth, and nothing but the truth?"

"I do so swear."

"Very well. The prosecution will proceed with questioning."

The prosecutor approached the center of the room.

"Sergeant Cooper, you commanded the police that initially discovered the deceased's body, is that correct?"

"Yes. I was summoned after some of my officers responded to cries for help near the banker's office."

"And what did you see upon arriving?"

Cooper shifted uncomfortably.

"I entered the room and discovered the body of the late Luke Thomas lying on the ground. His noose was still around his neck, but my officers had untied the rope and lowered him the floor, as they are trained to."

"And Sergeant—"

Alastair stood up.

"Your worship, if I may but quickly chime in, the prosecution keeps referring to this gentleman as sergeant, but for the sake of the jury's clarity, I must point out that he is no longer a sergeant with the Dawnhurst Police but has recently resigned from that post for reasons I dare not speculate."

"Fair point, counsel," the judge nodded.

"Mr. Cooper, then, were you not also the acting authority who expanded this investigation beyond a presumption of suicide?"

"I did," Cooper said stiffly.

"Why would you do such a thing?"

"There were certain elements of Luke Thomas' situation that I found unusual, aspects that I thought may or may not speak to foul play."

"Namely?"

"For one, we found no note from the deceased, and from all discussions with his associates, family, and friends, no one claimed to notice any sign that he was in dire straits or possessed by some madness. Often, before such a tragic event, the party in question behaves unusually enough to raise alarm in the mind of at least one of his social acquaintances."

"And what of his accompanying financial scandal? Is that not enough to drive a man in his position to desperation?" The prosecutor paced slowly, gesticulating with his hands theatrically.

"I know that financial scandal was reported at length in the papers, but after conferring with others in his field, it might more aptly be described as an oversight. The amount of money in question at the center of this so-called scandal was a sum too small to tempt a man of his stature."

"How do you mean?"

"Luke Thomas' associates knew him to be a man of exactness and correctness. As per the records that were unveiled by his competitor, he had committed theft by transferring the ownership of a sum of money to his own benefit. But the sum in question was about a year's pay to a factory worker. To a factory worker, that would be a considerable increase. To put it mildly, it would not have been much of an increase at all for Lord Thomas. It left me wondering why a man like him would risk the reputation he spent decades building in order to benefit in such an insignificant way."

I exhaled. If my article had caused Luke Thomas' death, I would have written about a sum of money I figured was great. But how could I know how much money the wealthy truly enjoy? A year's worth of factory pay? A year's worth of my father's time was more like it. Cooper continued.

"We also usually find in these situations, a platform or chair from which the deceased might have jumped. There was no such platform beside the rafter from which he hanged," Cooper said.

"Is that all?" the prosecutor asked, a smug expression on his face as he noted the whispers in the crowd.

"No, not quite. As I mentioned, these things in isolation are peculiar, but life is peculiar. Had it not been for a conversation I had later that day, I'd have thought nothing of it. Luke Thomas' son was an officer in my police brigade, and it fell upon me to notify him of his father's misfortune. When I arrived at the station, he was consorting with a reporter that had only recently taken a keen interest in him and his exploits. When I asked to speak with him in private, he insisted that she could hear whatever personal matter I had to tell him. When I told him, he responded as you might expect. But the reporter, Luella Winthrop, did not. She swooned and swayed like a drunkard, didn't respond to questions, and wandered from the building. This was the first moment I thought there might be a greater plot against Luke Thomas."

Alastair stood again.

"Your worship, again, I fear that my interruption is bold, but I must remind the prosecution that Luella Winthrop is not on trial today. We've yet to hear anything from this witness that touches on my client."

"Because I'm not finished," Cooper said, glaring at Alastair. "I pushed these thoughts from my head because they were wild thoughts. I happened upon Miss Winthrop speaking with Edward Thomas at the station soon after that date, and she turned hostile towards me, something I might expect from Edward, but not an unaffected party. I'd have expected Luella Winthrop to be delighted to have such a compelling story to write about. Later, Miss Winthrop's fiancé, a Byron Livingston, came to me with concerns that Luella had gone mad, citing irregular episodes of her personality. I took some officers to question Miss Winthrop, but when we arrived at her home, she fled the city, as has been well documented by the papers."

I blushed as I remembered the events Cooper recalled for the court. I wish he had told them incorrectly, at least then I could have hated him for it, but I could refute nothing.

"Months later, Luella Winthrop and Edward Thomas showed up at my office as an engaged couple with a man in their custody. The man was Bram Lowhouse. They told me Mr. Lowhouse would confess to the murder of Luke Thomas. When I asked how they knew, Luella Winthrop shared a story with me that fit it all together.

"Mr. Lowhouse had convinced her to try out what he called a magical pen that would turn her imagination into reality. To convince her, he guided her through writing foolish stories, all the while orchestrating con schemes to prove to her the magic was real. This he did in order to create a scapegoat for his ultimate crime. He convinced Luella to write a story detailing the demise of Luke Thomas. When her story turned out to be true, she had a nervous breakdown, foolishly believing that somehow she had caused the banker's downfall. Her erratic behavior distracted me and my officers while the true culprit ran off with his ruddy carnival."

The courtroom was gravely quiet as he finished. Clothes worn by the people around me rustled as they shifted uneasily.

"Thank you, Mr. Cooper. The prosecution has no further questions for you."

Alastair rose quickly, looking like he had an earnest desire not to let the shocked silence sprout into a conviction.

"Mr. Cooper. Why did you resign from the police force?" he asked.

"Frankly, after this case, I felt it my duty. It had been so public and so embarrassing for my professional career, it seemed only right to resign my post."

"Did you know Luella Winthrop before the Lord Thomas' suicide?"

"Yes. As I mentioned, she wrote articles chronicling one of my officers." Cooper wrung the brim of his hat. Alastair wouldn't let him wriggle free so easily.

"Did you know her before she started doing that?" he asked. Cooper hesitated.

"Yes. I had met her on one or two occasions as a little girl."

"Did you know Luke Thomas in any personal capacity?" Alastair asked. Cooper cleared his throat.

"I'm telling the truth," he hedged, looking discomfited.

"I didn't ask if you were telling the truth," Alastair said.

"Yes. Luke was an outstanding gentleman."

"How did you meet? It's not often a police sergeant and a member of the House of Lords have overlapping social engagements."

"As you know, Lord Thomas was also one of the city's more prominent bankers, and the police had more than one opportunity to come to his aid."

"So you went to escort rowdy customers from his premises, let's say, and you just happened to strike up conversation?"

Cooper narrowed his eyes.

"That was his way. He didn't look down on the rest of the world the way many of his station do. He cared. He asked after my family. He—"

"Did he ever loan you money, Mr. Cooper?" Alastair asked. Cooper nodded and stared at his lap.

"Do you mind sharing the details about that?" Alastair bent over to peer into Cooper's gaze when the prosecution stood.

"Your worship! What does this humble civic servant's financial affairs have to do with Mr. Lowhouse's culpability?"

Alastair cut in before the judge had a chance to respond.

"The prosecution means to present this man's testimony as a cornerstone for their case. The man paints them a pretty convenient picture, your worship. But this picture has one artist, and I suspect it's a forgery. Mr. Cooper had a personal relationship with both the deceased and a suspected participant of this crime, and the prosecution hid those facts from the jury. How do we know that this man isn't willfully blind about Miss Winthrop's involvement in his close friend's death?"

"If a police sergeant acting in his duty reports a confession, how can we call the honesty of such a sworn testimony, into question?" the prosecutor roared, pounding his fist on the table.

"For all we know, the resigned Sergeant Cooper might have a romantic relationship with Miss Winthrop!"

Alastair put both hands on his waist and relished the scandalized cries coming from some women on the first floor. I couldn't help but smile. There was no blame to assign Alastair. I had approved this strategy. Seeing it hefted so mightily, though, was a sight to behold.

"Order!" shouted the judge. It took several minutes for the room to calm down. The papers tomorrow would crawl with the drama.

"What was Mr. Lowhouse's confession?" Alastair asked Cooper.

"This is unnecessary, your worship. The confession is a signed statement already submitted as evidence," the prosecutor cried.

"I'm not asking what the statement said," Alastair went on. He looked Cooper dead in the eye. "Did Bram Lowhouse ever tell you the words, 'I killed Luke Thomas?'"

Cooper looked miserable. I imagined this public scrutiny was exactly why he'd resigned.

"No."

"What did he say?" Alastair asked.

"He said 'I am responsible for Luke Thomas' death.'"

"Responsible," Alastair echoed. "The way a parent might be responsible for a child's indiscretion." He walked to his chair and pushed it over to the floor. It echoed violently in the chamber.

"Am I responsible for the chair falling over?" he cried. "No! I pushed it over. Am I responsible for the actions of Luella Winthrop? No! She commits them. And is Bram Lowhouse responsible for the actions of Luella Winthrop?"

He turned to the jury.

"We would say no, but he may disagree. After all, he fell in love with her. A man in love does crazy things, we all know that. What is more likely? That Bram Lowhouse concocted an elaborate many-month long scheme to set up a working-class woman as a culprit for a heinous crime to which he has no personal connection? Or is it more likely that Luella Winthrop, now engaged to the banker's son, who vanished the night the banker's widow disappeared, inspired an infatuated man to take the fall on her behalf?"

Alastair turned back to Cooper.

"I'm grateful for your service, sir. I do not believe you to be a liar. I believe that you were eager to believe a story from a girl who has a special place in that big heart of yours."

Alastair turned and sat down. I had been so absorbed in his words that it didn't occur to me until he finished to feel self-conscious. He painted me as such a villain that the onlookers might well turn into a mob. If anyone were to recognize me now, they might rip me apart right then and there.

That's when Sergeant Cooper's eyes locked with mine.

I froze.

He sat quietly, staring for a long moment. Pain streaked his eyes, and fear rooted me to the ground. Finally, he stood slowly. My hands began to quake. Here was the servant of justice. I wanted to turn and run, but his eyes held me prisoner. I couldn't move.

The room hushed as he wet his lips to speak, fists clenched and jaw set.

"I, George Cooper, do not believe that Luella Winthrop is guilty of Luke Thomas's murder," he cried in a loud, breaking voice. "For whatever my thirty years in service to this city is worth, that is my final word on the matter."

The room rested, still as the dead, but a quiet tear escaped my eye. I nodded to him subtly.

He stepped down from the witness' stand as a broken man and retreated slowly through the door from which he came.

17

WINNER OF THE GOLDEN INKWELL

George Cooper's departure left a wave of solemnity in the room. Everyone seemed to understand that they had just witnessed a defense lawyer break down the character of a man who had served the city for decades. Somehow, despite the already heavy atmosphere of a murder trial, it added an even greater air of severity to the proceedings.

"Do you have more witnesses to call forward?" Coldworth asked the prosecution.

"We had hoped to, your worship, but it appears all Bram Lowhouse's associates have fled the city. That's to be expected of a vagrant as he is. We had heard he had some colleagues lodging in Reading and requested the Reading Police to round them up and send them our way. We only received one such transfer and only this morning."

I gritted my teeth. So that was the true reason the carnival's flat had been raided. I shook my head, remembering the rubbish the Inspector fed me about some type of sordid love affair.

"What is the name of this witness?"

"Sadie Le Gris."

On a gesture from the judge, the bailiff walked back to the witness door and led Sadie, ruffled and unenthusiastic, to the stand.

"Sadie Le Gris, do you believe in Almighty God?" the judge asked.

"Sure, I do."

"And do you swear by Almighty God that the evidence you shall give shall be the truth, the whole truth, and nothing but the truth?"

"If I have to."

"Miss Le Gris," the prosecutor said as he approached her. "I thank you for your willingness to attend this trial."

"Wasn't very willing, was it? You had the Reading police pull me out of home and throw me in a wagon."

Murmurs buzzed, quickly inciting the judge to pound his gavel.

"You told me I had to tell the truth." Sadie shrugged. The prosecutor cleared his throat.

"Do you know the accused?"

"What? Bram? Of course. We've worked together for years."

"And what is your responsibility in the traveling show by whom you are employed?"

"I'm a hypnotist. I put volunteers into a trance and then use the powers of suggestion to have them make fools of themselves. We'll be back here in summer, everyone!"

This elicited some laughs from the crowd.

"Miss Le Gris. Please. This is not a promotional opportunity," the judge said.

"Everything is with the right mindset, your worshipliness."

"Could you describe Mr. Lowhouse's character to the jury?"

"Certainly. Bram is a recluse. He likes to read books, listen but not talk during our nightly fires, propose big ideas but leave them for others to accomplish, and has a tender spot in him for animals."

"Have you ever known Bram to be violent or vindictive?"

Sadie folded her arms and chewed on her tongue as she considered what to say.

"Violent? No. Vindictive? Aren't we all? I've never known him to be classically vindictive. He always found creative ways to get even with someone that didn't matter to anyone else. If a guest at the fair called his act idiocy, for example, he'd talk to some of us and ask us to make sure that the guest thought all the acts were idiocy. That way, the gentleman or lady wouldn't enjoy any part of the show."

"So acts of planned revenge were not beyond him?" The prosecutor clasped his hands behind his back.

"I didn't say that."

"What was Mr. Lowhouse's act at the fair?"

"He's a magician. He does tricks where things vanish and reappear or look impossible."

"So more than the average man, he would know how to coordinate a scenario that appears to defy normal explanation?"

Sadie wore an apologetic frown and looked at Bram. "I suppose you could say that."

"Has he ever made a man levitate?" the prosecutor asked.

"Truly, or appear to levitate?" Sadie asked.

"I object, your worship," said Alastair. "It is beyond the scope of today's proceedings to determine whether magic is real or imaginary."

The prosecutor waved a hand in concession.

"I revise my question. Has Mr. Lowhouse ever deftly hoisted an individual into the air using a method that wasn't readily apparent?"

Sadie smiled wickedly.

"That's the thing about magic, though, isn't it? The explanation is not readily apparent until it is. If you're asking if Bram is smarter than the average person, he is."

"Do you believe him to be capable of taking another man's life?"

Bram and Sadie looked at each other. No words were exchanged, but much appeared communicated.

"I'll say this. I think the skills we all rely on individually can turn against us if people fear us enough. I'm not afraid of Bram. I have no reason to believe anyone else should be, either."

The prosecution leaned toward her.

"Do you believe him capable of taking another man's life, Miss Le Gris?"

"Aren't we all, sir?"

A somber mood filled the room. The prosecutor shrugged toward the jury and returned to his bench.

"Does the defense wish to question the witness?" the judge asked.

"We have nothing to ask, your worship, but we thank Miss Le Gris for coming despite the prosecution's rough method. I understand it was not her first choice."

"First choice? More like last choice!" she said. The spectators in the courtroom laughed again while the bailiff led her out. I smiled again. I doubted that went how the prosecution planned.

"We have a final witness, your worship," the Prosecution said. "But her connections to the case had not been made clear until recently, so we've not given her much notice."

"Is she here today?" The judge furrowed his eyebrows in worry, giving an impression that he did not want to drag out this trial any longer than was strictly necessary.

"She is."

"Then by all means, let's bring her forward and get to the truth of it."

"The prosecution invites Carolina Drake to come forward."

My insides turned over. The name Carolina Drake conjured up such strong negative emotions. It was her fault I had been captured and imprisoned, ultimately causing our plan to rescue Bram to fail. The crowd turned with me to identify movement on the balcony where she stood.

She stood indignant and proud, though her face was flushed. She gave off the appearance of being frozen in ice, with sharp facial features. Somehow, the attention gave her overly affected wardrobe an air of importance.

No one was more surprised than Byron. His mouth fell open, and I could almost see his pulse thumping from where I stood on the ground floor. Carolina whispered something into his ear and left his side.

What did she have to do with any of this?

The room parted for her as if she drew a stick through a pile of sand. The bailiff ushered her past the bar and guided her to the witness stand.

I caught a glimpse of Bram's confused stare before he turned forward again. Evidently, he knew as much as the rest of us. Or was that his failing memory again?

Her posture was impeccable as she sat down on the witness stand, her head poised as if she were Victoria herself.

The judge pressed the same vows of honesty on her as he did Cooper and Sadie. She responded more eloquently than the hypnotist.

Grace is rarely innate. Carolina was a practiced, polished figure who had prepared for a public moment like this for years. She looked more expensive and refined than the somewhat gaudy clothes she wore.

The prosecutor began.

"Miss Drake, am I correct in believing that you sit on the Golden Inkwell committee of Dawnhurst-on-Severn?"

"That is correct."

"Can you explain the responsibilities of that committee to this jury?"

"The Golden Inkwell is the city's most prestigious writing award. Each year, we bestow the honor on one deserving journalist and one deserving fiction writer, be they serialist or novelist."

"What recommends a writer for such a reward?"

Out of the corner of my eye, I noticed Alastair's leg bobbing up and down. His gaze was fixed on Carolina.

"We look for well-researched, progressive, and consistent writing. Usually, our winners have published a story or article that has pushed the civilized conversation of the city forward in an important way."

"Could you provide us with an example?"

"Certainly. Last year, we recognized a man name Arthur Paxton, for his story chronicling the life of coal delivery workers. His work inspired hard looks at our local economy and pushed forward the railroad improvement initiative that commands the attention of local leaders and regional railroad presidents alike."

The prosecutor nodded and leaned against his table with one hand.

"How does one become a member of this distinguished selection committee?"

"Appointment to the committee is by invitation only. In most cases, invitations are extended to previous winners of the Golden Inkwell."

The prosecutor smiled toothily.

"Are you a winner of the Golden Inkwell, Miss Drake?"

She drew in a deep breath of importance.

"I am."

"Which of your writings recommended you for such an award?"

"I wrote an article detailing the dangers of vagrants and transient lifestyles coming through the city. I used Mr. Lowhouse as the case in chief for my article."

My mouth went dry. Memories of my first meetings with Bram came rushing back to me in an instant. I noticed him go rigid in his seat beside Alastair. I wished I could see his face more clearly from where I stood.

"Then you believe that Mr. Lowhouse is dangerous?" the prosecutor prodded.

"I know him to be."

"How can you know that?"

"In my research for the aforementioned article, it was confirmed to me."

Even as my legs went weak, I found the strength to roll my eyes at her use of the word 'aforementioned.' I never knew how much I could dislike another human being.

"Please explain," the prosecutor said. He strode behind his table with purpose, as if it were a theatrical show of turning time over to Carolina to speak freely.

"This is not Bram Lowhouse's first time being accused of killing a Dawnhurst resident. Years ago, he was at the very center of a scandal many of you may remember. An attendant at a 'Display of Illusions' performed by Mr. Lowhouse met a most unfortunate and peculiar end.

"Mr. Lowhouse was performing a rehearsed presentation on the effects of what he called one of the lesser-known forms of magic, a field he called malicious ambition. In the presentation, he brought forward a volunteer from the audience, a strong, bricklayer in his forties named Stephen Hardson. Mr. Lowhouse bound one of his arms before instructing him to crank the gear shaft on a music box. Mr. Hardson did as requested, and spectators reported seeing a most unusual change come across the man. He entered a type of trance and kept going on about getting his money. He grew louder and more aggressive, shouting that Mr. Lowhouse get out of his head and forget about the, 'damn-them-all sovereigns.'"

She held up a hand at the end of her sentence to indicate they were not her words. As far as I was concerned, she made them hers by bearing them forward.

"Some people watching in the small crowd grew alarmed, claiming that a devil had entered the man. Some wanted to call a clergyman. But Mr. Lowhouse was said to have smiled in a peculiar and awful way. When the protests reached a zenith, he wound the music box gear shaft in the opposite direction and closed its lid. The man's fits abated instantly, but he was reported to have a dark and brooding expression on his face. He walked through the crowd and left the fair immediately."

Alastair pound his fist on the table and stood in a fury.

"Your worship, somehow we've arrived at accusing my client of black magic. This is utter nonsense! If my client was employed as a magician, it was his job to produce sensational effects for his audiences. How can we penalize a man simply because he does his job well? Behind a magician's illusions are simple methods."

The judge leaned forward paternally.

"Mr. McHenry, I understand your concerns, but they can be voiced when the witness has finished her account. Please, Miss Drake, if you have more to say, continue."

Alastair fumed and sat down in his chair like a hunched wolf.

"Your concerns are valid, Mr. McHenry," Carolina went on. "It was not my intention to prove Mr. Lowhouse's magical powers in that article. Nor is it today. Mr. Lowhouse's 'Display of Illusion' was only a precursor to the main event. Mr. Hardman reportedly hanged himself that night. He left no letter, and the peculiarity of his circumstances were similar to those of Lord Thomas."

I felt a chill. On glancing across the room, I was alarmed to see that the lamps had been lit. Had the sun just gone down? How long had this trial gone on? The people around me shuffled uncomfortably.

"When I conducted my own research, I discovered that a close friend of Mr. Lowhouse's had come to catastrophic financial ruin. Mr. Hardson had borrowed money from this friend with the pretense of using the funds as a loan to start his own bricklaying firm. In reality, Hardson used it to drink and gamble. Hardson's neighbors reported hearing a loud row about a week before the incident, in which a brutish voice shouted, 'You'll meet your end, Hardson. Mark me, you'll meet it!'"

She stopped here, and the prosecutor took his time before taking the conversation up, letting her words impress themselves on the minds of the jury.

"Do you believe that Mr. Lowhouse is responsible for the death of Luke Thomas?" he asked.

"I have no cause to speculate on his guilt in the case at hand. I know nothing of the facts or background beyond what has been presented in the course of this trial."

"But do you believe he has erroneously walked free from a crime committed those years ago? A crime which was ultimately ruled by our police force as a suicide?"

She set her jaw but avoided looking Bram in the face.

"I am sure of it."

"Because of your research for your award-winning article that won an award from such a reputable institution?"

She nodded.

"The prosecution has no more questions, your worship."

I swallowed. When I first met Bram, he warned me there had been an accident that removed him from his post as one of the fair's featured performers. An accident. I thought an accident meant a rope broke or someone set a gun off unintentionally.

He meant that he'd had an accident with the magic.

Hadn't Jeremy confessed to using a song that Hirythe feared to wake up a type of magic? Now, I learned Bram prompted a volunteer to play music during one of his shows...

Malicious ambition.

Even to me, this produced a very sour taste in my throat. Even I questioned his background.

"Miss Drake," Alastair began. His friendly and unassuming demeanor was gone. In its place lay furrowed brows and a tight mouth.

"Has anyone who has received the Golden Inkwell award had it subsequently rescinded?"

"No. Though it has been proposed on a handful of occasions."

"What about Golden Inkwell Committee members? Have any been removed from their post?"

"Not for some time," she said, stiffening.

"What would qualify a person for such a removal?" Alastair paced in front of the jury.

"If the committee were to find something in their conduct adequately detrimental to their character to tarnish the award's reputation."

"A scandalous affair, for example?" Alastair's pacing increased in speed and purpose. Carolina blushed.

"That may be adequate, yes."

"And if that member's earlier writings were proven to be false, disproven, or otherwise scorned? If it were to come to light that someone had fabricated a story for the sole purpose of self-aggrandizement?"

She glared at Alastair.

"I don't like your insinuation, sir."

"I just want to understand. If your story about Bram Lowhouse's involvement in the death of Mr. Hardson proved to be a sham, would your position in a prestigious institution be threatened?"

"It's not a sham."

"Can that be verified by someone else? A reputable third party? The Dawnhurst Police, for example? It sounds like there are two versions of the story of Mr. Hardson by two different entities. Yours, which catapulted you to respect in your professional community, and that of the police, who had little to no reason whatsoever to make Mr. Hardson's suicide into anything other than what they saw it to be."

She leaned forward and put both hands on her chair beside her.

"If there were someone else to verify my findings, I would not have to find them myself. That's what reporting is all about. We are the detectives when the detectives have given up. Are you quite finished?"

Alastair finally stopped pacing and stood tall.

"One final question," he said. "Are you married?"

She blinked, seemingly annoyed.

"Not yet. I'm engaged."

"To whom?"

"Mr. Byron Livingston."

Alastair smiled and turned to the crowd.

"Now, isn't that interesting? Byron Livingston was engaged once before to a woman with a name we all know. A woman who should sit where this man sits." He pointed at Bram. "Luella Winthrop."

The silence in the room was broken only by the loud and violent tinge of red that flushed Carolina's skin all over. I had to hand it to Alastair. He was vicious when required, unafraid to dive into the uncomfortable. I instinctively retreated a little further into the collar of my coat and pulled down the brim of my hat a little lower.

"I have no other question for her, your worship," Alastair said, sitting down. The bailiff escorted Miss Drake from her seat back to the crowd. I expected her to find Byron again, but she never turned toward the stairs, opting instead to march directly out of the courthouse.

Who could blame her?

"Does the prosecution have any other witnesses or evidence to bring forward at this time?" Coldworth asked.

"There is one person from whom we would all appreciate a testimony, your worship. The defendant, himself," said the prosecutor.

"Is the defendant prepared to provide such testimony?"

Alastair leaned over to Bram. They exchanged a quiet, albeit animated conversation. At the conclusion of which Bram shook his head.

"I fear the defendant will not be offering any testimony on his behalf."

This concession marked murmurs across the court from the crowd. Mr. Justice Coldworth leaned forward.

"Are you quite certain, Mr. McHenry? If he does not testify, the jury may take that into account when deciding the question of his guilt."

"Mr. Lowhouse has made it clear," Alastair said heavily.

"Very well. Then the task will soon turn to the jury to decide the fate of Mr. Lowhouse. But before I instruct the jury to do so, I would like to offer both parties a final chance to address this bench of fine gentlemen before they deliberate on the matter."

He nodded to the prosecutor, who stood and turned his nose up pedantically.

"Thank you, your worship. Gentlemen of the jury. I understand full well the difficulty of your decision. The penalty for murder in this the Queen's country, is hanging by the neck until dead. Voting to send a man to such an end is no light chore. It is not a pleasure. It is not an aspiration. We delight not in bloodshed. But it is for those reasons that you cannot shirk or be swayed to leniency.

"Bram Lowhouse is a murderer of the worst kind. His methods are, as of yet, undiscovered in full. We do not know how he put Luke Thomas in a noose to hang in his office. But we know some instrumental truths about this situation that cannot be ignored, and for that, Mr. Lowhouse must be stopped before he can kill again.

"Let me explain clearly the sequence of Mr. Lowhouse's dastardly and malevolent sins. He took employment with a disreputable carnival, where he undoubtedly made friends with undesirables. When one of these friends was wronged financially by a foolish bricklayer, Mr. Lowhouse stepped forward to avenge that friend's honor. Before he killed Mr. Hardson, he humiliated him publicly with a performance that unsettled his mind. I propose, as did Miss Drake in her award-winning article, that fear drove Mr. Hardson to lunacy in front of that crowd. Fear that a previous threat issued by Mr. Lowhouse would come to fruition.

"That night, Mr. Lowhouse hanged Mr. Hardson from the rafters in his own home.

"Years later, Mr. Lowhouse came forward to confess to a crime identical in all but the name of the victim. Why would he do such a terrible thing? The retired police sergeant was kind enough to explain it clearly. When Mr. Lowhouse devised his con and lured the perfect unknowing accomplice into his service, the unthinkable happened. He fell in love. When the proverbial noose tightened around his beloved, he did the first decent thing in his life and stepped forward.

"We cannot now allow such dignity to retreat. Mr. Lowhouse did the right thing by exonerating Luella Winthrop with his confession. It is time to put an end to this vile campaign. Bram Lowhouse cannot go free. He must die. If he does not, we invite all others to play similar games with God's justice."

The prosecutor clenched a hand, took a long last look at the jury, and took his seat. The judge nodded to Alastair, who stood up haltingly, taking a final glance at a paper on his table.

"When I was a lad," he began, "in my first factory job, we'd go to a pub after our day's work was finished. A worker's pay is slight, but to a young man, it's a dream come true. My pocket jingled with the promise of the future.

"When I got home that night, a wee bit more tipsy than I had planned on, I was furious to discover that my pockets had only a six pence remaining.

"My suspicion festered as I watched some of my factory fellows make purchases I thought were too elaborate and extravagant for the pay we received. It wasn't long before I narrowed in on a thief. I confronted him, and he protested. I grabbed him right by the lapels and swore that if he ever stole from me again, I'd beat him bloody. He steered clear of me after that.

"The next time we were paid, we went back to the pub, where the owner looked at me and said, 'Back again, are you? You made me a rich man last time.' Only then did I realize, I had misunderstood the price of a pint. It was my own bill that pilfered my pockets. But I had forever ruined the friendship with my workmate."

He put his fists on his hips.

"The prosecution asks you to kill a man today, and he asks you to do so simply because you should trust him and his parading band of witnesses. You heard those witnesses. One of them was a reporter who climbed to the top of her field by stepping on a poor man's head. It's convenient, isn't it, that the mysterious research that supported her award-winning article points fingers at the lowest among us? Bram Lowhouse was just doing his job when he performed for Mr. Hardson. Can you be cross with him for being good at what he does for a living?

"The other was a resigned police sergeant, who gave up his post in disgrace. But he said one thing worth exploring. Luella Winthrop told him Mr. Lowhouse is guilty. But Luella Winthrop is out there somewhere. She was arrested again by that same sergeant after giving her statement to him. Then she escaped from prison the same night that Lord Thomas' widow disappeared. She is the one who wrote that damnable article the night Lord Thomas died. She is the one we should be investigating. But the prosecution is only interested in looking competent. It wants this whole ordeal put away, and quickly, so that its offices won't be bothered any longer by insecure people requiring something like justice.

"We don't require justice. Justice makes requirements of us. Your requirement is this: if you cannot in full confidence state that you are certain Mr. Lowhouse snuck into Lord Thomas' private office, put a noose around his neck, and hoisted him into the rafters, then you have no God-given right to vote that he is guilty of this crime.

"The prosecution says that guilt pushed Bram Lowhouse to confess and exonerate Miss Winthrop. *Bah!* What a time to have a change of heart? He came forward out of love and a desire to take her fall. It was stupid and noble, but I *will not* let a man's good intentions thwart the true demands of justice. You cannot either."

Alastair energetically pounded the table on the word 'either.'

I wanted to faint. The prosecutor brought forward such evidence that even though I believed Bram to be innocent, I saw him differently. There was more to the Meddler than I knew, even though I'd walked through the valleys of his memory.

Why hadn't he defended himself? Was that decision from Alastair, who feared the skills of a deft prosecutor? Or did they fear that Bram's mental state had deteriorated so that his own testimony could only hurt him?

My world spun. I didn't even hear the instructions the judge gave to the jury, who retreated to a small room hidden from our view to deliberate.

I must have missed a good portion of the trial. There must have been more evidence. There was more I could have done to help Alastair, to help Bram. If only we hadn't lost the page to that diary.

It seemed impossible that his fate now lay in the hands of a handful of gentlemen who spent only a day deliberating the facts. Can a life be decided in so short a time?

I cut through the crowd to talk with Alastair again.

"You need to make yourself scarce," he said, trying to look as though he was not speaking to me. "I'm sorry for what I did to your name, but nothing I said in this trial can be used in a trial against you. I will defend you just as earnestly when the time comes."

"Why didn't Bram say anything?" I asked. Alastair hesitated.

"He's not well, Luella. You told me you didn't want him admitted to an asylum. The only way to prevent that was to keep him quiet."

I nodded, but I wrung my hands all the same. The gravity of that decision had an all-new bearing now that I was faced with the moment.

"I think we'd all prefer the asylum to a hanging," I said.

"If it comes to that, we'll see what we can do about appealing to the Queen."

"The Queen?" I asked. I doubted the fate of a transient carnival worker would command much of her attention. Perhaps if she knew the truth about his magic... Yes, the Queen could assuredly use a true magician in her court.

"It's more common than you'd think," Alastair said. "The Crown has pardoned many a criminal unjustly sentenced to death. It'd be tricky, but I think we could make for a good argument."

I bit my lip.

"It won't come to that, though. You'll see. But you need to clear out of here. Your little disguise may have kept you hidden during a dramatic trial proceeding, but now that the police have some downtime, the risk is much higher they take notice of a funny-looking girl covered in coal."

He smiled briefly before turning from me, a sign that he would not entertain further debate on the issue.

His words soothed me. It would take the jury some time to deliberate. Perhaps I could get home, bathe, and enlist Mrs. Crow to wait at the courthouse until a verdict was reached.

As I headed toward the door, I searched the balcony for Byron. I wanted some more information on Carolina. Had he been as surprised as I was to discover the content of her article years before? To think, months ago, Byron might have used her position to leverage my work for the Golden Inkwell.

How times change.

I sifted through the dense crowd but couldn't find Byron anywhere. He must have gone off in search of his fiancée. Disappointed, I turned to leave, but I only made it to the foyer before I heard a commotion.

The jury was back already. It had been perhaps twenty, possibly thirty minutes.

I tried to elbow my way through the crowd. I could hardly see a thing, just small windows of incomplete fragments on the proceedings. I pushed forward, but the crowd pushed back on me like an overwhelming tide. No one wanted to miss the announcement.

"Has the jury come to a conclusion?" Mr. Justice Coldworth asked in a loud, practiced voice.

"We have, your honor," said a man with light hair, neatly parted one side. He looked young.

"And what is your conclusion?"

"The jury finds Bram Lowhouse guilty of murdering Lord Lucas Thomas!"

18

COLLAPSE

Pandemonium, but it all played out before me in silence: movement and noise everywhere but in my ears. Time slowed.

Alastair jumped up in a rage. But to me, he appeared to move underwater. Bram turned toward the crowd, and I thought he might be searching for me. But despite how I tried to push myself through the mob, I didn't move any faster than the lumbering, unearthly crawl of the men in uniform.

The judge spoke through a theatrical mask made of distance, fear, and pity, but I did not hear his words.

I almost reached the bar by the time they hoisted Bram to his feet, all part of the silent ballet. He gazed at me with a longing crease in his forehead, folded in regret and surrender.

I wanted to hurdle the railing and wrench his arms free from those terrible, faceless men, but something held me fast. I shouted his name, but though I felt it in my throat, no sound reached my ears. He mouthed something to me before they stuffed him into a restricted hallway, a heavy door slamming behind him.

My gaze darted around the room. There had to be a way to get to him. Alastair had approached the magistrate's podium, the prosecutor directly on his heels. They looked so incongruous, so animated and dreamlike.

Alastair could help, but something dragged me through the crowd in the opposite direction. I glanced quickly behind me and saw the back of a police uniform as an officer pulled me along, heading for the exit.

So they had recognized me in the end.

It was difficult to care. My limbs hung lifelessly beside me, and my legs pushed mechanically. Good heavens. This was my fault. I had convinced Bram to confess. I had used the page to get back to the Netherdowns, cutting off his only exit.

I failed to secure him an adequate legal defense.

The officer marched me out the front door, ushered me into a black carriage, and locked me in. I followed without objection or complaint. I deserved it. Incarceration. I deserved to head to the noose in Bram's place. The door shut behind me, and the carriage abruptly lurched forward at a brisk pace. I looked through a small window behind me at the court building shrinking from view. Alastair stumbled out on the cobbles, searching desperately in all directions, searching for me.

He could not have seen through my small window, but he stared after my carriage before it rounded a corner and disappeared.

I slowly became conscious of noise again: the beating hooves ahead, the whip of the driver, the clattering wheels on the cobblestone. With the sound came a sharp shooting, overwhelming pain.

Sobs. My stomach heaved violently as reality crushed from above. This wasn't a game. Why did I think I could cheat the rules? Where was the magic in the world now? It died with Bram.

Time warped and stretched out like burned toffee. I visited hell itself inside that carriage, tormented with guilt, remorse, and the pain of loss.

When the horses stopped, the driver opened the door to a defeated woman. Edward. Edward opened the door to a defeated woman.

And Edward, despite everything, was at least familiar.

I practically fell from the carriage into his arms and continued crying. He was a ghost in a police uniform, fate mocking what it had dangled in front of me to start this mad road to misery.

"They're going to kill him," I stammered between hiccupping gasps for air.

"Come now," he said as he led me away from the carriage with gloved hands. I had hardly bothered to consider our surroundings. We weren't in town. There were trees around us. He pulled me into a wood, and my surprise was enough to arrest my cries for a moment. What were we doing here in the cold? Old snowbanks crusted near the edge of the wood, but beneath the canopy only irregular forms of ice littered the ground sporadically. I no indication that might designate our objective.

After shuffling under the trees for a half mile, Edward came to a stop beneath a tall oak and turned to face me.

"You're a mess," he said.

"What can you expect?"

"I mean, physically. I hardly recognized you under that layer of soot. You look positively like a shadow."

"I took a boat to get back into town," I said vacantly.

"Back into town from where?"

"Reading. Edward, where are we?"

"Somewhere private."

I screwed up my face, finding the courage to look at him.

"You should have helped him," I said.

He folded his arms. His features had changed. He had dark rings under his eyes. His gaze, once so stalwart and steadfast, now danced evasively.

"You had the resources, and you didn't because you were jealous." I stuck a finger into his face. I hadn't felt angry like this since Sraith left me. "You're a jealous, sorry excuse for a man."

He stood there, quietly, framed by the large tree behind him. His uniform had been hastily donned. I could tell from some unlatched buttons and the state of the shirt poking out underneath.

He didn't say anything. I pushed him against the tree.

"You ruined my life!" I shouted, pushing him again. Why wouldn't he say anything? Fight back. "Why couldn't you have been real? Why did you have to be so damn interested in magic? I would have loved you, anyway. You didn't have to bewitch me!"

He was like a statue, a mirror. Who cared if he knew I had uncovered his secret. Let him kill me, if that's what he wanted.

"Why couldn't you have seen that things were good the way they were, been satisfied with what you had!"

I beat on his chest with my fists.

"Why didn't you just walk away when he showed you that stupid pen!" I shouted.

But of course, Bram hadn't showed Edward the pen. And the anguish I threw at Edward, haphazard and careless, bent back on to its true target.

Somehow, regret, accusations, conspiracies—everything brewed together into a foul, ugly brew. The vertigo of grief came on suddenly as a tide.

I stepped backward, my shoulders slumped and heaving from exertion. Edward's brows furrowed in what looked like concern. But was it? I had just accused him of bewitching me, but he betrayed no sign of anger.

"I know what you are," I said, betrayal constricting my throat.

"You do," he confirmed.

"I do." I nodded, lip quivering from cold and fear.

"And?"

I wanted to trust him. The way he looked in that uniform evoked a longing for the comfort I used to find in him.

He held his arms apart in an invitation it took all of my strength to resist. How I wanted to curl up in the comfort of his embrace, to trust that somehow things would turn out well.

My strength crumbled as I fell into his arms. He wrapped them tightly around me, muffling my tears, rocking me gently.

"I'm so sorry," he repeated sweetly in my ear.

"It's my fault," I cried over and over again. He didn't correct me. He didn't offer a plan to rectify the situation. We both knew we were well beyond that. Bram had a sentence from an Assizes judge. Alastair had mentioned we could appeal it. With any luck, Bram might still have some time.

But these hopes were distant and flickering as stars.

Edward held me for another few minutes in silence, just long enough for my mind to clear. The fog of my devastation was not gone, and the world around me still swam like a dream, but at least my faculties cleared enough to navigate that fog. I noticed how cold my feet had become, and I wondered why Edward had brought me here of all places.

He grabbed me firmly by the shoulders and stared me in the eyes.

"Something is wrong, Luella," he said.

"I know that."

"Something is wrong with me," he added. "I fear I have little time."

I peered at him. Was this another act? Another trick?

"What are you talking about?"

"It began with what I considered frustration about our relationship, jealousy over Bram, grief over my father. There were many ways to catalogue those emotions."

"What emotions?" I asked.

"Longing. Guilt. Desire. It's hard to explain." He walked past me and looked carefully through the trees, back toward the route we'd used to get here. "The timing could not be worse, I know. Bram is special to you. I understand that. It's no time for me to parade my horrors in front of you."

He winced and leaned on a tree trunk. I noticed his frame was thinner than before.

"You once loved me," he continued. His jaw clenched when he looked back at me to see if I would correct him.

I closed my eyes to avoid his stare.

"Did you find your mother at Fernmount?" I asked. He scoffed.

"She was never there. You knew that. Why didn't you tell me?"

I started to protest.

"You're not a good liar, Luella. It's obvious when you withhold or deceive. It's your posture and the cast of your eyes. Gives you away every time."

I blushed, feeling a swill of resentment. If he knew me as well as he claimed, he would have recognized my waning affections for months. No wonder he'd been jealous.

"Where is my mother?"

I bit my lip. The bond between Edward and Charlotte was a sacred one. Did I have any right to interfere with it? Was there even any chance I'd be able to bring Charlotte back from the Netherdowns? If Bram died, all hope of returning there might be lost. Jeremy had won, after all. His plan for revenge went exactly as he wished. He might not return to the real world, either, but from the way he spoke with Hiry-the, he didn't seem to care.

"You must tell me," Edward insisted.

Perhaps the guilt wasn't all mine after all. If Edward had bewitched me, perhaps all of this stemmed from his own negligence. He was the one to disturb the hornet's nest.

Cause and effect.

"The diary," I admitted.

His face, already pale, blanched.

"The book was destroyed," he said, collapsing against a tree trunk. "Save for the page you used to escape your cell. We must find it."

"We've been trying to find it!" I spat. "Johnson ran off with it. Odds are he's in the Netherdowns, too. And if he's there, he's good as dead."

"Why?"

"Because Bram's greatest rival found a way in, and the whole place is at war. There! Is this what you've wanted to know so long? Yes. The diary is made of memory: the memories of Bram and a fae named Hirythe, all bundled up together."

"What happens to the world if Bram dies?"

I knit my eyebrows. What a question. Where did the memories of the deceased fly off to? Would the magic on the spell bind them to whatever was left of the diary?

"So this is what it will take to make you care about his fate," I said bitterly.

Edward blew out a frustrated sigh.

"My mother's life? Yes, Luella. That's enough to make me care about anything. It is not my fault that Bram was found guilty. Did I testify against him? If we had followed my plan, he would have never had to come out of his precious memory world in the first place, remember?"

He trailed off on the last word and started shaking his head as though water stuck in his ear. Then, I saw something that chilled my blood right through: his fingers twitched.

"Edward?"

"I won't accept that my mother is lost. There must be another way. Is the world located inside the book or does the book serve simply as a pathway to the world?"

His question caught me off guard. I didn't know the true answer. I supposed that if the Netherdowns did still exist, it couldn't be completely contained inside the diary. After all, the diary had been destroyed.

"I don't know," I replied.

"Then I need to question Bram."

"Question him? Edward, he's headed to the gallows!"

Edward shakily gained his feet.

"He's not dead yet, is he?" he said. "My mother might still be alive in that world. That means I have to get there and bring her back before Bram hangs and the whole thing collapses."

His plan stirred my conscience. Perhaps we could save Charlotte— she didn't deserve to die in the Netherdowns. But it made my stomach twist to think of Bram so coldly, as though he were a bit of cheese starting to go moldy and ready to be discarded. Plus, the thought of letting Edward into the Netherdowns made me incredibly uncomfortable, and had done so even before I'd learned of his involvement in high magic.

"Bram's mental state has deteriorated," I said. "Alastair told me."

"He may just need some help remembering." Edward's mouth stretched grimly. I shuddered, remembering the vicious hook he'd wielded to help Gerald "remember" in the boathouse.

"No, Edward. Please. He's already been sentenced to death. Don't hurt him."

"Hurt him? Luella, have I fallen so far in your eyes? I only meant that we should talk to him."

I wrapped my arms under my jacket.

"We? I'm wanted by the police."

"Let me take care of that," he replied. He motioned for me to come back to the carriage.

"So you're taking Cooper's post as sergeant, then?" I bit my lip. I had hoped he wouldn't. I hoped I was wrong about him.

"I must. It's the only way."

"The only way what, Edward?"

He shook his head and walked back to the carriage.

"You can stay at my family's tenement or Mrs. Crow's until it's safe."

"Where will you be?"

"Working," he muttered. I followed him to the carriage. He held the door open for me.

"Why did you bring me here? Why take me from the courthouse?"

"I didn't want you to be recognized. What if they had arrested you?"

"It'd be no more than I deserve."

His gray eyes locked on mine, and for a moment, he reminded me of the outstanding and kindly soul I thought I'd known so well.

"Why are you so convinced all of this is your fault?" he asked.

"Isn't it?"

"I was upset when I said I blamed you before. I didn't mean it," he said. His eyes shone with sincerity. But that was always what was wrong with Edward, wasn't it? He was too understanding. He was too good. He never blamed me, even when he should have. His affection was either unnatural, stupid, or, or...

Or the efforts of a man who actively chose love over doubt.

He turned away.

"Take me to Mrs. Crow's," I said quickly, before clambering inside. He closed the door behind me before the tears returned.

Something in Edward's eyes had blown air across a flickering hope inside me, despite the millstone dangling perilously from my heart. His resolve to find the diary had invigorated me. Perhaps we could still save Charlotte. Perhaps Hirythe hadn't turned into the monster Bram feared he would become.

And Bram—hadn't Alastair said he would appeal Bram's sentence?

Could I hope?

Could I hope?

Could I hope?

The question echoed off the cobbles in the wake of Edward's retreating carriage before I knocked on Mrs. Crow's door.

19

DOUBTING DOUBTS

"**M**rs. Crow!" Rebecca Turner, looking more herself than she had since my incarceration, burst through the front door the following morning, giving me a start and Mrs. Crow a complete jump. Even Cyrus gave a yelp. "Have you seen it?"

She had a newspaper clutched under her arm and the light of an angel about her. When she saw me, she buried any trace of joy in her face, but couldn't smother the excitement emanating from her eyes.

"Luella," she said, "thank goodness you're here. After the trial yesterday, I'd feared the worst."

"The worst being?" I asked.

"That you'd done something rash. Don't ask me what, but I can't imagine what the trial would have—"

"What are you so excited about?" I cut in. If there was a development, I wanted to hear it, and I was eager for a distraction from my endless ruminations over Bram's misfortune.

"It's Edward," she said, sliding the paper across the table. There, in black and white across the front page, was the headline.

THOMAS SPEAKS OUT ON LOWHOUSE CASE

I grabbed the paper with both hands and read on.

M*r. Bram Lowhouse was convicted for murder yesterday in an Assize Jury Trial, leaving open-ended questions about loose ends in the demise of Lord Lucas Thomas, banker and one of Dawnhurst's leading socialites.*

Through the dramatic case (in which several arrests were made and Charlotte Thomas, wife of the deceased, disappeared), Edward Thomas, son of the victim, has remained silent. Previously, an officer of the Dawnhurst Police Force, he has recently accepted the office of Sergeant, left vacant by the resignation of George Cooper, and assumed command of his colleagues on the force.

Now, the young Lord Thomas has broken his silence for a brief interview. We provide it below.

On the issue of George Cooper's resignation, Thomas said: "I will not comment on his reasons nor his previous performance. I can say that I'm willing and able to take his place and insist that the boys of the force will carry on in his name, performing their duty to the utmost."

On the issue of his father's death: "I was kept from many of the details of the investigation because of my proximity to the victim. As such, I learned about much of the evidence at the same time and method as anyone else. I will say, it confounds me to think that my father would have taken his life, but I imagine many such cases leave the family with similar sentiments."

On the issue of his mother's disappearance: "I am turning over every stone in England to find her. I fear that she may be in the hands of brigands or kidnappers who saw an opportunity to make a profit out of a family tragedy. They took advantage of the chaos my father's death brought to our lives. It may yet be connected to Bram Lowhouse. I plan to question him extensively on the topic before he goes to the gallows and urge that his execution be postponed until attempts to withdraw such information can be satisfied."

On the issue of Luella Winthrop: "As far as I am concerned, Miss Winthrop was in the wrong place making the wrong friends at the wrong time. I go on public record that as Lucas Thomas' son and Sergeant of the Dawnhurst Police, I consider the case against her closed, and unless further evidence comes to light, I will not be investigating Luella Winthrop or her friends any further. Frankly,

I'm appalled by the way our community turned on her. It is time to heal, let my father rest, and get to work finding my mother."

"Do you see?" Rebecca asked as I lowered the paper.

"What joyous news!" Mrs. Crow sang, clapping her hands and jumping up and down.

"Doug is elated," Rebecca said. "He's already back at the pub, of course, getting ready to open for this evening. He is so industrious that way."

I watched Rebecca cheerily going on about the pub, as though she couldn't be happier that things were going back to normal.

Whatever normal was.

I read a very different story than she did in this article. It read very much like we had bought our freedom with Bram's conviction. It was bold and daring of Edward to announce my exoneration publicly. I was grateful, if not disbelieving, that I no longer feared arrest. But how could I relish in it when I knew it was possible only through Bram's sentencing?

"You'll both have to come by the pub later—"

I couldn't handle it anymore, hearing Rebecca make plans as if Bram did not wait alone in a cell to be fitted for his noose.

"I don't care about the stupid pub!" I burst out. "What is he serving? Fish and chips? We haven't had those a million times over, have we?"

Rebecca recoiled and stared at me. My face burned at my outburst, even if I believed it justified. The room grew heavy with silence.

"It's not my fault Bram was convicted," Rebecca said. "I did everything I could. Surely, you can't say otherwise. You can hate me all you like for having good fortune. But Doug and I have been honest with each other, and I've never hid anything from him. I deserve my reward for that."

Her words stung as she threw my own shortcomings in my face. I wanted to lash back, to say that it was a good thing I'd kept secrets from Edward because in the end, he didn't turn out to be the shining knight we'd imagined.

But something held me back.

"The offer stands, Luella," Rebecca said. "But please, if you are planning something crazy, like an attempt to free Bram from prison or something, count me out. I can't. I finally have a life that I fear losing, and I've rolled the dice on it too many times already."

She nodded to Mrs. Crow and left the paper with us. Mrs. Crow, undoubtedly embarrassed by my temper, retired to the other room to dote on Cyrus. I sat alone, looking at the news story and fingering my now raven hair.

That afternoon, I visited Alastair's primary office. It took a deal of courage to walk about openly again. The skirts, blouse, and cape had almost felt foreign to me for how much time I'd been spending gallivanting in Edward's large coat and disguising myself over the past many months.

His office was located a few streets over from the Thomas family tenement. The receptionist, a wiry man with eyes older than the rest of him, politely told me to take a seat. I'd sat down for no more than ten seconds when the northerner burst from his private desk.

"Luella, we will appeal! It was a circus in that courtroom. They have no evidence! Nothing valid! These prosecutors always do the same thing, parade all the skeletons out of a poor man's past and frame him into a villain. And don't get me started with Carolina Drake, that worm of a woman!"

He ushered me back to his office and closed the door during his rant. As I entered, I nearly lost my breath.

Edward sat in a corner chair, wearing a false beard.

"Hello, Luella," he said.

"Edward." I nodded and curtsied. "What are you doing here?"

"He's been waiting for a few hours."

"I told you she'd come today," Edward said.

"Yes, yes, you're a fortune teller. Now, it's good we're all here," Alastair said, pointing at the chair beside my old fiancé. "And it was very good of Edward to put out his statements in the paper. At least Luella can walk about freely now."

"Beg pardon, but what is going on here?" I asked.

"Right. I forgot we hadn't shared the details yet." Alastair leaned back in his seat. "Edward came by a day or two before the trial started, after he heard I was representing Mr. Lowhouse. At first, I thought he'd come to run me through for representing his father's accused."

"I thought you'd gone back to Fernmount," I said.

"I did, but it didn't take too long to see my mother was not there. I left orders to make inquiries through the village and with her acquaintances and returned for the Assizes."

"Edward guessed my legal strategy," Alastair said, "that I'd need to cast you in a less than pleasant light in order to divert blame from Bram."

"Yes, though it didn't work, did it?" Edward said.

"I didn't know about Carolina Drake. The poor man is affected in the head somehow. I asked him if there was anything that may come to light like her story... Had he told me, I could have prepared."

"His memory is decaying," I said. They both looked at me.

"It appears that way." Alastair nodded. "It's not uncommon for the Crown to vacate death sentences. She's a pious woman, Queen Victoria, and if she had it her way, I imagine there'd be a great deal more compassion in her judicial system."

"Even for murder cases, Mr. McHenry?" Edward asked. Alastair's face drooped slightly.

"So you came to undermine Alastair's defense strategy?" I shot Edward a pointed glance.

"On the contrary," Alastair said, "he helped me prepare. I insist that had Miss Drake not given her testimony, we'd have had that jury acquitting Mr. Lowhouse. We had already prepared the statements Edward would make to the papers immediately after the trial."

"That's why you're in disguise," I said. "It wouldn't do to have the Sergeant of Police collaborating with a defense lawyer against the Crown's prosecution."

Edward blushed.

"When you say it that way, I feel very dishonorable," he said.

"So what now? Alastair appeals. We hope for the best. What are we all doing here?"

The northerner took a deep breath in.

"Well, we are running through hypothetical scenarios."

"Namely?"

"If there are any legitimate means of delaying an execution, removing a man to an asylum, or what consequences there might be for an individual should that individual unknowingly and without intention assist a convicted felon's escape from prison, should such an escape happen to occur."

I whirled on Edward.

"You're trying to preserve him? Why? In the paper, you all but said you were glad he'd been convicted. Last night, you told me—"

"I said that Bram is the key to finding my mother, and I meant it. I have a couple of strategies to entice the information from him, but the more varied those strategies are, the better."

"Why not just have me speak with him?" I asked.

"That's one of those strategies. But I'm not sure you'll share what you learn with me," Edward said frankly. "You've made it quite clear that you don't trust me."

"I never said that," I protested. He looked at me, annoyed.

"As I told you last night, you've never been good at lying."

I studied Edward. His appearance had improved somewhat since the night before, but the bags under his eyes contributed to his false beard disguise. He looked a far cry from the perfect police figurine I'd first met. The stress of our journey and the loss of his parents had taken their toll.

Or was it more than that?

I still didn't understand his motive for enchanting me. I'd crafted a story in my imagination, that he had wanted to use me as a scapegoat for eliminating his father and disgracing his superior to inherit all he desired. Perhaps somewhere along the path, he developed sincere feelings for me. If Bram could serve as his scapegoat, why not use him and try to maintain my affection?

But if my affection had waned, and Bram had taken the legal fall for his father's death, why bother trying to save him?

Jeremy kidnapping his mother must have come as a surprise.

"I thought it wise for the three of us to align our objectives," Edward said.

"Yes," Alastair added, "it would be good for the three of us to visit Bram at the same time. Even if we don't speak with him all at once. In my experience, his episodes appear to come in waves. If we can interview him consecutively, we can compare notes afterwards. He's unlikely to have a fit of forgetfulness through all three conversations. And, seeing three different people may rekindle some of his memories."

"But we can't show up together, can we?" I ask.

"No. I'll be at the jail tomorrow morning to inspect the facility and question Bram. I suggest that Luella comes with me. We can use a private room to rotate through our interviews."

The thought of Edward questioning Bram made my stomach turn. But how could I argue with his plan? I both jumped at and shrunk from the chance to speak to Bram alone again.

"Can we prevent him from going to the noose?" I asked Alastair.

"There are ways. But now, I think it's more appropriate that he's sentenced to an asylum. His mind is not sound."

Edward nodded.

"I better be on my way," Edward said, rising. "They will expect me at the station. Mr. McHenry. Luella."

He gave us each a curt nod as he left the room. I held up a finger to Alastair and followed him out of the building. On the walk outside, he turned.

"Yes?"

"Edward, why do you want to help him now?"

"How else will I find my mother?"

I bit my lip.

"And if you find and bring her back, what will happen to Bram, then? Do you believe he is innocent?"

"What does it matter?"

"It matters a great deal to me."

"Why should my opinion matter to you?"

I didn't know how to respond. He couldn't maintain eye contact with me for long. There was something otherworldly familiar in his countenance.

"Are you worried I will ensure his execution once I get what I want?" he asked.

I shrugged, and he clenched his jaw.

"I can only take so many slights to my character," he said. "You've made it abundantly clear that the esteem you once held me in has vanished. I don't know why that is, but its timing is positively dreadful. Luella, I need you now more than ever. My mother is gone, and..."

He drifted off, staring at a passing hansom cab to collect himself.

"And what, Edward? Why won't you just tell me?"

Despite myself, I reached for his hands.

"Yes. Why not unveil all of my secrets to you, the same way you did for me?"

His words stung, reopening the sensitivity Rebecca's rebuke inflicted that morning. But I shook it off. I didn't trust him. I couldn't afford to. Why should I care to know his secrets?

"I apologize for my unharnessed emotions," he said. "Recent events have taxed them. I will be by Mrs. Crow's in the morning to collect you on my way to the jail."

He turned around and hurried down the street without another word. I re-entered Alastair's office, welcomed by a pitying expression.

"We're all worked up over it, lass," he said. "He means to help."

I sighed.

"That's what worries me."

20

PERSPECTIVE

The next morning, I sat in a carriage bound for the Dawnhurst jail. Edward, dressed in a police uniform now embellished with a Sergeant's stripes, drove the horses casually.

Although I was not filled with the same panic as my last carriage ride to this building, I had a palpable sense of dread all the same. Bram would face three interviews. I didn't doubt Alastair would be forthright in sharing the details of his interview, but he didn't know the magical nature of our predicament, and I didn't expect him to ask the right questions.

I had no idea what information Edward would share with me. He seemed sincere about wanting to save his mother, at any rate. But I'd already proved a hundred times over that I could not trust myself around him or accurately read his intentions.

I wanted to save Bram from his death sentence. If that meant an asylum, so be it. It was better than the alternative.

Second, I wanted to find a way back into the Netherdowns to stop Jeremy and save Charlotte. Alone, preferably. If, for whatever reason, I had to bring Edward with me… I'd cross that bridge if it came to it.

In the worst case, Edward would discover how to enter the Netherdowns despite my failing to understand the same. There was already one party hostile to Bram loose in there.

The carriage pulled to a stop, and Edward opened the door. He glanced about furtively.

"Quickly, now," he said as he ushered me inside the jail.

The few officers there, his officers now, stood at attention. I noticed an air of formality in their demeanor that wasn't present with Sergeant Cooper. How much more difficult would it be for a Sergeant as young as Edward to command respect and discipline from those in his charge? An old war bear could afford to be congenial, allowing his age to lend him distance from his colleagues. Edward, it appeared, had chosen another tactic.

None of them looked at me.

He led me into a small office beside the door that led to the rows of cells in the next room. It was tidy, cold, and formal as rooms went, exactly as I might have imagined a jail office to be.

"You'll go first," Edward said. I nodded, fumbling with the items in my purse. Alastair had surrendered them to me the previous afternoon, and though I hadn't ascertained their designed effects, I practically sensed the magic emanating from them.

Edward disappeared, leaving me in the office while I tried to quiet my heartbeat and listen for Bram's approaching footsteps.

When he walked through the door, chains on both wrists, looking weak and undernourished, a ghost of a man. I fought back a sob.

His honey eyes had dulled to a confused attempt at hazel. His hair was greasy, his clothes dirty. Still, he smiled at me poorly.

"Luella," he said, "it's good to see you."

I crossed the room and wrapped him in my arms, allowing the sobs to communicate emotions words could never express. He tried, once or twice, to unravel me from around his neck, but my arms were a vice grip.

"How much time do we have?" he asked.

"A half hour," I responded. "How are you? Are they treating you well?"

"As well as you can expect them to treat a condemned man."

"Alastair tells me you have fits of memory loss," I said, trying to smooth his hair or stroke his arms with my hands, as if this were all a wrinkle in his shirt I could simply massage away.

"Yes. I assume that's Jeremy's fault."

I nodded.

"Well, you seem very coherent now."

He smiled again and sat me down in one of the small chairs in the office beside the desk.

"I hope that doesn't change soon, but for caution's sake, perhaps we should hurry. What happened?"

I related the whole story, the moment I used the page to get back to the Netherdowns, the brewing storm between Jeremy and Hirythe, Charlotte entombed in a painting, returning into the Severn River, the lost diary, singing the song to Edward, and the wandering police receptionist.

Bram shook his head sadly through the whole tale.

"I was such a fool. Hirythe was right this whole time. I underestimated Jeremy. He must hate us profoundly."

"Bram, what is to be done? Is there any other way into the Netherdowns?"

He squinted hard and squeezed my hand.

"What is it?" I asked.

"It's just so frustrating. There must be. Why didn't I installed a back door? But I can't think of it. The pieces float together in my head, but they won't coalesce."

"Please try."

"I am. Jeremy's destroying the Netherdowns from the inside out, just as he told you. Or worse, Hirythe is hell bent on destroying Jeremy, and he's burning the house down to stop him. I'm sorry. I'm so sorry I can't remember."

I stroked the back of his knuckles with my thumb, uncomfortable with how bony they felt.

"I should be the one apologizing," I said. "You wouldn't be here if I hadn't asked you to come and confess on my behalf."

"Oh, Luella. I was planning to, anyway," he said.

"You what?" I blinked vacantly.

"That day you came to the Netherdowns with your plan, Hirythe and I had already been discussing it. It became more and more apparent that you planned to come back here to settle the matter of Edward's family tragedy. If I didn't step forward as a scapegoat, you'd likely be off to the gallows in my place. Hirythe was against it, but when you came up with a plan to execute an escape from the prison, how could he prohibit me?"

My heart reeled. I'd been working under the assumption that Bram's imprisonment was exclusively my fault.

"I wouldn't have let you," I insisted.

"But you did," he replied.

What did this mean for me? Did it exonerate my conscience? Complicate it? I shook my head, trying to focus. The time slipped away from me, and I needed answers more practical than insight.

"Jeremy said he stole things from your chest."

"My chest?" he said.

"He thought he could hurt Hirythe with some of your trinkets."

Bram's face scrunched up again.

"You showed me some at the trial."

"Yes. Do you think that's how Charlotte became a painting in Hirythe's office? Did you have an item capable of that?"

"Most likely. I made so many. I was so irresponsible. Why did I think that magic was so easily contained?"

He wrung his hands miserably.

"What about these?" I emptied my purse onto the desk. The dolls, the cheesecloth, the rings, the locket, and the rubber sphere. "Do you remember what these are?"

He handled the items gingerly, probing each one, careful not to open the dolls.

"I remember seeing them, making some of them," he replied. He gritted his teeth. "I'm slipping again. I can feel it. It's like remembering that I read a book a long time ago, but forgetting all about its plot and characters."

"Stay with me. Perhaps I can help," I said, touching the doll. "I used this in a conversation with the Inspector of the Reading Police. When you open it, another doll the exact same size and dimensions is inside. I didn't test to see how many times it would work, but the

Inspector and I didn't find the end. He broke down crying by the time we were only a few dolls deep. When I opened them, I had the most curious and deep desire for a brutal self-examination."

Bram stared at the dolls.

"I don't remember the magic," he said. "Hirythe and I made it after meeting a man named Sergei, though I'm not sure how. Hirythe stole a painted doll from one of his rooms. It wasn't enchanted then."

He looked at me in a mix of confusion and apology. Before Jeremy invaded the Netherdowns, he'd already confided in me that there were large holes in his memory, holes I later learned that were created by Hirythe.

It must have been maddening to know you've forgotten something.

"It's all well," I said, quickly removing the doll and putting it back in my purse. "What about these others?"

As he touched the rubber sphere, he laughed.

"This one is familiar, but you may be disappointed to hear it's not magical—at least not to us."

"What is it?"

"It's a ball. Cyrus loves it. I mean really loves it. I had to hide it in my chest to get a moment's peace. He'd do just about anything for this."

I gaped at it and blushed. In my ambition, I couldn't recognize what were now obvious bite marks. We both laughed. It was the first time I'd laughed since Alastair had given me hope for Bram's salvation before the trial, and although it felt natural and good, as soon as we stopped, a heavy sense of foreboding settled on both of us.

"These objects won't save you," I muttered. "Or Charlotte. Or Hirythe."

"You never know," Bram said. "If you could get them to Hirythe, they might help."

"Yes, but I don't have a way of doing that, do I?" I grimaced as the guilt reared up in me again. "I should have never taken the page from you—"

He stopped me by putting a hand on my knee.

"Have you considered, Luella, that this was beyond either of us? I made a good deal of Crimson Ink," he said, nodding at the cheesecloth.

"With this?" I asked, holding it up.

"Yes, I don't think I will ever forget that piece of cloth."

"How did you do it?"

He smirked.

"Just because I remember doesn't mean I'll tell you. You might do something crazy like make more. We just got the magic out of you. Why would I give you the tools to bring it back in?"

"When did you know I was no longer enchanted?"

"Hirythe told me before I left the Netherdowns. It's good news, even if it's troubling."

"Why is it troubling? I thought you'd be happy Sraith left me."

"You aren't a little curious why you woke up one day with no magical illness?"

I swallowed.

"To be honest, I've been so distracted with your case and learning about Edward's betrayal. I've hardly had time to consider myself."

"Well, consider this. Hirythe didn't look thrilled when he told you, did he? There's a reason for that. We were looking for a cure so we could cure you. If we'd managed that, we would have expelled the magic, banished it. Instead, we have no idea what happened to it. High magic doesn't just wander around with no purpose."

The scrutinizing gaze in his eye made me uncomfortable, but I didn't want to talk about more of his theories on high magic.

"That will be for another time," I said. "Alastair and Edward want to have you put in an asylum. I think I agree with them, if just to save you from your execution."

He sighed uneasily, emitting a hesitant groan.

"I don't know, Luella. In an asylum, if I lose my mind, there's no telling how my knowledge may be used against me. I may be a danger to the asylum staff or other residents. It may be better if..."

He trailed off and stared at his feet, nervously forming fists of his hands. I stood.

"Better if what, Bram?"

He maintained his silence, and I slapped him. He stared up at me with foggy confusion as he cupped his reddening cheek.

"How dare you give up, Bram? We need you. I need you. Charlotte is still in the Netherdowns trapped in a portrait! And Hirythe is doing who-knows-what in there. Have you considered what may happen to all of them if you die?"

His brow darkened.

"If only you knew how much I considered it," he muttered. "You don't need to remind me of my mistakes. I made a world tethered to my mortality and sent my best friend to live there. I do not know what would happen if I died. Perhaps I had an idea once, but I just can't remember."

"Then fight! Fight this like I know you can!"

"Fight what, Luella? What do you expect me to do? I'm in a jail cell, convicted of murder, awaiting my execution. If I could escape, I would, but you don't know what it's like being a chronic addict to magical solutions."

He picked up the cheesecloth and passed it between his fingers.

"Do you have any idea how many years of my life I turned into ink in an effort to save my wife? I don't. It wasn't like an arithmetic set, one for one. It was impossible to measure how much of the feeling sucked from my body equated to days, weeks, or years. I might die tomorrow because my time has simply run out. My life has been a constant parade of horrors, knowing I doomed everyone I love with my half-brained, sloppy meanderings through powers too great for my understanding. So yes, in some ways, the idea that there is a scheduled execution is a major weight off my shoulders."

I bristled. I refused to accept how he embraced defeat. His chest puffed in and out, agitated from his outburst, and his eyes were wild, like a caged animal. I recognized the fear in them. What man wouldn't be afraid? His life's passion had crashed down around him into ruin for himself and those he loved.

Suddenly, I understood what Hirythe had feared when I first asked Bram to confess to the police. Bram sought atonement. Deep down, perhaps he had hoped this would happen. It'd be a way to wind up the mess that quickly grew beyond his control while still rendering the end of his life productive. Through Bram, I gained my liberty.

Bram's story had so little to do with me. I came in during the last act of his drama. There was so much I didn't know about him.

I put my hands on his shoulders, my gaze resting intently on his face until he met my eyes. They calmed a little.

"You said you loved me once. Do you remember that?" I asked.

He swallowed.

"I'd convinced myself it was a dream."

I kissed his cheek. His skin was cold and rough with whiskers.

"It wasn't. And if you meant it, I need you to see this through. You once promised you would heal me, and though the malady is gone, you haven't finished with your promise yet. You said you would hold me when the fits came. Well, here I am, holding you. This is only a fit, and there's a mess out there I need your help with."

I hoped my speech would rouse him into an emotional acquiescence the way a general might inspire troops on the battlefield. Instead, behind his eyes, the struggle raged on. He was with me one moment and gone the next.

"Can you do that?" I asked.

He nodded along with me.

"What must I do?" he asked.

"I need you to remember how to get back to the Netherdowns without the diary and figure out how we can rescue Charlotte Thomas. She never wanted to be mixed up in any of this. She only wanted to protect her son. You'll have to stay alive long enough to do that, which means cooperating with Alistair and Edward."

"How can we trust Edward?" Bram asked. "If what you say is true, he's been lying to you."

"We don't trust Edward. We use him to defeat the magic and never bother it again."

He looked up at me in surprise.

"Never bother it again?" he asked, distant.

"Never again. I've had my fill, Bram. I want all of my adventures from now on to be found in novels and in the company of loved ones. No more magic. No more interfering. No more meddling."

He shrunk backward, a hint of disbelief in his gaze.

"I couldn't live without magic," he replied.

"We found a cure for me. We can find a cure for you."

"No, Luella. You don't understand. I don't want to live without magic. It's everything to me. I need it, and I always will."

I bit my lip.

"But I don't," I replied.

We stared at one another for several seconds until a brusque knock interrupted our conversation.

"That's my signal," I said awkwardly. He shuffled his feet.

"I hope to see you again," he replied.

"You will," I said as I embraced him. It was difficult to walk away, so I busied myself collecting the objects I'd brought for his inspection and forced myself not to look back on my way out. He called after me.

"Luella, will you make me a promise? If I can do what you asked, promise me you'll go on."

I didn't promise. I didn't turn around, only opened the door and continued.

Standing just outside was Edward. He was sweating and his brows knit together aggressively.

"Your turn," I said to him.

Edward looked past me at his dejected prisoner, shoulders heaving.

"Edward?"

His hands balled in and out of fists, and the skin all over his face grew red. I noticed a small vein bulge in his temple.

"I must go," he said, turning abruptly to head out the front door. He barked at one of the prison guards on his way out. "Lock him back up until his lawyer arrives."

I brushed past the incoming guard to follow Edward out the door, but by the time I reached open air, he had already mounted a horse and was galloping down the street, leaning over the saddle as though wounded.

When I turned to re-enter the jail, the door was barred.

"Sorry, miss. That'll be enough visiting," the guard said through the door.

I slumped down the street, not dressed appropriately for the long walk back to Mrs. Crow's.

21

CYRUS

I was a miserable mess by the time I arrived. I fumed through the streets, my mind a dizzying destructive cycle. Thankfully, Mrs. Crow had gone out.

I was furious with Bram and all the guiltier for it. How could I accept the blame after learning he planned to step forward in my place before I'd asked him? Nevertheless, I'd still taken away his escape route in the prison. Was I not still at fault?

What haunted me more was the bleak, blunt understanding that Bram and I had different objectives. I saw him in my mind, encased in chains, all the while protesting that he could not live without magic. What about safety? What about me?

That was Bram, though, wasn't it? He'd never be content unless he was working out a new theory, making a new trinket, or thirsting for deeper magical knowledge.

Since the magic had left me, I'd longed for it. I couldn't deny that it was beautiful, but it was beautiful like stars were beautiful. I was happy to admire them from a distance. Bram wanted to control the stars. He wanted to make his own.

I threw my purse onto the table. The trinkets spilled out. The rubber ball I'd so stupidly thought was a magical artifact fell on the floor with a gentle bounce. Cyrus poked his head up with more excitement than I'd seen from him in weeks. He padded over and collected it in his mouth.

Whatever glimmer of hope Edward and Alastair had woken inside of me had been smothered like the embers of a small cooking fire. I wanted to slap Bram and wake up his sense of vitality. I wanted to shake the fate destined martyr idea right out of his head. I wanted him to consider the beauty offered by a normal life without magic.

Cyrus nudged my hand with his nose, urging me to play. I waved him off, but he persisted.

I tossed it into Mrs. Crow's room and slumped into a chair. If Bram didn't care, why should I? This house had been my prison for weeks. I was a free woman now, wasn't I?

Cyrus returned, begging me to throw the ball again.

"Stop it, Cyrus! Get out of here!" I took the ball, opened the front door, and threw it as hard as I could down the street. The dog went chasing after, not caring in the slightest that I slammed the door behind him.

My goals had been simple: rescue Bram, rescue Charlotte. What was I supposed to do if Bram refused help? He'd said he loved me. Perhaps he did, just not as much as the magic.

I choked back thoughts of my conversation with my father. He too had left in the end, claiming it was for my benefit. They didn't know. Those who leave don't know how hard it is to remain.

Cyrus barked outside. I ignored him, but soon he was scratching at the door and barking louder. The neighbors would be furious before long. Cyrus and Mrs. Crow had become best friends. She'd be upset to find him locked outside.

I opened the door and took the ball.

"We're finished. No more ball." I put it in a kitchen drawer, doubting Mrs. Crow would mind the drool. The pointer immediately began whining and staring at me expectantly. Bram was right. No wonder he'd locked it in his chest.

"No! No more! I refuse to be the only one who wants to keep going. Bram is the one who left you, not me. So if you want the ball, go ask him! Perhaps you could get through to him, you stupid mongrel!"

Cyrus stopped whining and crooked his head as though he understood me. My words were foreign to him, but I'd heard somewhere that dogs are adept at understanding the moods of their caretakers.

We stared at one another, my guilt swelling for taking my lot out on him, until he padded away into Mrs. Crow's bedroom.

Now, even Cyrus had left me.

I buried my head in my arms, leaned against the table, and found I was too exasperated even to well up tears.

But Cyrus came back almost immediately, poking my leg with a wet nose. I absent-mindedly reached out to scratch behind his ears. When he poked me again, I looked up from the table and froze.

In his mouth was a dirty, tattered, nearly destroyed sheet of paper.

I collected it from him gently, scarcely breathing. But as I uncrumpled the note, I saw the familiar lines of poetry scrawled across them.

I don't know where the wind come from
Or where trees hide in seed.
The origins of the running stream
Are mystery to me
I can't explain the pendulum
That undulates the sea
But at least I know to find you
Where dreams meet memory

Cyrus whined next to the drawer again.
How?

I sifted through my memories like lightning. I'd found Cyrus guarding the book in a Reading alleyway. Hadn't Hirythe once told me he'd trust Cyrus over Bram? And when I'd come out of the diary, Edward told me the pointer had blocked his entry into the house and led him to the docks where Gerald was about to toss it overboard.

I gaped. Cyrus pawed the drawer.

"You're the book's guardian."

He whined.

"And you love your rubber ball."

He sunk into his hind legs and let out a bark until I relented and took out his ball. He took it from me and jealously stalked off to the other room, worried I might hide it from him again.

I was halfway to Doug's Fish and Chips Pub before I managed to collect my thoughts.

How had Cyrus retrieved the page? Why didn't he give it to me earlier?

He must have found it during one of his walkabouts with Mrs. Crow. She never mentioned him bringing home any rubbish, though. I glanced at the paper. Given the state of it, smeared in some areas, crumpled all over, and missing a corner or two, I supposed Cyrus might have quietly had it in his mouth without arousing suspicion on a walk back to the flat.

That was the best answer I had.

It didn't matter. I had it! Everything was different now. I could get back into the Netherdowns...

Doug's familiar pub rose before me, and I stopped.

Why wasn't I bringing the poem immediately back to Bram? Hirythe had told me not to return without him. But I doubted the police would let me speak with him again. I'd only left a couple of hours before.

My heart pounded beneath the stays of my bodice. I needed to calm myself and think through this clearly. The excitement and bewilderment of finding the page had been so staggering that I'd moved on instinct.

Time to think, not to act.

I took a deep breath and took in the world around me. Horse hooves beat on the street over, the sound of the river called from down the avenue, and the sun had already started descending from its zenith.

I'd used the diary too often without considering time or place. This time, I needed to be more careful. Yes. This was why my mind had taken me to Doug's unconsciously. Where else could I disappear for twelve hours or more, if needed, and still expect the page to be tended?

I pushed through the door and was delighted to see Rebecca near the front.

"Luella." She smirked. "Now I hate to be one to gloat, but I knew you would come around."

I held up the piece of paper.

"I need a private booth, one with curtains."

Her eyes stretched wide.

"Where? How?" she asked.

"Cyrus. The dog simply brought it to me in exchange for a rubber ball."

She laughed aloud and put her hands over her mouth.

"Well, there's one of those high magics you're going on about! The love of a dog for its favorite toy."

"Apparently, there's not much stronger. Where's Doug?" I asked.

"In the kitchens, but there's no need to bother him. I practically run this place now."

She led me across the pub toward a back corner behind the bar. I'd sat in this booth once before when Rebecca confronted me about the news article that became a key piece of evidence in Luke Thomas' murder. Back then, I was still infected with high magic, and I'd lunged at her.

She climbed into the seat behind me and drew the curtain closed.

"What are you going to do with it?" she asked.

"I don't know."

"You're not going back in?"

"Hirythe told me not to return without Bram."

She pinched her chin.

"That's tricky, considering Bram is locked in a cell," she replied.

"Tricky, but manageable. If I can sit down with him again, it's actually quite simple. He reads the poem and enters, then I follow immediately after."

Rebecca hummed out a long, thinking tone.

"But then the paper is just left in the room. Isn't that how you lost it last time?"

I bit my lip. She was right.

"Presumably, Johnson is lost somewhere in the Netherdowns, as well." I sighed. "Hopefully, he hasn't been harmed. The irony that after all those times he asked me if I was at the station to report a missing person—"

"—he became the missing person?"

Rebecca attempted, unsuccessfully, to hold back a chuckle.

"It's not very funny for him!" I said, trying to hold back my own amusement.

"I'm sure Johnson is fine. I'm just trying to imagine what the encounter between him and that fae must have been like. If only I could have seen it. That boy had no imagination at all."

I wanted to treat the matter seriously, but my lips turned up in a smile, more of a relief that I finally had options again.

"You're right. If Bram and I both read the poem, it will just sit in that office until who knows who finds it."

"In that case, we both know Edward would end up with it. Are you ready for that?"

Was I ready for Edward to enter the Netherdowns?

Certainly not.

"I have to go in by myself, then."

Rebecca nodded.

"How long do you want the booth undisturbed?"

I sighed.

"It's difficult to say. Won't the pub be busy tonight?"

"In the worst-case scenario, I will just take the page with me. You're in good hands this time."

As she said it, my anxiety melted away. It was such a boon to have Rebecca on my side.

"I'm sorry for what I said earlier," I muttered. She elbowed me.

"See how wonderful life can be when you don't hide a bushel of secrets from the people you love?" she asked. "Now go on. I'm sure Charlotte is tired of being a painting in some ruffian's memory land."

She left and pulled the curtains tight behind her.

22

OF HOPE AND GUILT

I appeared on Willow Hill.

Below me, currant bushes spread out in all directions, all fruitless.

I knew in an instant the Netherdowns had changed. Columns of smoke rose from pockets in the forest and from buildings in the village. The agricultural land looked barren, torn up, frozen in some places, burned in others, large chunks of stone and timber debris littered throughout. On top of it all, it appeared as though a massive flood had swept through the valley, with silt deposits and mud drifts tracing awkward arcs across the landscape.

A jarring fear gripped me. Caught up in my excitement of finding the lost page, I had not considered the real danger present in the Netherdowns. I had no armor or weapon, and even if I did, I wouldn't know how to use them. More importantly, I had not considered that Hirythe might have lost possession of his stock of the familiar scent that anchored me to the real world.

But now that I was here, the only way back would be to find Hirythe or find a store of the perfume they used to anchor me to the world.

I descended the hill in awe of the destruction. The wood, which had always filled me with dread, now looked sick, as though lumber from its trees might not weigh as much as it used to. I couldn't decide which was more unnerving, an abundant and sinister forest, or a desperate one.

No colorful birds flew openly through the air as they had on previous visits, and fruit and vegetables previously ripe on flora were scattered and mutilated on the ground.

The eeriest part of it all was the suffocating silence everywhere. I didn't even hear the wind through the long meadow grass as I used to.

I made it to the edge of the village without encountering another living soul—or, I supposed, another living memory. The buildings, once eclectically beautiful, were now broken and crumbling in staggered states of decay. The streets were a mess with the remains of burning lumber and piles of stone set in mortar. Bricks of different colors lay everywhere, covered in dust and straw.

The fountain in the plaza that marked the middle of the village had been cleaved in two as if by a thunderbolt. It lay barren and dry.

It was a wonder that Bram had any memory left at all.

Hirythe's study had been smashed in from the outside. An enormous boulder lay on the ground beneath its shattered second-story window. No light came from within.

How had one man caused so much harm? I had known Jeremy as Brutus. His critiques had wounded me once as well. I wondered what he could have done in a world made of my memory.

I turned and walked toward the tower, tall on a hill near the center of the village. Now, finally, I saw glimpses of movement.

I walked through the gates of the complex, unmolested. The mirrored soldiers worked like silent machines, maintaining their camp. None paid me any attention. On closer examination, I found only some of the reflective panels on their armor functioned. The others reflected nothing—just a window to whatever lay behind them.

I climbed up the hill to the tower entrance, remembering my first time here escorted by Drycha. I'd accidentally brought in loneliness brought to life as a monstrous cat. That cat had done significant harm to these soldiers. Before, I hadn't realized the destructive power of loneliness.

When I arrived at the tower door, I turned again to survey the town that Rebecca, Anna, and I had all considered one of the most beautiful places we'd ever seen. Taking it in now filled me with melancholy. Could beauty ever return to such decay?

I entered the tower.

Inside, Hirythe sat alone at his great table, the topographical map in front of him. His face drooped heavily on one hand, his elbow propped up on the table for support.

His eyes drifted up to assess me.

"Did you bring Bram?"

I shook my head.

"Damn." He stood up shakily.

"What happened here?"

"We're losing." Without preamble, he approached me with an embrace. "It's good to see you, Luella."

I awkwardly reciprocated. I'd never expected to receive an embrace from Hirythe.

"You as well," I said as he pulled back to scrutinize me again.

"You look terrible. That hair color is a nightmare on you. Truly awful."

I hit him.

"You don't look well either."

"I've been doing battle against Jeremy Evans and his organized band of monsters. I look battle worn. It's rugged and handsome."

"Is it?"

We stared at each other for a long moment. His frankness reminded me of our first meeting. I considered him so dismissive. Yet, as I saw him interact with Bram, his personality grew in endearment. There was charm embedded in his deprecations.

"Where's Bram?" he asked.

"In a cell, sentenced to death for the murder of my fiancé's father."

"How is he taking things? Is he desperate to escape or has he interpreted this as a sign that his time has run out?"

"He's back and forth, losing his memory more every day." My next question caught on my lips, coming out stilted and abrupt. "Why didn't you tell me Bram planned to confess to the police before I presented my plan to both of you?"

Hirythe winced.

"So he told you that, too. What did it matter in the end?"

"I wouldn't have felt quite so beastly," I replied. "The self-loathing has been difficult."

"Then what? Would you have worked less earnestly to secure his escape?"

"No—"

"It's not true, anyway," he continued. "You'd have still felt beastly because he's in a cell, and you couldn't stop it."

He folded his arms. There was something odd about the subtle blue in his skin. At moments, I'd have sworn flickered, like a sputtering candle.

"I'm surprised that none of the diary pages worked well enough to bring him back," he said. "Jeremy has wreaked havoc on his memory, yes, but I hoped I'd preserved enough vital remembrances between us to keep the reading effective."

"The diary is lost. Jeremy hypnotized a man and instructed him to toss into the River Severn."

Hirythe's eyes narrowed.

"Then how are you here?"

"The page we ripped and planned to use for Bram's escape. Things went sour. I was imprisoned as well. When you last saw me, I'd escaped from the cell through that page, but Bram was left without an escape route. We lost track of the page for some time, and I feared that was the end."

He sighed and leaned against the table.

"That explains Johnson, then."

"You found the police officer?"

"Of course I found him. He nearly got himself killed, traipsing into the middle of a battle. A stag with flaming daggers for antlers nearly ran him through."

I folded my arms in displeasure, trying very hard not to imagine a stag with flaming daggers as antlers killing the lanky redheaded man.

"Where is he now?" I asked.

"I wasn't about to have him roaming the Netherdowns. I sent him back."

The thought of Johnson appearing on whatever street corner the page lay amused and weighed on me. Who knew what lasting effect the experience would have on the poor lad. He probably thought he'd gone mad.

"And Charlotte?" I asked, dreading the answer. From the state of the fae's office, I feared that the portrait might be damaged beyond repair. The way into the study had been blocked sufficiently to deny me passage.

But Hirythe motioned to a spot on the tower wall above the front door behind me.

"I assume you mean the severe-looking woman immortalized in a gaudy art form."

I turned around, relieved and horrified all at once. There she was, looking as if she was about to teach me a grueling lesson at The Sheldonian Theatre.

"Who is she?" Hirythe asked.

"She's my prospective mother-in-law. Well, *was* my prospective in law. It's complicated."

Hirythe raised his eyebrows.

"Edward, you said his name was? Your gallant knight somehow got his mother into a mess, didn't he?"

I ignored the sneer on his lips.

"Is there a way to reverse the enchantment, get her out of the painting and back to her life?" I asked.

Hirythe stretched his neck and started up the staircase lining the wall in a great spiral to the top of the tower. I followed, just as I had the first time we met.

"Jeremy brought no small number of Bram's old enchantments with him. Under the best circumstances, their effects would be unpredictable. You remember the disastrous luggage you carried in, yes?"

I swallowed and nodded.

"You only brought things into the Netherdowns one at a time, and we were able to manage the monsters you introduced discreetly, then teach you the error of your ways."

I kept with him stride for stride up the stairs. Either he had slowed since our last ascent or I had grown more agile.

"It seems Jeremy brought the trinkets he imagined would be most destructive. Imagine a miner or a stone mason purposefully sabotaging a chemist's laboratory with the chemist's own equipment."

"I'm not sure Bram would do well with chemistry," I quipped. As I noticed the fae's fatigue, a desire to bring him some comfort or levity surfaced in me. He had been trapped alone with an enemy for weeks. He wasn't himself.

My quip was rewarded with a smirk.

"In any event, Mrs. Thomas—"

"Lady Thomas," I corrected. Hirythe stopped and turned toward me on the narrow stairwell, giving me an incredulous look.

"Sorry. It doesn't matter," I said hastily.

"Lady Thomas," he went on with sarcastic emphasis, "is trapped in what you might call a manifestation."

"What's a manifestation?" We were nearing the top now.

"Some forms of high magic are difficult to conceptualize. That's why Bram was so interested in finding and creating trinkets to render them more solid, easier to study and understand. Each type of high magic has its own set of conditions, properties, personalities...

"Take the Crimson Ink, for example. It derives power from the arbitrary relationship between the true, expansive nature of cause and effect and the binding power we assign to certain steps along its chain."

"And Charlotte? What type of high magic has her trapped in a painting?" I asked.

"Let me finish. Different interactions between highly magical principles give way to unexpected results. If I'm correct in my analysis of her painting, she's alive, though she's frozen in a manifestation of fear. For some, fear is a paralytic, and when that is combined with the magic of memory binding the Netherdowns together..."

My head spun as he pushed open the door at the top of the tower.

"You're saying that the power of fear and the power of memory clashed together to render her a portrait?" I asked. He swung his burdened shoulders around to face me.

"As you know, I'm only correct most of the time. But Bram once found the handle of an artistic instrument used by some northern tribes for human sacrifice. The sacrifices may have had little substantive effect, but these northern groups successfully imbued the artistic instruments with concentrated reserves of fear. Our idiotic friend refashioned the handle into a paintbrush.

"I think Jeremy marked Lady Thomas' skin using this brush and then brought her into the Netherdowns."

A chill coursed through me.

"But why didn't I ever experience a similar effect? I brought in my sister's letter and the destructive spell laced with jealousy."

"You did. But having an ordinary object charged with a bit of loneliness in your pocket is not the same as being marked by a paintbrush purposefully filled with concentrated fear."

"Still, shouldn't it have just summoned a creature as I did by accident on both occasions," I asked.

"Luella, try to understand. She is the creature. She is the manifestation. Fear is a paralysis. The brush amplified it. Then she tried to enter living memory. She's manifested into what she fears her legacy will be."

Once, on Christmas, Charlotte had indulged in enough wine to confide in me that her greatest fear was being forgotten altogether. That no portrait of her would hang on the wall. That she would just vanish into the waters of time without a ripple. Now she hung as a portrait on a wall made of memory. It made the hair on my neck stand on end.

I followed Hirythe to the tower edge and saw afresh the devastation of the Netherdowns. The rooftop was now lined with cannons pointing out menacingly from the ramparts.

Intuitively, I looked toward the stretch of forest where I found the Church in Belford Square. A silver currant had grown there, enabling a conversation with my father's pure memory.

"It's defended the best I can manage," Hirythe said as if he could read my thoughts. "I figured Bram would insist on diverting some resources there, given that it is such a sacred memory."

My eyes widened as a thought struck me.

"Where is Olivia?" I asked. Hirythe set his jaw strongly.

"I don't know."

We looked out over the landscape for some time in silence. Everything felt colder than it had before.

"Somehow, Jeremy is inciting the legions of our darkest memories to do battle against us. The scars you see on the land, in a way, are self-inflicted. It's our own defense mechanism. You may have noticed that when one of my soldiers kills a monster, it vanishes."

I nodded, remembering the battle I'd witnessed at the village gates. Soldiers' bodies littered the road afterward, but the enemy's casualties had disappeared.

"Is it better to let a bad memory consume you or to wipe it from your mind altogether?" he asked. I waited for him to go on, but for the first time I got the sense that he was asking in hopes of an earnest answer. Despite his attempts at our usual banter, his whole bearing slumped as if with a heavy burden.

"Surely there is some middle ground," I said. "We can't forget the past altogether, or we may be doomed to repeat it. Is there not a way to split the difference?"

He smiled sadly but kept his gaze trained on the landscape.

"If only they would meet us halfway."

It was easy to be swept away by grief, knowing that I witnessed firsthand the destruction of not a life but a lifetime. It was one thing to die, another to have no recollection of living. Perhaps Bram's choice of surrendering to his sentence was not so abhorrent as I had believed.

"What will happen to the Netherdowns if Bram is executed?" I asked.

"Will his memory preserve beyond death, you mean?" His tired eyes went glassy, perhaps from the wind. "We all wish we knew, but I'm afraid to find out. I hope it does. I've known too many that have departed. It would be comforting to know they're not gone."

Our conversation grew more spiritual than I had intended, but I could not blame Hirythe. How many of his own memories had he lost in the past few weeks? How many of Bram's? All in an effort to ward off being completely overcome by them.

It was then I understood the true beauty of the Netherdowns, with its village carved from the surrounding forest and the waters calling from beyond. It wasn't the good that rendered it magical, but its preservation despite the dark pressing in. But to eliminate the dark altogether—there would be no beauty at all.

Perhaps Bram was right to demand a magical life.

I shook my head to snap out of my spiraling ruminations.

"How can I free Charlotte?"

"I wish I had an easy answer for you. I think you will need to resolve her fear," he said grimly.

"How am I supposed to resolve her fear of being forgotten?"

"That's for you to discover. I don't even know the woman."

I clenched my hands. I came here for answers. I thought Hirythe could help me. Every step took me further from my goal.

"Then again, if she's no longer your prospective mother-in-law, you can always abandon the cause."

"That's not funny."

"Why did you break your engagement?" he asked. "I hope it wasn't for Bram's sake."

I considered the rough stone of the tower ramparts under my fingers, waiting for the answer to form.

"My hell," Hirythe said. "I was joking. Was it really for Bram?"

I wanted to say yes. I wanted to say that Bram had captured my heart and, because of it, I had turned my back on Edward. I wanted to say that the kiss I shared with Bram on Willow Hill had caused my world to topple and that his honey eyes made everything else disappear. I wished that Bram had filled me with the passion to do courageous and noble things.

It was a cold understanding. I'd wanted to it to be Bram. But even before he had confirmed our fundamental differences in the prison earlier that day, I knew it couldn't be. I'd met the woman who had once held his heart. I was no Olivia. She loved magic as much as Bram, and she was fierce and adventurous.

Hadn't Bram asked me to run away with him? I refused him once, and I had no reason to believe my answer would ever vary.

I broke my engagement with Edward because Edward betrayed me, and his betrayal broke my heart.

"No," I said. "Edward was the man who enchanted me. Your song identified him. The chorus was deafening. He had the mark of high magic on him. I met him right before I had my first magically influenced dream. Since his father's death he's gained so much. All signals point to him."

"Ah," Hirythe replied. He studied the landscape silently for some time, though his unusual quiet signalled to me that he wanted to speak.

"What is it?" I asked. He sighed.

"Well," he began, "the relationship between our two species, races —whatever you'd like to call it—has always been murky and fraught with misunderstanding. The very reason there's none of my kind left is because the fae never trusted humans. We thought we could manipulate you, that you were inferior to us. I fear such tricks became so central to our cultural interactions with humans, that customs were passed down in our blood like hair color or personality traits.

"Not all fae are like me. Some are wild," he faltered. "I try ardently to ensure those less desirable tendencies don't surface in myself. In most cases, I can keep it under control, but when allowing a human to borrow a portion of my own magic, it's possible that the ensuing results were unpredictable."

I cocked an eyebrow.

"What?"

"Don't humans believe that the fae are tricksy folk, always baiting unknowing victims into unwinnable contests or wagers?"

"Well, if you subscribe to what's described in fairy books, I suppose many humans would consider fae nothing short of magical cons."

Hirythe grunted.

"The root of the matter is that fae believe they understand things in full, when often we overlook possibilities that seem obvious in hindsight—"

"Just get on with it."

"Fae magic is meant to inhibit. Human magic is meant to expand."

I furrowed my brow.

"What do you mean, human magic?" I asked.

"Have you considered that the song may have misled you?" he asked. "Fae magic is built on the concept of contract. If you didn't follow my directions exactly, your results may have been, well, not incorrect, but misleading..."

I blinked. I'd only considered it when I didn't want to admit to all the evidence that implicated my fiancé. Since administering the test to Edward, I didn't allow myself the luxury of doubting the magic. Bram had told me that fae magic was incredibly powerful. I believed it.

"The chorus sang, Hirythe."

"The same way it sang for your sister?"

I shook my head.

"You said my sister was different because we were family. We found out that she'd transgressed our sisterly bond by telling Byron I'd gone mad."

"Yes, she was marked by high magic, but not because she bewitched you."

My mouth went dry. I stumbled back from the rampart and shook my head.

"You don't even know Edward. I do. Or I thought I did. Why would you defend him?"

Hirythe turned and leaned against the stone wall beside him.

"Has he shown any other signs of manipulating high magic? Any symptoms of magical maladies?"

"Heavens above..."

Edward was practically wasting away now. His eyes were sunken, his strength sapped, his cheeks becoming gaunt. But that was because he was so worried over his mother and, possibly, because I had withdrawn myself from him. His plans were falling apart.

"How long have you known him?" Hirythe asked. "How well? How would you describe his magical proficiency?"

Hirythe walked slowly toward me.

"He's always taken an interest in magic, since his boyhood. His mother hoped that I might shake him of it."

"And did you?"

"No. He still wanted to go to the library to dig up old musty tomes. He was the one who gave me the spell that summoned the bull by Echo Lake."

"Why would he do that?"

My back hit the wall beside the stairwell door. It surprised me.

"He wanted to sever my connection with Bram, so he said. But it was all a trick. He was playing dumb so I wouldn't uncover the truth."

Hirythe stopped a pace away and stared into my eyes like he did when diagnosing me.

"You may be right," he said with a shrug. "But I find it odd that any trace of the magic in you vanished, and now you're convinced the man who you claimed stood beside you and supported you through all of your difficulty is actually someone who meant you harm from the day you met."

I tried to respond several times, my breath faltering before finally grabbing hold of my vocal chords.

"Hirythe don't do this. I beg you. It tore me apart to discover him. It would kill me to hope I was wrong and lose him all over again."

A deep, soul-bending horn sounded three blasts from the hill far below. Hirythe turned to examine the horizon.

"If you bring him here, I can tell you for certain," he said before heading back down the stairs.

"What if he means the Netherdowns harm?" I called, following behind. It took my eyes a moment to adjust to the darkness inside the tower, and I stumbled on the first step.

"What more harm could he do? It's dying already."

A feral glint took hold of his eye, and he hurried away. Anxiety gripped me. I tried to remember everything I had been dying to ask him, but it all slipped from my recollection.

"I had some of Bram's trinkets to show you!" I called out. "He can't remember what they do."

Something large and heavy struck the outside wall of the tower. I screamed, and my pulse started racing. Suddenly, I mistrusted the steps below me. Dust fell from the wooden beams holding the ceiling up high above us.

"Hopefully, you can show me next time. Adventure calls. You can find your anchor in a cabinet drawer by my map. Mind not to hold the bottle when the magic takes you back. I wouldn't want it to fall and shatter."

The terrible gleam in his eyes grew more robust, as if he were excited by the prospect of the danger outside. I tried to ignore the urgency with which Bram had insisted I stop Jeremy from entering the Netherdowns, how he'd hoped I could prevent Hirythe from doing something.

Perhaps from becoming something.

The fae sped down the steps.

"And your silver currants?" I called after.

"They've been quite useful," he called back before exiting the tower door.

His response sent a chill through my veins. I wanted both to be very far away from him and linger to witness the oncoming confrontation all at the same time.

I rummaged through the cupboards until I found a familiarly etched bottle. I dabbed a portion on my wrists and stopped it again, careful to keep my wrists limp and hanging by my sides.

Even removed from directly beneath my nose, the magic still frayed my vision. I hurried to the tower door and flung it open.

At the bottom of the hill, monstrous creatures with dark pelts patterned in a mesmerizing texture clashed into Hirythe's troops of memory. Screams already polluted the air, cold and inhuman.

But as I looked more closely, it wasn't the mirror-paneled soldiers or hideous, hellish beasts they confronted that made me tremble.

I had seen Drycha swiftly and gracefully dispatch the monsters with a dancing, smooth style of combat. Hirythe was something different, altogether.

I wasn't sure which was worse, the savagery with which he butchered limbs from the monsters, the way he took generous bites of their shadowy flesh, or the perverted smile on his face.

23

THE HALLWAY

I came to my senses in the same booth at Doug's pub, but I couldn't stop shaking. It had been one of my shortest stays in the Netherdowns, but the state of it unraveled me. Small wonder Bram's mental state was in question.

The pub was lit by candles and a roaring hearth on one end of the dining room. Light tugged at the curtains drawn around my booth. The absence of any gas lamps gave an impression of years passed, as though Doug either refused to change with the times or he couldn't afford to.

Doug's pub had always felt comfortable and homey. But in the dark of that booth, I shook. The path forward looked clear and terrifying.

With the page from the diary, I could escort Bram into the Netherdowns, away from his death sentence. But he would walk directly into the ravaged waste that was once his memory. I wasn't sure what would become of his sanity.

But what other choice was there? If Bram hanged, any chance of rescuing Charlotte and Hirythe was out of the question.

I bristled, catching myself as I considered Bram's life as if I were a logistician. How else could I? Facing the reality of his loss might break me.

But of course, there was a lot I refused to dwell on at present.

Edward...

I put my head between my hands, refusing to admit Hirythe's suggestion. I'd spent so long insisting Edward could not be my enchanter. Now, a selfish, fragile part of my heart insisted he must be. After how cold I'd been to him, after how purposefully I'd sabotaged our relationship, after how neglectful I'd been toward his welfare...

It was finally time for Edward to enter the Netherdowns—should his purposes be nefarious or benign.

I missed my simple life. Yes, I had never truly loved Byron, but we would have enjoyed a modest and pleasant existence together. My sister would have still married Jacob, and we would have readily and easily visited one another.

It pained me to think about it.

I had grown so much when compared to the woman who had to scramble up enough courage to go to a police station or attend a carnival by herself. But perhaps strength and competence comes at the price of greater depth of feeling. With risk comes reward. With strength comes opposition. With love comes fear.

No, I never loved Byron, but I'd found love since. Was it worth all this?

Only Edward would know how to remedy his mother's greatest fear. If I needed his help, I had to face the truth, even if it killed me.

I pulled back the booth's curtains and climbed from my seat. Rebecca walked with a tray of mugs between tables speckled with patrons. I caught her eye, and she immediately changed course.

"I didn't expect you back so quickly," she said. "What was it like?"

"It's a ruin," I replied. "The buildings, even the landscape, it's all torn apart."

Rebecca paled.

"And the fae?"

I blinked and shook my head, trying to clear it of Hirythe's haunting savagery in battle.

"Before I escaped from my cell, Bram feared that if Jeremy found his way into the Netherdowns, Hirythe would become something terrible, a monster or a shadow of his former self. I'm afraid it's already begun."

"How do you mean?"

"He was feasting on terrible memories even as they tried to attack him. The look in his face—it was feral, wild even."

The clinking of cutlery and scraping of chairs accompanied a somber void between my friend and me.

"What are we going to do?" Rebecca asked, finally.

We, she said. Not you. I considered the spat we had at Mrs. Crow's. It was selfish of me to expect Rebecca to risk all. She had already done so much...

I cast a glance toward the kitchen. Out of sight, Doug made his presence known constantly. If not for the sounds of him barking at his employees, then from the overflowing spirit of joviality emanating from that direction.

The resolve came on like the warmth of a good pint. I could ask nothing more from Rebecca. Her name was clear, her heart was full, and her future bright. She was the purest embodiment of friendship I'd ever known, and finally the time had come to repay her.

"I am going to talk with Alastair about Bram's chances at getting into an asylum. Then, I'll get Bram to the Netherdowns and see if we can stop Jeremy. Perhaps he knows a method to restore memory."

"And me? What can I do?"

I smiled at her. Rebecca had always possessed grace and confidence. Even working in a pub, her beauty was unquestionable, inside and out.

"You and Doug should stay here, and ready some fish and chips for when I return."

She jutted out her bottom lip.

"There must be something more."

I took her hand and squeezed it. "It's time for me to fix my own problems. I hope you are happy here. I want every happiness for you."

Silent tears leaked from her eyes.

"You speak as if you're marching to the gallows yourself," she said.

"There's no telling where I'm marching off to. I'm holding a lantern and taking one step into darkness at a time."

She embraced me.

"I won't let you go alone," she said. "Doug will understand."

"Doug loves you," I said. "That's high magic, my friend. If you offend it, I fear what demon may come after you."

She pulled back with a look of worry.

"I'm joking," I said with a laugh. "At least, I think I am."

"Oh, Luella," she sighed.

I placed my hands on her forearms.

"Since my father passed away, I've always wanted to be the woman he dreamed I would become. I thought that meant achieving something, like winning a writing award or marrying a man I truly loved. It's not about pathways or destinations, though, is it? It's about magic, a magic you once told me was the only type you believed in."

Her chin trembled as she tried to control her emotions.

"I couldn't remember how important it was to love someone until I met you," she said. "When I fell out with my family, my heart stopped loving altogether. But now look at me, surrounded by people I'd give the world to protect. It's so easy not to be afraid of the world when you let little matter to you."

"But you matter," I said. "Doug matters. Please, be careful. And no matter what happens, live well."

She gave me a last embrace before I forced myself quickly out the front door.

I'd see this pub again. I'd eat with her and Doug and laugh, carefree and warm. I hoped.

But first, it was time to face what I most feared.

My heart pounded as I marched through dark streets, across Thompson's North Bridge, and into the west quarter of the city. I would not enjoy the homey comforts of Mrs. Crow's flat tonight.

When Edward's doorman saw me, his eyes widened. He covered up his surprise quickly, though, and nodded me in.

Apparently, legal exoneration did not have a restorative effect on one's reputation.

I climbed the stairs and knocked on Edward's door. Waiting awkwardly for a response reminded me of the time I'd knocked on

Byron's door after I'd all but ended our engagement. Life is circular, at any rate. It is left for us to improve each time around.

There was no response, so I knocked again. Edward had acted so erratically lately. I wondered if he was even in the city. I'd seen him last that morning, when he fled the prison in a rush.

I knocked again, and after a few moments, had to admit I was relieved he wasn't home. Despite all the courage I'd screwed up to face him, a last-minute reprieve was not unwelcome.

I had turned to head down the stairs to retreat to Mrs. Crow's when I heard a crash from inside.

"Edward?" I called. He did not respond, but another crash sounded from within. "Edward!" I tried the doorknob and, relieved to find it unlatched, crept inside.

The flat was dark, illuminated only by a perseverant dining room candle and stray streaks of light filtering through the windows from the streetlamps outside.

The crashes came from above, near Edward's bedroom. I ascended a small set of stairs and found his door closed. Something thrashed about inside, banging against the walls.

"Edward!" I tried the handle, but this one was firmly locked, and it would not budge. "Edward!" I banged my fist on the wood, eager to get his attention. "Let me in! Let me in!"

He did not respond, however, and the lock on the door would not yield. Desperately, I found a candelabra and tried to smash the door handle. I injured my hands in the attempt, and the door still held fast. Perhaps he had barricaded it from the other side.

The pounding on the floors and walls seemed to have a personality of their own, syncopated, disjointed, and insistent. It was a familiar personality to me. I had known and feared and fought against it night after night. Some nights, Edward had sat on the other side of my wall or across my room—restraining me on occasion—to ensure I did not injure myself.

Was that the mind of a man who meant me harm?

"Edward!" I pressed my face against the door. "Don't give into the dark!"

I sank to the floor, each new crash or slam like a battering ram to my heart.

Slam.

The hope gnawed its way through my callous resolve to distance myself from him. I was convinced that because Edward had somehow been marked by high magic, he'd done so purposefully, perhaps maliciously.

I had been so scared that night in the stormy Netherdowns, then in the river. My rescue was so implausible. A last-second discovery, led by a dog. A hypnotized bruiser like Gerald. It could not have been...

Slam.

"Edward, please!"

Why didn't I give Edward the benefit of the doubt? He might have stumbled into magic as clumsily as I had. He carried me when I was too weak to go on. How had I abandoned him?

Slam.

And even if he had purposefully enchanted me, was his motive necessarily irredeemably vile? Anna had betrayed me by telling Byron I'd gone crazy, and my forgiveness flowed to her even before I'd learned the extent of her indiscretion. Should I not have as much love for a fiancé as I did for my sister?

The pounding did not stop. How many nights had Edward endured this alone? As I sat on the other side of the door, the hope blossomed, ripened, and spoiled. There was meager joy to be had if he was innocent, as Hirythe suggested. I could never deserve him.

After all this time, there I was again. When Edward and I first started our journey together, when he saved me from the Dawnhurst Police, I didn't think I would ever deserve his love. I'd never comfortably believed otherwise. But there were moments I hoped the question didn't matter, that the gap might be made up with devotion, the debt paid with loyalty. But now?

Tears streaked my face, my fists balled in anxiety as I sat in the ruined corridor. The commotion in Edward's room reverberated within me. His bruises were my bruises. They were memories of hot nightmares, searing poison behind the throat in the early morning hours.

When the test marked him, when the signs of magical dependency appeared in his face and posture, which was easier to believe: that Edward planned to use me, the way the world and even fate had used me for its own purposes, or that Edward was interested in me for no other reason than that he deserved to love someone, and I, in turn, deserved to be loved?

The pieces of Hirythe's suspicion came together like magnets while I sat on the cold floor in that hallway.

Edward had not infected me. I had infected him.

And because I didn't believe in myself, I was fooled into thinking he deserved it.

The dark magic of despair worked its way on me until I lost all track of time.

I must have fallen asleep at some point. The glow reaching up the stairs from the dining room candle was extinguished. I stretched my neck through a painful kink, courtesy of the hard wall I'd rested against.

That wall now lay silent, but with my ear against it, a bedframe creaked inside.

I wearily stood up and tried the handle. It was still locked, so I knocked gently.

"Edward," I called. "Edward, it's Luella."

There was a stretch of silence before weary footsteps crossed the floor, accompanied by grunts and the scrapes of moving furniture.

The lock clanged open, and Edward cracked the door.

"Luella? What are you doing here?"

I could only make out his silhouette in the dark, but I saw him in a new light all the same. I struggled to find words.

"How long?" I finally choked out.

"How long what?" he said.

"Why didn't you tell me?"

His swallow was loud in the dark where I did not breathe.

"You didn't want me," he said plainly and painfully.

I wanted to deny it but had not the courage to lie. Instead, I swallowed down a painful stone rising in my throat.

"You would suffer alone?"

"Can I help you with something?" he asked with a quiet groan as he shifted his weight.

"You left the jail because you were about to have an episode."

"Luella, please. Don't."

I stared at his barely distinguishable features as he tried to push me away. I had tried to do the same to him when I first learned about my attacks. Every time he had to clean up my mess, I stomached a new helping of humiliation.

"May I come in?" I asked.

"It's the middle of the night," he said. "It wouldn't be proper."

"Edward—" I held out my hand to push him backward, but he caught it. I gasped.

I realized that the past several times I'd seen him he wore a pair of gloves. Now I saw his hands were callused and cut, covered in lesions.

"Your hands," I whispered. He tried to pull them away, but I would not let him. Instead, I unwrapped the clumsy bandages he had fastened and studied their skin, discovering each scar painfully. Some of his fingernails were chipped and ragged. The flake of newly dried blood came off under my fingers at the wrinkles on his knuckles

With this discovery, something in him surrendered, and he opened the door wide. I entered, and even in the dark I saw the outlines of smashed furniture, broken glass, and torn cloth. Not long ago, the value of the trinkets in these rooms made me feel small. Now, many of them lay in pieces on the ground, and I felt all the smaller.

Porcelain crunched beneath my shoes. I turned about and was grateful for the dark. I was afraid to see by light of day what had become of my Steely-Eyed Detective.

"I didn't want to attack Bram," Edward whispered. "When the episodes come, it's so hard—it's like I've no control at all."

"I know," I replied, then gently added. "I always saw my father. Do you see yours as well?"

He took his time responding but eventually gave up an answer.

"I see you. More cruel, yet close enough to be real that, in my darkest moments, I can't tell the difference."

I steadied myself on a bedpost, overwhelmed, drowning in something sticky and corrosive. Why me? Of all the people the fog creature could have chosen to manipulate him... When I spoke with the creature in my dreams, at least I knew to doubt it from the start. My father had been long dead. If it had chosen Anna, would I have handled it as well?

I would have given more deference to the ghost of my father than I would to any version of my sister trying to give me counsel.

Was that the trick, then? The fog creature embodied whoever would have greatest sway over a mind? But if that were true...

"At first, I thought I was just dreaming about you," Edward whispered. "That's not all that unusual, is it? A man dreams about a woman he cares for."

"When did it start?" I asked.

"When did I start dreaming about you?" A pained chuckle lined his voice. "Do I have to say?"

"When did things change, then?" I asked, grateful that the dark masked the color spreading across my cheeks.

"Not much earlier than when we went to Fernmount for Christmas. In my dreams, you started suggesting things to me. At first, they were innocuous, but helpful. You suggested I give you a typewriter for Christmas. I feared it might be a painful gift, but you encouraged me you were ready."

His Christmas gift to me had taken my breath away. Rebecca called it a husband gift. In a peculiar way, it stung to know that the typewriter may have been nothing more than a tool the fog creature used to manipulate him.

"What then?" I asked.

"Then, you had more daring ideas. I've had my issues with George Cooper, but I would never have invented a scheme to discredit him publicly on my own. We argued about it for some time—well, not you and I—but in the end you insisted it was best, even if it were harsh. You told me not to let you dissuade me. I woke from that dream with the same conviction as if I'd thought of everything myself."

He sat down on the floor and put his face in his hands. A damaged picture frame scraped beneath him.

"My mind is not my own. My judgment is compromised. Both versions of you tell me that my mother went into the diary. But why would she? For my entire life, she detested magic, scolded me for taking any interest in it as a boy. Did she just want to leave me? What have I done that merits such abandonment by everyone I care for?"

I knelt beside him, my knees resting on something sharp. I hardly cared, though. Enough was enough.

"She didn't go willingly," I said.

He jerked his forehead upward.

"What?"

"Oh, Edward. There's so much to tell you. She's trapped in the diary. We may yet save her, but we'll need to free Bram to do so."

He leaned away from me.

"Edward, what is it?" I asked. He stood up and crossed the room.

"It's strange, is all," he said. "Why did you come here tonight?"

"I just came from the Netherdowns. I hid things from you because —I was afraid—you failed a magical test devised to identify the person who enchanted me with my illness."

He scoffed.

"How did you come from the Netherdowns? The diary is lost, as is the page you stowed away in the prison."

"Cyrus found the page. He brought it to me."

Edward hit his head with open-palmed hand several times.

"You're asking me to break a convicted felon from prison. How do I know you're real? This is the type of thing you ask me in dreams. I thought I just woke from one, but what if I didn't?"

"You can trust me."

"I can't trust you!" he cried fiercely. His words echoed in the darkness. I stood calmly and approached him.

"Your mother waged war against me when we met. I know why she fears magic as she does. She would never forsake you. She loves you. We can save her, but I need your help, and I need Bram's help."

"Freeing him would be an abuse of my power," he replied.

"Edward, you don't really believe that Bram killed your father. I know you don't."

He withdrew another step.

"To hear you say that, when so often you've said the opposite... You soothe. You incite. Which is sweeter? Which is more authentic?"

I knit my brows together in a deep furrow. The magic was already so deeply engrained in him he was losing his grip on reality. Why would the fog creature encourage a belief that Bram killed his father?

I stepped toward him and grasped his hands.

"It doesn't matter what I say," I said. "The only thing that matters is what you believe."

He looked down at me, and I was close enough to breathe in his scent, warmed and expanded by his recent exertions. His brow glistened with perspiration.

"It's up to you, Edward. I deserve whatever consequences sprout from the deeds I've sown."

After a final bloated silence, he nodded.

"It would be best to go immediately."

24

TOWERING OBSTACLES

Edward looked weak as we made our way to Dawnhurst Jail. A pale color shaded his features as we passed through the streets, only an occasional streetlamp left lit. It wasn't a long ride to the other side of the city, yet I was grateful that he kept his own carriage, ready to depart at a moment's notice. Convenience is a luxury of the wealthy.

He rode inside this time, eyeing me from across the cab as if I might vanish into smoke at a moment's notice. Perhaps he had lived out this scene before with the fog creature or he still didn't believe that I was sincere in my well wishes toward him.

I tried my best to avoid his gaze, staring out the window at shifting shadows. My mind reeled from our conversation in his apartment. Why would the fog creature choose to imitate me? Was there no one else? And he'd suffered like this since before Christmas. I didn't notice anything. His suffering was a symptom of my neglect.

My faithlessness.

Everyone had begged me to test Edward, and I refused, insisted it was unnecessary. Yet, when the test of that faith came, I crumbled.

I still had questions. Why? How? But faith isn't a lack of curiosity.

It's a trust that the answers themselves are less important than knowing that there are, indeed, answers.

Of all the things he told me, what stung the most were four hopeless words: "You didn't want me."

Lord Edward Thomas, the Steely-Eyed Detective, now sergeant of the Dawnhurst Police Force, tried for months to trust in my affection. He persevered through the death of his father, through my pathetic search for another man, and I was sure it would have persevered through the disappearance of his mother had I only allowed it.

Misunderstanding pushed me away, not disgust. It hurt to be apart from him because I wanted him.

But how could he possibly see that?

I wanted to explain everything to him on that carriage ride to the jail. I wanted to dissuade him from any belief that I chose Bram over him. My relationship with Bram was complicated. That much was true. But I once heard someone say discovering what is most important in life is more an exercise of subtraction than comparison. In a world with Edward and Bram, I admit Bram held fascination. He introduced me to magic. But in a world without Edward, there was no magic at all.

Edward needed a woman of stronger moral fiber than mine, with a backbone that would not bend and snap in the face of adversity. I could not dream of winning his heart again. But at the very least, I could clean up my mess and allow him to move on.

At the very least...

The carriage pulled to a stop.

"How is this going to work?" he asked.

"To enter the Netherdowns, you need to lose yourself in the poem on this page." I pulled the folded, weathered paper from my purse. "Once you do, you will be taken up and vanish from our world. Inside, you'll appear at one of three hilltops." I paused, considering the current state of the memory world. "I must warn you. It's possible that we will arrive in the midst of a great deal of violence."

He put his hands on his knees.

"All the more important that we save my mother."

"When we go into the jail, we're counting on you to get us out. The three of us can enter his cell, or the office I used to speak with him last. Then, Bram and I will go. You take the page back to your tenement, or another safe place, and start reading. We will wait for you inside."

He chewed on his cheek, accentuating his jawline.

"How do I know you're telling the truth? You and Bram might use it to escape, and when I go to read it, nothing happens."

He looked pained by asking, and it was hard to hear it. How could he know I was telling the truth?

"I feel unworthy to ask it, but you'll have to trust me. The transportation is rooted in a high form of magic, the sensation you get when reading a good book, and you just get taken away... Have you ever experienced that before?"

Though he had stared at me the whole ride over, when I looked at him, he didn't meet my eyes.

"I'd be a fool to say I haven't. Very well. We'll go in. I'll come out."

"If we are split up in the Netherdowns, head toward the tower in the middle of the town. You'll see it from the hilltop, I'm sure of it."

He nodded and opened the door.

I followed him inside the jail. The guard at the front office eyed me suspiciously, but he didn't question his superior's orders and handed over the keys. We walked to Bram's cell. I glanced at the empty one beside him where I once sat prisoner. A chill passed through me.

Bram shrunk away from Edward's imposing figure, but a wave of confusion spread across his face when he saw me.

"Luella? What's going on?"

I glanced back toward the office.

"We're just here to talk."

The clang of the cell door lock echoed in the prison. Edward and I both stepped inside. Bram stood up, misery compounding his features.

"Sergeant Thomas," he said. "I swear to you, I have no recollection of killing your father."

It was brave to apologize as he did, but the wording left something to be desired. Edward winced.

"You have no recollection—"

"Please, there's little time. I'll explain more soon. Bram—" I pulled out the page, "—Cyrus found this."

His eyes lit up as they settled on the words of his poem.

"Is Hirythe all right?"

"He's trying his best, but he needs your help. Lady Thomas is stuck inside as well."

Bram looked at Edward again.

"Then we must go at once." Awkwardly, he put a hand on Edward's shoulder. "Don't worry. If Hirythe is still alive, I'm sure we can bring her back."

"If?" Edward asked. It was my turn to wince.

"Here, Bram. You first."

I handed him the page, and he looked at it, glossy eyed.

"Thank you, Luella."

"Just read, please."

I had feared that because of Bram's deteriorating memory, he would have a more difficult time connecting to the words and losing himself in their meaning. The opposite was true. It took only a moment before I'd misplaced Bram, and Edward and I were the only ones in the cell.

Edward picked the page up off of the bench.

"You promise you're not simply running off with him?" he asked.

I gripped his arm firmly.

"I promise I won't rest until we've done everything we can to save your mother." And, I added to myself, to expel the fog creature from Edward. "Even if it costs me my life."

An icy breeze swept through the jail.

"Let's pray it doesn't come to that," he said, handing the page over.

By now, I about had the poem memorized. That, combined with my nerves, made it all the more difficult to focus on the meaning and intention. I took a deep breath, closed my eyes, and on my third read through, the Netherdowns meadows stretched before me.

Bram sat childlike on the grass, both legs before him in a V shape, looking at the world he made. What must he be feeling? Freed from a death sentence only to discover his refuge of cherished memories was coming apart at the seams.

And coming apart it was. More now even than my trip earlier that day, I could nearly taste the decay in the air. The first time I had entered the Netherdowns, it welcomed me with the warmth of a security blanket, chasing out the dark magic which possessed me.

The air was thinner now. Less substantial.

"This is all my fault," I said as I knelt beside him. "If I'd never come here or requested your help, Jeremy would have never found you."

He vacantly traced shapes in the dirt, dragging his finger through acorns that littered the ground beneath the Oak.

"It's not your fault," he said. "That first night we met, I sensed something magical about you. I thought I'd found someone like me."

His eyes glazed in a trance, as though the memory spread delicately like wine over his tastebuds. "Someone who would never stop chasing magic," he continued with a shrug. "Besides, it was only a matter of time until Jeremy found us."

A question tugged at my conscience. I hadn't asked Hirythe. I feared the answer.

"What will you and Hirythe do to Jeremy?"

Bram lumbered to his feet.

"I don't want to kill him. I don't want to let Hirythe kill him, either. That was why I asked you to leave me in the cell to warn Hirythe."

The hair on my neck prickled up like matchsticks.

"Hirythe has killed before," I said.

Bram set his jaw and surveyed the landscape.

"Sophisticated society limits the severity of punishment for criminals. Can you think of any deed that justifies eternal misery? We hang killers in England. I've always wondered why. Is it to balance justice's scales? Does a killer's death honor the victim? Does it bring satisfaction or closure?"

"I've always understood it to prevent society from committing the same errors. It discourages imitation of evil," I suggested.

Bram sighed.

"No one knows how close they are to evil choices until it's too late," he said. "And when it's difficult to discern if a choice is evil or not, our conscience is so adept at finding hiding places."

I put a hand on his shoulder.

"You're waxing philosophical. It's frightening me."

He attempted a smile.

"I don't know if I will make it back out of here, Luella. When I made this place, I always was afraid I'd get lost inside and never emerge."

"Well," I hoisted him to his feet, "at least you remember being afraid of that. Besides, it doesn't matter what you're afraid of. I need your help."

He laughed, and I took heart.

"Luella Winthrop, why do you always need my help?"

I slung his arm over my shoulders and urged him down the hill toward Hirythe's tower.

"Enjoy it while you can. Edward will be here soon, and I'd like a good vantage point to see which hill he arrives on."

Bram stopped.

"Edward is coming here? I thought you told me in your letter that he was your enchanter." He sounded disappointed.

"Your selective memory is curious, Mr. Lowhouse."

He smiled bleakly.

"It appears to be recovering somewhat now that I'm in what you might call its homeland," he replied.

"Hirythe and I have come to believe that Edward is infected with whatever magic resided in me," I continued.

"Not Sraith," he said. "There was no more ink left, and it's difficult to manipulate cause and effect without it."

"No. Whatever hid behind Sraith. It left me—"

"—and attached to Edward?"

I nodded and swallowed. The trail was making itself more clear the more I thought about it.

"Jeremy claimed he woke up an evil power with a song of some kind. He used the power to kill the other member of your team. That was the death I first reported on when I wrote the Steely-Eyed Detective."

Bram took a step in front of me, cutting me off. He wore a haunted, fearful expression.

"He claimed to use a song to wake the magic?"

"Yes. He said you and Hirythe were afraid to sing it."

Bram put a hand to his forehead, as though he had committed an egregious error. "Of course. He woke a Dúil. An evil Dúil."

"Dúil?" I asked.

"The song Jeremy referred to was a safeguard we used to tame it. Jeremy woke up malicious ambition, unhinged desire. That's what infected you before. Sraith, yes, with its distortion of cause and effect, amplified by a Dúil. It preyed on what you wanted most, what you aspired to become. It feasts on your hunger, and the more your character morphs and changes to accomplish your ends, the stronger it grows."

My ambitions. His words chilled me. Small wonder I had seen it as my father in dreams. What I'd wanted, more than anything, was to make him proud, to make his sacrifice worth something. Of course it would have pushed me to write more daring articles. Of course it would have pushed me deeper into the magic.

But if Edward saw me in his dreams...

"We need to get to Hirythe," Bram said, studying my face. "Especially if Edward is coming here."

"Why should that matter? When I came before, I was free of my magical enchantments. And it looks like its having a restorative effect on your memory. Isn't the Netherdowns a temporary balm on this type of magic?"

Bram pulled me down the hill with a strength he didn't have moments before.

"It's breaking apart. There's no telling what that means for magic traveling into its confines."

I stuffed my hands into my purse. If that were true, and Bram's memory was coming back, perhaps he could shed more light on the trinkets from his chest that Jeremy had left behind.

"Bram, I—"

A deafening boom cut me off, followed by a crack reminiscent of a cricket paddle. We both searched for the source of the sound. When I found it, my heart dropped to my knees.

Hirythe's tower, standing tall and battered above the Netherdowns village, had been struck by a cannonball. Its top leaned over, as if bowing to its enemy, before succumbing to gravity in a terrible fall to the earth, splintering and crushing its lower half beneath it.

It fell from our view, engulfed by a growing cloud of dust, expanding outward in every direction like billowing fog. At its epicenter was the last place I'd seen Hirythe. The last place I'd seen Charlotte Thomas.

We both stared, speechless, until the dust cloud dissipated, and we could see pockets of the town through its veil. Bram lost his strength and stumbled to his knees, some invisible poison seeping through his veins and toward his heart. I wondered what significance the tower had for the strength of his memory, for his resolve.

"Bram," I called, crouching beside him to place my hands on his shoulders. "Are you all right?"

A dark shadow fell over his face, and he stared at the forest behind us.

"You'd better hope Edward arrives here on Oak Hill," he said. "Things are about to become much more difficult."

🥀 25 🥀

TRINKETS

The realizations came after the dust cleared. I'd last seen Hirythe holed up in that tower. He once told me magical protections buoyed it up. I experienced one of those first-hand: climb a few flights of stairs and arrive on the pinnacle of a tower taller than it looked from the outside.

When did the Netherdowns monsters procure a cannon? How would they operate one? I shuddered, imagining one of the unsightly creatures with enough dexterity to manipulate human tools. Or had Jeremy set it off himself?

Charlotte—I'd last seen her portrait in the base of that tower. Did she lie among the rubble? Had she been torn and smashed, and if so, what did it mean for our chances of restoring her?

But even those crushing concerns did not compare to the smoth-ering fear that with the collapse of the tower, we were losing. All I could do was hope the collapse of such a symbolic hold on the land would not be a tipping point in the enemy's favor. If Jeremy won the Netherdowns—destroyed the Netherdowns—there was no hope to get Charlotte, Bram, Edward, or even me back home. I'd always relied on the magical prowess of Hirythe and Bram. Did they have anchors in reserve to send us back, or methods of discovering new anchors for the Thomas family now they were here?

And what were we to do now? I had planned to keep a lookout for Edward from the tower. Bram was right. If he didn't appear on Oak Hill, where we stood now, it would be a trek through dangerous, hostile memory to find him.

Even if I found him, what would I say about his mother?

I started down the hill toward the ruins of the town.

"Where are you going?" Bram asked.

"Charlotte Thomas was in that tower," I said. "I can't leave her."

"You don't know what's down there."

"I know what might be, and it's my fault she's stuck here in the first place."

Bram rounded in front of me, cutting me off.

"You can't be faulted for what Jeremy chose to do," he said.

"Don't start with me like that, Bram. I'm not possessed by Sraith anymore. I have a very firm grasp on cause and effect. I chose to be a part of her life. I brought the magic into it. This is my mess."

"But you didn't choose to be infected. You didn't—"

"Enough!" I cried. "This is your whole routine! It always is. Hirythe told me you are infected with magic worse than I ever was. *You're* the one who doesn't understand cause and effect, Bram. What's worse, I think you purposefully misunderstand it to get what you want. You've made it abundantly clear how much you value magic over others. I will never make that mistake again."

He stepped backward, as though from a blow. I bit my cheek. My rebuke came out swift and sudden, a continuation of our awkward conversation in the prison. Although in ways it came as a relief, it still hurt me to know that I could never play first fiddle for him. I would always be second to the magic.

"Are you going to help me, or not?" I asked.

He swallowed before responding, looking at me as he never had before with a guarded air.

"If you die trying to save Charlotte, you can't very well save her, now can you? Our best chance is to hope Hirythe is still alive, and if he is, he won't be in that pile of rubble. If the Lady Thomas is in there,

there's nothing a timely but feeble attempt at extricating her from the remains can do to help her chances."

There was a sting to his voice, salt in his defense. For the first time since I'd known him, it felt like he was speaking down to me.

"And the next time you accuse me of valuing magic over others, I'll be pleased to take back the years of my life you spilled on a rug."

He brushed past my shoulder and stalked off in the other direction. I blinked back tears. His retort disturbed emotions I'd tried so hard to suppress. He had done so much for my case, and at significant cost. Yet, he'd made the ink before he ever met me, and he never told me what I wasted when I wrote those stories with it. Was it fair for him to lord that over me?

"Where are you going?" I asked.

"Into the wood," he replied, form shrinking against the treeline. "If Hirythe is alive, and that tower has fallen, he will be dangerously close to becoming what we've always feared."

"Which is what?" I ran to catch up to him, more to stay within earshot than with an intent to follow into the wood beyond. "You keep mentioning that Hirythe could become this terrible something, but you won't tell me plainly what that is."

Bram stopped and turned to me, his face a portrait of hard lines and determination.

"Wild."

Wild? I thought of the words in the song Hirythe taught me, the resonating feeling of the fae chorus, and the drawer filled with silver currants. Where had the wood folk gone? What was it about Hirythe that enabled him to live beyond his kin?

Bram marched off toward the trees, and I had two choices. Soon Edward would be arriving. I promised him I wouldn't just run off with Bram. Yet, I didn't know which hilltop he would arrive on. Without Bram, I'd be wandering the Netherdowns looking for Edward alone. If I came across any of those terrible monsters... I was no Olivia.

If only I knew how long it would take Edward to read the page, or if he would even do it at all. I needed to stall for time, just in case he appeared on that hillside.

"Wait! Bram!" I ran to him and yanked his sleeve, which was still filthy from his time in his cell. "I'm sorry," I said. "I want to help Hirythe just as you do. Before you go in, please." I knelt and emptied the contents of my purse on the ground. "The last time you looked at these, you couldn't remember much. What about now? Can they help us? I mean, when I brought the Uncantation spell into the Nether-downs it transformed into a charging bull. Can we manipulate the magic in any of these?"

His shoulders eased, signaling that my apology found at least some purchase on his conscience. From the way he rolled his head, I could tell my idea seemed insignificant, but as it was months ago, he found it in him to play along and explain.

"It's unlikely," he said, sitting beside me. "I made these, so they're at least a little more stable in a world of my memory than another object you brought charged with who knows what type of magic. Have you opened the locket?"

"After the ink and the uncomfortable phenomenon with the dolls?" I shook my head. "I was afraid to."

He smirked, thumbed its compartment open, and peered in.

"It's a Lover's Eye."

I slumped my shoulders.

"Well, that's not uncommon. You can buy those from any street peddler."

"Not quite," he insisted. "Open this one, and you'll see a painting of an eye belonging to whomever holds your heart. Presumably, it might change over time. If you can find one from a street peddler that does the same, I'll eat my hat."

My strategy was working. As he talked about his magical trinkets, the same youthful excitement filled him up again, an exuberance I had never provoked in his demeanor without the aid of our shared interest in magic. I wondered if Olivia ever had. He extended the locket to me.

"Care to see?"

I closed it without looking. I didn't need a locket to tell me my own heart.

"What high magic did you use for it?" I asked.

"Loyalty." He took it back from me, lifting it by the chain. "It's amazing the effect loyalty has on a person's resolve."

"What about these?" I asked, pushing the rings toward him. When he saw them, he failed to suppress a proud smile.

"Rings of Regret," he said.

"Regret? That doesn't sound very nice. A dark magic?"

He made a tsking sound with his tongue.

"It's unpleasant, but it's not dark. I'd often wondered over how quickly regret spoiled. Time is the great healer, so they say, but it wipes the past away without scrutiny. The good. The bad. All fades away eventually. I thought if I could protect regret from the effects of time, one might be less likely to commit the same mistakes over again."

I grunted, wishing he had told me about these a long time ago. Perhaps if he had, I wouldn't have made such a mess of things.

"Why are there two?"

"Popular demand," he said. "There were more. Hirythe has one. I hope he is still wearing it. If he is, I hope it still works."

He slipped one ring on. I took a breath and did the same. I slid it on a finger beside the engagement ring Edward gave me after Christmas.

"How do you feel?" I asked.

"No different. My regrets are too fresh. I don't need a reminder."

He leveled his gaze at me. I met his eyes without waver. Some time ago, this exchange would have spurred a giddy, heady reaction from me. Now the eye contact made me remember everything that hung in the balance. Was that because I had changed or because of the ring?

"Still," he said, standing, "can't hurt to keep them fresh. It may come in handy if hard choices lie ahead."

Hard choices. Life was a series of hard choices.

Since my time visiting Bram in the Dawnhurst Jail, my outlook on him had morphed. With ample opportunity to reflect on our time together, some details became clear to me.

I liked Bram because I fancied myself similar to him. If I wasn't, I wanted to be similar. I wanted to believe in magic and adventure, chasing the unknown despite where it led.

Before, I thought the unknown was attainable in a vague sense of the word. That eventually it wouldn't be the unknown anymore because I would know it. But the unknown is limitless, and many gravestones line the road into the abyss, expired in the quest to reach the next horizon.

Bram wanted a traveling companion for that next horizon, and the one after that, and the one after that.

All I wanted was a horizon of my own. Meaning, I didn't look for a traveling companion, but someone with which to build a home in its view.

But what I wanted mattered little now. There was nothing for me but to do all in my power to right the wrongs I had wrought on the Thomas family.

Bram started again toward the woods, leaving me to sit staring after.

"If you thought he was quickly ducking back to his flat and hurrying into the Netherdowns, then by now, he either appeared on another hilltop, or he won't be coming at all," he called over his shoulder.

I looked longingly back to the Oak tree standing on the hill like a stooping sentinel. Bram was right. Edward would have come by now. Perhaps he had another episode.

A chill ran through me. Or perhaps I was wrong, and now Edward controlled the only exit point from the Netherdowns, where Bram, Hirythe, his mother, and I were all trapped inside.

My finger seared underneath the Ring of Regret.

I regretted distrusting Edward before. He would come. Or he needed me to find him. In either event, Bram was right. We'd need Hirythe.

"Forgive me, Edward," I whispered. "I'll find you."

I stuffed the locket, dolls, and cheesecloth into my purse, and hurried after Bram.

26

IN THE WOOD

My only time entering the Netherdowns woods before had been a sprint to discover the source of the moondust trail, a trail that had since grown cold. I wondered if the shimmering particles were merely a byproduct of my magical infection, a type of hallucination that stemmed from an enchanted fever.

Still, it led me to my silver currant, and Hirythe had promised me I could trust the exchange I had with my father after eating it.

Now, the wood was dark, almost black, punctuated with glass-like shards of Netherdowns moonlight raining through the canopy and pooling on the forest floor. A thin and menacing mist curled around our ankles, stronger in the dark than when touched by the pockets of illumination.

We made our way slowly away from the hill. Eventually, beyond, a sea lay in wait for us on the other side, but there was no telling how far we'd have to travel before the trees would thin to reveal the lapping of glimmering waves.

"Bram, where are we going?" I asked in a whisper. Speaking too loudly in this place seemed all but sacrilegious.

"Deeper," he replied.

"Is there a hideout deep in the forest you and Hirythe planned to escape to if your situation devolved?"

He shook his head.

"No shack, like the one by Hollow Lake?"

He shook it again.

"No, but if Hirythe has reverted, this forest would be the closest thing he could find to home."

Reverted? I stumbled over a protruding root with a snap. Bram turned and caught me before I toppled to the ground.

"Be careful," he said, standing me back up.

"I'm trying to be."

He let go of me, but he kept my hand in his to lead me through the dark. I wanted to fight the warm reassurance it offered, but I couldn't deny Bram had always been able to calm me down.

"Hirythe was one of the wood folk," I surmised, gingerly picking out my next steps through the gnarled terrain of what I thought were raised Ash roots. "When he was... wild?"

"When I first met Hirythe, I was convinced I'd found a ghost. He was dressed in the tattered remains of what looked to be an aristocratic dueling outfit from the early 1700s. It hung in tatters from his shoulders and waist. They were vestiges of a civilized, though dated, life. For all I knew, he was the deceased spirit of some German Viscount or some other similar figure, roaming the woods. That wood wasn't altogether that different from this one."

The scattered light illuminated the perspiration beading on his forehead in small flashes when we strode underneath. The air smelled of cold moss and decaying leaves. I squinted. It appeared as though translucent tattered clothing hung from the trees as he told me the story.

"When I invited him to talk with me, Hirythe circled, wary as an animal being offered food. Wild fae, by then, had grown so suspicious of humans that it was a miracle he stopped to speak with me at all. I suspect he might have sniffed out some trace of magic on me. In those days, it would have been faint. I fumbled in my attempts to unravel magical principles or bind powers to objects. He'd have smelled errant traces on me the way you might see milk stains on the shirt of a new farmer.

"As we spoke, it became evident that he wasn't a ghost. For one thing, he didn't believe he was dead. Then, as he offered some very compelling and paradoxical discussion on everything from the stars to systems of governance, I recognized his kind from my research.

"After talking for about an hour, he stood up, and I realized he'd stolen everything but my underclothes, switching them with the rags he wore when I first encountered him. He wore my jacket, held my satchel up like a prize. I looked like the destitute 18th century nobleman. Clever fae magic. Then, he told me my time had come to a close because I'd not been able to stop him from stealing what was closest to me. To his great surprise, I started clapping and laughing. I couldn't help it. It was like watching a magic trick.

"He suspended whatever plan he had to kill me and asked what I thought was so amusing. I told him I was delighted to meet a fae, that I'd always dreamed of doing so, and that I'd found his conversation civilized and enchanting."

The snap of a branch off to my right froze me in my tracks, pausing Bram's story. We both peered into the darkness, counting our breaths and waiting for something to emerge. After several minutes, it became apparent nothing planned to jump out and attack us, and we trekked on.

"So you flattered him? I can imagine Hirythe responding well to that," I said.

"He did," Bram continued. "He sat back down, inquiring why I wasn't angry he had stolen my clothes. I didn't know what use anger would have been. And, if clothes were the price of such an immeasurably rare conversation, I was happy to pay it. At this, something in his face flickered with conflict, as though an identity inside him was trying to break out. He lunged at me, then threw himself backward. Then again. He tried to protect me from himself, somehow."

I nodded. I understood that feeling. Once, I'd attacked Rebecca, despite the prospect being absolutely abhorrent to me.

"Before long, he was on his hands and knees, heaving great breaths of self-control, muttering something about me being worth the debate.

Then, a passage from a book I'd read came to mind. The author made outlandish claims that the fae could be—well, not tamed or domesticated, but convinced to make bonds with certain human beings. I knew the fae loved making bargains, so I tried one.

"It was simple. I asked if he would trade his hostility for something else of mine. At first he scoffed, thinking he'd already stolen everything of value from me, so I offered the boldest thing that came to mind. Protection.

"The convulsing stopped immediately, and he peered at me with terrible suspicion. 'From other humans?' he asked. I assured him, especially from humans. And, as what might only be natural for one of his folk, he made the bargain obscenely serious. He stretched out his hand saying, 'Swear that, upon the value of your life, you will protect me from all humans who ever would wish harm against my kind, that you will spend your mortality defending my immortality, that you will devote your days to my preservation.'"

The way Bram rattled off the words made me believe they were etched into his heart, and he recalled them often like a personal credo.

"I told him I would make the deal, so long as he was open to considering our relationship to be one more elaborate than just a subject and its protector, that we might not seal off camaraderie or even friendship. This request piqued his interest, and I thought I saw fear in his face, but he agreed."

I had often wondered about the nature of their relationship. Bram and Hirythe bickered like brothers, and they postulated over magical theories like overly acquainted work comrades. Knowing that Bram was bound to his protection cast new light on Hirythe and the Netherdowns as a whole.

"You made the Netherdowns to protect him," I considered aloud. "But now it's falling apart."

"With an enemy in the gates," Bram added. "You must understand, when I found him, Hirythe had never enjoyed friendship, at least not as we understand it. After a time, he feared I would not uphold my end of the bargain, not because of a desire to cross him, but through negligence and arrogance. More importantly, he began to value my life over his. If I fail to protect him, my life will be forfeited, as per the deal we made together. But Hirythe doesn't want our friendship to end, so he's been adding his own precautions, especially after noticing what he considered cracks in our agreement."

"You mean Olivia?" I asked.

"Hirythe was threatened by her. He would never understand love. That is not the source of fae magic. We quarreled often about my feelings—my weakness, as he put it—reminding me constantly of our deal. The poor creature couldn't understand that the magic he discussed with me was infinitely more seductive and dangerous. I often wonder what might have happened if I had allowed myself to love Olivia without reserve while she still lived. Would I have formed the Phantom Battalion? Would I have become so obsessive over new strains of magic, or could she have been enough for me?"

Bram stopped walking. The shadows swirled around as figures of his past challenged and taunted him. The magic felt palpable and familiar. I drank the same atmosphere with the Reading Inspector. This reflective magic had broken him, but Bram stood bravely in its midst now.

A circling darkness formed in front of us, swelling into a tall oval shape like a whirlpool. As the darkness bent and curved, it pulled in reflections of the moon streaks, and before long I recognized the coloring and patterns that I'd seen time and time again on the monsters of the Netherdowns, a texture that killed or devoured memory.

The realization came nearly too late.

"Wait! Bram!"

A blinding burst of light shot through the plate of darkness in front of us. I tackled Bram to the ground. We watched the light burst into a tree, dousing it in fire not of orange and yellow, but the same awful black, white, and gray patterns.

He turned to the tree for only an instant before pushing me back to the ground with one arm and reaching for my bag.

"Whatever you do, stay hidden," he whispered before jumping to his feet. In his hands, I could barely make out the small stretch of cheesecloth he'd used to make the Crimson Ink. He looked closely into the darkness before his eyes went wide and his hands shot up, clumsily using the cheesecloth as a shield.

Another burst of light hurtled toward him, and I nearly cried out, but when it collided against him, the outstretched cheesecloth dissipated the energy entirely, as if it had just eaten the light altogether.

Another burst came to a similar end, pushing Bram backward one step at a time. Then another. And another. Soon, Bram had retreated dangerously close to the peculiar flames licking at the brush and limbs at the base of a group of trees.

"Is that all you have?" Bram called into the dark. There was a pause, painfully long as I expected whatever it was in the forest to respond. But then, two streaks of the queer fire stripped down the forest floor, creating a wall of the flames about knee-high. Bram scrambled to one side, and the streaks of flame curved in a large arc, separating us and surrounding him in a semicircle.

"I have more," a voice replied. "You should know. They're your relics."

I barely recognized Jeremy's features in the dark. He was a shadow of himself, the scant, dirty light provided by the flames illuminating only the peaks of his features and silhouette. Jeremy Evans. Brutus. My greatest critic.

My memory rushed back to the conversation we had in the Oxford tea shop. He'd insisted that his job was to help my writing improve. To help me improve. He seemed so kind then, in a professional, difficult sort of way. How long had this anger brewed inside him?

Bram's words resounded in my ear. No one knows how close they are to committing atrocity.

Jeremy hunched with what looked like a large magnifying glass in his hands.

"How did you escape the noose, Bram?" he called.

"I have friends in high places," Bram replied. "Didn't you know?"

"I just destroyed the high place. Did you see the tower come toppling down?"

"You've gone too far, Jeremy," Bram said. "You trapped an innocent woman in my memoryscape, as a portrait no less. Your brother would not have condoned involving strangers in your personal vendetta."

"That was an accident," he replied. "You should consider better labeling. I thought the paintbrush would gently rearrange her memory. How was I supposed to know it dripped with fear?"

"I didn't label them because they weren't intended to be used by anyone."

"Anyone but yourself, of course. You always thought you were so exceptional, Bram. You spoke like we couldn't understand your lofty theories. They're not that difficult. But Bram Lowhouse is in control of everything. You can afford to play with other people because you *know*. You've *researched*. You *understand*." Jeremy laughed bitterly. "You understand nothing."

From my hiding spot in the brush, I reluctantly considered Jeremy's words. Bram asked me to use the ink the first time he met me. He endangered me. He was fortunate that his meddling uncovered a greater malady that required his attention. But he couldn't have known that at our first meeting. Later he insisted he knew small doses should not have been so dangerous. Jeremy was not lying.

The fire around Bram spread slowly in his direction, smokeless and menacing with the heat of forgetfulness. Hirythe and I had wondered what would happen to the Netherdowns if Bram were executed. It was a different fear entirely to think about what would happen if Bram was killed in the Netherdowns.

He had admonished me to stay hidden, but I couldn't let him face Jeremy alone.

"What happened to your brother was an accident! An error. I wish I could take it back. Damn it, man! I would take it all back!"

"But you can't," Jeremy said. "And now, I will ensure your arrogance and deceit never hurt another person."

Jeremy raised the seeing glass like a weapon. What could I do? I was too far away to stop him. The flames licked up in front of me, anyway.

My mind went completely blank, but I had to do something. Reaching out with instinct, I opened my mouth.

Do you hear the echo?

. . .

I forced the words out in an awkward attempt at singing, but my voice was rough and breaking. Still, it accomplished its end, and Jeremy startled. He turned, looking for the voice. A swift breeze stirred the smoke and mist and leaves. Finding nothing, he refocused on Bram. So I tried again, this time more clearly.

Do you hear the echo?

"Who is there?" Jeremy called.

My voice had rung out more clearly the second time, ringing like a bell, far more melodious than I'd ever heard myself sing before. Bram tried to jump forward, lunging at his rival, but Jeremy spun back around and another blast of the modulating light shot from the seeing glass. Bram barely raised the cheesecloth in time, and he took the blow awkwardly, the impact staggering him from his feet. The cheesecloth fell from his hands into the dark brush. Jeremy advanced.

"No more tricks, Bram. Singing voices in the woods may have been enough to frighten me when we first met, but I've learned since then."

Bram scrambled backward, as close as he dared to the creeping line of gray flame. The breeze returned, making the fire dance, as if taunting me, daring me to help Bram survive this.

"Jeremy, please," Bram said, his forearm raised as a shield in front of his face.

I stood, caution be damned. I doubted the song would work another time, but perhaps if Jeremy saw me, it would stop him long enough for Bram to do something—anything.

My side hurt from where I'd landed on a tree root, but I took a big breath in, trying to muster the volume to make my location unmistakable.

Do you hear the echo?

The sound was deafening, emanating from the forest like a shock wave. The full force of the fae choir at my back like a furious gale, skirts whipping around my legs, accompanied by an army of pipes as pipes had never been heard before. Power and sound knocked Jeremy over sideways. My heart raced as the force of it choked the flames to the ground. The music blasted from every trunk and limb of the wood.

On the crags and in the barrow?
And do you see the moonlight mellow
In the cracks and in the burrow?
But where have the hillfolk gone?
And where have the woodfolk gone?

No ripple in the water,
No stirring of the vines,
No trouble in the torpor,
No mischief in the mines,

No hexes in the hayfield,
No music in the song,
The earth will not recover
When the folk, at last, are gone.

As the song roared on, I sprinted to Bram, a hand on my skirts as I jumped over the flames. Nearby, Jeremy scrambled to his hands and knees, tripping over himself to make an escape.

"Bram! Are you all right?"

He waved me off and bounded for the scrap of cheesecloth, which now lay draped over a small bush, twigs catching it at funny angles. He whirled to hold it up as a shield again. But Jeremy had vanished.

I spun around, my clothes still dancing in the music's wind. Squinting, I caught sight of our enemy sprinting to the edge of the wood in the distance.

"What is happening?" I asked Bram, my voice straining over the music.

"Luella, you're brilliant!" Bram replied, crossing to me protectively but unable to keep the awe from his face. "Hirythe imbued that song with a part of his soul. Singing it in this forest—you've woken the fae!"

"I thought Hirythe was the last left alive."

"In the world, yes. But we're in the Netherdowns. I made it in large part from his memory."

"That can't be all bad, though. Weren't we looking for him?"

The music finally faded, the woods quieting and still. Final breaths from the pipes persisted like settling clouds of dust. We stood quietly, afraid of the dark air around us. The awe on Bram's face turned dark.

"It's as I feared," Bram whispered. "He's reverted to the wild."

In front of us, a shadowed figured stepped from behind a tree. The silhouette lined the familiar figure of our friend, but it moved all wrong, slow and menacing.

In his hand, I saw the ripening shine of a handful of silver currants. Hirythe stepped into a shaft of moonlight.

"You made a promise, Bram," Hirythe said. "And as before, when Olivia threatened our bond, so has Luella. Too many times, I've paid the balance for your failure."

"Hirythe, I'm sorry. I can do better!"

"You told me I was strong enough to resist my baser motives, that I could enjoy the fruits of civility as you did. But how can you be trusted? It's time to test your work."

"Hirythe! No!"

Bram reached a desperate hand forward, but too late. Hirythe threw his head back and stuffed the entire handful of currants into his mouth. Then the trees began to glow.

27

WILD FAE

When the trees stopped glowing, I thought we'd somehow transported to the study in the middle of the Nether-downs town square. The room was untouched. Around me were the furnishings, the fireplace, the windows, the tartan blankets, and hanging weaponry. But when I turned to see where the door should have been, the trees had turned black behind us like cooling magma.

We were still in the forest, only under the power of the silver currants.

Hirythe strolled around the office.

"This is the first test," Hirythe said. "The first proof of my humanity. It lies somewhere in this room. Find it, Bram. You do not have long."

So this is what he meant by a test of Bram's work. We would simply have to find some hidden objects that held significance to their relationship. That wasn't so difficult. My mind instantly raced to the intricate slithering lock magically hidden on the desk.

"Bram, I think I can help," I said. "There's a locking mechanism on the desk. It's where he kept his most cherished possessions."

I ran over to the desk, running my fingers along the wood, vainly and hurriedly attempting to pick up a trace of the lock. Bram interrupted my frantic search with a calm hand on my shoulder.

"I remember those early days, well," Bram said to Hirythe. "But we didn't have access to an office like this for many years. You certainly loved the artifacts you adorned the room with. The textiles and the tools. The art."

Bram paced the room, carefully examining everything from framed bat skeletons to crystals growing in glass bell jars. The hearth displayed a heatless fire frozen in time.

"What is civilization if not civilized taste?" Hirythe asked rhetorically.

"You became quite a gentleman the longer we were together. Your fine-tailored suits and obsession with human culture made that clear. When weren't you reading books or studying musical scores?"

I leaned against the desk, a feeling of apprehension growing in my chest. Bram was moving too slow. Hirythe's admonition that we didn't have long gnawed at my anxiety, perhaps because I already waited for Edward's arrival on bated breath. What would happen to us if Bram did not pass Hirythe's examination?

"You don't know what you're looking for, do you?" I asked Bram.

"It's a private thing," Hirythe replied to me. "I've never shared it with him before. I would wager that your friends or family would struggle to identify the mark of your maturity as well. It lives within us, a marked item in our memory."

"Then how is it fair for you to expect Bram to find yours?"

Hirythe watched Bram silently. The magician had sauntered over to the hearth.

"Of course, collector's items and cultural products aren't civility themselves are they?" Bram said. "If I remember correctly, you made your greatest early developments in understanding humanity during late-night conversations, near fires like this one." Bram sat in one of the armchairs and motioned for Hirythe to sit across from him.

"For a creature of mortal duration, I never sensed in you a hurried demeanor while we spoke." Hirythe sat down. "At first, I considered you must have gratefully spent your time communing with a fae with such a longer lifespan than your own. But it didn't take me long to understand that the length of a life does not dictate its value."

Bram looked up at the hearth, where sat a small clock I hadn't noticed before sat.

"Yes. You would keep it somewhere close to our discussion chairs, wouldn't you?"

I crossed to them.

"Yes. You taught me discussion is not about subservience or conquest," Hirythe said. "It's about connection. That was such a novel idea. It awakened something frightening."

Bram nodded at me, indicating that I search the clock. The face of it sprung open, and a tattered photograph tumbled out, ripped on one side. I flipped it over and saw a younger, brighter version of Jeremy's face.

"The rest of the photo?" I asked.

"The Phantom Battalion," Bram said. "You had kin before, but you'd never known what it was like to want to belong to a family of your own choosing."

Hirythe gazed intensely at Bram. I took the scrap of photo back to the desk, unstuck the rest of the image from its compact frame, and put the pieces together. The scrap sprang from my hand and reattached as though it had never been separated. The full roster of the Phantom Battalion stared up at me, the photograph smooth under my fingers. There he was, Jeremy Evans, standing proudly beside his brother, looking happier and lighter than ever I had seen him. His expression did not have the gaunt, tired creases they did now.

For the first time, I considered just how painful the death of his brother must have been not just to Jeremy, but to the entire company. When Jeremy had blamed them, the sorrow would have compounded significantly.

"You've passed the first examination," Hirythe said.

The room retreated like ice melting beneath an afternoon sun. In its place, I was reminded that we were not in the office at all. The dark gnarled roots of the wood reclaimed the ground plane, but the fae's magic was not finished yet. A coat of leaves fell from the dark canopy above us in a shimmering, silvery show. Soon every surface around me was blanketed. It looked as though the air peeled back like the skin of a carrot to reveal a new panorama. Instead of the wood, I was surrounded by an aged and worn kitchen in what appeared to be an abandoned estate. There were no fires in the worn hearth, no stoves lit, or water boiling. Dusty crates of dark bottles were stacked haphazardly by a doorway with no door on its hinges. Leaves and other growth had invaded the space to reclaim it. Early morning sun shone through, chasing shadows from nooks and crannies.

Frozen in time, standing to one side of the central countertop, stood Bram. A book lay open in front of him beside what appeared to be an alchemical apparatus. A funnel, stretched over by a cheesecloth, snaked into winding tubes which eventually led to a small bottle—an inkwell with which I was all too familiar.

Across from him, gripping both edges of the counter with strained hands and forearms, was Hirythe. He was dressed in a loose shirt, half undone, under a black waistcoat. A coat hung on a meat hook behind him.

On the shelves was a mess of trinkets. Dolls, miniature siege machines, a rapier, crystal bottles, pocket watches, marble busts of strangers, codices... It looked like a disorderly antique shop.

The scene, though detailed, did not look altogether real, due in large part to its eerie stillness. It reminded me of the stone version of the Forbury Gardens I'd once dreamed.

"Surely, you remember this?" Hirythe said. Suddenly the tableau before me sprang to life, Hirythe assuming his place at the counter. When Bram spoke, he was at the book and the cheesecloth apparatus.

"I will never forget it. The night I made the ink."

"Where is the proof of my humanity?" Hirythe asked. "Did I not employ all manner of tricks to convince you not to create the ink?"

"You did." Bram nodded. He traced the pages of the book with his fingers. "Though you didn't need to. You could have told me no."

I walked through the room, searching on the shelves for anything that could be considered proof of humanity. Perhaps it was hiding in plain sight this time.

"At the time, I didn't know your power would be inadequate,"

Hirythe said. "I didn't know how much of yourself you were willing to give in order to save your wife."

"I would have given more," Bram replied.

"Look at them, Bram!" The fae motioned to the shelves. "All the time we spent together gathering these trinkets. You siphoned power from all of them to find some force strong enough to fuel your incantation. Years of your life's work, reduced to a collection of forgotten rubbish."

I reconsidered the items on the shelves, noting how some lay on their sides or cramped in corners like they had been discarded or thrown there. Were each of these items once magically imbued? I had accused Bram of loving magic more than people. If he had discarded so much of it to help Olivia...

"You didn't understand, Hirythe," Bram said evenly, as though he explained this before to no effect.

"When you met Olivia, I watched you change. Your heart split in more than one direction, and the motivation and drive you once showed toward magic waned. What weakened the attraction you and I had in common? I didn't understand what allure could be stronger than magic."

"It was painful for you," Bram recalled, rolling up his sleeves. "That much was clear."

"Of course!" Hirythe spat. "I loved finding these treasures with you. I loved learning new truth about magic, seeing other magic reduced to oddities and antiques. But you threw it all away."

"I didn't throw it away, Hirythe. I used it. I loved Olivia. There wasn't any choice." Bram picked up a rusted knife on the table. "We could make more trinkets. The magic could be rediscovered."

"Not all of it," Hirythe countered.

"But much of it. Fear is plentiful and powerful. It was in this knife, as it was in the paintbrush Jeremy stole from my chest. And wasn't creating the ink an interesting experiment in its own right? Didn't it interest you to know, that only fear was strong enough to power the distillation of my life?"

Hirythe stared at him icily.

"Is that fear laden knife the proof, then, of my humanity? Is that your submission?"

Bram wanted to offer it to him, but hesitated. I held my breath. What would happen if he was wrong?

"Fear is not civility. It is wild," he replied.

"Your time is running short, Bram. You must submit an answer."

They stared at one another. The Meddler and the fae. One friend trying to talk another down from the grips of crisis, but Bram could not bring himself to extend the knife as his answer.

Then, I noticed something in Hirythe's demeanor, a shift of his brow I had seen him exhibit once before while speaking with Jeremy, a frustration of being misunderstood.

I crossed beside him and looked across the counter at Bram as he did, taking in the room from his perspective.

There was Bram, knife in hand, book of research open, and a flimsy contraption on the table. What was Bram to this fae, aged and so well-versed in magic? How pathetic the scene was! Bram did not espouse power. He showed desperation, a willingness to try to do anything that might offer even a slim chance of restoring his wife to her full faculties. Bram was a wounded animal. He didn't hold a knife filled with fear. He was filled with fear.

"Bram," I whispered, understanding at once. There was a magic that made Bram's sacrifice possible. A magic Rebecca once told me was the only kind she believed in. "It's not the knife."

"I don't think so either, but do you have any other ideas?"

"No, Bram. I mean, it wasn't fear that allowed you to distill years of your life to save Olivia. It was love."

Hirythe's faced drooped.

"But I felt the magic leave the knife."

I scrutinized Hirythe, doubled over now in a very human pain.

"He sympathized with you. He felt love." I whispered.

I reached across the counter and plucked the inkwell from the apparatus.

"He saw you in pain, and not able to relieve you of it using any other method, he gave up what he treasured most."

Bram looked puzzled.

"What did he treasure most?"

"Years of your life," Hirythe finished. "Is that not what love is? Sacrifice?"

There was a long silence. A tear fell from Bram's cheek.

"Hirythe—"

"You've passed the second examination," said the fae bitterly. "Prepare yourselves, now, for the final."

Again, the room melted away like shadow, and soon the ominous silhouette of the trees in the wood revealed themselves again.

Bram and Hirythe still faced one another, once more wearing the clothes they'd earned through imprisonment: Bram in his dirty jail clothes, Hirythe in his battle-weary uniform.

I wondered how the wood might transform now, and I reflected on the first two examinations Hirythe put us through. Marks of his humanity. The items we found along the way were signposts on his transformation to understanding the human condition. The first was an evidence of friendship, or at least a sense of belonging. Second was a symbol of sacrifice and love. What followed that? What could be more human than love and friendship?

The silence stretched on, and the wood did not change again. If anything, the trees and dark around me came across, somehow, as more concrete than before. It was a subtle difference, like comparing the Netherdowns to the real world, or somewhat more nuanced than discerning dream from reality.

At first, I expected Hirythe planned to use a riddle for Bram's third examination. I'd read something about the fair folk attempting to confound humans with riddles, games, or perhaps a puzzle based in logic.

But the hair on my neck rose slowly, and I saw them in the darkness. Figures emerging from the trees, human figures, not clad in mirrored armor like Hirythe's army was, but in damaged clothing. Some wore torn jackets, shirts slashed across. One woman's dress appeared in a state of decay, as though it had been underwater for many years.

As Bram had mentioned in his story about Hirythe, their clothing marked different periods of history. Formal wear from the 1700s. A soldier's uniform with a steel breastplate. A ruffled collar over a velvet jerkin.

The figures advanced, slow and threatening. As they passed through shafts of moonlight, I saw in their eyes terrible anger, a hunger for something that eluded them.

All of them were dead, and they blurred the line between ghost and memory, if such a line ever existed.

They formed a circle around us, stopped, then all at once produced weapons, drawing them out from hidden scabbards and holsters with grave sloth.

"What magic is this, Hirythe?" I asked, my heart rate climbing. Warning about the real dangers of memory in the Netherdowns clambered up my throat and hung from my tonsils.

"What is the examination?" Bram asked. "Where is the humanity in this?"

Hirythe's eyes swept across the ranks of these ghosts, this true phantom battalion.

"Just tell me!" Bram cried. "I'll do whatever I must. What am I looking for?"

Suddenly, a thundering crackle sounded from across the Netherdowns. I turned to face the direction from where the sound had come, and a wave of gray light swept over me, coursing through the ghosts and out the other side before dissipating altogether.

"What was that?" I asked Bram, my eyes straining for the source of the flash through the canopy.

"Hirythe?" Bram insisted.

The fae's shoulders sagged as if under a great weight.

"You must go, Luella. Bram, you may accompany her if you feel it's right."

"What about the final examination?" Bram asked.

"The final examination is mine, and there is little you could do to help me. She will need you. Something just entered the Netherdowns —something less friendly than Jeremy Evans."

I glanced about, eager to leave, if it were possible. I would have preferred to face almost anything other than the dreadful spirits before me.

"They're not here for the two of you," Hirythe said. "Walk on through and see if you can keep the Netherdowns intact for a while yet. There's still more to do."

I grabbed Bram's arm and pulled on him to leave, but he resisted. A knowing look traded between them, a calmness to Hirythe's features that I didn't know was missing before. It was like looking at someone after they had a good night's sleep.

"Are you back, old friend?" he asked Hirythe.

"If I'm still here in an hour, I will be." Hirythe held up a hand, and I noticed a ring on his finger glow faintly.

The ghosts closed in, the circle shrinking on us before Bram relented, and we sprinted directly through the spirits in the direction of the sound that had nearly deafened us before.

"What were those people?" I asked Bram as we hurried along toward the edge of the wood. I wasn't sure which direction we headed, but any direction would suit me better than standing before those specters. Intuition tugged at me, suggesting of their identity.

"You asked me if Hirythe had ever killed before?"

I winced and swallowed.

"It was before he met me," Bram hurried to explain. "Before he knew humanity."

I bit my tongue. I knew there was a side to Hirythe which had been shielded from me. We had enjoyed conversation together, ruminated over magical principles—he'd offered me tea. And yet, in his ever-stretching past, I now had the faces of his victims burned into my mind.

Brams words from earlier cut at me. How many years' punishment could be appropriate for a killer? For a life? A life for a life? Did the quality of the lives matter or the nature of the victim? What singular moment could ever merit an eternal punishment?

Behind us, a dreadful moaning mixed with the sounds of clanging blades, shrieks, and the impossibly deft pipes which had shaken the wood not long before.

28

———— ⬧ ————

THE DÚIL

My lungs burned. My legs ached, but we finally burst out of the wood, and as we breached the perimeter, the pipes fell silent to our ears. I suspected that in the forest they played on.

I would never look at a wood the same way—Netherdowns or no.

We both collapsed on the ground, trying to recover from our clumsy sprint over vines and roots in the dark. We'd stopped talking after Bram confirmed the identity of the ghosts to me. He likely felt uncomfortable, as if I'd discovered a nasty truth about him.

In some ways, perhaps I had. Was it incumbent upon him to have divulged the true nature of his friend before introducing us? That was Bram, though. Perhaps all his time with a fae had rubbed off on him, and now it was in his nature to conceal facts when making deals or arrangements with other human beings. Bram was inflicted with his own maladies, and I doubted he was aware of all of them.

But the truth about Hirythe's past notwithstanding, the Netherdowns had a different weight to it now than even when we had entered hours before. The world held less color. Someone had wrung it out like a wet rag.

As my thoughts collected, I realized I sat in an area of the Netherdowns I had not been before. There was an unmistakable sound, described to me by my father and authors.

"Bram," I gasped between breaths. "Did we run through the wood?"

He nodded, appearing weak after his confrontation with Jeremy.

In front of me, a grassy knoll abruptly ended in a cliff. I crawled to the edge, and the ocean spread before my eyes. Its beauty crushed me. The moonlight glistened off the water like a kiss. Below me, white-capped waves crashed on a beach interrupted by jagged boulders coated in algae, seaweed, and lichen. The water seemed endless. Terrifying, beautiful. In a very odd way, it reminded me of Olivia. I looked back at Bram. An ocean made in his memory that had the aura of his late wife. Given how she died, it was only a fitting tribute.

My father had once promised to take me to the sea. I ached to see what it was like in the real world, without its color drained, outside of memory and dream.

"Something's wrong," Bram called. "Look at the sky."

I did. The Netherdowns sky was usually clouded over in a parchment texture, but now I saw that parchment tear gaping holes—holes through which no light was visible at all.

"What is it?" I asked. He rose, shakily, to his feet.

"The protections we built into the Netherdowns against outside magic must be breaking," he said. "Something has come in."

My mouth went dry.

"Or someone?" I asked.

He nodded, slack-jawed. He didn't need to say Edward's name. I understood. The flash of light in the wood, the ripple of energy. Edward was here now, and on his back rode a powerful malicious magic.

"We have to find him," I said. "There must be some way of ridding him of the Dúil."

"A Dúil that feasts on the reaching ambition of others. Now, it arrives in a land created of memory in a desperate attempt to protect the last of a dying breed—and in that world is a fae trying to become more human, a man bent on revenge for his brother's life, and an aristocrat who wants nothing more than to marry a version of you since outgrown."

He shook his head.

"We've all built our lives on borrowed possibilities. Edward has unknowingly brought a wolf to the flock, and once it's done eating, I'm not sure there's anything we can do. Hirythe's fae magic is powerful," he swallowed, "—as are our desires. But the Dúil is leeching that energy from us now. I was such a fool to think I could make something like this and keep it hidden forever."

I bit my lip. Bram looked ragged and pathetic. An expression of defeat painted his features. Perhaps it was my upbringing, always fighting for what was mine, or perhaps he understood something that I did not. But his surrender was intolerable. There was too much at stake. I still had amends to make, and there had to be a way.

"Come now, Bram," I said, grabbing him by both shoulders and peering into his downtrodden face. His eyes glanced furtively up at mine, all but extinguished of their former exuberance. "You've forgotten yourself. This Dúil fears you. It knows you. It called you the Meddler in my dreams."

His tired brows perked up, betraying his interest.

"You're the man who civilized a fae, who traveled far and wide to understand magic. This is a puzzle, that's all, and your mind is capable of the task. Jeremy may deserve to be undone in here. Hirythe may deserve to be undone. Hell, you and I may deserve it, but Edward does not, and his mother certainly does not. There must be a way to save them, and you can figure it out."

He shrugged.

"I need Hirythe—"

"No. You don't." I said, shaking him. "Edward and Charlotte need you. You can do it. I believe in you."

Baffled and awestruck, he stared at me. The honey of his eyes, the same honey that had attracted me to him that night we met, regained its color. My words were sincere. For all of Bram's faults, I needed his proficiency for solving magical problems.

For a moment, the corners of his mouth turned upward, and he stood a little taller.

"Ow!" he said, scooting away and grasping his hand.

"What is it?" I asked.

"It's nothing." He shook his hand up and down to ease whatever pained him. "Of course, you're right. Edward and Charlotte deserve to go home. This is not their fight. We will have to act quickly."

"Would it help if you had a blackboard?" I asked. He let out a small laugh, and I knew he was committed, the same tenacious energy coming back into his words.

"And, if we're fortunate, we can yet preserve the fae."

I bit my lip. It was hard to consider wasting energy to save Hirythe at present. The truth of his past still stung afresh, and I had not weighed out how my heart sat on the issue.

"What can you tell me about Edward?" he asked. "How is the magic working on him?"

"Since you were imprisoned, he has slowly crumbled into a wretched state. I thought he had enchanted me, so I closed myself off to him. I've been staying with Mrs. Crow. Throughout your trial, he was in and out of Dawnhurst, looking for his mother. The day of the assizes, he took me to a forest, and he had undeniably changed. Since then, I've discovered his city lodging in shambles and Edward himself experiencing a terrible fit as I used to experience when the Dúil and Sraith were in me.

"He's seeing manifestations in his dreams, just as I did. With me, the fog creature came as my father. For him... Well, it appears as me."

I looked down, a little embarrassed to divulge this bit of information.

"And you're sure he's telling you the truth?" Bram asked.

I stopped.

"He was having an episode."

"Did you see the episode?"

"I saw the aftermath."

Bram stared at me.

"Please, Luella, I know this is hard. I need you to think more like a logician. Are you sure?"

I shook my head. I wasn't. It could be still a lie. Edward might have still brought the Dúil here on purpose, perhaps to distract Bram and Hirythe while he rescued his mother.

My finger burned beneath the ring I now wore, a ring that sat beside the one Edward had given me. I had doubted him once. My greatest regret.

"I'm not technically sure. But I believe it's true with everything I have," I said.

Bram nodded.

"Very well. And his mother?"

"As I've said, Jeremy stole your paintbrush. She entered the Netherdowns and turned into a portrait. I'm not sure if Jeremy used the brush before or after they entered."

"But why would Jeremy want to bring her inside the Netherdowns in the first place?"

"Perhaps it was the easiest way to deal with her while Gerald took the diary," I said with an exasperated shrug of the shoulders.

"Gerald? He hypnotized Gerald?" Bram's hands balled into fists.

"Yes. But Gerald is well now."

"Why a painting?" Bram asked, turning to study the sea. I searched for an answer.

"Charlotte once told me that what she feared above all else was to disappear from the world without a trace, without a portrait or a legacy."

"But you're saying she is a portrait. Why would her greatest fear of not having a portrait transform her into a portrait?"

He brought up a fair point.

"Could she have been lying to you?" Bram asked.

"Why do you suspect everyone is lying to me?" I replied.

"Well, if not lying, then hiding something embarrassing or that she didn't want you to know."

I threw up my hands.

"It's possible. Is it necessary to know in order to save her?"

"It might be," he said, turning back to the wood. His eyes narrowed as he calculated possibilities. "Right. Well, let's start with Edward. He's possessed with malicious ambition, and from the sounds of it, the Dúil has a very firm grasp on him. Can he discern which Luella is the real one?"

I wrung my hands. The waves crashed below. The smell of the brine reached us on the cliff.

"He's losing the ability quickly." It was an honest, painful answer.

"Then we will need to sever the magic from him."

I bristled.

"I don't want to hurt him," I insisted. Bram eyed me dubiously.

"You may not have a choice. It will be difficult to understand how to sever the bond between him and his ambition unless we know what he wants."

"He wants to save his mother," I said.

"That might be true, if the Dúil attached to him after his mother disappeared. Did it?"

I furrowed my brows. Edward said he'd started to have disconcerting dreams just before Christmas.

"No."

"Well, we can only assume that it left you and attached to him. It would only leave you when it grew tired of what you were longing after and found his desires more hopelessly fixed."

I shut my eyes tightly. I had infected him. It was me. My fault. Hirythe had first told me I was free of the magic after I ate the Silver Currant. Charlotte hadn't disappeared yet—she was waiting for me when I got back. How long had I been free before he told me?

"She was still there."

"Then there must be something else that Edward wants. Something he wants but couldn't hope to have. His father back?"

The answer was plain as the sound of the waves below me. I had infected him two times over.

"Heavens above. It's me," I said, fighting tears that wormed their way up from my chest. "He wants me."

Bram grew quiet, either because he was concentrating or because he wanted to respect my fresh, aching discovery. When the Dúil infected me, I'd wanted to be Dawnhurst's top writer, be married to Edward, and spend all my time with Bram. That was exactly the type of hopeless, impossible desire Bram referred to as satisfying to the Dúil.

When I finally reached my breaking point and committed to Edward at the risk of Bram's life, the Dúil had had enough of me and transferred. But if I had just abandoned that which stood in the way of my union with Edward, why did the creature find his ambition so appealing?

"That might explain why you appear in his dreams," Bram suggested gently. "But it complicates how you will sever the tie between him and the magic."

"Complicates it?" I asked in a shaky voice.

"Well, you may need to convince him to fall out of love with you."

I laughed aloud.

"After everything, that shouldn't be so hard."

"Speaking as a man who has had his heart broken before, it may not be as easy as you suspect."

I kicked my foot through the dirt, begrudgingly.

"It won't be pleasant, but I think I can manage it if I can only sit down with him. But even if I sever the tie between him and the monster, it's already here. That will let us save Edward, but hardly the Netherdowns."

"I may have an idea for that," Bram replied.

"At any rate, first I will need to find him," I said.

"I don't think that will be too difficult."

"Why not?"

"The Dúil will keep him close. Why part with your favorite food? If we can find the Dúil, we can find Lord Thomas."

I crossed my arms. Being so close to the water exposed me to cold ocean breezes.

"And how do we find the Dúil?"

"Oh," Bram said casually, "just follow the source of the fire."

He pointed at the wood, and on the horizon, I could see the trees catching fire, growing with the peculiar black, white, and gray flame.

"The wood!" I cried.

"Apparently, the Dúil has already started to eat the Netherdowns," said Bram slowly.

The fire burned, slow but steady. Without a second thought, Bram started walking toward it. I followed in his trail, wondering, in a small corner of my mind, where I might have been in that moment if I had decided to simply marry Byron Livingston.

29

JEREMY EVANS

We walked along the cliff between the forest and the sea and soon discovered a small meandering path. This part of the Netherdowns had not suffered the same destruction as the terrain closer to the town. The eclectic variety of plant life was inspiring even as it paled in color. Beside sea grass and gorse grew tropical plants I did not recognize.

The Netherdowns was a horticulturist's dream.

As we walked along, my feet hurt. I wished I'd had the foresight to don a more comfortable pair of boots.

"How will I distract the Dúil long enough to speak with Edward?" I asked.

"You may not find that possible."

"Why not?"

"I don't know if the Dúil is capable of distraction. The trouble with ambition is that it narrows your view until you see the world as though through a pinprick in a sheet of paper. You may point the paper at something else, but don't think you can dangle something shiny just out of view to gain its attention."

Bram often spoke in these metaphors when referring to magic, and I was never sure just how much of them I should discard as flowery language. For all I knew, I might take a piece of paper, prick it with a pin, and somehow control the Dúil the same way his cheesecloth absorbed whatever Jeremy shot at him earlier.

After a half hour of walking, we neared the fire. Slow-moving smoke billowed into the air. As with everything in Bram's memory world, the fire wasn't quite right. The flames licked at the sky with the wrong dance steps.

Bram stumbled to a stop to take it in, a weight settling back onto his shoulders. These weren't just trees, not just a wood. Inside it were wild memories, dark memories, but Bram's memories nonetheless.

I put a hand on his shoulder.

"It's all ablaze. I made this place to protect my memories. Now, look what's become of them."

"Are you aware of what's burning?" I asked.

He shook his head.

"That's the worst part of losing your memory. You can't even mourn what's gone."

"But the wood was full of things you couldn't readily remember, or didn't want to. Wasn't it?"

He squeezed my hand and pushed it from his shoulder.

"Yes. It was full of the most dreadful, painful memories. Those strong enough to make them all but unbearable. The most important memories of all."

From the fire line, I noticed movement. A creature emerged, one of the monsters that Hirythe's soldiers fought against. This one looked distantly familiar. I may have seen it, or a similar creature, at the first battle I'd seen in the Netherdowns: a large stag with antlers that moved like tentacles.

As it emerged from the wood, it looked in our direction. Its hide shimmered with the same shifting black and white patterns as the other creatures I'd seen in the Netherdowns. Bram and I met its stare, and I couldn't resist the notion that it was calling to us, asking to be let out of the wood. Bram held it prisoner. Was it better to let it perish or let it out?

Bram walked toward it, slowly at first, then at a run.

"Wait!" he called, but as he neared, the creature retreated, hesitantly, back into the wood. "No! Wait! Please!"

"Bram! Don't go near the fire!" I yelled after him and followed. The creature had practically retreated into the flames, and Bram wasn't slowing down. My blistered feet protested as I kicked the ground. I was still a way's off when he stopped, close to the fire, and fell on his knees. He gripped the dirt and grass beside him.

The sight would make its way into my own wood, the unpleasant and painful view of a man whose life's work crashed around him with self-destructive menace.

Then another creature sprinted out of the wood. But it wasn't a stag.

Jeremy tackled Bram to the ground before he could get back to his feet. In the critic's hand was a knife—the knife I'd just seen in Hirythe's second examination, a knife made forged from fear.

"Bram!" I rushed forward, but they tussled dangerously. *Fear.* Fear had paralyzed Charlotte, turned her into a portrait. If Jeremy cut Bram with that knife...

They struggled with the same ferocity I'd seen in Hirythe's soldiers. Jeremy tried to work his arm free to slash and stab, but Bram had one hand clutched on either of his wrists, preventing him. I arrived and started beating my fists against Jeremy.

"Get off of him! Let him go!"

Jeremy struck out with his foot and caught me right behind the knees. I fell to the ground.

I gasped. The ground expelled the air from my lungs, but I kicked a foot of my own at him in retaliation, hard.

Jeremy twisted, and my foot connected with Bram's stomach.

"Bram!" I called, hoarsely. He grunted and rolled in pain. His grip slackened, giving Jeremy an open opportunity to attack with his knife. I clawed forward, lunging from my spot on the ground, and caught his arm just before he brought it down on Bram's body.

I wasn't strong enough to stop the strike altogether, but I redirected it to the dirt. Jeremy snarled and slapped my face with the back of his hand. The shock of it set me reeling, and I tasted blood on my lip.

I looked back at Jeremy through the strands of my raven hair. There was an evil gleam in his eye. But when he saw me bleeding on the ground like that, something tugged at the mania, a shred of humanity struggling for air. I pulled on the loose thread.

"You told me your job was to help me become a better writer."

He ignored me, turning back to Bram, who gasped for breath on the ground beside him, and raised the sinister knife into the air.

"No!" I screamed.

He plunged the knife down into Bram's back. My vision blurred, but Bram writhed on the ground, shouting in agony.

"What have you done?" I cried.

He drew the knife free, painted with Bram's blood and backed away. Jeremy's face was awash, as though he asked himself the same question. He stumbled backward, eyes wide.

I crawled to Bram and turned him over. His torso heaved in pain, and his eyes flickered about as if possessed.

My limbs moved so slowly. The world around me fell away in muddy pieces. The judge was pronouncing Bram's sentence all over again. I thought I could rescue him by bringing him here. My eyes blurred with hot, tenacious tears. I shook them free.

My hands clumsily grasped at his shirt, inching to the wound. How do you heal a stab wound? Pathetically, I tried to rip pieces of fabric from my skirts. I could try to use them as bandages. But my arms were so weak, so disconnected from my torso.

The knife. If I could get the knife, I could cut strips free and perhaps then...

"Give me the knife," I shouted. Jeremy took another step backward. I rose, ready to spit venom from my glare. "Jeremy, the knife."

"I can't give it to you," he said. There was genuine fear in his expression. After so much time pursuing Bram to exact vengeance, I didn't know if he'd ever considered how terrible it would be to succeed.

"Jeremy, he's dying!"

"He must. He's walked free for too long."

"I need him!" I yelled, the shout raking my throat raw.

"You don't. He's only convinced you that you do."

I lunged at him, not caring that he held a dangerous weapon, a weapon that gleamed with magical toxin. My fingers found his face and scraped, peeling skin beneath my fingernails. He cried out with a yelp, but grabbed my wrist forcefully right after and threw me to the ground.

I sobbed and crawled back to Bram. The blood spread over his shirt so quickly. He moaned and whimpered weakly. I struggled again to rip a length from my shirt before giving it up and removing it altogether, pressing it awkwardly in a clump against the bleeding gash in Bram's back. It was difficult to apply any pressure; he kept spasming beneath me.

"Stay with me, Bram. *Please!* Please stay with me."

If I couldn't harm Jeremy, I wished he would just leave. He was an intruder on this delicate vulnerability. He violated the smokey air.

"Luella," Jeremy said. I ignored him. "Luella."

He walked forward and tried to jerk my hands free of the wound, to stop any progress I might make at stemming the damage.

When he had both my wrists again, he pulled me toward him.

"Luella," he said, "we are all of us slaves to different masters. This is the only justice my brother will ever have."

"And what justice will I have?"

That was not my voice.

I blinked up, looking past Jeremy, and saw a figure who had emerged as if from the air. Olivia Lowhouse, dressed in full armor save her mirrored mask, grasped Jeremy by the scruff of the neck and pulled him from me.

His face went white. He whirled on the voice of the woman he'd taken overboard years ago and raised the knife in desperate self-defense. Perhaps once he might have overpowered her, but this was a world of Bram's memory. She seized his wrist and turned it backward, churning the bones and cartilage in an uncomfortable direction. The knife fell to the ground. I seized it instantly.

"Olivia," he sputtered.

"Yes. Olivia Lowhouse. You remember my face well. Do you remember that night on the boat, Jeremy? Do you remember how helpless you made me feel? Were my cries in the dark music to your pernicious little ears?"

His bottom jaw cranked fruitlessly, silently, but the horror betrayed every sentiment hidden in his soul.

"I wasn't well," he sputtered. "I was grieving. I had lost my brother."

"Then let us end your grief by reunion."

She hoisted him up with inhuman strength. Jeremy shrieked as she dragged him to the cliff's edge.

"They must be stopped," he screamed. "Luella! Hear me! Bram and Hirythe must meet justice!"

My eyes shot wide as Olivia hurled him off the edge. I didn't get up from where I knelt, cutting strips from my shirt to make bandages. But the shrieks faded quickly and stopped abruptly.

I didn't need to peer over the cliff's edge to conjure the image of the jagged rocks pocketed with sand bars and buffeting waves far below. I had eyed them warily for the past hour.

I'd never watched a man die before, let alone watched someone kill another human being. I expected to feel anguish or nightmarish adrenaline. I expected pangs of regret to course through me. But when Jeremy Evans went over the cliff I was... indifferent. Neither here nor there.

Olivia rushed back to my side.

"These won't help." She surveyed the patchwork strips of cloth I'd cut apart.

"I have to stop the bleeding."

"The blood is the least of our worries. Fear is racing through his veins. I sensed it enter him. It's what drew me from the wood."

"Drew you? How?"

"All of us have a safe place to go when we feel afraid, a sacred memory."

She cradled Bram in her arms.

"I'm here, my darling," she whispered to him, rocking him back and forth. The sky above me rumbled, threatening to storm. Lightning struck out across the sea. The fire raged, consuming more of the wood. The mixture of electricity and smoke in the air made breathing uncomfortable and my eyes burn.

But more immediately still, sections of the cliffs near to where we sat crumbled.

The Netherdowns was being torn apart. Bram's memory could only take so much.

"I'm here, my darling," she repeated. "Nothing can take me from you."

Bram looked up at her with clouded eyes, but she placed a hand on his cheek and nodded.

"Olivia?" he asked. He heaved deeply. "It's bad, isn't it?"

She nodded calmly.

"Hold on a little longer, my love."

"Is Hirythe safe?" Bram sputtered. "Have you seen him?"

She looked at me for the answer, but I shook my head.

"It will depend on how he faces the examination," she said.

"I know that," Bram cried. "Has he already faced it? Did he survive?"

"It's not about surviving," she said. She turned her face to me again. "Hirythe must believe he can withstand the pains of humanity. As a wild fae, his past doesn't haunt him. It's so very human to live with regret. Hirythe is learning his limits."

Bram's teeth clattered together as though he were in a snowdrift.

"You can't forgive me," Bram said, tears streaking from his cheeks. His hands clutched Olivia's wrists furiously. "You'll leave. You'll hide from me again."

I put a hand through his hair.

"Bram, you're shaking," I said, trying to calm him.

"He will continue to shake. It's the fear. Combined with the Netherdowns' destruction, all of Bram's fears are coming true. Hirythe may be lost. His memory of me may burn. And despite his best efforts, you may suffer the same fate. This fear will manifest differently as they are confirmed or rebuffed. Resentment, hatred, relief, exhaustion. It remains to be seen. For now, he must survive the paralysis."

The sound of the burning wood grew louder, popping, cracking, crunching as though the fire chewed a piece of crusty bread.

"What can we do?" I asked.

"I'll stay with him, but you're running out of time. Go to the beach below. I think you'll find them there."

"Will he live?" I asked.

"Perhaps not."

My mind raced. Even if I managed to free Edward from the Dúil, what about his mother?

Olivia put a hand on my shoulder.

"You can't save everyone," she said. "To live with regret is so very human, and that is no accidental magic." She nodded at the ring on my finger, the ring that had already kept my mind from wandering dangerous avenues even in the brief time I wore it. "Hurry. There is nothing you can do here," she whispered. "If Hirythe makes it through, he will find us and prolong Bram's life the best he can. Go."

I stood awkwardly and backed away, leaving Bram struggling for life in the arms of his late wife's memory. It hurt like a dagger in my own gut, but as my tired legs bound forward, searching for a passable trail down the cliffs and to the sand, I tried my very best to believe I wasn't leaving him alone.

30

SAND AND STORIES

Tears slipped numbly down my face. I stumbled along the cliff's edge for nearly a mile before I found a passible, shallow slope to the sand below. I put one foot in front of the other, concentrating on solitary movements and my aim, chasing out the mental painting of Bram suffering in a field above.

I came to the Netherdowns to save Edward and Charlotte. I knew there was a risk to Bram and Hirythe, but I'd hoped... Even if I saved Edward, Charlotte's portrait still lay under a pile of rubble in the town. There was no telling what damage it had already suffered.

Olivia's words urged me on.

I couldn't save everyone. The implication was that I might save someone.

I tripped over wiry grasses poking through the hillside and fell down to the sand below. The course grit worked its way under my corset. That's right. I had torn my shirt free to bandage Bram's wound. I must have looked a right mess, stained with splotches of blood in a state of undress.

I shut my eyes tight, trying to let the sound of the buffeting waves drown out the images of Bram's wound that sweltered in my memory.

Edward. I had to find Edward.

When I looked up from the spot on the beach where I lay, I found eroding footprints in the sand heading down the beach. Two sets of footprints. One of them looked like my own. They stretched just along the bottom of the slope I'd traversed.

I placed my foot in gently, to be sure. It was a perfect fit. My gaze traced them as they faded into the distance. Edward and the Dúil.

How had the Dúil caused the forest fire if it still walked with Edward on the beach? Did its power transcend place and time while in such a magical arena? In my dreams, it had done whatever it pleased with my consciousness. The Netherdowns, I supposed, were not unlike a dreamscape.

I trudged on after the footsteps. For some time, I tried to match the Dúil's gait, putting my foot in each of the prints before me, but it didn't take me long to tire of the game.

After half a mile, there was no sign of the trail's end, and a sickening thought occurred. If I continued this way, might I not encounter whatever remained of Jeremy Evans on the sand? The thought sickened me, but I had no choice but to continue. I gained the second half of a mile much more slowly than the first, and sure enough, before long, I came across Jeremy's body on the sand, broken and twisted and—

—still moving.

"Jeremy?" I asked. In response, a gut-wrenching groan grumbled from his underbelly. His face lay crooked, halfway sunk into the sand, his arms and legs protruded at funny angles, and his pant leg was beginning to wet as the tide came in.

I put a hand to my mouth to keep from retching and turned away, but the sight of him was just as vivid with my eyes closed as it was looking directly at him.

What was there to do in such a situation?

He appeared to me now as no threat to Bram or Hirythe, despite the damage he'd already done.

"Winthrop." A ragged and weathered croak escaped his mouth as an unmistakable cry for help. And despite the hatred that had burned in me less than an hour before, my legs brought me to him of their own accord.

"Jeremy, can you hear me?"

He wheezed in response, his eyes darting like a trapped fox. The look in his eyes was so similar to the look in Bram's eyes just above on the cliff.

I looked about, pathetically, searching for something to bandage. I didn't have my blouse, but I had skirts I might rip still. But mended sails can't salvage a shipwreck.

"Winthrop," his voice scraped out again, "please."

"I don't know what to do." My voice came out in an exasperated panic. My understanding of cause and effect faltered, his death inexplicably attaching to my guilt. I couldn't save him, and not long before I would have pushed him off the cliff. Did that not make me liable?

"Please," he croaked again. I stood, the panic cresting. My hands shook. There was nothing to do for him, other than pray perhaps, and his accusing eyes weighed on me like millstones.

Just as the weight on my shoulders became too heavy a bear, I felt a hand on them.

I whirled around.

"Leave him to me," said Hirythe, calm and composed as a clear morning.

He walked past me, and I froze, unsure if he intended to end Jeremy's misery or use some type of magic to make him whole. He knelt and started to cover Jeremy's body with sand.

For a long moment, the only sounds were the scrape of his hands in the sand, the buffeting waves, the occasional crack of thunder, and Jeremy's wheezing, now accelerated that he was so close to one of his sworn enemies.

"What happened in the forest, Hirythe?" I asked. He didn't look at me, only continued his digging.

"I'm sorry you had to see them," he replied. "How can you even look at me without disgust?"

"Bram is above," I said, choosing to focus on more pressing matters, "with Olivia. Jeremy stabbed him with the knife I saw in you examination. He needs you."

Hirythe did not hurry his task.

"This is more important."

"More important? Bram is your friend. He's dying."

"There are some things worse than death," he replied. The words chilled me through my thin clothing. Bram had said the same of Hirythe once. "We've been spending so many years hiding from Jeremy. We were afraid of what he might do to us, but more importantly, we were afraid to face what we'd done to him."

He had finished digging around Jeremy's legs. They sunk into the sand in trenches the fae built. He leveled the sand over them to create a smooth flat surface. One might not even think his legs were beneath at all.

"Did you kill his brother, after all?"

"Ned. His name was Ned." Jeremy seethed hotly through clenched teeth, but Hirythe continued as if there had been no interruption.

"Bram met Jeremy at an exposition of ancient volumes of peculiar history, Bram there for practical research, Jeremy there for research of a more scholarly nature. After a discussion about a volume on fae history, Bram invited him for a drink. Jeremy thought the book was fiction. Bram challenged him and challenged and challenged him until Jeremy admitted there was no way to disprove everything in the book.

"Soon, Jeremy joined Bram, Olivia, and myself for weekly dinners, where we speculated on the possible magical properties of trinkets available at antique auctions. Jeremy was very adept at ferreting out fakes, but back then only I was proficient at identifying what had been touched by real magic. Bram learned soon enough, then Jeremy, but even when they learned to identify the trace of magic, they could not push the items' boundaries, probe and experiment to understand it more."

Hirythe had dug out a good portion of sand from beneath Jeremy's torso, and after Jeremy sank into it, he leveled the sand over. Jeremy appeared to be vanishing slowly beneath the earth.

"We tired of auctions quickly, as Bram used his new skills to identify magical trails that led us to items not yet discovered. At first, these expeditions didn't take us far, only around England, Scotland, and Ireland. But we became more bold, venturing out through France, south through Italy, even as far as Egypt, and as far north as Russia. We found magic, and while the others contented themselves on the acquisition, soon Bram wanted more. If these trinkets influenced high magic, he was curious to see what effect they would have on human subjects. At first, I was against it, but I couldn't deny that the concept piqued my curiosity. If conducted in the correct way, we might learn insights my kind had only ever dreamed of knowing.

"But then Bram and Olivia did something foolish. We'd found a quill in an Italian hillside, likely of Roman origin. It was endowed with the magic you know as Sraith."

"She wrote with it," I said.

Jeremy's arms were buried now, and though he couldn't turn his neck from its painful, distorted position, he glared at the fae.

"The nature of the group changed. While in Italy, Bram had put our ideas in the ear of a wealthy benefactor, someone who might help fund our journeys."

"Roberto," I recalled, the man the Dawnhurst Police failed to identify after the reported ghostly attack.

"We had our eyes set on the north. But after Olivia's symptoms manifested, Bram became distracted, and that frustrated Jeremy, who felt that the addition of an investor brought a new legitimacy to what we were doing. As Bram searched more desperately for a solution to Olivia's new condition, he left preparations for our journey to the Nordic countries lapse to Jeremy and myself.

"But Jeremy had a new companion. He insisted his younger brother, Ned, come along on this voyage, if only to pick up some of the more ordinary jobs that Bram now neglected. For whatever reason, Ned stuck to me like a moth to flame. Jeremy had explained in minor detail the nature of our activities, but evidently not the specifics. Ned pestered me relentlessly for stories of our travels and findings. He was so trusting, so ready to believe magic was real."

Hirythe stopped digging. Jeremy was buried from neck to toe, only his head protruding now from the sand. Hirythe scooped large piles of sand from around him, moist from the rising tide. Soon, the waves might reach Jeremy. The fae started molding the sand into long, blocky shapes on top of Jeremy's body.

"Bram's ideas about testing magic on humans ate at me. He and Olivia had been foolish, but surely I could be more careful in my attempts. It didn't take long for me to elaborate on our stories with Ned, pose difficult questions to him about reality, and show him some of the trinkets we'd discovered. I did what my kind has done for over a thousand years. I toyed with him.

"By the time we arrived in the north, although I'd prevented him from developing any similar condition to what ailed Olivia, Ned was ravenous for magic. We unearthed the entrance to a hollow hill, and inside he behaved like a child in a confectioners. Bram had identified the location as the resting place of an ambitious Jarl, and he thought that the source of his ambition rested in an old sword that should be buried with him.

"There was no sword, but Ned found a flute, and before any of us managed to stop him, he set to playing the damned thing. I think the artifact called to him. Though he was not a musician, a haunting, evil melody came from the old flute, and at once I knew where the Jarl had found his ambition. A Dúil burst from the music, formless as a vapor, and trapped Ned. His eyes changed instantly. He let it inside of him, and the ambition took his faculties captive. Hungry for more magic at an intensity his body could not withstand. He took hold of a ceremonial axe and attacked us.

"While the others were concerned for their physical safety, I had heard about the power in Dúils, and I worried it might try to jump from Ned to one of the rest of our party. I tried to sing an old fae tune to ward it off, but by then Jeremy had become hysterical. He ran up to his brother as if to shake him free of the power that held him. But as they scuffled, Ned slipped. He fell off a slab of stone and cracked his head sharply on the rock below. He died in an instant.

"I knew the Dúil would search for another host, and we ran, dragging Jeremy behind us. I sealed the door in our wake to trap the magic from chasing us."

At this point in Hirythe's story, Jeremy's breathing slowed, exhausted and weak. The fae had formed a crude sand sculpture of a person atop Jeremy's buried body. He stood and turned to me.

"By now, you know that I have killed humans before. Please understand, with Ned it was different. I should have recognized what was happening to him. I've been running from that memory for over seven years."

I could predict the rest of the story.

"Jeremy snapped. He killed Olivia on the boat ride back to England," I said.

Hirythe nodded.

"After the initial shock wore off, we spoke with him at length. He hid his hatred well. Only Olivia suspected something was wrong before it was too late."

My brows knit in understanding.

"Jeremy used the song his brother played to awaken the Dúil back in England," I said.

"He didn't know how fickle ambition can be, and what type of hunger the Dúil savors most. When Roberto died, it tired of Jeremy."

"And jumped to Edward," I concluded. My mind raced. "But Edward didn't have any unusual or unattainable ambition. He'd given up a life of greater wealth to content himself as a constable."

"So it jumped to you. Upon hearing his claim that he saw a ghost, the Dúil recognized a hunger in you, a hunger that would take a life-time to satisfy. You wanted to honor your late father through profes-sional accomplishment, an impossible tool for such a task," Hirythe said, shaking his head. "When Bram saw you at the fair, the magic called to him, but he failed to recognize the nature of the attraction. By the time he recognized you had a problem, the Dúil hid safely behind your misunderstanding of cause and effect, acting as a catalyst to speed your dependency."

I leaned against a weathered log worn by sand and waves.

"The Dúil jumped back to Edward," I muttered, "when he believed he could no longer compete for my love, after we were engaged. What's more pitiful than the longings of a husband who believes he plays second violin in his wife's heart?"

"Then, the magic in the song I taught you identified the Dúil in your fiancé."

"And I shut myself off to him." I shuddered. Exactly when Edward needed me the most, when my love would have been its most powerful to his wellbeing, I lost faith.

"I'm sorry, Luella. It's my fault that you were ever infected. If I had understood—if I had never worked up tales in a mind so impression-able as Ned's or infected him with magic like a mouse in a laboratory, he would have never played that flute. He'd still be alive. Jeremy would have never awakened the Dúil."

"And I'd be complacently married to Byron Livingston by now..."

Bittersweet feelings swelled in my breast. My skin prickled from the cold blowing off of the sea. The waves inched closer, and Hirythe knelt beside his enemy.

"I'm sorry," he whispered.

Tears leaked from Jeremy's eyes. He closed them, squinting. The fae turned to me again, but he spoke loudly enough for us both to hear him. "What price can be paid for another's life? There is no price. There is no balance. The effects are exponential, but when the guilty party remains, and perseveres in remorse, his wasted life only adds to the misery. I hid from my deeds for so long. Hundreds of years in some cases. Those are years wasted. I need to live for Ned, for the good he would have done. As do you, Jeremy."

The next wave lapped over the sand sculpture foot Hirythe had made. The rolling water pulled away, and I doubted my own eyes. This was a new magic altogether. I thought the sculpted foot looked a little more realistic.

Another wave came, and I was sure of it now. The foot took on a more human characteristic. The grains of sand becoming pores of skin.

"You're not here to end Jeremy's misery," I said in disbelief.

"Not by ending his life," Hirythe replied. "He may not forgive me for what I've done. That is his choice and his right. But I have enough souls waiting in the wood. I will find a way to live more for those who have departed."

I shook my head and stood. As beautiful and transfixing as the sand's transformation was, Edward and the Dúil waited.

"Hirythe, what does it matter if the Netherdowns are still destroyed with all of us inside?"

"We will leave," he replied frankly. I stared.

"And just leave Bram's memories behind to be devoured?"

"Outside, we can collapse the magic of the Netherdowns, the same way I sealed Ned's Dúil in the hill. It will live on in Bram's memory, and he won't be the same, but I'd rather have half of Bram and save you and Jeremy than risk the alternative."

"What about Edward and his mother?"

Hirythe grimaced.

"If the Dúil still has Edward in its grasp, I'm afraid there's not much I can do."

I stalked over to him.

"Can't you use some of your magic to fight it for me?"

"My recent trials have left me all but exhausted. It will take time for me to replenish my abilities. But even at my full strength... You don't understand, Luella. The fae were decimated by Dúils summoned by man. If there is a predator for fae magic, this is it. It's magic's cruel joke against us. We preyed on human ambition through cunning deals and bargains. In turn, the monster we used to torment them bent back to destroy us."

"How am I supposed to stop it, then?" I asked. "Bram told me I had to sever its connection, make him fall out of love with me."

"That is a type of magic, I'm afraid, I'm only beginning to understand." He looked back down at Jeremy. "There are remedies for pride and ambition, but they don't lie in fae magic. They're found in the depths of humanity."

A wave crept over my own foot now, soaking through my shoe and stocking. I backed up instinctively. The smoke of the fire above me cast the whole beach in an eery light. The footsteps in the sand marched onward.

"Go, Luella. The fire is only going to grow more quickly, feeding the Dúil's power."

I folded my arms against the cold, wishing I had Edward's heavy coat.

"When you're done with Jeremy, Bram needs you above," I said.

I trudged through the sand, feeling small and alone. I had no sister, no friend, no father, nor fae. Only the magic of humanity could free Edward now.

Whatever the ruddy hell that meant.

31

THE ONYX DOOR

The beach became rockier, more hostile the deeper I probed. Smoke in the air multiplied just as Hirythe had warned. The fire must have been growing at an alarming rate, eating the magic that held the land together.

The tracks stopped when the sand did, but they had pointed directly into the rocky outcropping, and there was no other direction they could have led. Soon, the rocks grew slimy with algae, and sharp lichen tore at the wet leather of my shoes. As smoke blocked out the moon, a blanket of fog rolled in from the ocean. I hunched over to use my hands as tools to help navigate the maze of slick stone, and finally, ahead of me, I saw a clearing. A small, sandy cove appeared below, and gratefully, I descended into it. In the sand, waves had licked the pair of tracks clean, leaving only indistinct and vague footprints. They did not lead in a straight path as they had before. It was as though someone had paced the cove in endless debate. The half-eroded imprints were everywhere.

I closed in on where they were most concentrated and stopped.

There was something eerily familiar about where I stood, and it chilled me through. I looked around at the rocks and cliffs imposing around me, the fog, and the impending waves...

It was a scene taken directly from my dreams with the Dúil. The only thing missing was the onyx door carved into the stone—

My heart skipped.

It was there. The door from my dreams, the door the Dúil had tried so ardently to convince me to open. Every night I had this dream. I would stand in this very spot and debate with the Dúil as it masqueraded as my father. As we debated, the tides washed in and the fog thickened until I drowned or opened the door.

When I'd opened it then, the Dúil did not follow me. It told me it couldn't follow me.

But now, as plain as the water behind me, I saw the vague impression of footprints leading to that door, and no footprints coming back.

I hung my head. I'd told Edward many times about this door after I woke up from my fits. Judging by the prints all over the sand, he had similar deliberations with the Dúil before finally going forward.

In my dreams, that door led to an iteration of Bram's yurt from the carnival. Would it be the same in the Netherdowns? Or would it lead to some location of significance for Edward, or Bram, or even Hirythe?

There was no telling, but I refused to deliberate or fear my imagination. Edward was behind that door, and there was no waking from the Netherdowns. I needed to get him out.

I marched up, gripped its heavy handle, and swung it open.

The cold of the beach instantly gave way to the warmth and familiarity of Bram's yurt. It was just as I remembered it from my dream. The door swung closed behind me, and across the eclectically furnished tent was another door, one I'd never opened before.

Edward stood at the writing desk, his back to me. Across from him, sitting on Bram's bed as I had done many times, was an image I had only ever before seen in a looking glass.

It was me. At least, it was a version of me, slightly more beautiful, better dressed, and laced in an intangible aura of allure.

When the Dúil saw me, its eyes narrowed, and it stood, crossing to Edward.

"Edward, I'm frightened," it said as it grabbed his arm affectionately. "It's—it's me."

Edward turned around and took me in. He didn't seem surprised.

"Oh," he said.

"Hello, Edward," I replied. "You made it into the Netherdowns."

His gazed swept up and down my body, and I was embarrassed to remember that I'd discarded my blouse for bandages. I was still covered in blood as well, though some of it had faded from my sojourn through the slick rocks between the waves.

Edward moved to the bed and pulled a blanket free to cover me.

"What are you doing, Edward?" the Dúil asked.

"She's freezing," he replied.

"Edward, it's not a she at all. That is a monster." The Dúil drew Edward's hand backward, away from me.

Edward peered at me, his face slack with discomfort.

"If I were the monster, why would I come dressed like this?" I asked, opening the blanket to reveal myself.

"It's trying to evoke pity from you. Edward, please, we are so close to finding your mother. Don't let the fog creature pull us off course."

My protests caught in my chest. Of all the difficulties I imagined facing to sever Edward from the magic, I didn't expect to have to prove my own identity. But I should not have been surprised. The first time it appeared as my father in a dream, I'd fallen for it. The only way I knew better was because my father had been long dead.

But if Edward could not tell in a moment that I was Luella, how would I convince him?

"Edward," I said, raising a hand. "I've come to take you home. The Netherdowns is collapsing. We have to get out."

"You see!" hissed the Dúil. "It's trying to keep you from finding your mother. Quick, we must open this next door."

I winced. The very thought of trying to manipulate Edward, or lying to him again, made me nauseous. After all, I had resolved not to do that. My half-truths had spoiled him. But what if I needed to misdirect him to save him? Surely, that could be forgiven.

Even the thought of it caused my finger to burn beneath the Ring of Regret.

"Edward, I'm not lying. I wanted to save your mother. You must understand, Bram has been stabbed," I said.

"This is Bram's yurt," he declared, "isn't it?"

"The door you came through was the same door from my dreams," I said. Honesty. It was time for honesty, though it would break his heart. But then, wasn't I trying to break his heart? "Bram lived here when the carnival was at Dawnhurst."

"You told me in Reading. But you never explained why Bram's lodgings were behind the door in your dreams." Edward said.

I clasped my hands together and nodded.

"She's trying to hurt you," the Dúil chimed in. "I've told you before. Nothing romantic ever happened between me and Bram."

I winced again. Hearing my own lies from the mouth of this monster made the ring burn. How could I fight against the very person I'd presented to Edward for months, for that was what the Dúil embodied now: the Luella I wanted Edward to see.

"Don't listen to her," the Dúil continued. "Come, let's go quickly. Your mother is just behind this next door. Let's rescue her and leave this place."

Edward stared at me sadly. I didn't know what to say, and the silence condemned me. He allowed himself to be led by the Dúil toward the next door.

"It's detailed, isn't it?" I called to him. "The room we're in. It's enough to make you wonder whether you can trust me at all. How is the room so detailed?"

He stopped and turned back to me.

"What do you mean?"

"Come," hissed the Dúil. I pressed on, daring a few steps forward.

"This room appeared in my dreams in vivid detail because I spent so much time here."

"She's trying to make you jealous. Don't believe her! I never did any such thing!" called the Dúil.

"Look." I crossed to the desk. "This is where we wrote the stories using special ink Bram prepared. It made my stories come to life. This is exactly where I sat when I was caught up in a fever dream, writing the article responsible for your father's death. A dream brought on by this creature."

I nodded angrily at the other Luella. Its eyes were fire, and I saw its face ripple like a cloud, the same way my father's face had in the stone version of the Forbury Gardens in Reading. If only Edward had been looking.

"Here," I said, crossing to Bram's bed. "I sat here, next to Bram, for many hours, reading, talking laughing. Yes, even on his bed."

Edward turned his head, bracing himself for whatever blow came next.

"Look at you," the Dúil said to him, clutching his shoulders. "She is beastly. She's a monster made of evil magic. Please, stay with me, Edward. I'm yours. I would never do the things she's accusing me of."

"I kissed him, too!" I called. "And what's worse, while you and I enjoyed our time together, when you proposed, during our engagement, all that time I was still searching for him, and no, I didn't understand my feelings. He was the only one who knew how to heal me. At least, that's what I thought, and my heart was confused, Edward."

"Stop," he said, shaking his head urgently. The Dúil's lips pursed furiously. "Just stop."

"On Christmas, after such a wonderful day with you and your mother and our friends, I snuck into the Netherdowns to speak with Bram. To check on him."

"Would you please stop?" Edward called. "If you love him, just tell me. Don't draw it out any longer."

"I don't love him," the other Luella said. "Edward, search your heart. This isn't right. I'm *here*. Your mother is here somewhere, and if we can find her, we can leave. We can be married. Everything can be as we want it to."

He put his face in his hands.

"What is true?" he cried.

It stroked his hair and cradled his face to her bosom.

"Don't let the monsters steal our happiness," the other Luella whispered. "We are so close."

It led Edward toward the door again. I knew the Dúil wanted nothing more than to open it, just as it had wanted nothing more than for me to open the first door in my dream. But I suspected another door lay beyond the one they approached now. And another after that.

That was the way of ambition. Never ending bends in the road. Countless horizons to chase.

I needed to persuade him to see the truth, to see me. And honesty was my only tool left—but it was as painful to speak as it was to hear.

"We can't be married," I cried, tears dotting my eyes. "That's the truth, Edward. We can't be. All this time I've been hiding things from you, and you don't deserve that. I wanted everything. I wanted you and Bram all at once. But that isn't love. That's the opposite."

"You can't listen to her—"

"I will listen to whatever I wish," Edward spat back to the Dúil. "You will have to trust that I can discern for myself."

"The fog creature that infected me infects you now. It jumped from me to you because I didn't give you my heart as I should have. Your mother isn't through that door. She's at the bottom of a pile of stone because of my carelessness."

He trembled. His mouth worked silently to stammer or protest, but I went on.

"Edward, how much more must I cost you? How many more lies must I tell you? We can't be married. I'm no good for you."

Reluctantly, painfully, I plucked the engagement ring from my finger. It was a simple band, one that belonged to his mother, one that despite everything I had not removed. Until now.

"Please, take this back, let me get you free of this place, so you can start healing and move on."

The expression on his face was too much to bear. The energy drained from his whole body, palpably. His steely grey eyes took on a dull, murky hue as they stared at the outstretched ring. But the finger of my other hand, beneath the Ring of Regret, was not burning.

This was the truth Rebecca had egged me on about for so long. My stomach churned at the sight of him. My head spun, but my conscience flew finally free.

It wasn't fair, of course. I had often wondered if someone like Edward Thomas could exist. He was too picturesque, perfection in so many aspects. And because I believed a man like that could not exist, my heart ran into the arms of a flawed and rough alternative.

That was the sad story of Luella Winthrop.

Edward's hand trembled as he plucked the ring from my hand. His arm fell heavily with it.

"Luella," he whispered to me. "Why didn't you tell me before I made such a fool of myself?"

Tears ran down my face now, openly.

"I'm the fool, Edward. There's only one fool, and it will never be you."

"Another lie," he replied, shaking his head.

Motion behind him caught my eye, and the other Luella burst into the dense magical fog. It swarmed Edward, but there was no ambition left in him. He was crushed.

Instead, I heard a terrible noise, a cross between whistling wind and guttural scream, and it burst through the door behind me, back out to the beach. Instinct told me that it was not running away, but instead hastening its work. If it could not feast on Edward Thomas' misguided attempts at love, it would consume the Netherdowns in a fury.

"Come on, Edward," I said. I pulled on his arm. It hung limp like dead weight. "Edward, please."

"Why bother?" he asked. "Out there I'm just a fool. What Dawnhurst must think of me, pining over the woman accused of my father's murder."

"It doesn't matter what they think of you," I said.

"Then whose opinion matters?" he asked. "My father's? My mothers?"

"Yes. And even though your father is gone, you still carry his name."

He scoffed.

"And I'm not sure your mother is gone yet," I continued. He tilted his head upward, confused. "But she's not through that door. She's at the bottom of my mess."

He turned toward the closed door set opposite the one I'd entered through.

"What is through that door?" he asked.

"I don't know, and frankly, I don't care. I know what was through this door." My head nodded toward the beach. "That's enough for me. But the fog monster was right about one thing. We have little time, less still to have any chance at saving your mother."

He relented, finally, and I tugged him toward the door. Before we went back to the beach, he grabbed my arm and stared me in the eyes.

"If my mother is lost, I will never forgive you," he said gravely.

A sad smile worked its way to my lips.

"I'm beyond hoping otherwise."

32

ANCHORS

Whether due to the brief time we'd spent in Bram's yurt or the Dúil's newly focused attention on destruction, the Netherdowns was a different place when we emerged. Burning fragments of the parchment that hid above the sky rained down as slothful comets.

Moonlight flickered in and out like a sputtering candle. The trek back through the slick stone was treacherous for it. Progress went slowly, but Edward helped me along. When he grabbed my hand to help me over a rock, there was no romance in it, no spark as there used to be. I knew fully that he kept me beside him for strategic purposes. I was his only way to find his mother and then back to the real world.

We hadn't spoken since we closed the Onyx Door behind us, and as I ruminated over my plan, I realized Edward still did not know his mother was not a corporeal being, but a painted portrait. At least Hirythe had not succumbed to his wild nature. If I could reunite with him, I would plead for his help restoring her.

But the last I'd seen Hirythe, he was hell-bent on leaving the Netherdown and sealing the Dúil within. To do that, there still had to be enough Netherdowns to keep the Dúil occupied, and judging by the landscape, that left a very short fuse. Even the cliffs that we canvassed were eroding, small trailings of pebbles slipping to the water beneath. In others, large chunks of rock broke free, tumbling dangerously by. More than once, Edward had to grab me by the waist and pull me back to safety before being flattened by such a boulder.

When we finally achieved sandier pathways, the tide beat furiously against the beach, reaching past signs of previous erosion, and a rain beat down heavily. My shoes sunk deeply into the wet sediment as though it were quicksand.

We passed the weathered log that marked the location of Jeremy's fall. There was no sign of him or Hirythe. I continued without mention of it.

"Where are we going?" Edward called through the storm.

"Bram was wounded up on this ridge. He and Hirythe are our only way back to the world."

"And my mother?"

His mother lay still much further on. We'd traveled through a wood from Oak Hill to arrive at the beach. We'd have to go back through to get there again and further still to find the tower. I eyed the sky.

"Still quite a way off at the center of the Netherdowns Town."

He set his jaw firmly and continued on, faster than before. I struggled to keep up with him. When at last we found the trail I'd used to get to the beach, it was pockmarked with open craters and wept streams of loose dirt onto the sand. We climbed it anyway, Edward helping me behind him.

At the top, I turned around and my eyes stretched wide. Out over the water, the horizon looked like it was on fire. The sight of it filled me with a heavy dread. The land was turning against us, and whatever fire the Dúil used to consume the Netherdowns didn't seem to care what it fed on. Not even the water was safe.

My friends weren't much further on. They'd backtracked from where I'd left them, and it only took us a few minutes before we saw them, a few spots against a backdrop of smoke and decimated forest.

"You succeeded," Hirythe surmised when I was in earshot. He noted Edward with a nod. "That explains the acceleration. We saw a burst of cloud fly from the beach and spread into the air."

"How is Bram?" I asked.

"Fading," Hirythe replied. "I know what fear is working in him. He's afraid of losing Olivia."

"He already did," I replied.

"Not her memory. We're leaving the Netherdowns and closing the door behind us, but I can't bring a memory back to life." He looked over his shoulder at Bram, cradled in Olivia's arms.

"Will Bram have any memory left on the other side?" I asked. Hirythe shrugged.

"Believe it or not, I've never done this before," he replied.

"What about your memory?" I asked. "This whole place is made with your memories as well."

He smiled and surveyed the crumbling world around him.

"I've got enough to spare."

"Where's the town?" Edward cut in.

"I beg your pardon?" asked Hirythe.

"The town. I need to retrieve my mother."

"There's no time for that," the fae replied. "We need to leave immediately. It'll take long enough to make an anchor to pull you back. You can't go traipsing around—"

"I'm not leaving without her."

I put a hand on Edward's arm.

"You may have no choice, Edward. The town is on the other side of this burning wood, and another mile or two still." I pointed toward where I knew the town lay far off. "Look around. You won't make it."

"Then, I'll find my own way back."

Edward took off at a run toward the smoldering remains of the wood.

"Edward!" I called, uselessly after him. I shouldn't have expected him to behave any differently. It was in his marrow to put others before himself.

"That damned fool!" Hirythe hissed, turning to watch him go. "We can't wait, Luella. The longer I wait to seal off the Netherdowns, the worse Bram's condition will become. I'm sorry."

I wrung my hands and paced furiously, casting furtive glances between Bram, Hirythe, and Edward's shrinking form.

This was no decision, though. No decision at all.

"My anchor." I stretched out my hand to Hirythe.

"What?"

"I know you have some, give me a vial."

"This is ridiculous!" Hirythe rolled his eyes. "The anchor will only work for you. Even if you caught him, how do you intend to get him back?"

"I'll hold on to him tight enough," I replied. The plain and ugly foolhardiness of my idea stunned the fae into silence. I knew what he couldn't seem to say, though. It didn't work that way. But I knew that already.

"No, I won't give it to you!" Hirythe face contorted into a pained grimace. "If that man wants to throw away his life, that's his choice, but it's too dangerous. I won't risk you like that."

"Hirythe! I don't have time to debate it. He's already running too quickly for me. I'll lose him if I don't leave now. Give me the vial."

"Then I'm afraid you'll have to lose him," the fae replied.

I glanced over my shoulder. Edward's form retreated quickly. Soon, I would lost track of him altogether. Without the vial, I'd have no way back to the real world. But without my help, there was no telling what would become of Edward.

It was a decision I'd already made in my heart. I threw my arms around Hirythe in a firm embrace.

"One thing about being human," I said in his ear, "is that we make our own choices."

I ran off before, ignoring Hirythe's cries to stop.

My wet shoes steamed as I ran through the burned wood. Everywhere around me, pockets of the fire remained, eating away at the remnants of tree branches, stumps, and logs. The rain must have cooled the ground considerably, but even so, it was devilishly hot, and I did not enjoy the added protection of Edward's boots, nor his speed. Instead, I ran as quickly as the devastated terrain would allow. If I tripped, I feared I might fall into the oddly colored flames. There was no telling how it might burn, or what else it might do to me.

The wood, while wide, was not nearly as deep as it felt when I journeyed through it with Bram. I was confident I could make it through before my feet took on any irreparable damage, despite how hot the soles of my shoes were quickly becoming.

My muscles spasmed sharply as my foot caught an ashy branch, and I feared I would fall, but the branch gave way like a bit of sand.

Soon, I saw Oak Hill, standing like a sentinel over the valleys that led to Netherdowns town. To my horror, the tree burned like a candle, spewing smoke and ash into the air. Looking around to the hills that marked the other entries into the Netherdowns, it was the same. Candles on hilltops.

It distracted me so much that when I turned my head straightway again, I was surprised to find Edward had stopped.

"Where is my mother?" he asked when I'd caught up. His breathing was labored. Mine wheezed all but beyond repair. I doubled over and collapsed to sit on the grass, clawing at my shoes. They were singed on the edges. My feet felt like they were on fire. I managed to point at the town. It wasn't just the tower, now, that lay in a heap of rubble. Most of the buildings laid in a terrible state of razed debris. Some structures that still stood intact lit up before my eyes, catching from sparks in the air.

"Edward," I gasped, "I need to tell you something. She's not as you imagine. When Jeremy brought her into the Netherdowns, she transformed."

"What are you talking about? Is she not lying helpless, waiting for us?" Edward crouched down and helped me rip the shoes from my feet. Steam billowed off my bright red skin.

"She's a painting." I clutched a stabbing cramp in my ribs. "Jeremy paralyzed her with a dose of fear, and it manifested as a painting."

Edward scrunched up his face at me, bewildered, disbelieving, but too deep into magic to question me.

"I don't care," he said instead, coughing on the smoke. "I won't leave her."

"You may need my help," I said. "The town is disorienting even when whole. Now it's likely a maze."

"You can't walk like this," he said. I gritted my teeth.

"I can try." I stood, but every pebble was a razor, and I fell again.

"Ah! It's useless. Go on without me. She'll be at the bottom of the rubble on the hill in the center of the town."

Edward turned to leave, but paused.

"What about you?"

"I'll wait for you here. Then we can find a way back to the world." The words stuck painfully in my throat. I knew that wasn't true, and likely as not, this would be the last I'd ever see Edward Thomas. The thought brought any resolve I had crumbling down. Quiet tears betrayed my eyes. Still, Edward could not die in the midst of the frantic desperation he embodied now. He needed to die having seen the truth for himself, holding his mother's painting or using all his energy to get to her.

"What if I can't make it back?" he asked. I was shocked to find that despite the pain in my feet and the cramping of my side, the Ring of Regret burned my finger all the same.

"Edward, it's likely hopeless, anyway. Hirythe was the only one who could create an anchor for you."

His shoulders slumped.

"Then I'm trapped here?" he asked. "As is my mother."

It was painful to confirm such fear in his eyes, but I nodded. His muscle in his jaw worked as he considered my confirmation.

"Do you have one of these anchors? Did Hirythe make one for you?" he asked.

"He did. But he wouldn't give it to me when I followed after you." I ignored the panic that bit at me as I said this. This would be the end.

"Why not?"

"He thought following you was a foolish idea and if he kept it, he would keep me from running after you."

"But you did, anyway?" Edward asked.

"I couldn't leave you," I said, voice breaking.

His mouth went slack across his face, and for a moment, it seemed his eyes took on a kind, sympathetic sheen, the same expression he'd first had for me when learning my father had passed on, the first day we'd met. Then, his brows quirked up.

"What's this, then?" He reached behind me and plucked a crystal vial from the lacings of my bodice.

My mouth fell open. I sucked in bittersweet relief.

"Hirythe!" I cried. "He must have stuck it there when I embraced him."

Edward paused before extending the vial to me.

"Can we both use it?" he asked dismally. By the expression on his face, I predicted he already he knew the answer.

I reluctantly plucked it from his hand, wishing beyond hope for some method to alter the magic so that it might benefit Edward instead of myself.

"I'm so sorry," I muttered miserably.

"How long does this vial take to work?" he asked.

"Only an instant."

"Well, then, there's no helping it."

He bent over, scooped me into his arms, and together we bounded down the hill toward the town.

Cradled so close to his chest, I discerned all too easily how much more exertion was required in carrying me. His frequent stops to catch his breath did not surprise me. Each time he set me down, more ash and perspiration mixed on his face, down his neck. He undid the front of his shirt to cool down, but it was no use. The fire I'd first noticed on the horizon now gained speed and momentum, heating the very air of the Netherdowns.

I spied it behind us, creeping closer. I also spied it beyond the town behind the other entry hills and realized it was a ring. A ring growing smaller and smaller, closing in on the town. Like a several-course meal, the Dúil was saving the best for last, the most cherished cultivated memories.

When we passed through the burned remains of the town gate, cinders rained down around us. I directed Edward through the mismatched streets, lined with actively burning or recently torched eclectic architecture, amassed from Bram's and Hirythe's many adventures. I wondered at and mourned their loss.

Edward barreled through, red-faced and determined, stepping over stone and wooden rubble in the streets. We passed by the fountain, still split by magic, but now trickling with filthy, ashy runoff that spilled into the square in toxic rivulets.

By the time we reached the hill, almost every step sounded like excruciating effort. The remains from the tower explosion had rained down the sides of the hill, and at its base was only a small portion of the rubble. That encouraged me. Perhaps we could recover Charlotte after all.

But then?

"You can leave me here, Edward," I said. "The base of the tower is just at the summit. Whatever remains of your mother will be buried there."

He didn't reply, only soldiered onward and upward.

"Edward, you'll have no strength left! Leave me here!"

His silence was a response of its own. He had no intention of setting me down until we reached the top.

When we finally arrived, he put me down abruptly, and I assessed the damage. Although the tower was in ruins, the cavernous main room in which Hirythe had hung Charlotte's portrait was partially intact. Portions of the roof had crumbled in, but some vestiges of the lower walls still stood.

Edward dug in at once, clawing at rocks and rubble with his bare hands. He heaved smaller boulders aside, strained against some that were too heavy, and investigated alternative routes through the wreckage.

"Mother!" he called repeatedly. I stopped myself from explaining that she couldn't hear him. As he worked, I understood the calls to be a type of war cry as much as an attempt to make contact with her. It fueled him, and as he called out for his mother, his efforts redoubled, his muscles taking on new strength.

I turned my head and coughed, inhaling a sharp gust of smoke. The fire had eaten through the fields at a terrifying rate. The ring licked at the city walls like a hungry jackal and as it combined with existing fire from the buildings in town, its strength multiplied.

Even before the flames had breached the boundary, eclectic buildings reacted to the heat. Glass windows burst in their frames and thatched roofs caught fire as though from the power of suggestion.

We had so very little time.

There was nothing more to do for Edward, but I could not bring myself to open the vial. I would not miss a single moment of him.

He ploughed on tirelessly.

"Luella! She's here!" The relief in his voice dripped palpably with relief and enthusiasm. "Help me with this rock!"

I limped over, the pain in my feet still sharp, but even I enjoyed a thrill at seeing the corner of Charlotte's canvas. It was wedged beneath a stone the size of Edward. He braced his back against and pushed off another. It did not budge, not even when I did the same beside him.

We both collapsed from the effort. We were so close. I looked at him. Edward was crying.

"Not like this." He shook his head. "Not like this."

I took his hand.

"Just take a moment to rest," I said. "We'll try again. You don't need to move it all the way off. Just tilt it, and I'll try to pull her out. It may scrape the paint, but at least she'll be with us."

He stared at me.

"Then you can open that vial."

I swallowed. Beyond him, the flame had reached the base of the hill.

"That would be the time," I said. "One more, then? For the Lady Thomas?"

He clambered back to the rock and put his back firmly against it, searching for new footholds. I knelt in the dust, ready to reach under and pull.

He pushed, and the rock barely lifted on one side. I urged my hand in, scraping my knuckles between the soil and its rough underside, but as Edward continued, I caught hold of the canvas. My neck and back throbbed as I pulled with all my strength.

"A little more Edward! I've almost got it!"

Edward let out a lionlike roar, and the stone budged another inch. It was enough. With a small ripping noise, it came free, and Edward let the rock fall.

His chest worked like a bellows, struggling to make deep breaths in and out. The fire licked up the hillside.

"Here, Edward," I said, crawling to his side. "Your mother. I'm so sorry. At least, you'll have her at the end."

Weakly, he took my offering and cradled it to his chest. I wanted to kiss him. I wanted to hold him.

Instead, I crawled to the edge of the rubble. Above me, the Dúil's fog stood out, awkwardly distinct from the fire's smoke. In the end, it would have Edward after all.

But if that were true, I needed him to hear the truth, to tell him what I'd never been brave enough or felt worthy enough to say before.

"Edward!" I cried, turning around.

But Edward was gone.

I glanced about. The heat from the flames was palpable on my skin now, rendering me feverish.

"Edward?" I called again, to no response. "Edward!"

He was gone. There was no trace of him at all. I looked for him until a tearing, gut-searing sound wrenched high in the air. Above the Dúil, a streak of lightning, frozen in a moment, cracked across the sky.

I unstopped my vial, cupped my hands around it, and breathed in the unusual scent of Bram's carnival.

33

EDWARD'S DECISION

I opened my eyes to shafts of morning sun in an otherwise shaded room. I was stretched out on the ground, my face pressed flush against floorboards. Everything hurt. My feet. My hands. My lungs. My ribs. My heart.

It took a moment to orient myself, head still reeling from the closing fire and collapsing Netherdowns world. I pushed myself to sit up, and as the world shifted from the horizontal to vertical plane, the cluttered mess of Edward's Dawnhurst tenement came into focus. I was in the dining room, with its table marked by cluttered documents, errant money, gloopy candle remains, and a body.

I wasn't alone.

Hirythe worked over the body, and rising, I recognized it as Bram's unconscious form.

"Come on, you devil," Hirythe said, hurriedly working his hands over Bram's knife wound. There were several sheets of blood-stained bedding cut into pieces around them.

"Hirythe?" My voice croaked. "What's wrong?"

"Everything," he said. "I can't stop the bleeding."

I stumbled over to his side, knocking a chair over on my way. Hirythe's hands shook violently, panic set deep in his face. I was no nurse, but even I could tell the way he bunched up wads to dab at the bleeding would be ineffective at best, counterproductive at worst.

Still, as I tried to assist him, it became apparent my attempts were not much better. I had to lean heavily on the table to keep painful weight off my feet, and my own hands were scratched and arthritic from my effort with the tower rubble. I depleted our stock of bandages faster than Hirythe could cut them.

"He's losing so much blood," I cried, exasperated. "We need to get him to a doctor."

"That will take too long. The bleeding wasn't as profound in the Netherdowns. It's gotten worse," Hirythe replied. "And if I must remind you, this man was headed to the noose. The hospital would save him just for his appointment at the gallows."

"Well, he'll die anyway if we don't do something."

"Here." A calm, resigned voice interrupted. Edward Thomas parted us and quietly set to work.

"Edward!" Before I could stop myself, I'd thrown my arms around him. He was here. But how? He pushed my arms gently from his neck and set back to work.

"Sergeant Cooper always treated the police force more like the military," he said. "He was criticized for it by some other jurisdictions, but we benefitted from more expansive training. I'll do what I can for Bram."

Edward's fingers worked deftly, finding a needle and some thread in a nearby drawer, stitching Bram's cut together, and wrapping the wound tightly. He did it with no sense of pleasure, nor anxiety. He appeared all but numb.

Hirythe peered at him under speculative eyebrows. Perhaps the same question burned in his mind. How had Edward left the Netherdowns? The last I'd seen him, he'd—

"Your mother?" I asked.

He nodded toward the hallway unceremoniously. Hirythe followed behind me.

She sat against the wall, still a portrait of her former self. The only difference between Lady Thomas in the Netherdowns and the Lady

Thomas before me was a nasty rip across the bottom corner of the canvas. A chunk of the painting by her hand was missing.

Hirythe set to studying it immediately, muttering to himself in hushed tones.

"She came back the same," I said, kneeling, "still frozen from the fear toxin."

"Yes," he replied, running a finger along the back of the canvas and touching it to his tongue. He paused for a second. "Evidently, her greatest fear remains unresolved."

"What do you mean?"

"The fear toxin is done with Bram," he went on. "That's why I suspect the bleeding worsened as it did. For all the damage fear can do, apparently it slowed his blood loss. Perhaps it slowed his heart."

"What was it he feared exactly?" I asked.

He grew still for a moment and whispered to me.

"Losing Olivia's memory," he whispered. "That fear has been resolved."

My mouth fell open.

"You mean he doesn't remember her at all?"

"I suspect he has some memory of her, but not the memories he used when making the Netherdowns."

I slumped against the wall.

"That's awful." The thought crushed me.

"It is if you're aware the memory is missing." He slumped down beside me. "That's comforting, isn't it? What's more frightening than knowing that even our most cherished memories might leave us one day?"

He turned back to analyzing the portrait.

"Anyway, the fear is gone. The outcome decided. Although it's not the outcome he desired, the fear can have no more hold over him. Now comes the aftermath."

"Which is?"

"Likely resentment. Bitterness. Listlessness." He glanced back to the room. "Assuming he survives the wound itself. You don't suspect Edward is trying to kill him, do you?"

I shook my head.

"No. Though I would like to understand how he came back without an anchor."

Hirythe set the painting down and leaned against the wall. He looked contemplative, relishing the opportunity to puzzle out a new magical principle despite his exhaustion.

"All I have is a working theory," he said. "I've always used high magic with strong links to something palpable in the real world to allow a departure from the Netherdowns. Scent has this euphoric melancholy quality to it, transitive even. But as you know by now, Luella, there is more than one way to produce a magical outcome, and magical methods sometimes have unpredictable outcomes themselves."

"Like the awful song you taught me."

He squinted out the sides of his eyes at me.

"The song worked. It was just too sensitive. If you had come back more often as you agreed, we might have been able to fine tune it so that—"

"As you were saying, Hirythe..."

"Right." He took a breath. "The Netherdowns is a world of memory. My anchors worked on the assumption that these scents were the best way to pull someone from one area of consciousness to another. But I think when Edward touched this portrait, a similar effect occurred."

I leaned over and watched Edward work, stoic and resolute, still the blank stone I'd seen a moment ago. Perhaps he was simply exhausted, emotionally, physically, mentally... But I knew him well enough to tell that this stretched deeper.

"The last he'd seen his mother, she was alive in the real world," Hirythe continued. "When he saw what happened to her in the Netherdowns, it was different from you seeing the memory of your father, Bram seeing the memory of his wife, or me seeing the memory of my victims. It had all the potent, heart-wrenching grief of a child discovering the fate of a lost parent. Nothing will rip consciousness like that. Touching the portrait, embracing the reality that his mother was lost..."

"It was grief," I finished.

Hirythe nodded reverently.

"Sudden, fresh grief. Not even I could foresee an anchor like that. We stretched the Netherdowns beyond what it was intended to accomplish. Several living individuals entering at once, substantive changes to the real world originating in memory..."

I stared at Charlotte in the portrait. She looked so unlike herself, her expression blank and witless.

"And you don't think Charlotte's fear has yet resolved?" I asked.

He shook his head again.

"But then, what do I know? Every time I think I understand something about magic, it changes."

"And what about Jeremy?" I asked. "What did you do to him?"

"I healed him," he replied. "And I'm lucky it worked."

"You couldn't heal Bram, too?"

"Jeremy didn't get stabbed with a fear toxin knife. He only fell off a cliff. It's different."

"So you sent him back as well?" I asked, leaning my head against the wall.

"He was gone by the time we arrived. I can't say I'm not thankful for it. I'm committed to what I learned in that forest, but it doesn't make facing those I've wronged any more comfortable."

Edward appeared in the doorway.

"I've done what I can for him," Edward said. "He's lost an awful lot of blood, and he'll probably wake up with a hell of a headache."

"Thank you," Hirythe said. "He means a lot to me."

Edward gave a curt nod, almost imperceptible. Edward's face showed conflict, and a terrible thought struck me.

"What happens now, Edward?" I meant with Bram, and I asked the police sergeant. He chewed on the inside of his cheek, considering his options.

"I don't care," he replied. "Do what you want with him."

It should have come as a relief that Bram yet had a chance to escape the noose. But knowing that it came at such a cost to him, that his memory would never be the same—there was no victory in it.

"I'll see what I can do about finding transportation out of the city," Hirythe said.

"He's too weak to travel," Edward replied. "You should both stay here until he's better. There should be some money left around for food, if you need it. Then, take caution. He'll be a wanted man, and I can't erase his conviction."

"What will you do?" I asked. Edward's shoulders fell. He turned his head toward his mother's painting, but he didn't look at it.

"I'll take my mother home," he said, "or what's left of her, anyway."

"When?"

"At once. I need to—there's so much to... At once." He swallowed hard, outlining the muscle in his clenched jaw, shut tight to keep emotions at bay.

I closed my mouth, a response failing on my lips. What could be said? The silence stretched on.

"Thank you, Edward," said Hirythe. "I'll go sit with Bram now, if you need anything from me, you have only to ask."

He left Edward and I alone in the hallway.

"How long will you stay at Fernmount?" I asked.

"I have no idea."

"Of course."

He shifted from one foot to another.

"You're a free woman now. There's no specter of the law hanging over you. What will you do?"

"I don't know."

He nodded with a stern brow.

"So then, this is goodbye?" I asked.

"I believe so, Miss Winthrop."

I folded my arms across my chest, blinking back tears. Farewell came so suddenly, and I wished I'd been more prepared somehow.

"It will never amount to anything," I muttered, "but I can only profess how very sorry I am for everything. You didn't deserve any of this. You deserved—well, so much more."

"I expect you will get back to writing," he said in a stunted cadence.

"Oh, Edward."

He cleared his throat.

"Right."

There was nothing to say. We both knew it. This was the end of a long, treacherous, and involved road. Without waiting for any sign of approval, I threw my arms around him and kissed his cheek.

"Thank you," I tried in a broken whisper.

He took a step back from me, and our eyes met for a cheap instant before he broke away.

"I'll just change my coat and be on my way."

He collected the portrait of his mother, stopped for a moment by the coat rack, and left.

A part of my heart left with him. Nothing had changed, and I didn't lie in that cave on the beach. I was no good for him, but it didn't make his departure hurt any less. As his steps sounded down the stairs, memories gushed of the nights he watched over me, the ridiculous disguises he donned during our investigations, the heroic adventures he never shied away from, the good-natured boyishness and enthusiasm, the disarming sincerity, the handsome smile, the steely grey eyes...

I could not bring myself to chase after him. I was stayed by crushing understanding that some woman, one day, would truly make him happy. But it wouldn't be me.

No tears came, but I took my time collecting myself anyway before walking back into the room.

Hirythe sat dutifully by Bram's side, toying with a piece of paper. I took a chair beside him.

"I can see why you wanted to marry Edward," Hirythe replied. "He had every reason not to help Bram, but he did anyway."

I swallowed hard and decided, immediately, to change topic.

"What's that?" I nodded at the piece of paper in his hand. It was old, battered, creased, but blank.

"This? Well, this is that troublesome page. The Netherdowns are now sealed shut, but they're still here."

"You mean the poem is gone? You erased it somehow?"

He nodded.

"No high magic in reading if there's nothing to read. But just because a poem is erased doesn't mean it's gone. You've likely committed it to memory by now."

I recited it quietly:

. . .

I don't know where the wind comes from
Or where trees hide in seed,
The origins of the running stream
Are mystery to me
I can't explain the pendulum
That undulates the sea
But at least I know to find you
Where dreams meet memory.

"Bram's finest," Hirythe whispered.

The words toyed with me, taking on new meaning. I'd understood it before to mean that Bram could find Olivia in the Netherdowns, a place made of memory but woken from like a dream. But now the words made me pine after Edward. I'd found him through the Onyx Door.

I shook the thoughts from my head.

"Magic doesn't make sense," I muttered. Hirythe smiled.

"That's why it's beautiful and worth protecting."

Beautiful. Terrible. Frightening. Inspiring. My hands hung by my sides, some of my fingernails chipped from where I'd helped Edward with the tower rubble. My feet still throbbed, despite the cool tile floor beneath them.

"What now, Hirythe?"

"I'm sure you'll come up with something."

"I mean for you and Bram. Edward's right. He will be a wanted man. He's been condemned by the Queen's Court." I coughed bitterly. "Condemned for a crime he may not even remember and never committed in the first place."

Hirythe leaned his cheek on one hand. The blue of his skin was less distinct, whether that was because he had spent so much magic and energy so recently or because the real world lessened its effect, I didn't know, and I didn't find it appropriate to ask.

"Ah, us. Well, I imagine we will try to rebuild his memory."

"Can that be done?"

He shrugged.

"Who knows? Memory is very deep magic. I'll retrace the steps we've taken together. We will visit those places again. I've never believed that memories truly die." He smiled, considering the challenge before him. "At any rate, he will need time."

"Yes. I imagine he will." I squinted at our friend, breathing shallowly on the table.

"You're welcome to come with us," Hirythe said. "It'd be nice to have someone with full mental capacity along with me."

I chewed my lip. My instinct was to decline. I'd had enough adventure. But when I reached for polite excuses, I drew up blank. What did I have to look forward to here? I had no prospects. No home. No fiancé. No reputation.

"I'll consider it," I said. "But first, I'm going to bathe, find another outfit, and sleep." I put a hand on Hirythe's shoulder. "Wake me if you need me."

34

THE LOVER'S EYE

Sleep was restless and dreamless, one of those slumbery spells that last long but restore little. In contrast to the rest of the flat, which had been subjected to the Dúil-inspired fits Edward suffered, my room had remained untouched, preserved perhaps.

It unsettled me to wake in Edward's house without him here. I ruffled through an armoire, staving off memories of the night in Reading where he hid me from his mother in a similar piece of furniture. I found my old clothes, sensible skirts and waistcoats in wool herringbone, gifts from Edward to protect me from the cold.

Beside them was Edward's heavy coat I had worn in and out of the Netherdowns. It was battered and dirty. I bit my lip, and in a rush of desire to prolong any sense that he was still with me, I enrobed myself in those memories.

Thankfully, the pain in my feet had diminished significantly overnight, and though I still took care to double wrap them before putting on stockings, walking was bearable, at least for short distances.

Hirythe sat reading in the dining room, precisely where I'd left him the night before.

"How is he?" I asked.

"Hasn't woken, but for everything I can tell, he will survive this. Are you headed out?"

"I'm starving," I said, picking up some money from the table Edward instructed us to use. I'd have to pay Edward back. I'd taken enough from him.

"Bring me something sweet, if you don't mind."

I waved a hand as I headed out the door, down the stairs, and out into the open air. Winter's bitterest cold was behind us with only a cruel, blurry border with spring to look forward to. I hailed a hansom, my feet already protesting my activity. It wasn't hard to find transportation in this more affluent side of my hometown, and soon I was bound for Mrs. Barker's bakery, not a little nervous to face the bakers after my public debacle.

"Luella Winthrop!" Mrs. Barker cried as soon as I'd come through the door. "I was wondering when you'd come back around. What a fright with that trial! We were always cheering you on. That Luella Winthrop was capable of what you were accused of—well, call me Irish for what nonsense that is."

"Hello," I replied sheepishly. "Thank you for your kindness. I've just come by for some of your iced buns, and perhaps some meat pies, if they're ready."

"But what a brute you mixed yourself up with, dear!" Mrs. Barker didn't stop babbling her opinion for a moment as she bagged up my order. I worried that if she wasn't careful, it might get on my food. "That Lowhouse seemed a rascal. You best be careful with who you trust. There are scoundrels out there who will chew you up as soon as look at you. Believe you me, I have to sell scones to some of those scoundrels! And they don't ask for the currant variety, if you have a mind to my meaning."

I didn't have an inkling what a scone preference had to do with anything, but there is a peculiar wisdom in the proficiency of bakers, and I nodded along. I had no energy to explain that Bram was not at all what the papers made him out to be, and so I offered her my money.

"My treat today, dear. Please send your sister my regards!"

My sister. What I would give to share these buns with her like old times...

I dropped off the buns with Hirythe. He took a bite and shrugged, deeming them adequate, but not sweet enough. This was proof enough to me that though he was a genius when it came to magic, he was a ruddy idiot in other areas.

I set out again, this time for the comfort of friendship. I'd been to Doug's pub not two days before, but it seemed like weeks. Rebecca's reaction when she saw me indicated the feeling was mutual.

"You're safe!" she exclaimed, squeezing me tightly before demanding details. "Doug!"

Doug Tanner lumbered from the kitchen.

"What?" he barked, but when he saw me, his face lit up.

"Little Luella! Rebecca had me praying, and I don't pray!" He laughed coarsely and scooped me into his arms, lifting me off the floor and plopping me painfully back down on my sensitive feet. I winced.

"Be careful! She's just been through an ordeal!" Rebecca said, hitting him on the arm when she noticed my grimace.

"I'm sorry! It's just I'm happy to see her. The way I did those prayers, I feared I'd condemned her. I kept mixing up my words, and you know me, I swear when I make a mistake by instinct. Can't imagine God was right happy about those prayers..."

"Don't blaspheme either, you big brute!"

"You're the one who insisted I start praying!"

Watching them bicker brought a reluctant grin to my mouth. Perhaps the whole experience wasn't a loss. Though I had ended worse off, someone had found love and kept it.

Rebecca and I sat at our usual table. The pub was not crowded, and we drank tea together for at least an hour before I succumbed to the smell of the troughs bearing Doug's signature dishes from the kitchen.

Rebecca had few words as I recounted everything. She shifted in her seat constantly, made uncomfortable by the exchanges I described in the wood, pained to hear about the Netherdowns' destruction, and downright frightened by my encounters with Jeremy and the Duíl.

"You gave the ring back," she finally said, shaking her head.

"I didn't see how else to do it," I replied. "How else could I show him that I was serious? I should have listened to you all along, been honest with him, told him everything every step of the way."

Her eyes glossy, she leaned forward.

"But you still love him, don't you?"

I clenched my jaw and stared out the window, down the street, toward the river. A painful stirring took hold of my stomach.

"What will I do now?" I sighed. "Hirythe asked me to accompany him and Bram."

"That would break my heart," Rebecca said. "I'm not capable of noble sacrifice, as you have learned to do. If you leave me, I can never forgive you."

There was no guile in her words. She was lying, but it warmed me to feel such affection. I was happy that at least I'd never done irrevocable damage to my friendship with Rebecca or Doug. They were members of a family of my choosing.

"You can always take up your life here again," she continued. "You must be a better writer now than you were at the start. Think of all the life experiences you have! Why not fight the war for women's recognition in literature? You might even try your hand at fiction."

"Write again? My word. I don't know what fiction is, after seeing what I have." The prospect was daunting. "Who would even give me a chance? I'm not going to talk to Byron again. What a mess of a man."

"And you nearly married him," Rebecca said with a wicked smile. "You may be surprised at any rate. After all, you're an infamous celebrity now."

"Don't remind me." I stuck my finger into a remaining blob of Doug's secret sauce. "What about the pub? I could help around here, couldn't I?"

"Of course," she said. "I can't imagine you would be happy doing it. Even I don't like it that much."

She snapped her fingers at a serving lad and pointed to a table where two men had just sat down.

"You seem to enjoy leadership," I countered, teasing a guilty smile from her.

"Yes, that's the part that keeps me here."

"I'd have thought it was Doug that kept you here."

"Leadership of Doug is what keeps me here. I can imagine no more pleasurable occupation."

. . .

The days crept by with only incremental improvements to the state of my feet and my friend. Hirythe, now adequately rested, kept Bram sedated by using some fae magic he refused to explain. I kept myself busy making rounds to Mrs. Barker's, Doug's, and Mrs. Crow's, where Cyrus still lived.

When I returned to Mrs. Crow's flat the first time, Cyrus was overjoyed. He appeared lighter, acting so much more like a dog than ever before. He'd always possessed an unusual poise and purpose. Now he was more playful, more eager to beg for a walkabout. I wondered if this change was caused by the sealing of the Netherdowns or Mrs. Crow's incessant affection.

The two were inseparable.

But her improved mood did not prevent my scolding.

"This isn't some boarding house, Luella. I hate to say it, but you've had me worried sick. No word! Gone for days! I almost reported your disappearance to the police."

The idea made me smile. If Johnson had ever made it back to the precinct, it'd be his first question for someone like Mrs. Crow appearing at his desk.

But as is the way of older generations, the scolding subsided and an increase in motherly concern took precedence. I explained I was staying at Edward's for the time being and not to worry about propriety because he was not in the city.

"Speaking of Lord Thomas, you'll never guess what has happened!" Mrs. Crow nearly bounced where she stood in the kitchen. "All the payments he made to cover the expense of funding your little secret society—"

"Secret society?"

"—well, we all know he gave in excess, but when I went to count my figures, Mr. Stringham came round. He was in an awful way."

"Good heavens, Mr. Stringham. And how is his ailing mother?" I asked. My old infuriatingly plain landlord. I hadn't found an opportunity to speak with him since the night he told me he needed more rent.

"She's healed quite well, I would say. Well enough to gamble in any event!"

"Gamble?"

"And not well! The man was in ruins, long of face and desperate for means to pay off his mother's debt, one she accumulated from her near-nightly game of cards."

I laughed, rudely. I couldn't help it. Imagining Mr. Stringham bound by a mother given to vice was downright ridiculous.

"Cards! I can't believe that," I said.

"Oh, it's not as uncommon as you might suppose. Even Mrs. Barker and I have tried our hands on occasion—mind you it was in very private circumstances with very small sums, but we love to have fun as much as anyone else."

"What a tale!" I cried, clapping my hands.

"Well, to jump to the end of it, I bought your old flat!"

My hands froze together.

"You what?"

"He was desperate to sell, and there weren't many offers for him, so I told him I could at least take the flat across the hall. And would you believe it, he was just desperate enough to agree! And at such a bargain! Would you like to go see it? For nostalgia's sake?"

I pursed my lips. Anna and I had lived in the flat across the hall for many years. Happy and desperate memories haunted the rooms. But I wasn't ready to face memories at present.

In fact, the longer time went on, the more uncomfortable I felt in my old life. Making my old rounds was like putting on a garment I'd grown out of. Hirythe's invitation lingered constantly in the back of my mind, not as a tempting cry to adventure, but as a protected, friendly shield from the present.

I didn't want to see my old flat. I could hardly stomach seeing my old city.

"Perhaps another time," I mumbled. Still, considering my old life reminded me of something. "Mrs. Crow, didn't you say that Anna had written me before I left for Reading?"

Her face soured.

"I was afraid you were going to ask about that," she said. "I'm so sorry, but Cyrus found a stack of letters and chewed them all to bits. I had no choice but to throw them away."

Irritation jabbed me from the inside, but after all Mrs. Crow had done for me, I didn't consider myself worthy to scold her.

"I'm sure she'll write again," I murmured.

Cyrus barked, as though proud of himself. Mrs. Crow tossed him a bread roll.

Two nights later, Bram woke. It must have happened while I was calling on Rebecca, for when I returned to Edward's flat, he sat on a chair eating a meat pie while Hirythe made an absolute mess in the kitchen. Bram looked up at me from his chair, blankly, calling to my attention that this was the first time we would have spoken since he was stabbed.

I stared back.

"Do I look that bad?" he asked. My reserve swept away, and I collapsed on him in a large embrace, squeezing more tightly than prudent for someone on the mend from his injury. Still, I ignored his protests and hid tears of relief in his shoulder.

Hirythe heard Bram's yelps and pried me off of him.

"What's the matter with you, Luella! He's healing!"

When the fae pulled me free, I noticed an apron tied round his waist, a sight that left me flabbergasted.

"Oh stop," he whined. "I don't want to get anything on my clothes while working in the kitchen. This is a very practical device!"

"It's not a device, Hirythe. It's a simple apron," Bram said, laughing.

"I'm aware. You are both ridiculous. It's not that strange!" He continued muttering as he headed back into the kitchen to continue his culinary experimentation. I wondered how much of Edward's sugar he'd used.

"You're alive," I whispered to Bram. "I was so afraid."

"I'm alive," he replied. "Hirythe tried explaining it all to me, but it's difficult to remember."

"That's to be expected. What do you remember?"

"Well, I recall making the Netherdowns, and I remember going in and out and all of that. It's just the details that are gone. What it looked like. Names. Faces. What we did there. Things I said. I wish I could feel bad over it, but I don't know what it is I don't remember."

"What about outside of the Netherdowns?" I asked.

"I'm not in prison anymore. I imagine that was not because the police had a change of heart."

I tilted my head.

"Well, you may be surprised..."

"Everything before making the Netherdowns is vague and blurry. I remember you, though. Luella, I'm so sorry. Hirythe explained about the Dúil, how Jeremy learned to wake it from our expedition north. If you don't mind me saying, our friendship has been a tennis match of guilt. I thought I was responsible for infecting you. Then we thought my interference was a Godsend, now... it's come full circle. I have to take the blame."

I shook my head and grasped his hand.

"Take it from someone who has a firm grasp of cause and effect, it doesn't matter whose fault it is."

He nodded and took another bite of his meat pie.

"I just hope Jeremy doesn't seek more revenge," he said.

"I doubt he will."

"Even if he does," Hirythe appeared in the doorway, now without the apron, but holding a small pot of soup, "we will be long gone. Will you be joining us Miss Winthrop?"

Bram turned to me, startled, and I stood formally.

"About that," I said. "Some time ago, you two created a merry group of friends on a never-ending quest to discover new magic. I don't know if I can pursue the same purpose, but as I've retraced my past life here in Dawnhurst, it's become clear that I've outgrown it. There's nothing for me here but sad and broken memories."

I took in a deep breath. Bram leaned forward, food frozen halfway to his mouth.

"So, if you'll have me, I would be happy to go with you."

Hirythe raised the pot in celebration, sloshing some of the soup on the floor.

"Splendid!" he cried. "Look at us. Three enterprising individuals ready for new adventures!"

Bram stared at me.

"Look at him," Hirythe said. "Stunned with happiness."

"Could you give us a moment, Hirythe?" he asked.

The fae's smile fell before returning to the kitchen, all the while grumbling that secrets were hardly an appropriate start to a new union.

"You took some things of mine, trinkets from my sea chest. Do you still have them?" Bram asked.

"Not all of them," I admitted. "We lost some in the Netherdowns."

"The locket. Do you have that?" he asked. I nodded, and in a quick moment, I'd retrieved it from a bag in my room and returned.

"You can't come with us, Luella," Bram said.

"Are you uninviting me?"

"You have the warmest invitation, but as your friend, I can't allow it."

"Why not?"

He took the locket from me, put it around his neck, and opened it. I peered inside it and saw a well-drawn brown eye. I recognized it in an instant. I had seen it on a moonlit hilltop, behind a mask, and beside a burning wood.

"Olivia's?" I asked.

"Is that right?" Bram responded. "I hoped this might work. This may be about all I have left of her." He gazed at the locket longingly. "What a beautiful image. How strange, that though my memory of her is so hazy, her eye still shows in the locket."

"Has it always?" I asked. He smiled.

"For as long as I can remember."

After indulging for a prolonged moment, he closed the small jewelry compartment, took the locket off, and gently placed it around my neck.

"You wouldn't open this before," he said. "Are you ready now?"

I stared at the small gold box, its tiny hinges and clasp so delicately arranged.

"Must I?"

"I have to see what's in it before I allow you to come with us."

I sighed and pinched it open, unsurprised to see a distinct, steely grey eye staring back at me. I sniffed, trying to hide my face from Bram by staring at the floor before he was contented to let me close the locket again and take it off.

"It's funny," Bram said. "Something about having your worst fear come true is that it gives you such a healthy dose of perspective. I have many regrets, and even more I'm sure that I can't remember. Perhaps this ring will remind me of them, and I can use that as a way to unravel the past. Do you believe regret outlives memory? I hear that soldiers who have lost limbs in combat sometimes experience an itch where an arm or leg used to be."

"I wouldn't know," I mumbled.

"I don't remember much of Olivia right now, but I still miss her." He smiled. "I cannot make you happy, Luella. I wanted to try once, but I think I just hoped that I could prove to myself I'd learned my lesson, that if I had love again, I wouldn't mess it up a second time."

I held his hand.

"But we had a deep connection, did we not?" I asked. "Even if I can recognize it now as more familial than romantic, that should be enough to make me happy. And Hirythe, too. My friendship with him can grow and blossom, and you can't say that I won't be happy."

He finished his meat pie in an effort to hide his emotions, but despite the time he gave himself to chew, his voice was not whole when he replied.

"Family and friends are what we leave for love," he said. "What else could tempt us away? If you'd never known something sweeter, perhaps I'd believe you. But no matter where we go, the eye in this locket will follow you."

I shut my eyes and gripped the arms of my chair.

"But he doesn't want me," I said.

"Are you sure?"

"Even if he does, he shouldn't."

Bram pulled my ring finger straight and touched the Ring of Regret.

"How about we try a magical experiment? In one year, if this ring burns when you think about letting us go without you, leave a message for Hirythe in the wood nearby. Bury it under a tree root. We'll come collect you."

"Very well," I said, swallowing. "You're just forgetting one thing."

"I'm forgetting a lot of things," he corrected.

"How can I say goodbye to you both?"

Bram put the locket back around his neck and opened it to stare at Olivia's eye.

"There are no goodbyes. Memories live in our surroundings, and the very Earth keeps those who have left us nearby, if we'll allow it."

"I can't explain the pendulum that undulates the sea, but at least I know to find you where dreams meet memory," I muttered.

"That's beautiful. Who wrote it?" Bram asked. I smiled, unsure if his question was a jest or not.

"An old friend."

Hirythe appeared in the doorway again.

"Am I allowed to come out, now?"

"She's not coming," Bram said. Hirythe's chest deflated.

"She's not?"

"No, at least not for now."

"Well, damn. I'm stuck with you, then?" the fae asked in a quick effort to mask his disappointment with sarcasm.

"I'm afraid so."

I closed my eyes and pretended the three of us were back in Hirythe's study in the Netherdowns, enjoying a cup of tea and hypothesizing about how to cure my magical dependency.

It was hard to believe, but I wished I could be back in that study.

"Well, then we best leave," Hirythe said as he put a lid on the soup pot. "Bram, gather your things."

"What things?" Bram replied.

"Right."

"You're leaving now?" I protested. "Bram has just woken up! It's dark out, night has barely fallen."

"Why do you think I woke Bram up?" Hirythe asked. "And night is the best time to smuggle a fugitive out of the country."

"The country?"

"Yes. Oh, and something else." Hirythe reached for a blank piece of paper on the table. The diary page. "This is for you."

"I can't take this. Isn't it dangerous?"

"Less so in your hands than in his or mine. Just don't write on it, at least not anytime soon. Monsters like the Dúil simmer and lose power after they sit idle for too long with nothing to eat."

Hirythe picked up a satchel I hadn't noticed packed by the door, tossed a coat to Bram, and placed a hand on both my shoulders.

"Goodbye for now, Luella," he said, staring me poignantly in the eyes. "I'm sorry to rush out, but these separations are easier this way. Trust me."

Dumbfounded and caught off guard, I defaulted to embrace him.

"I will miss you, Hirythe. You're always welcome where I am."

He patted my shoulder and pulled away.

"Please give Relkavich my regards."

He stalked out the front door, Bram on his heels.

"Bram!" I called. He stopped in the doorway and turned around.

"I do love you, you know," I said. "I wouldn't be who am I today without having met you, and though I'm not proud of who I was, I'm proud of who I am."

He smiled.

"Then I am sure your father would be proud, too." He shrugged. "Who knows? Perhaps I'll see you in a year."

He smiled, and the Meddler walked out, leaving me alone in Edward's entry hallway.

35

NEW LIVING ARRANGEMENTS

I lingered on at Edward's for another few days. I spent the time tidying it all up. It was the least I could do. After all, how many times had he helped me clean up after my own episodes, sometimes at his own expense?

The tenement did not boast the stately appearance I'd first been introduced to, but at least it was clean. One morning, I closed the front door, locked it behind me, and left.

Bram's words haunted me, and I resented him for refusing my request to come along. I was Hirythe's guest as much as his, after all. But if he needed a year to see what I already knew, so be it. I'd have to content myself until then.

Meanwhile, I distracted myself by cleaning up some other things...

"It's just not prudent," I said to Rebecca at the end of our lunch.

"No one is paying any mind," she replied.

"It doesn't matter. You're living with Doug as if you were married when, in fact, you're not. It's unwise, and unlikely to inspire any greater commitment on his part."

She scowled and sulked as if being lectured by a parent, an expression I recognized and missed from my time bringing up Anna.

"What? You suggest I simply live on my own?"

"No," I said. "I want you to live with me, in my old flat across from Mrs. Crow's."

Rebecca's expression tore between joy and hesitation. And why wouldn't it? On the one hand, it'd be great fun living together, for a time, but if she loved Doug, why part from him?

"Mrs. Crow?" Rebecca asked.

"Yes. She would be our landlord, and it will be a good test of boundaries for your newfound romance. Doug will have to pay you wages for your help at the pub to help cover the cost. It's a chance to see how much you're really worth to him and how badly he'd miss you."

She stared at me, but I avoided her gaze. We both knew Doug's intentions were pure, and my suggestions had much more to do with my plea for a companion than a desire to safeguard Rebecca's romantic investment.

"Please," I said, finally finding the courage to look at her. Sweet Rebecca took my hand.

"Of course." She sighed, looking sweetly resigned. "But if Doug proposes, and we're married—"

I raised a hand to cut her off.

"If, if, if," I said, pretending to be unaffected.

R ebecca tried her best, but it was apparent from the start that the arrangement wasn't going to work. For one, waking up every morning in my old flat pained me. I expected to see Anna at every turn, and though my friend tried to make for a cheerful living companion, she took every opportunity to spend time with Doug or work at the pub, leaving me with a lot of time to sit alone and stew over what I would do with myself.

After returning from a walk about with Cyrus one day, and sitting through another session of town gossip from Mrs. Crow about people I didn't know and didn't care to know, I came to the inevitable conclusion that I wouldn't make it a year carrying on like this.

So, uncomfortably, haltingly, and dreadfully, I turned back to my typewriter, or at least, the prospect of my typewriter. Perhaps Rebecca was right, and some publication in Dawnhurst might be willing to take a chance on me. I didn't mind writing under a pseudonym if necessary, and awkward as it might be to beg for a position, people did this type of thing every day.

It bristled against my sense of loyalty to knock on the door of *Langley's Miscellany's* greatest rival, *Mansfield's Weekly*. But what loyalty did I owe to Byron now? Presumably, he was now engaged to Carolina Drake of the Golden Inkwell Committee. Surely his publication could handle a little competition from a discrete, humble author as I was.

"Luella Winthrop," Mansfield's editor bellowed when he heard my name from his receptionist. It was a small office, not much larger than Langley's, but enjoyed much more organization. The editor was a stout man in a waistcoat, halfway into a morning cigar. "I'll be damned! What a blessing!"

I took an instant dislike to him, and not just for his careless mix of infernal and celestial exclamations.

"Thank you for seeing me," I said. He laughed raucously.

"I should be thanking you! To what do I owe the pleasure?" He let out a puff of smoke before setting his cigar down.

"Well, you see—" I coughed through the smoke, "—I've come seeking work. I wanted to inquire if you might have use of another writer on your staff."

"Yes." He grinned at me broadly, revealing a nearly black front tooth.

"Yes?"

"Yes, I'd love to have you," he said.

"You would?" I sputtered, the conversation going wildly better than I imagined. "Just like that?"

"Look at you all befuddled." He chuckled. "It's not that surprising. I was already planning on sending someone to track you down for an interview. But to think 'Luella Winthrop's Exclusive Comments' on *Mansfield's Weekly's* front page. We will sell by the bucket load."

My heart sank.

"My comments on what?" I asked.

"The trial, of course. You were acquitted in Dawnhurst's largest and most mysterious criminal case in years. The city is itching to hear the story it from your point of view. Let's talk about remuneration."

I blinked. How could I even begin to explain my perspective on the trial in writing? How could I expose the private details of Bram's or Edward's lives? Charlotte was still a painting, for heaven's sakes.

"I'm sure there are other topics that might interest your readers," I suggested. "I don't have much to share in terms of the trial or my imprisonment."

"Other topics?" he bellowed. "This is the topic. This is all anyone has cared to read since you left the police scratching their heads over your escape from Dawnhurst months ago."

"Please, sir. There must be—"

"What will it cost me?" he asked. "I hate to insist, Miss Winthrop, but I can't let this go."

I stood up, staggered and offended. This man didn't want my writing, he wanted to make me a spectacle.

"I'm afraid that I have nothing to offer you," I said. "Good day."

"Miss Winthrop, wait!" The editor yelled after me. "Stories are meant to be told! Why not tell it to someone who will pay you well?"

I whisked the door open and stormed onto the walk outside, indignation fueling every step, cursing myself for considering working with a long-time rival. I'd always known *Mansfield's* to publish rubbish. If I was going to write again, it would need to be at a publisher with values similar to my own.

But throughout the day, though the tone of the conversation varied, the substance was always the same. Publication after publication made their desires expressly clear. My firsthand account of the most scandal-filled criminal proceeding in Dawnhurst's recent history appeared to be the only value I offered the publishing world.

By the time night fell, not even signs that the sun was lingering longer in the sky brightened my mood. It was a very unfortunate evening, indeed, to have a visitor.

"Luella!" Mrs. Crow greeted me on the steps, Cyrus in a lead. "We're just out to enjoy some spring evening. You have a visitor. I hope you don't mind, I let him in to your kitchen to wait."

"A visitor?" I did mind. This was one of my preoccupations about submitting to Mrs. Crow as a landlady. Her nearly familial connection emboldened her to do things that other business acquaintances wouldn't dare. Allowing a man in my flat to wait for my return was just such a grievance. The last time this had happened, Mr. Stringham wanted to raise my fees.

"He's handsome, too!" she called back after me as Cyrus pulled her toward the open street.

Handsome?

I tried to shake off my foul mood as I walked up the steps, banishing thoughts of wanton wishing from my mind. It was not him. It could not be him.

Still, my heart beat faster as I opened my door.

It wasn't Edward.

"I'm very happy to see you, Luella." Alastair stood. "After the trial, I searched for you, but feared the worst." He looked uncomfortable, embarrassed even to face me.

"Alastair, what a surprise," I said, quickly masking my disappointment. It was ridiculous to hope that Edward would be in my kitchen, and I let my warm feelings for the northerner smother my delusion. I swept across the room to embrace him.

"This is a much warmer greeting than I expected," he replied.

"Don't speak nonsense. You've been nothing but a friend to me."

I sat beside him, and he poured me a cup of tea. I noted a plate of Mrs. Barker's iced buns on the table and smiled. He really had been worried.

"But I failed," he said. "Thank heavens he escaped again. Our appeals weren't looking promising. I presume you know where he's gone."

I smiled and shook my head.

"I knew where he was, but I can honestly tell you his location is a mystery to me."

Alastair exhaled slowly.

"That's probably for the best," he said. "Should the police get smart and try to question you again—"

"They won't, Alastair. The issue is dead. You might blame yourself for failing Bram, but I think he's come to grips with the outcome. I think somewhere deep within him, he did feel guilty for the death of

Edward's father. But the scroll has passed, and he's living with his own penance."

Alastair sipped his tea.

"And you?" he asked. "How are you managing life after the notoriety? I've been concerned for you, to say nothing for Edward. Has he found his mother, by the way?"

"Yes and no," I said sadly. "He's found her, but she's in a terrible way."

"Is there any hope that she might improve?"

I took my time responding. Hirythe had said that the same toxin ebbed in Bram after he saw the outcome of his greatest fear resolved. In his case, it was resolved in the way he'd feared. It followed that Charlotte was still in her current state because her fear had not yet resolved either way. Or else, something had simply gone wrong with the magic, and her portrait was the resolution of her greatest fear, as she had hinted to me once before. Hadn't she said that she was afraid of having no portrait, no legacy? Perhaps her true fear was that her legacy would be only a portrait...

"I don't know," I said, shivering. "Who can say what is going to happen."

He peered at me, precise and piercing.

"That sounds cheery."

I put my hands together and shrugged.

"You are an excellent judge of character," I replied. We sat in silence, taking sips of tea, not touching the buns. Alastair seemed to be working up the courage to say something, and finally, with a great clearing of his throat, he managed.

"Luella, if you don't mind me saying, I'd be very happy to help support you however I may, be that financially or otherwise. I did not lie when I said your father changed my life. And it warms my heart so to see that you have followed in his footsteps."

I set down my teacup.

"What do you mean?"

"The way you defended Mr. Lowhouse, the way you fought to find him a lawyer, and the lengths you endured to ensure he had a fair shake... It reminded me so much of your dad."

My cheeks burned, unprepared for the comparison.

"It's different. I was partly at fault that Bram was imprisoned in the first place. My fate was tied up in his," I protested.

"And you think that occasionally your dad didn't find himself with those same feelings? Or that sometimes he wasn't tangentially connected to the schemes that landed his friends in with the coppers? The truth is Luella, some people run and some people fight. Your dad would be so proud to know that he raised a fighter. Even if your lot seems rough now, take comfort in that at least."

I looked away, out the pitiful window at the street.

"I don't feel like a fighter," I managed with breaking voice. "I feel wasted and lost."

Alastair scooted his chair beside mine and wrapped me in his arms.

"As do all warriors after a battle," he said, wiping a tear from my cheek, the way my father may have. "Take whatever time you need to heal. As you do, the comfort of doing what's right will warm and right you. Then, when it's time, fight again."

I didn't deserve his words, but I succumbed to his comforting embrace before regaining my composure.

"Thank you, Alastair," I said. "Now, please, can we talk about anything else? Your work, perhaps?"

He laughed and stood.

"We can't, I'm afraid. That's one of the tenets of my line of work. It's a professional skill not to share it with others, a facet I'm sure you can appreciate."

"I certainly can." I stood and shook his hand. "Alastair McHenry, please don't be a stranger."

"Ha!" he said. "I was about to say I hope I don't have to see you again soon, but I meant it in a professional context."

I saw Alastair to the door. He held a hand out to test a light drizzle of spring rain, laughed, and made his way home.

Mrs. Crow and Cyrus came back wet, and Mrs. Crow prattled on and on about unpredictable weather before reminding me she was hosting Rebecca and me for dinner.

Rebecca didn't arrive until we were halfway through the soup. She insisted that she'd already eaten, as was her custom, but graced us with amiable company and listened attentively to Mrs. Crow's ramblings about the speculated romance between a nearby thatcher and the fish-monger's wife.

"I did as you said," I told Rebecca after the food was cleared and Mrs. Crow had retired. "I tried to drum up some writing business, you know, rekindle my old passion."

Rebecca's face brightened, eager at the idea that I was taking steps to get on with my life and allow her to get on with hers. Doug had not appreciated how quickly I stole her away, and I was surprised he hadn't overcome his pride and proposed already.

"And? How was it? Should you have been taking notes on all of Mrs. Crow's stories?"

"It leads nowhere, Rebecca. No one is interested in Luella Winthrop. They're only interested in the scandal behind my name."

"How much were they paying?" Rebecca asked with a piqued eyebrow.

"Does it matter? I can't do it. It would be disrespectful."

"It wouldn't have to be. I'm confident that if anyone could find an appropriate way to share the true side of this story with the public, it's you. And after all, after everything you've been through, don't you deserve to share your side of things?"

I pursed my lips, folding my arms in disbelief.

"And what? Do I simply parade around Bram's misfortune and Edward's private family life? How can I give the public any satisfactory response and still respect the people I love most?"

Rebecca stood and shrugged, wandering over to the kitchen counter.

"Who said you had to give a satisfactory response? They just want to sell papers, don't they?" She smiled and sifted through a small pile of envelopes. "Oh, look here. Did Mrs. Crow tell you that Anna wrote?"

I jumped from my chair and plucked the letter from Rebecca's hand, tearing it open to read. My dearest sister. How I hungered and ached for news of her life. After hearing that her last letter had been ruined, I craved word from her all the more.

"Well, what does it say?" Rebecca asked.

I looked up from the page, positively glowing.

"She's with child. I'm to be an aunt."

36

OUTGROWN

It didn't take long for me to give up Rebecca as my prisoner. Once I'd learned about Anna's pregnancy, I wrote back immediately, with a new purpose, saying I would be there to help her through every stage of confinement and the early years of the child, at least. If she would have me, that is.

She would have me, as things turned out, and requested that I don't dawdle on my way there.

Mrs. Crow understood.

"Should I keep the vacancy?" she asked.

"I don't think so. If I do return, it won't be for a long time, and besides, you'll need the rent."

"And Cyrus?" Mrs. Crow asked heavily. The pointer lifted its head from its makeshift mattress in the corner of the room. "I'm sure he'll love the country."

I laughed. Cyrus had enjoyed himself at the Rigby home, kenneling with the other hounds. I was certain that Mr. Rigby could make good use of him.

But it was like tearing a page out of a library book.

"Not quite as much as he loves it here, I imagine."

Mrs. Crow's eyes welled up with tears, and she bawled as she hugged me. I withheld a giggle. As fond as I was for the dog, Mrs. Crow had become his family.

"I'll take excellent care of him," she promised.

That much was true, much better care than the transient life Bram had offered. I wondered, with Bram's reduced life expectancy from the ink, who would pass first, my neighbor or the Meddler—a grim and sobering thought.

Before leaving the city, I visited the pub for a last farewell to my dearest friends. It was full of woeful warnings against being gone too long, admonitions to visit often, and more embraces than I felt necessary.

In turn, I chided them about making things legal, which produced a ruddy red color in Doug's cheeks and a saucer-like hope manifesting in Rebecca's wide eyes.

Then, I had a final stop to make before leaving: Alastair McHenry's legal offices.

As I walked through the familiar streets of my home, I gazed on the brick and cobbles, breathed in the spring-crisp river air, noted with nostalgia and fondness the various print stands that checkered the avenues and corners. I didn't imagine I would return to Dawnhurst, not in any permanent capacity, at least.

The consideration was not laced with resentment as it had been once. In the midst of my accusations, the street-going strangers came across to me as enemies, traitors even. This was the home that brought me up, and in my dire straits, I could not rely on its hospitality to know and protect me. I wanted to run from it, hate it, rebel against it.

But now, a deeper melancholy played on its stage. As I walked, it felt as though I'd left it for years and now came back to see the city for what it was. Dawnhurst had never betrayed me, but its humble gates could never have kept me in. My feet weren't the right shape for its walks, my face the wrong shape to look like its child.

In the end, though, if I was to leave, I wanted to explain to the city why. It might not matter to anyone, or it might meet gossip, but I wanted to make it clear to myself that I left on terms that were my own.

Alistair wasn't in his office, so I left my note with instructions that he find the best, most reputable buyer on my behalf, and to forward any payments to the Rigby's address, minus whatever professional fees he deemed appropriate.

I had written what all of those editors begged for. They would want revisions, more clarity, more details and indulgence, but this was not to be requested.

My words were my own.

As the carriage the Rigbys sent for me drove from the city, the words of my article circulated on an endless loop in my head. Farewell to my streets. Farewell to my home. Farewell to the past.

I didn't look back when we reached the bend on the city's outskirts. It was either too painful or not painful enough. I didn't need to know which.

37

LUELLA'S LETTER

Why I Must Leave Dawnhurst-on-Severn

Thoughts by Luella Winthrop

I grew up in Dawnhurst-on-Severn. I lived on both sides of the river. My father and mother are buried in the church's graveyard. I worked in many capacities trying to support my sister in modest straits. It may surprise you to learn that I wrote under the pseudonym Travis Blakely for the publication of *Langley's Miscellany*. I tasted the city's finest food, both in rich establishments and humble pubs. I reached for the golden rings it had to offer.

And now I leave it.

I know many of you are interested to read the sordid details about my arrest, my associations with Bram Lowhouse and the Thomas family, or even hear me lament the burden of my now infamous reputation.

I cannot satisfy any of these desires.

But I could not leave this fair city without at least saying goodbye, and in so doing, leave with you the knowledge I have pertaining to it. If you feel it your business to dive into my words to find insight and inference, the choice is yours.

But it is my opinion that if Dawnhurst cannot accept the suicide of Lord Lucas Thomas, the city itself is to blame for his end.

I've been fortunate to know some of this city's most wonderful inhabitants, and it's not my purpose to list them all here, but I would be remiss to refuse an opportunity to make use of the public's attention in order to repair some of the damage that gossip and scandal has unjustly sewn.

Bram Lowhouse was a wandering fair worker. He scratched out a living from humble beginnings through an obsession with natural phenomena he called magic. He theorized, hypothesized, experimented, and followed this obsession to ludicrous ends. I will be the first to admit that this aim has, in the past, led him down difficult avenues to painful consequences. But to think he would ever purposefully harm another individual is sheer lunacy. It is my personal conviction that Mr. Lowhouse would sooner build a world of his own than come against another in violence even in self-defense.

That a jury from Dawnhurst convicted him of murder will forever stain the city's history. We chose the easy lie over the difficult truth. Bram had no motive to kill Luke Thomas and no desire. What he had was a reputation as an outsider, and a mob willing to jump at the merest hint of past transgressions. I've come to believe our past actions do not define us, and those who do not enjoy the stable and domestic lifestyle to which we all aspire bear that specter of past wrongs heaviest. I don't know where Bram Lowhouse is now, but I pray he finds some place that may appreciate him for what he is, instead of condemning him for whatever he was.

George Cooper was a friend of my father's. I met him when I was a young girl. When my father's friends found themselves in minor scrapes against the law, my father would inevitably march down to the station to plead their case. Although he and the old sergeant didn't always see eye to eye, on numerous occasions they reached fair and equitable solutions through compromise and a willingness to consider that their position might not be without flaw.

Years after my father passed away, I met Cooper as I worked in journalism. I always knew him to be a correct and true man, dedicated to principles and cognizant he could only do his part to make the city run. I'm inspired that a man can persevere in good conscience with his principles even when the immediate outcome troubles his intellect. Many of us know genuine goodness in the abstract and struggle to apply it to everyday life. Cooper did not adjust reality for the sake of what he recognized were his own limitations on understanding. I do not and never will bear George Cooper any ill will, and pray he finds peace and rest for the remainder of his days.

Edward Thomas, the new Sergeant of the Dawnhurst Police Force and son of the late Lucas Thomas, is the most inspiring man I've ever met. When I think of sacrifice and dedication to loved ones, his face will forever guide as an example. I hesitate to elaborate on his good nature, as it may distress him. He's not one to accept public praise with ease. Suffice it to say, I doubted Edward Thomas. I did not believe men came with such distinguishing good built in their hearts. I've paid for that doubt and learned that whatever weaknesses lie within him are for God to judge alone.

I think it's difficult to accept that some among us are what they seem. It can be so frightening to trust that a good man, or a good woman, will not falter, will not crack. Of course they will! But with such individuals, the fissures are so few and far between that rather than allow ourselves to crumble on their discovery, I would rather now take from myself to buoy up and support them. Above all else, if Dawnhurst can keep Sergeant Thomas, it will count for more than any railway, electrical innovations, or any other sophistication which may yet come through future's door.

The trial of Bram Lowhouse will haunt me forever, as will all of its adjacent ordeal. But life's end is not to spend our days avoiding evil, but to find it within us to grow from trauma.

Finally, dear Dawnhurst-on-Severn, I pray you will continue in prosperity and beauty. I will visit in the future and long for the streets of my childhood, when my sister and I played with my parents near the churchyard.

Oh, and should you ever find yourself in need of an unforgettable meal, Doug's Fish and Chips Pub will inevitably become a landmark of the city and famous round the country. Some may insist that fish and chips are food fit only for the streets, prepared by the impoverished hands of migrants. I insist that Doug's dish has been enjoyed by pauper and aristocrat alike. When I return to visit, I hope that finding room in that establishment is difficult at least, impossible at best.

Farewell.

Sincerely,

Luella Winthrop

38

ANNA'S CONFINEMENT

My sister waited for me on the front steps of the house as she had the winter before when I arrived with the Thomas family. This time, though, it was only her, and there was much less ceremony than when welcoming aristocracy.

The country was brimming with spring life. I arrived in the evening, but the darkness did not linger as it did even a couple of months before. Driving in, I was greeted with budding trees, the sounds of livestock, and the thrill of running streams.

She embraced me as soon as I'd set foot out of the carriage. I held her, unable to pry my arms free. It took all of my fortitude to keep from breaking down. Somehow, being with her made me feel safe in a way I hadn't in months.

"Easy now, Luella," she said, laughing, "mind the baby."

Mention of the pregnancy shocked me out of the embrace, and I stood back to examine her. Her stomach protruded beautifully, despite her fitted skirts and corset.

"A dog ate your first letter," I said, exasperated.

"Oh, it's fine. You know how it is. It took me a while to realize myself what was happening. Yes, there are the signs, but you want to be certain about a thing before you become too excited."

"I certainly don't know how it is!" I cried. "I'm afraid, baby sister, by now, you've accumulated mountains of experience that I do not have!"

"Don't have *yet*," she said warmly, and she wrapped her arm around mine. I opened my mouth to protest, but she didn't give me the time. "Come along. You've arrived early enough for me to show you the budding gardens. I've instructed the rest of the family to allow me all the time I desire alone with you."

"Instructed them?" I laughed. "You have the house under your thumb, then?"

She smiled mischievously. "Oh Luella. One thing to look forward to when it comes to pregnancy, is that few are bold or brave enough to cross your wishes."

She led me around the estate, pointing out her favorite spots beneath tree canopies or benches beside small ponds, until it was too dark to make out much of the nature. She didn't ask about the trial or Bram or Edward, and I didn't volunteer the information.

She ushered me inside, where warm food and a warmer welcome waited from the Rigbys. Jacob swept me into his arms and kissed me happily on the cheek. The euphoric glow that emanated from Anna's pregnancy had spread not just to her own personality. The entire household acted as though they awaited Christmas.

High magic. High human magic. I smiled, as I enjoyed the familial chaos picking up the dinner table: exuberant conversations, unguarded smiles... It was a heavenly scene.

But even in the midst of the joy, a small strain of regret and grief pained me. I would never have this, not of my own. I'd likely cost Edward the same. Bram and Hirythe would not enjoy a meal like this either. We were the hopeless, having spent our passion for adventure and traded our futures for excitement.

Anna noticed my dazed expression and took my hand, banishing the thought quickly. I helped myself to some buttered parsnips. If Anna could banish my demons with a gentle squeeze of the hand, my future might not be all bad.

Time stretched on at the Rigbys, and piece by piece I told my story to my sister. Like Rebecca, she shared in the disappointment of the

Netherdowns' destruction, and I could see a disturbed concern in her eyes when I recounted how I'd lost faith in Edward.

She replied the way any loving sister might, full of unabashed loyalty for my own heart, notwithstanding its flaws. There is no greater champion than family for our own causes, but in the end, my sister knew little about my plight. I was grateful for her love but took no heed of her counsel.

Despite what she said, I did not deserve Edward. And even if she could convince me otherwise, it didn't matter. I doubted I would ever see him again, unless I happened to bump into him while visiting Rebecca or Mrs. Crow in the future.

And if that were to happen... The prospect filled me with dread.

Anna grew more uncomfortable the closer she came to delivery. I hadn't enjoyed much opportunity to be so close to a pregnancy, and seeing just how large my sister's stomach grew was nothing short of astonishing. I did my best to make her comfortable, accompanying her on walks through flowering meadows or reading to her. But the closer we came to delivery, the less effective these measures proved.

One morning, while she was laying out on a sofa, and I read aloud a delightful adventure from the United States of America called *Little Women*, Mr. Rigby interrupted us.

"The post came in," he said, filtering through a series of letters.

"Not now, Mr. Rigby! We were reaching a crucial juncture in our novel reading," Anna protested. Mr. Rigby smiled broadly.

"Sorry to interrupt! It's just that the post pertains to Luella. Apparently, there was a bit of mix-up. I'm afraid some of these letters are a bit tardy."

He placed three envelopes on the side table and whistled on his way out of the room.

"What a quandary!" Anna said. "I'm not sure which I'd rather hear, news from outside the estate or the next chapter for Jo March."

"Let me answer for you," I said, opening the first letter. "I don't think I can wait another second. It's from Rebecca."

My heart skipped with anticipation.

"Dear Luella," I read aloud, "well, there's no point in beating the bush. It's happened. I'm to be Mrs. Doug Tanner. It took no more than a week after you left. Something about your parting sat poorly with him, and after reading your article in the paper, I think he felt it was time for him to something equally bold. I cannot describe how happy I feel, but I plan on saving every detail of the account of his proposal until I can see you in person. The wedding will be in just two short months. If you aren't there, I don't think I'll ever speak to you again."

I dabbed my eyes. There's magic in a proposal. Rebecca Turner, the woman I'd met as a police station typist, older than myself, and ever-inspiring for the growth of my character... If she could find love at her age, perhaps love knew no bounds after all.

"You must go to the wedding, then!" Anna said happily. "Don't worry about me. I'm sure you can make it back in time for the excitement."

"Two months? That will be uncomfortably close to the baby's delivery. I don't know what to do, Anna. How can I leave you at a time like that? Surely Rebecca will understand." I shook my head, bewildered. It's funny and inconvenient how life often packs everything important into a rain cloud and showers it down at once.

"But that's not true at all. You heard Mr. Rigby. There was a delay with the post. What is the date on that letter?"

I glanced quickly at the top of the page.

"Gracious, this was written in March. That would put her wedding in May."

"That explains the other letters," my sister said, eyeing the stack.

I sifted through them quickly, each a reproachful and anxious missive warning that the wedding date was coming quickly, and that Rebecca was worried she hadn't heard from me and finally a desperate plea to respond, or at least surprise her with my attendance.

It hardly seemed fair that a problem delivering these notes could threaten such an important juncture.

"The wedding is next week," I said, pale and panicked.

"Thank goodness you haven't missed it then. You will have to borrow something of mine to wear. Heaven knows I haven't fit into my best dresses in months. A spring wedding! How beautiful it will be! I only wish I could accompany you."

The thought of returning to Dawnhurst already weighed on me. I wrote my parting article with the intention that greater time might heal whatever ill feelings it left with my readers. Having Anna beside me would certainly ease that misgiving.

"You couldn't make the trip, could you?" I asked.

She laughed.

"I was just saying something nice, Luella. You're always so literal about things. I can't go. What would I wear? And thinking of sitting in a carriage for half a day sounds miserable. You will have to give the couple my regards. Tell them we'd be more than happy to host a visit if they ever feel up to traveling."

I nodded meekly. I would be traveling alone then. I wondered who else got an invitation. The wedding party would not be unseemly large. Then again, Doug was not unpopular amongst his employees or friends.

"What's that last letter there?" Anna said, noting a final envelope still sealed on my lap. Clumsily, I picked it up and noted immediately that its weight differed from the others. On the envelope's edge was a gold border, and the seal was made with fine, crimson colored wax.

When I read its contents, I nearly fainted.

"What is it?" Anna asked.

"Heavens above. I've just been nominated for the Golden Inkwell..."

39

VOWS

My hasty return to Dawnhurst-on-Severn came before I knew it. I was surprised to discover just how quickly time passed when spent in good company and pleasurable occupation. After writing to secure a bed for a couple of nights with Mrs. Crow and Cyrus, I traveled by Rigby carriage, dressed in something borrowed from my sister, a green, fashionable gown that she insisted brought out the color of my eyes. I pushed down memories of a green gown Edward had once dressed me in.

To make the wedding ceremony, which Rebecca graciously scheduled later in the morning, I had to leave early, well before the sun had come up, dressed and ready to attend when I arrived. The bustle bunched behind me on the narrow seat while traveling, and the under-layers and corset, although flattering, made the trip less comfortable than I'd have preferred.

I tried to occupy my mind while traveling, even attempting to read to pass the half day it took to return. But it was no use. A singular question ate every idle moment. Who would be there? What would I do if *he* were present?

But soon, the nerve-wracking wait ended, and I was entering the Church at Milford Square with hardly a moment to glance toward the graveyard where my parents lay. Still, it was impossible to miss the gravestones. Travis Gerald Winthrop. Emma Jane Winthrop. The headstones were fresher than many of the others in the graveyard. It'd been too long since I'd paid my respects. My mother would have been upset by it, but my father would have been happy that I was busy living.

The memories rubbed at my emotions before I'd even entered the chapel.

I was wrong about the intimacy of the affair. The church was nearly full. I was fortunate to find a spot on a pew near the back and just in time. Minutes after I'd arrived, Rebecca and Doug entered, and everyone in the room craned their necks or stood to have a good look. She was beautiful, wearing a white dress with ruffles and lace that must have cost an absolute fortune. I'd rarely seen a dress dyed white in person before, and the effect was nothing short of angelic. I couldn't imagine a more fitting aesthetic for such a wonderful person. Doug beamed beside her, glossy eyed from his first step into the building.

I had already predicted how unique Rebecca's wedding would be. But to have so many in attendance at the church was astonishing. The whole affair spoke to a wealth and prominence I was unaware my friends enjoyed.

Once the clergyman began, and my relief at arriving in time settled, my eyes wandered to examine the surroundings. The church was just as I remembered it as a girl. I suppose that's one purpose of a church. It's not a ship that bobs in the waves of change, its value lies in its ability to stand firm like a lighthouse.

But it didn't take long for my wandering eyes to find what I feared and looked forward to most. Edward Thomas sat near the front, dressed in a crisp ebony frock coat. From my safe distance across the room, I allowed my gaze to linger on his features, trying to place it over my memory of him from more than half a year before.

His ordeals had matured him, and his expression, though pleasant and supportive of the event at hand, carried a natural, nested exhaustion. His once sharp eyes looked wary and wise. In place of the well-trimmed mustached I'd known on him were freshly shaved whiskers, which somehow rendered him more distinguished than young.

A lump formed in my throat at the sight of him. Hundreds of questions buzzed inside me. I hoped he was well. I hoped he was moving on and finding some satisfaction in his work.

As if cognizant that eyes were on him, his head turned in my direction, and I quickly jerked my attention back to Doug and Rebecca, trying to stifle a blush.

The ceremony passed by quickly and beautifully. Who could maintain dry eyes when Doug fumbled the words of his vow or when his voice broke through his rugged beard when he promised to honor his new wife or when close inspection revealed just how tightly Rebecca grasped his hands or when her shoulders heaved from suppressed, happy sobs?

Marriages go poorly so very often that it's easy to forget how powerful one may be when rightly done.

Soon, we all stood, and the couple exited down the aisle, paying strict attention to look none of their guests in the eyes, as tradition dictated. I'd never seen Rebecca so reverent, her cheeks streaked with quiet streams of tears.

I was grateful to be sitting toward the back, and thus one of the first of the congregation to leave the church. I was afraid of accidentally bumping into Edward. Despite how many ways I envisioned it in my head, I could not see the interaction ending gracefully for me.

We followed the couple through the streets to Doug's Fish and Chips Pub. As guests entered, Doug and Rebecca warmly shook hands and exchanged embraces, happy as clams, looking younger than their age by far.

When Rebecca saw me, she yelped with joy and threw her arms around me.

"You came!" she said. "I was afraid you didn't receive my letters."

"I nearly didn't. Let me say that delivery of notices in the country is not as reliable as the post we enjoy in the city!" I kissed her cheek. "Look at you! How lucky Doug is. Your gown is breathtaking."

She smiled, blushing.

"I have you to thank for that."

I knit my eyebrows. "I beg your pardon?"

"Your article. It was all anyone wanted to talk about. You have a knack for that. Soon after its release, the pub enjoyed a steady stream of business that has filled Doug's head with such imagination. You should see the changes he's planning. It'll be more a restaurant than a pub before you know it. Your recommendation will make him more wealthy than he ever imagined."

My mouth must have dangled open.

"I'm shocked, too," she continued, "but happy for it. It was so kind of you to think of us."

The surprise burst from my stomach as laughter. Rebecca laughed with me.

"Well, that's for the best. Consider it a wedding present, I suppose."

Soon after, I lost her to the rest of her guests and awkwardly found space at a table far enough from the wedding party's so as to avoid contact with Edward. I imagined that if I had received Rebecca's letters earlier, she would have asked me to be her maid of honor, as Doug asked Edward to be his best man. I said a silent prayer of gratitude for it. The thought of interacting with Edward in such a close capacity still made me shrink.

"I'm glad to have found the bashful table," said an older, feminine voice behind me. I turned and faced a woman who bore familiar characteristics, though I couldn't place them. Beside her sat a woman of about my age.

"Am I that obvious, then?" I asked, nodding at an invitation that they join me.

"Well, kindred spirits are not so difficult to identify. I'm just happy to have received an invitation."

"Mother!" the younger woman said discreetly.

"What? I am!"

They sat beside me and we watched Rebecca and Doug interacting with guests, eating, and laughing heartily.

"She is so beautiful, isn't she?" the daughter asked. "She was always beautiful, even as a girl."

I turned again. Their shared angular jawlines and bright eyes suddenly made sense to me.

"You're Rebecca's mother? And sister?" I asked.

"I am." She nodded. "I'm Beatrice. This is my daughter Diana."

"It's a pleasure," Diana said politely.

"And you are?" Beatrice asked.

"Luella Winthrop, I'm a good friend of Rebecca's. In fact, I hope it's not too bold to say she is my closest friend. Though, I've only known her for a relatively brief period."

"Thank you, then," Beatrice said, grasping my hands. "I may have you to thank for our presence here today."

"Me?" I scoffed. "What on earth did I do?"

"Perhaps nothing intentional, but Rebecca and I have quarreled for many years."

"Mother, I hardly think Miss Winthrop is interested in our family drama," Diana cut in.

"Nonsense. I won't miss this opportunity to express gratitude," her mother countered. Diana shifted uncomfortably in her seat. "If it bothers you, you can take a turn around the room."

"I think I will," Diana replied, standing and leaving us to privacy.

"Propriety," Beatrice said, "ever in the way of what's important."

"Wise words," I replied, my eyes lingering on Diana as she masterfully entered conversation with strangers.

"Yes. Words I paid dearly to learn. I'd given up any hope of hearing from my Rebecca again, but a few months ago, I received the first letter from my daughter in years." She smiled. "Something changed."

I nodded as I puzzled over this information. Rebecca never mentioned to me she wrote her mother. I thought back to our conversation overlooking Fernmount when she confided in me she'd lost her mother. She'd never explained why. She'd once told me she took to my friendship so easily because she'd lost a sister, as well.

"Please forgive me for asking," I said, "but Rebecca never explained what caused a rift between your family. My mother passed away many years ago, you see, and I'm so close with my remaining sister. It's difficult for me to understand what could merit such a divide."

"Nothing should," she replied. "I've regretted it very much since. If I knew then that my convictions would have such consequences, I'd never have pushed them so strongly. I thought I knew what was best for her. I wanted her to marry a nice young man capable of providing a comfortable home."

I nodded and tilted my head.

"That seems the heartfelt desire of every parent, does it not? Marriage, comfort, happiness. No one wants to see a child struggle through life."

"Of course," she went on. In the center of the room, Doug danced a small jig with some of his mates. Rebecca clapped and laughed. Diana settled beside her, a smile escaping her own lips. They looked so alike. "Rebecca wanted to struggle. She thought that if she did things her way, some magnificent treasure awaited her at the end of her road. How was I to know she was correct?" Mrs. Turner laughed. "I mean look at him. Who could not be enthused by his easygoing manner?"

"He only gets better, as well," I assured her. She smiled and patted my arm.

"I gave Rebecca an ultimatum. She either found common sense and married the man her father and I had chosen, or she must leave home... I feel filthy just recounting it, but I hope my penance is paid. As I said, I was elated to have received the invitation."

I leaned back in my chair.

"If I know anything about your daughter, I can only say that you should look forward to her goodness. She will not have invited you here just to neglect your relationship henceforth."

Her voice broke as she replied, "I hope so."

We lapsed into silence, and the rest of the morning played on. Many rounds of food—not only fish and chips but several surprisingly sophisticated dishes—circled the tables, and drink was shared by all. Edward was nowhere to be seen, and I busied myself getting lost in trance-like considerations about the cyclical nature of family, love, and friendship.

Finally, the happy couple made their way to a waiting carriage, one I recognized from the Thomas estate, to whisk them away to a secret location for the rest of their marriage celebration. I joined in the rest, throwing handfuls of rice, while some of Doug's more chummy companions tossed shoes.

In their wake, the celebration party was left in a pool of bittersweet melancholy. While the couple had lit the atmosphere with unbridled joy, the rest of us were left to consider life, longing, and priority. Many of these guests went back into the pub, their wedding present a stimulus to Doug's business venture through drink. I stood watching after the carriage, smiling, and wishing there had been some way to preserve the memories of the day, the way Bram had with the Netherdowns.

The crowd peeled until I was nearly alone. Someone else looked after them several lengths from me—someone with steely eyes.

"Rebecca was gutted when she came to grips with the fact that you would not be beside her through every step of the wedding day," Edward said abruptly, his eyes still watching the road.

My heart pounded. I had feared this interaction from the moment I received Rebecca's invitation. How could I trust myself to speak? I was grateful he did not turn his eyes on me.

"There was a problem with the delivery of her letters," I stammered quietly after an awkward beat. "I only heard about the wedding last week."

"I had assumed as much. I assured Rebecca that were it in your power, you'd have crossed an ocean to be here."

"Thank you."

Silence.

"That was one hell of a farewell letter to the city," Edward continued, eyes unflinching from the road. The carriage had already disappeared from view, but we both looked on. The street was safety. It did not hold my heart in its hands. I had never wronged the street.

"It wasn't intended to be. I only meant to clear the air on my way out."

"Congratulations on your nomination for the Golden Inkwell. You've chased that prize for a very long time."

I couldn't tell if there was bitterness in his voice. Did my nomination anger him?

"I don't think I will be accepting it," I said. This, finally, elicited a turn of surprise from him. I held my gaze fast on the street, though, and noticed him only from the corner of my eye. After studying me for a moment, he retook his position again.

"You don't think that might come off as snobbery?"

"I don't much care how it comes off. It doesn't feel right to accept it. If I'm scorned for that view, so be it."

He clasped his hands firmly behind his back. This conversation had gone so differently than how I'd imagined. As he shifted on his feet, suddenly, I was afraid he would leave, and despite how much I'd dreaded this reunion, being in his presence again was like finding water in a desert. I gushed desperately to prolong his stay.

"I'm sorry, Edward."

"Please—"

"I can't express how sorry I am for everything."

"Luella—"

"I keep looking back in horror at every point I should have—"

"Enough!" he hissed. I turned to him in alarm and bit the inside of my cheeks. He cleared his throat and continued. "What's done is done. It cannot be undone."

"Your mother?" I asked.

"The same. Just a ruddy, torn portrait hanging on the wall. I thought to have the painting restored but I'm too afraid to interfere with whatever power lies within."

"Of course."

The river swam noisily by down the street. Birds eager to enjoy the midday spring sunshine chirped overhead. The smell of wet cobbles drying reached my nose. He took in a breath to start another sentence but aborted the attempt. I picked up a different strand.

"How is your work with the police force? Do you enjoy your new position?" I asked.

"I resigned," he replied. "Did you not hear?"

My eyebrows shot up in surprise, an expression that seemed overly emotive and ungraceful in my sister's fine dress.

"I did not," I said clumsily.

"It was time for me to uphold the semblance of my family's legacy. My mother was right, after all. There are many who depend on Fernmount's management for their livelihoods. I spend most of my time there."

"That is noble of you, to turn down a position you might well have loved."

"Noble?" He scoffed. "If I'm honest, frankly—well, after Bram, the police work wasn't the same. His case, I mean."

I bit my lip. "I imagine as sergeant you were called on to make more discretionary decisions. A step toward judging who should go free and who deserved prison."

He drew a circle on the ground with his fine boot.

"It wasn't for me," he replied plainly. His mannerisms and willingness to share some parts of his life, even his eagerness to do so, reminded me of a young boy trying to prove he was a man. I didn't find it off-putting, only unfortunate. Once, Edward had allowed me into his feelings so openly. Now, he was a cold, closed window.

"And you?" he asked. "What is it you spend your time on? Has Bram rehabilitated well enough?"

"I don't know. He and his friend left. They didn't tell me where they were going. I'm confident that if there is a remedy for Bram, or even a treatment, Hirythe can administer it. But that's for them to discover."

"You did not go with them?"

I shifted on my feet.

"No." Beneath the ring on my finger, my skin warmed. "I was invited, and I considered it. At one point, I felt there was nothing here for me. But in the end, Bram insisted I stay."

"He did?"

"Yes. He helped me see that, though my life is not what it was, I would regret forever leaving some things behind."

My response soothed the ring's effect, and I found it in me to turn toward him, finally meeting his eyes. They were as deep as I remembered, wiser now, older, but they were Edward's. He looked back at me, daring to linger and decipher my meaning.

"Your sister," he concluded, turning away again. "It would be hard to leave family. I regret bitterly the distance I put between my parents and me."

Like a whip, his comment snapped and stung me, a subtle reminder that he had lost all dear to him.

"Yes, my sister. She is expecting a child at the Rigbys."

He snuffed out a small, ironic laugh.

"I imagine the household is thrilled."

"They are. It's refreshing to be around such hope for the future."

He was hurting. I could feel it in the air between us. He had already shut down my attempt at apology, but I could not simply stand there and bear his pain. I turned and stepped toward him.

"Edward, I don't deserve the privilege, but if you need anything, I would acquiesce in a heartbeat."

"I best pay the clergyman for his services and see to Doug's other affairs. Good day, Miss Winthrop."

He turned on his heel and quickly strode down the street. I watched after him, hurt, alone, but at least the ring on my finger did not burn.

❧ 40 ☙

FATE

Dawnhurst held no more surprises for me. After spending a night giving Cyrus some scratches behind the ears and listening to the latest gossip, again, from Mrs. Crow, I headed back to the Rigbys.

Despite my best efforts, the conversation I had with Edward replayed in my mind in a never-ending loop. Hadn't he looked at me like he did once? Was it hard for him to give up his role as police sergeant? It was honorable of him to perform as Doug's best man, despite the clear difference in social class. Of course, that was the type of unique approach to propriety that marred the Thomas name in aristocratic circles, the type of thing his mother would have reluctantly warned against while secretly supporting.

I hadn't seen him in months. It wasn't as terrible as I'd imagined. Perhaps, I'd find occasion to see him again one day. Perhaps with time, we could become friends once more.

The weeks passed quickly. I recounted everything about Rebecca's wedding to Anna on countless occasions, leaving out my conversation with Edward. I felt it was private in a severe sense of the word. There was no need to parade my guilt in front of my sister. Edward wouldn't hear my apology. What greater condemnation could there be of my character?

By summer, in the fresh heat of the country, the day finally arrived. It started with cries of pain in the middle of the night, but Mrs. Rigby and the midwife set to work with impressive efficiency and accuracy. While I was busy fumbling about back and forth between the washroom and her bedroom with clean linens, trying to hold back tears of fear and anticipation, they guided her through what I learned to be one of woman's most trying, God-given ordeals.

As I was the one going in and out of the room, Jacob continually pestered me with questions. A veritable litany of *How was she's*, *What could he do's*, *Did she look well's*, and *What should he be doing's*.

Who knows what I said to him—something reassuring, I hope. The truth was, with every contraction, I had to bury the fear deeper inside of me. Women died in childbirth. It was not uncommon, and here in the country, although there was a doctor in a neighboring town, there were no resources available like there were in the city.

If I lost Anna...

I understood, now, how Charlotte felt when she told me her husband's death was a penance for her interference in a magical ritual. If I lost my sister...

Hours into the morning, I sat quietly with Jacob and Mr. Rigby in the dining room, when Mrs. Rigby came out.

"She's still a ways to go, yet, I'm afraid. We're all tired, of course, but none as much as dear Anna. She needs our support. So buck up, everyone. A baby is coming!"

We all straightened in our chairs, weariness chased out by the reprimand, and recommitted to the task, whatever that task was. The most tiring part for the rest of us was simply being so helpless.

A knock rapped at the front door.

"Did you call for the doctor, dear?" Mr. Rigby asked.

"A doctor? Has she taken a turn?" Jacob asked, panicked and pale-faced.

"No, though if he is here of his own volition, I'd not say no to the comfort of his presence. Feed him pheasant. Feed him brandy. I don't care what you feed just don't let him leave."

The Rigby parents left the room in two directions. Jacob's leg bounced nervously.

"My sister is stronger than even you know," I said, putting a comforting hand on his arm. "She's been looking forward to this for her entire life. Have faith."

He smiled at me, a strand of loose hair dangling over one eye, when Mr. Rigby returned. He rubbed his temples and muttered with a bewildered tone.

"Um, Luella, I'm not sure what to make of it."

"Make of what?"

"Lord Thomas is at the door asking to see your sister."

I stood.

"What? Lord Edward Thomas?"

"Well, certainly not his father," Jacob remarked. "He can't see Anna right now, that much is obvious!"

"Why would he want to see her at all?" I asked.

"I don't know," Mr. Rigby replied. "He said it was private. I'm at a loss. I don't want to put you out, Luella. Things must stand dreadfully between the two of you, but what am I supposed to say to the man?"

One of Anna's cries sounded from the other room. The sound jolted my nerves like a lightning bolt.

"Of course, Mr. Rigby. I'm sorry to put you at a disadvantage. Please, let me take care of it. At the very least it will give me something productive to do."

"Thank you, my dear. If you need me, merely call."

I strode to the front door and swung it wide open. Edward stood, his riding outfit spattered in mud. His hair was not neatly combed, but a mess from the wind and travel.

"Luella?" He stood back in alarm as if I were a snake. "Of course, I knew you were staying here, but—well, I asked to see Anna."

"Your timing could not be worse, Edward. She's laboring now to bring her child into the world."

"Good heavens! Surely you jest."

Another cry from inside the house sounded.

"Clearly, I do not. So whatever business you may have with my sister will have to wait or else you can tell me a message, and I can relay it to her. But I'm afraid the Rigbys are in no state to entertain you. Mr. Rigby was just too bashful to say it himself."

He started awkwardly and cut himself off.

"Of course, I can return at a better time."

"And a message for her?" I asked.

A commotion of raised voices inside drew our attention. I retreated from the step and withdrew to hearing distance.

"Mr. Rigby, the baby is not right! Tell me you maintained the doctor!"

"It wasn't a doctor. It was Lord Thomas!"

"He won't do us any ruddy good. We need Doctor Marvins as soon as he can come!"

My knees buckled. The baby wasn't right. What did she mean? I'd have rather been reinfected with the Dúil and Sraith twice over than hear those words. They settled into my ears, spiraling me down. This was a nightmare. I lost track of the floor and fell into a chair. Oh, not Anna.

"He's a ride out still," Mr. Rigby said.

"I'll go at once," Jacob declared.

"You won't. You're not the rider your father is," Mrs. Rigby countered. "And you may want to be here, in case..."

"It's not a question of rider. I only hope our best horse is fast enough." Mr. Rigby swept through the room, his frock and crop in hand. He almost collided with Edward, who had crept into the foyer behind me.

"I'll go," Edward said. "There is no faster horse than mine west of Oxford. Doctor Marvins, you said?"

"In nearby Stroud."

Edward sprinted from the house and climbed atop his horse. With a shout from him, its hooves thundered on the dirt and faded from earshot.

"Luella, with me," Mrs. Rigby said, grabbing me by the wrist. "Don't let the fear in. There's still much to be done."

Back in Anna's bedroom, a pile of blood-stained linens sat in a basket, and my sister, wet with perspiration, ground her teeth.

"Luella, what's the matter?" she panted. Absent an answer, I looked to Mrs. Rigby.

"The baby is facing the wrong direction, and we're struggling to right it," she said.

"Will it be all right? Will my baby be all right?" Panic rose in Anna's voice. I smothered her hair in heavy caresses and grabbed her hand.

"Come now," I said. "We've sent for the doctor. You need to stay with us until he can get here."

I put my forehead to hers, and my tears mixed with her sweat. Agony is to be helpless in times of trauma.

As the minutes wore on, the strain on Anna's body grew terribly evident. Her skin lost nearly all color, and her lips started to blue. How far was it to Stroud?

No greater strength could ever be demonstrated than how Anna ferociously fought to keep her baby and herself in limbo while help arrived.

As we waited and struggled, she weakened. My faith and courage dueled with fear. But I would not show it, not where Anna might see. I drew on the high magic that I knew existed in our sisterly bond.

"Luella," she called in a hoarse voice. "Please, there's something I want to tell you."

"You can tell me after," I said, patting her brow with a cloth.

"It may be best if I tell you now." Her voice shook. "In the event—" She coughed.

"In no event. Do you have any idea how beautiful this baby is going to be?" I asked. "If it looks anything like you and Jacob, the stars will shine brighter for it."

"I just want you to know," she went on, ignoring me, "that you did so well. I owe everything to you. You may think a single mistake ruined all the effort you spent raising me, but it didn't. By then, you'd already taught me that people are human and make mistakes, and that does not define them."

Her eyes fluttered, and she groaned as another contraction came on.

"Stay with us now, Anna," Mrs. Rigby said. Her face was grim and slack-mouthed. I lost track of the walls of the room. They were like the walls beyond the Onyx Door, or the fog on the beach closing in on me, pushing toward darkness.

For all my interference with magic, could there not have been some trinket to help my sister?

"There is redemption," she went on. "There are clean slates. Do you believe that, Luella?"

Her question stuck in my ribs, where I struggled to keep my emotions in check. Did I believe in redemption?

"Yes," I said, nodding. "Yes, of course."

"Those chocolate flies worked, Luella. You can count the months. This baby was conceived before we were married. Will it be damned?"

I shared a terse expression with Mrs. Rigby. She shook her head and started crying. She felt as I did. We didn't care. Not now. We just wanted Anna and the baby to make it through, and Anna's eagerness to bare what she must have considered her most shameful secret was not a good sign.

"No. No, no, no. Of course not," I said.

She nodded, willing to agree, if not convinced altogether.

"Will I be?" she asked.

The fear in her eyes demanded a straightforward answer. No scripted refusal would do.

"Not if I have anything to say about it," I replied. "And if you are, think what must come of me? We'll tame the devil and turn hell into a paradise. Just look what we did on the east side of Dawnhurst. It can't be worse than that."

She laughed and coughed and tried to breathe.

"I love you, dear sister," she said, her eyes surrendering to slow blinks.

"Anna. Stay with me now. Anna. Anna!"

The rest was a blur lost to memory, damned to the same void of the burning Netherdowns ashes. A door opened. Doctor Marvins rushed in and immediately set to work. I collapsed on the chair beside the bed. There was such blood. Such distress. Did I weep? Did I wail? Did I call her name?

Is that what brought her back?

The sound of a child's crying worked on me like smelling salts, and I saw the most beautiful niece I could have imagined. Anna's eyes shot open as the cries activated some primal maternal instinct, and she stretched weak arms toward the cries.

"It's a baby girl," Doctor Marvins said. He handed the child to the midwife, who set to work cleaning and wrapping it beside an exhausted Mrs. Rigby. A baby girl. A new baby girl. The relief on Mrs. Rigby's face was overwhelming.

"What about Anna?" she asked.

"I don't see any early signs of infection. We will have to keep a close eye on her for the next few days, keep her in bed and well-tended to, but I don't think recovery is out of the question. She did remarkably well, considering how late I arrived. Small miracles." He smiled.

The midwife placed the baby in Anna's arms, and my sister's face transformed in an instant. She'd always been my baby sister, obsessed with fashion, immature at times. But now she was different. She looked more like our mother.

"Is there a wet nurse?" the doctor asked. "I fear after this ordeal, Anna may not be up to feeding the child."

"There is," Mrs. Rigby replied. But by the time she said it, my sister had already let nature work through her, and the baby's cries quieted to sounds of sloppy suckling and Anna's motherly whispers to her child. Perhaps it was only my weary eyes, but my sister had a glow around her, pure, angelic, and majestic.

The doctor smiled.

"Perhaps send for her just in case, but I think we can leave these two to the able hands of your midwife for now. Hopefully Anna and the baby can get some rest." His voice was quiet, nearly reverent. Mrs. Rigby nodded and followed the doctor from the room. I kissed my sister's forehead.

"Well done," I said. "Oh, Anna, she is beautiful."

"Emma," Anna whispered. "After mother."

I smiled.

"It suits her," I smiled.

I lingered for a while longer before letting Anna and Emma fall asleep. I quietly thanked the midwife and newly arrived wet nurse and left the room.

Outside, the doctor spoke quietly with the Rigbys. Jacob looked up at me.

"She's sleeping now, though I imagine she'll need some bread brought to her soon. Jacob, you should see your daughter."

He beamed, sweeping me into an enormous hug, and I was so grateful for the Rigby family. Jacob had come so far from his boyish arrogance around the Bunbury's dining table. And his parents were good to the core. He picked up a plate of bread and cheese and entered the room behind me.

"What happened?" I asked the doctor.

"I was just trying to explain to the Rigbys. The baby had turned around in the womb and could not make a clean exit. It was stuck. The midwife and I were able to help the child shift into the proper position. The stress on Anna's body must have been immense. Usually, a midwife can correct a baby's position on her own, but in some cases it's necessary to have more pairs of experienced hands."

"And once it was righted, it just came out? Everything went from dire to functional in a moment?"

"Not quite a singular moment," he replied, "but yes. Isn't life extraordinary?"

The quiet in the room bespoke a miracle. Life was extraordinary.

"Still, it's a good thing I arrived as quickly as I did," he went on. "I must say, I've never in my life sat a horse at such a speed."

That, too, seemed to invigorate him in a youthful way.

"Will we be traveling back at the same pace?" he asked, laughing.

"Best we give old Embers a break," Edward replied. I hadn't noticed him before. He leaned against a wall close to the foyer, respectfully distant. "But if you're ready, I can accompany you back to Stroud."

As Dr. Marvins gave instructions to the Rigbys to care for Anna, and promised to return twice a day for the next few days, I stared at Edward. He met my gaze firmly with an enigmatic expression.

How can you say thank you from across a room? How can you say thank you for something so important to someone you care for so deeply?

The doctor finished, but before Edward accompanied him to the courtyard, he gave me a weak smile, my first smile in ages. Then, he was gone, and I collapsed on a sofa, allowing the sheer weight and variety of emotions I'd just experienced to knock me out entirely.

41

THE HIGHEST MAGIC

Anna's spirits recovered more quickly than her body, and it wasn't long before she was begging to go out for some movement, at least small turns around the gardens.

"Please, it looks so lovely out there!" she whined.

But the doctor's orders were clear, and she was confined to bed well beyond the duration of her patience.

Emma was healthy and beautiful, settling in as well as any newborn might into a stark and large world. Anna, Jacob, the Rigbys, and I all spent many hours admiring her little hands, how her face scrunched into delightful expressions, and standing watch for the beautiful sight of an accidental smile or opened pair of eyelids.

In the following days, I also had ample time to try unraveling my emotions. What Anna believed to be her deathbed admonitions haunted me. Can people be redeemed? She spoke of damnation in death, but it seemed to me that the question was ever more important for mortality.

If people can be redeemed, could I be?

About a week after the birth, the Rigbys received another knock on the door by Lord Edward Thomas. He asked after Anna, and upon hearing that she was in high spirits, humbly renewed his request.

"I won't be long, and I hope not to distress her," he explained to Mr. Rigby. "I just find myself eager to settle something between us."

"After what you did for our Anna—for us," Mr. Rigby replied, "I would give you anything. I will check to see if she will receive you."

Edward was admitted to the living room and sat across from me on a sofa. I put a finger in the book I'd been reading and offered a warm smile. He did not reciprocate, instead offering a curt nod and choosing to study the rug beneath us.

His manner made it clear that he did not invite conversation, and I bit my tongue to languish in a truly awkward atmosphere.

It didn't last long, as Mr. Rigby came back promptly to retrieve him.

"She will see you, Edward." Edward let out a heavy breath, clenched his fists a few times, as though from nerves, and followed the man back to my sister's room.

Mr. Rigby, his wife, Jacob, and the wet nurse, Emma in her arms, all filed into the living room a moment later and took confused seats. None of us spoke, all straining our ears to perhaps catch a word of their conversation through the walls.

Twenty minutes later, Edward returned. Mr. Rigby stood.

"She wants to talk to you, Luella," he said.

My eyebrows shot up as all eyes turned on me. I stood, curtsied to Edward, and went into the room.

When I closed the door behind me, my sister met me with a hard expression.

"Sit," she said.

I obeyed.

"What is it?" I asked.

She leveled her eyes at me.

"It can't be," I said, shaking my head.

"And why not?"

"It's just not right." Tears pooled in my eyes. "Why?"

"Because he loves and admires you."

"I don't deserve him, Anna. After everything... his parents, his career, my deceits..."

Anna collected my hands in hers.

"Do you love him?"

I closed my eyes. I so rarely allowed myself to consider that question. What did it matter?

"People can be redeemed," Anna said, "but only when given a chance. A chance from him, and a chance from yourself. I can't tell you I want Edward as a relation or that I want him as Emma's uncle or that I want him to take care of you until you die and perhaps after that. I can only tell you, that I give you permission to consider it. He wanted my blessing. I give it to you."

A spark of hope lit in my heart. My sister's eyes were not playful but full of intention and well-meaning.

"He said he has something he wanted to show you," she said. "Will you at least hear him out?"

I nodded, trying to clear the painful knot rising in my throat.

"He told me he would wait for you near the bridge."

I squeezed her hands and looked at the door.

"What would Dad want?" she asked.

E dward sat beside his coat under an elm tree by the bridge, surrounded by summer grass and the gurgling stream. He stood when he saw me approach. I meekly closed the distance, arms folded.

"You came," he said when I'd come within earshot.

"I did. Anna said I should hear what you have to tell me."

"I'm grateful."

I shook my head ruefully.

"You have nothing over which to be grateful to me."

He frowned.

"Is that what you think?"

"What I know. Edward, what you are doing is noble and sweet, but I've hurt you so deeply. Whenever I'm around you, terrible things happen. I was neglectful of your feelings. I hid the truth about my relationship with Bram. I'm to blame for your parents' misfortune. And perhaps worst of all, I didn't have faith in you when you needed me most."

He rubbed his clean-shaven jaw.

"These are your objections?" he asked.

"They are not small," I replied.

He put his hands behind his back, accentuating the torso beneath his waistcoat. Evidently, he had recovered from the physical strain of housing the Dúil and was back to fighting figure.

"If I may, Luella, the grievances you bring against yourself are not new to me. And I confess they have caused me no small amount of pain."

"Then how do you expect this to work?"

He took a deep breath. "When I left Dawnhurst, I was miserable, wretched. Everything was dark. You occupied my thoughts endlessly. I didn't want to see even the sun for how bitter I was. But as the days stretched on, and I lived at Fernmount, alone and isolated, I grew to understand some things. Every morning, I saw my mother's torn portrait on the wall, where my father's portrait used to hang, and little by little my perspective shifted.

"At first, I considered it an insult to put my father's image beside my mother's on the wall in my home. I spent so much time begrudging him for what he did to me, how he neglected my mother and me. I instructed his portrait to be covered and hidden in a spare room. But seeing my mother alone grated on me. As I woke up alone and spent my time trying to prolong much of the work he'd tried to accomplish in life, I recognized the real wound between him and me came from the distance between us. Now that he's gone, that wound will never heal."

He cleared his throat and took a step closer to me.

"I began to think about you differently, to reassess what I considered your faults, to reconsider how you had hurt me. I hurt you as well, in my own ways. I pushed you. I didn't believe your initial claims about the Netherdowns. I grew so jealous of Bram."

"Those are nothing in comparison with what—"

He held up a hand to stop my protests. "My errors are what pushed me to improve. Or rather, recognizing my errors is what pushed me to improve. At times, when I was down on myself for being weak, the weight of my errors made me feel unworthy of love. Then, I thought about you and how you, after recognizing errors in conduct, might feel the same way. Perhaps even worse. But even a mental image of you, somewhere, cursing yourself for your weakness, feeling unworthy of love—"

He swallowed. My breath heaved in my chest.

"Perhaps it's the same instinct that drove me to police work, but a protective sensation swelled inside me. Nothing—no one—ever has my permission to make you feel like that."

My instinct protested against his words, but the hope in my heart kept my tongue silent, forced me to keep listening.

"As I worked, helping tenants with their land, holding meetings with my father's old associates to expand the estate's interests, my conviction took root, and slowly, reluctantly, expanded even to my father. I considered perhaps he too felt unworthy of love. It opened my heart afresh. I had withheld that from him, and in the end, I only hurt myself. I retrieved his portrait and decided to hang it beside my mother. That's when I found this."

He produced a rolled piece of paper from his coat pocket.

"What is that?" I asked.

"His farewell letter." His voice broke. "It confirmed everything I feared. My father realized his errors too late. His path to redemption was too much for him. He was not a good man, and because he recognized that, he didn't give himself a chance to become a better one."

"Edward, I'm sorry." My instinct to comfort him, to alleviate the sorrow bounding from his eyes, overcame any inhibitions. I grasped his hands. "Oh, I'm so sorry you had to discover that alone."

"It's bittersweet. The sadness and relief all at once. I don't know why he hid it behind his portrait. He apologizes for a life he regretted, even detailing the economic scandal you reported on. Every word hurt to read, but when I finished, I was blessed with at least some sense of closure. Bram did not kill my father. You did not kill my father."

Tears filled my own eyes, and I couldn't place the source of them. Relief. Empathy. Sadness. Everything wrapped into one. "Seeing Rebecca reconcile with her mother and sister at her wedding, watching how thin mortality wore for your own sister while bringing a baby into the world... I won't stand for it, Luella. Forgiveness is power, and I won't let my life be dictated by bitterness. I've lost my parents. I won't lose you, Luella Winthrop."

I shook my head. My walls were crumbling, but they couldn't. It could not be.

"There are other reasons not to have me," I stammered.

"I look forward to discovering them, if you'll allow me too." He moved closer.

"Please, Edward, what if I fail you?"

"Then you will try again," he said, another step closer. "And what if I fail you?"

"You never could," I whispered.

"Why is that?"

"Because I love you, Edward."

My relief, confusion, astonishment, all overflowed, running down my cheeks silently. People can be redeemed. I could be redeemed. Edward was giving me an opportunity to prove it. I had no strength or will left to fight the hope, the desire, or the longing to collapse into him. After seeing Anna so close to the veil of mortality, after seeing Emma's beautiful face, after knowing that my first and primary desire was to honor my family in love...

"Then will you please take this back?" he asked. He held up his mother's wedding band. I held out a hand numbly, and he slipped it on my finger.

"Never take that off, again," he said.

I threw my arms around his neck and kissed him, welcoming a sensation I'd never had before. There were no reservations, no hidden corners, no doubts or misgivings. I would give the rest of my life to Edward Thomas, and his joy, his pain, his life would be mine as well.

The desperation and commitment flowing through the arms that held me promised a future of happiness and fidelity. His words were made true by his heart. Our past errors were sealed by the promise that we would continue on, never surrendering, never parting, growing together, forever.

We lingered under the elm tree by the bridge until the sun set, at last welcoming joy, grief, hope, and love.

42

PEACE

Our marriage was quiet, an intimate ceremony at the church in Milford Square, just Edward, the pastor, and me. On our way out of the church, we paid respect to my parents' resting places before going on to celebrate at Doug's pub.

When we arrived, seeing my own relations and friends around the tables to celebrate our union looked like paradise. The Rigbys sat at one table, my sister and Jacob with young Emma in a pram beside them included. Alastair and Mrs. Crow sat beside them talking with George Cooper. All three clapped loudly and gave speeches about how surprised they were that Edward and I finally tied the knot. Some of their language was bawdy and irreverent, leaving us blushing bright.

Doug and Rebecca served everyone fish and chips and Mrs. Barker's iced buns. We danced. We laughed, and every moment I feared I would wake, that this was a fever dream caused by the Dúil or some other cruel magic. I'd never known such happiness.

In the end, though, Rebecca was right, and Hirythe as well. The magic in human beings is not based on the same power as other magics. It's built on love, and through it, miracles abound. Forgiveness, gratitude, redemption, mercy.

After the celebration wound to a close, Edward asked if I'd be interested in traveling for our honeymoon, but I was only eager to return to Fernmount. I wanted to see the fields, see Greenlake, have a home without a landlord for once in my life.

"Besides," I whispered, "what good is traveling when we'll be so wrapped up in one another, anyway?" He grinned and blushed and kissed me well. Then a shoe hit him, thrown by George Cooper.

"You call that a kiss?" he bellowed. Our friends laughed, and he kissed me again.

W hen our carriage arrived at the estate, the house staff applauded us until we stopped, and the door opened. Edward helped me out of the carriage a fair way off from the front door, specifically as though to introduce me anew to each of them. They all curtsied and said, "my lady." In turn, I hugged each of them, lingering a little longer with Rose.

"I have a dress to return to you," I said. She smiled brightly.

"That'd be most kind, my lady."

When we came to Mr. Crawling, the butler, he bowed and took Edward by the hand, his face excitable.

"You must come at once, sir. I'd have written you earlier, but she forbade it. I can't believe it. I can't make sense of it."

"What is it?" Edward asked.

"Your mother."

Edward looked at me, bewildered.

"Well, let's not just stand here!" I said.

He sprinted inside. I followed after as best as I could in my skirts. When I turned the corner to the dining room, I nearly ran straight into my husband's back. He gaped and trembled.

Charlotte Thomas sat beside the head of the table, sipping a cup of tea, as though she'd never left. She looked as plucky and sharp as ever, but her left hand, where the portrait had torn, was withered and crippled.

"Mother?" Edward asked, choking with disbelief.

"Oh, tell me it's not as ugly as I think it is," she said, raising the misshapen limb, but even she could not maintain her well-humored wit. Edward hurried across the room and cradled her in his arms, where they both broke down.

She motioned to me with one arm, an invitation, and I joined the embrace, taking my place among my new family.

"How?" Edward asked. "When?"

"Just yesterday," she replied, putting a hand on both our cheeks. "Right around the time they tell me you were married. I wish I could have been there. Luella, tell me you didn't wear that outfit."

Charlotte had once told me her greatest fear was to pass on, leaving nothing more than a portrait on a wall. It took me too long to under-stand that her fear was that of any other parent. Legacy is not always wrapped in shallow ambition. Charlotte's greatest fear was for her son, that he might not find happiness. Rebecca's mother had shared the same fear. My father had the same fear as well. What more can a parent desire for a child than they be cherished and loved?

As Edward and I committed to our vows, promising to each other that we would forever cherish our marriage, her prison of oil gave way. Our union was Charlotte's greatest hope, the balm to her greatest fear. Edward had saved his mother through his noble act of forgiveness, by not giving up on me, and instilling in me the courage not to give up on myself.

L ife carried on in something very near bliss. Having known the bad, we appreciated even the mundane. Our days were filled with visits from friends, finding joy in the hard work that comes with running an estate, and enjoying every morsel mortality had to offer. We built Fernmount not just to be a respectable estate of commerce, but one of culture, friendly to the arts and sciences, eager to rejoice in gratitude for God's abundance and quick to help those who may stand in need. Edward became beloved by all who knew him, but by none more than me.

As the months passed, the anniversary of Bram's and Hirythe's parting quickly arrived. I traveled to the wood near Dawnhurst, found a tree root, and buried the Ring of Regret beneath it. I hoped that Bram and Hirythe had found peace somewhere. I hoped that, wherever they were, Bram could finish his days rediscovering the joys of lost memory.

As I rode back from that wood, I understood my journey was never theirs. Their magical adventure, quarrels with rivals, experiments with nature, were all pathways that branched off my road to happiness, as I was to theirs.

As for the Golden Inkwell, I turned down the award despite Edward's insistence to the contrary. It was bittersweet, but I was happy to understand, finally, that my father's sacrifice for literacy had nothing to do with acclaim, as I'd once thought, but the power to improve my station, to improve myself.

Instead, I took Rebecca's advice to try my hand at fiction, publishing under the name of Luella Thomas. Edward was more than supportive, dedicating an entire room at Fernmount as my working office. That room alone was larger than all the offices at *Langley's Miscellany*.

On one desk in that room sits the Remington typewriter he once bought me as a Christmas present. I've since purchased others, wearing them out with endless drafts and revisions of my humble novels. His gift remains mostly untouched, set specially aside.

But sitting in a drawer beneath it is a single, creased, battered sheet of paper. One day, I will write on it, after it's had time to cool, when I'm ready to go back and see the parchment sky and ruins of the eclectic town. When I'm ready to see what happens to memory once lost.

I hope it goes on. The longer I live, the more I believe it will.

43

EPILOGUE

"I told you," Bram said. Rich soil fell from my fingers as I handled the ring. The magic spoke to me from within, resonating in my fingertips with the invitation to come play. I sneered and stood up. "She's not coming, nor should she."

Abandoned again. I wasn't surprised, but it was a shame, all the same. I had never bonded to a human as I had Bram, but he was only a shell of his former self. I considered Luella Winthrop, through some surprising turn of events, to be the perfect specimen to replace Olivia.

Well—not replace. That was cold fae thinking. Olivia could not be replaced. But Luella might have taken us from one and one half beings to three.

"You didn't tell her to simply bury a letter or a coin or something?" I asked without looking back at Bram. My gaze settled on the horizon, taking in the glittering waters of the Italian coastline. The beach far below our green hillside swept aloft into a wide bay. Smoke drifted from chimneys from the nearby village which fought for a permanent place amidst the verdant sloping forest.

Aromas of savory breads and melting cheese reached my nostrils. I shuddered. How I wished I could love the smells of such food. Instead, I was filled with a longing for the mushroom wines of centuries long over. Memories of old feasts of the forest sprang up from the neglected past, nights filled with the plunder of cunning and trickery back when man had yet to discover any method to manipulate the weakness of my kin.

Time never moved faster. A century crawled by as centuries do. A failure to embrace adaptation is what killed them all. I'd be with them, if not for the human beside me.

Bram pushed off from the tree he'd been leaning against and sat on a rock to take in the view.

"It seemed appropriate to tell her to bury the ring. I thought it'd be a chance for her to heal and move on," he said.

"As you have?" I asked.

"Don't start."

I gritted my teeth and closed my eyes. The magic from the trees around us worked its remunerative effects on me with unusual sloth. I didn't envy humans' necessity to sleep so many hours of their short lives, but I wished the choice were mine. The trees served as my restoration, but living in the humans' modern world meant woods were becoming more and more difficult to have at the ready, especially while traveling.

We'd found a small cottage removed enough from town so that we wouldn't be bothered, and I'd spent most of the weeks we'd been here recovering from my seven years in the Netherdowns. The forests in the Mediterranean were foreign to me, overly dense with shrubs and ever-embracing of the sloping ramps toward the sea. Perhaps for those reasons, their magic restored my powers and energies more slowly, but I had no will to complain about that. I was happy for the chance to reflect.

"Asking her to send the ring was foolish," I said after a few deep breaths. "It's..." I trailed off. It was nothing. My caution was a relic of a different time.

"Dangerous?" Bram asked. I bit my tongue. Despite how young he was, his rate of understanding was impressive, and he paid close attention to me.

"You're concerned about the ripple caused by sending an enchanted ring through tree roots?" he continued. "No one is listening. You've convinced me. I doubt we will ever see Jeremy again."

Jeremy. The death of his brother Ned still weighed on me. My related, almost spiritual experience when facing him in the Nether-downs had made far too contemplative.

I had decided I needed to live and do good in the names of those I'd robbed of the opportunity. It sounded right at the time, despite its all but blasphemous nature toward fae magic. Even so, the conviction did not come with any instructions. How did I plan on understanding what *good* was, let alone doing any of it?

Bram was right. No one was listening.

I stuffed the ring into a coat pocket and turned back toward the wood.

"Oh, come on," Bram complained. "You're going back in? Can't we head home?"

"There is nothing preventing you from returning by yourself to that shack." I narrowed my brows. This was why I needed the wood, it wasn't simply to replenish my magic—I needed to ponder and plan. I was alone. Bram had only a portion of his memories, and frankly, I didn't know what to do next.

"You'd abandon me to my own devices? What if Francesca comes sniffing around again?"

"Then you might need to be civil and invite her in. Who knows, you might have a pleasant evening talking together," I replied, massaging my temples. In addition to my own problems, Bram's humor had deteriorated in the past twelve months. He turned more and more reclusive, clinging to me for all social needs. And humans are very social, indeed. It was exhausting talking all the time. Interaction with someone after his own kind would do him much good.

"I can't speak her language," Bram said.

"You may not need to. She seems interested enough."

"An evening of sitting and staring at one another while she giggles awkwardly is not my idea of a pleasant time."

"Lies! I had to sit through countless evenings just like that when you and Olivia were courting." I bit my tongue, but it was too late. Bram failed to hide the wound. It was still too fresh. He still wore a stranger's gaze around his neck in the lover's eye locket. I had failed him thus far. We'd gained no ground at rediscovering the memories of his late wife.

"Francesca is not Olivia," he said quietly.

I sighed and took a final glance at the trees behind me. I'd been dipping into the energy of thickets and woods between here and Gloucestershire since we left Dawnhurst, trying to make up for seven years. It could wait another day.

"Very well," I conceded. "Let's return."

We hiked quietly through the brush until we found the small, curving dirt road that led back to our cottage. When I first met Bram, silence in social settings did not bother me. He had to teach me that in civilized society, silences wax awkward. It took him longer still to re-teach me that among friends, silences don't always wax awkward, especially when performing a task together.

All the better, as I felt my mind on the brink of understanding something. We'd come to Italy before, when Olivia was alive. At first, I hoped visiting the same locations as our first visit might renew Bram's memories of her. But time had changed the people in the towns we'd frequented nearly a decade prior, at least enough to ruin his chances at rediscovering his wife. The town nearby was new to us, but I had hoped our experience here might be closer to what we enjoyed in the past.

I was wrong, and our excursion to Italy might have been a complete waste of time.

As the roughly thatched roof of our cottage appeared around a bend in the hill, my thoughts turned back to what Bram said about Luella's Ring of Regret. Usually, using almost any kind of magic sends a ripple out to those who know how to listen. Like a swimmer, those skilled in its use have the ability and mastery to minimize the effect of those ripples. I once had kin who performed magic so adeptly that even standing beside them, you might mistake the ripple for a slight breeze or a distant birdsong.

As much as I loved Luella, she used magic the way an elephant paddles through a deep river.

But Bram was right. No one was listening. It should have been a relief, that after all this time, Jeremy no longer hunted us. Instead, though I hardly dared to admit it, it felt lonely.

"Home sweet home, for the time being, at least," Bram said with a congenial smile. I rolled my eyes.

"It appears you have already missed Francesca's visit," I said, pointing to a basket full of oil-laden, salty breads on our doorstep. A folded note sat atop it. "I must say, if you're not interested in getting to know her better, you really should not accept such generosity."

Bram took a deep breath. "I'm allowing myself time to see if her generosity can inspire my interest. Stop looking at me like that. Yes, it's devilish of me, but this bread is just so delicious..."

He put the basket under his arm and flipped open the note before heading through the plain wood door. No doubt he would insist I try the bread, deeming it impolite to do otherwise. I wrinkled my nose. I'd tried similar breads before. I had hundreds of years of experience trying foods. I knew what I liked.

Adapt or die. I sighed as my personal motto came to mind unbidden.

But as I started toward the door, my eye caught something resting in the corner, under an ambitious tuft of grass growing where the rough stone walls of our cottage met the wooden porch.

A Black Beacon mushroom about the size of my fist. I hadn't seen one in many, many years. It resembled what humans called the common toadstool, but the cap was a rich black that glowed bright green under a new moon.

A magic mushroom. This mushroom had been kept sacred, hidden from humans for centuries.

At first, I doubted my eyes, but as I crouched down and probed it with my finger, the unmistakable sensation of magic coursed up my hand. My vision clouded over as my ears heard silent melodies.

I recoiled. This was impossible. These mushrooms had died out with the rest of the fae. My mind reached for explanations.

"I know you have such high and mighty tastebuds, but this bread is amazing, Hirythe. Get over your pride and take a bite." Bram came back through the door, half-eaten roll in hand. He stopped when he saw me. "Hirythe what's wrong?"

I knit my brows, remembering all of the purposes the fae had for these mushrooms. They were used as symbols of vows. They were used in recognition of great accomplishments. They were used as announcements of intention and hostile warnings.

"Hirythe? What is that?" he asked.

"It's a Black Beacon," I replied quietly. His shoulders sank. I had taught Bram to sense magic, and surely he picked up the ripples stemming out from this mushroom by now as easily as I did.

"Where did it come from?"

"I'm not sure."

"What does it mean?" he asked.

I stood and turned toward the forest, scanning it with my eyes, trying to penetrate its magic. The trees here did not restore me as quickly as they should have. I credited that to differing topographies and unfamiliarity. But what if something else was feeding from them? What if...

The realization smothered me, struck me dumb with conflicting emotions. Joy. Fear. Anger. Relief.

A smile crept slowly across my face.

"I am not the last."

REVIEW

Thanks for reading!

If you enjoyed the book, I'd really appreciate it if you took the time to leave a review to let others know. A simple review or rating on Goodreads, Amazon, or any other book outlet goes a long way to helping readers take a chance on new authors.

Thanks again.

Kenny

ALSO BY KENNETH A. BALDWIN

The Shards of Lafayette Series

Book One: Drops of Glass

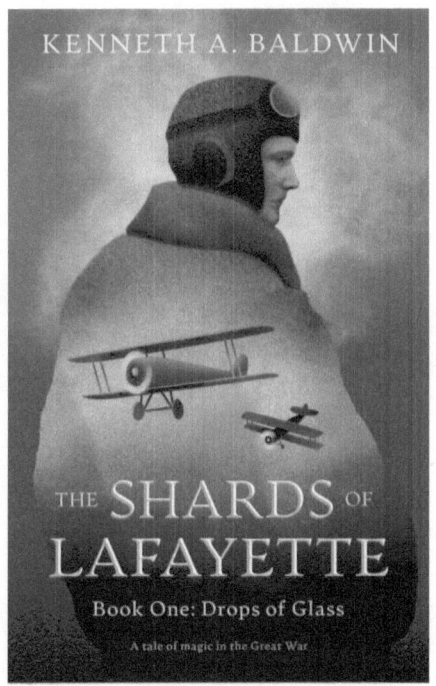

A magical artifact hunt through WWI.

"Baldwin's masterful writing flows seamlessly, allowing the reader to forget his narrative voice and get lost in the events."

Start the Adventure Today

ABOUT THE AUTHOR

Kenneth A. Baldwin writes stories that blur the lines between history, magic, dreams, and reality. He loves finding oddities in history books with unbelievable tales or unexplained phenomena. His first series, *The Luella Winthrop Trilogy*, takes place during just such a time when late 19th-century Victorians struggled to balance a surge of occultism and never-before-seen scientific advancements.

Before he started writing novels, Kenny paid his way through law school by writing, performing, and teaching humor. You can still catch him on stage or in corners of the Internet that feature sketch and improv comedy. Now, he lives nestled under the Wasatch Mountains with his wonderful wife, sons, and Golden Retriever.